T0268581

the
FRIEND
ZONE
Experiment

OTHER BOOKS BY

Zen Cho

the FRIEND ZONE

Experiment

Zen Cho

BRAMBLE

TOR PUBLISHING GROUP

NEW YORK

This is a work of fiction. All of the characters, organizations, and events portrayed in this novel are either products of the author's imagination or are used fictitiously.

THE FRIEND ZONE EXPERIMENT

Copyright © 2024 by Zen Cho

All rights reserved.

A Bramble Book
Published by Tom Doherty Associates / Tor Publishing Group
120 Broadway
New York, NY 10271

www.torpublishinggroup.com

Bramble™ is a trademark of Macmillan Publishing Group, LLC.

The Library of Congress Cataloging-in-Publication Data is available upon request.

ISBN 978-1-250-33039-0 (trade paperback)
ISBN 978-1-250-33040-6 (ebook)

Our books may be purchased in bulk for promotional, educational, or business use. Please contact your local bookseller or the Macmillan Corporate and Premium Sales Department at 1-800-221-7945, extension 5442, or by email at MacmillanSpecialMarkets@macmillan.com.

First Edition: 2024

Printed in the United States of America

0   9   8   7   6   5   4   3   2   1

To Alina Choong, who loves a good rom-com

1

When Renee woke up, she wasn't in her room at home. It took her a moment to remember where she was. Then she smiled.

She sat up and leaned back against the plush velvet headboard, looking around with pleasure at the suite her boyfriend had booked for the fortnight. There hadn't been time to check it out last night. She'd only been able to shuck off her shoes and dump her bag in a corner before Jason had distracted her.

It was the penthouse suite, with a wraparound terrace—the most expensive set of rooms in the hotel. Fresh white carnations were set out in a black vase on a side table by the bed. Next to the flowers was a card—Renee leaned over to look at it—saying how delighted the hotel was to be hosting global pop sensation Jason Tsai. Morning sunshine streamed in from the adjoining conservatory.

It was the kind of place Renee wouldn't have splurged on even in the days when she was spending on her father's dime. Despite Dad's wealth, he had an appreciation of the value of money that ruled out certain extravagances.

Jason had a different attitude, but then, it wasn't like he couldn't afford it. His last album *EXTRA.ordinary* had been a huge success in China, Hong Kong, and his native Taiwan, as well as across Southeast Asia.

"Wang Leehom for the TikTok generation," the *South China*

Morning Post had called him, to Jason's chagrin. He liked to think he was in a class of his own.

And he *was*, Renee thought loyally. Their relationship wasn't public—his fans wouldn't be happy about it, and Jason had his endorsement deals to think of. But she sometimes entertained herself with imagining the reaction of people back home in Singapore to the fact she was dating Jason Tsai. It would impress her parents' friends and her old schoolmates more than anything else she'd ever done.

She got out of bed, wriggling her toes in the carpet, and wrapped herself in a crisp white hotel bathrobe, before wandering out to the sitting room.

Jason was taking a phone call out on the terrace, already dressed in a Comme des Garçons hoodie and distressed jeans. Behind him unfurled the lush green expanse of Hyde Park. The city skyline rose up beyond, prosaic and beautiful in the sun. Brown, white, and grey office buildings, Victorian red brick, the ever-present cranes, and in the distance, the geometric glass shapes of the City's skyscrapers, looming over the squat onion dome of St. Paul's Cathedral.

Renee's heart rose. She never got sick of London. She might have been born in Singapore, but she'd chosen this city.

She was admiring Jason's ass in those jeans when he turned and she saw he was frowning. His face cleared when he met her eyes. He said something into his phone, wrapping up the call, and came in.

"Good morning, handsome," said Renee.

"Morning." Jason smiled. A little thrill of anticipation shivered through Renee.

Sometimes she worried about their relationship. Her business kept her busy, but Jason was on another level. He was always touring, or recording, or visiting his parents in their giant suburban house in California, festooned with photos of him at every microstage of development—from kindergarten concerts in Taipei, to his first day at elementary school in Walnut Creek, to that weird Korean magazine shoot he did when he debuted, where he was draped suggestively over a horse.

It was hard to connect the way Renee felt one should in a serious relationship. There were video calls, but either they spoke when it was nighttime for her and Jason had just woken up—and he was not a morning person—or it was nighttime at Jason's end, which tended to lead his mind towards the bedroom.

Renee had nothing against FaceTime sex in principle, but it was hard to get in the mood when it was the middle of the afternoon and Jason was booked in between a call with suppliers and a session with the tax accountant. And then his feelings got hurt, and she felt bad . . .

But now they were going to have a whole two weeks with nothing to do except focus on each other. Jason was in town to shoot a music video, and he'd extended the trip so they could have a holiday.

It was going to be amazing. Renee would make sure of it.

Jason sat on the sofa opposite her. "How do you look so good when you've just gotten out of bed?"

"Thank my dermatologist," said Renee. "Are you hungry?" She picked up her phone, navigating to the hotel's online menu. "They serve these gorgeous breakfast spreads here, with cute little waffles. I saw them on Instagram. Are you off carbs at the moment? We could get you an English breakfast—or ooh, grilled lamb kidneys, that's interesting. Or we could go out? Have you thought about what you want to do while you're here? Don't laugh, but I made a spreadsheet."

Renee swiped away from the breakfast menu on her phone, bringing up her spreadsheet. "There's so much you never get around to doing when you live in London. I thought we could do a champagne flight on the London Eye? Kind of cheesy, but fun?"

Jason held up his hands, laughing. "Hey, slow down."

"Sorry," said Renee, penitent. "You must be jet-lagged. We can get room service and chill. Whatever you want to do." She set down her phone, smiling up at him. "I've been really looking forward to this."

"Yeah. Totally," said Jason, but his eyes slid away from hers. He rubbed his thighs, clearing his throat. "Listen, Renee . . ."

Renee waited, but nothing further was forthcoming. Jason avoided meeting her eyes.

Foreboding swept over her, like the shadow of a passing cloud.

"What is it?" she said. She glanced at his phone, in his front jeans pocket.

Maybe something had come up. He was going to have to fly off early, or reshoot the music video . . . "Was that your manager on the phone?"

"No," said Jason. "I was talking to my mom."

This wasn't surprising; Jason spoke to his mother daily. It was one of the things Renee liked most about him. And it meant the call was probably nothing to do with work.

Warm with relief, she said, "You guys are so cute. How is your mom? Are her feet better?"

Jason blinked. "Her feet?"

"You know, the warts on her feet," said Renee. "We've been texting, she told me about them. She said they were caused by the wind entering her liver or something. She was using these weird herbal plasters to get rid of them, but she was running low, so I got some shipped from Singapore. They were a different brand, though. Did the plasters work?"

There was an ominous wrinkle between Jason's eyebrows. "Why are you texting my mom?"

Renee felt cold suddenly, insufficiently protected. She wished she'd got dressed before coming out into the sitting room. She pulled her bathrobe closer around her, folding her arms. "Her friends at church have a son who's coming over to do his Ph.D. in

London. She wanted advice on where he should stay. Should I not text your mom?"

Jason's forehead smoothed out. "No, it's—I didn't realise you guys were so close, that's all." He attempted a smile, but it didn't reach his eyes.

He was picking at a stray thread protruding from an artistic rip in his jeans. Renee's hands itched to stop him. She would have done it any other time, but somehow she was reluctant to touch him just then.

"I didn't mean to overstep," she said. "Your mom texted me first, so I thought . . ."

"I said it was fine," said Jason, with a trace of impatience. "Mom will talk to anyone. She's still in touch with my high school janitor. They trade gardening tips." He rolled his eyes.

Renee laughed, though she could hear the ring of nervousness in it. She couldn't tell what, or who, had made Jason impatient. His mom, because she was too gregarious? Or Renee, because of whatever it was she'd done to send this bright morning off course?

It must be the tiredness making him cranky. They'd gone to bed upon arriving at the hotel, but sleep hadn't been Jason's top priority last night.

He was coming straight off an intense few months of touring and publicity. Renee needed to be supportive.

"Mr. Vazquez?" she said lightly. "The one who sells Jason Tsai memorabilia on eBay?"

"He rescued her dying bonsai once, so now it's like she owes him her life," grumbled Jason. "He's probably got dibs on my firstborn."

His mood seemed to be passing. The tightness in Renee's chest eased.

"That might not be so bad," she said. "Our kid will be a bonsai master."

She knew immediately it was the wrong thing to say. Jason's face twitched.

She could change the subject, try to smooth things over. Instead, Renee said, a hollowness opening in her chest:

"Jason, what's wrong?"

A muscle spasmed in Jason's jaw as he came to a decision. He squared his shoulders, letting out a breath.

"Mom was hassling me about this house she wants me to buy back home," he said, gesturing at his phone. "She's been nagging me a lot lately about settling down. It's made me think about the future, and what I really want."

He leaned forward, resting his elbows on his thighs, and looked her in the eye.

"I want you to know, you mean a lot to me," said Jason. "Nothing's ever going to change that."

"What do you mean?" said Renee, but she already knew.

There would be no lingering over lavish hotel breakfasts, feeding each other cute little waffles; no ambling around her city with their hands in each other's pockets; no champagne flights on the London Eye or anywhere else. Jason having to cut their holiday short for work would have been the *good* outcome.

"Look, Renee," said Jason. "I love spending time with you. You're gorgeous, you're smart, you're funny. But what you and I want out of life, it's too different. I don't see us working out long-term."

He sighed, glancing away, before looking back at her. "I've known this for a while, but I wanted to wait till we could talk in person. I felt you deserved that much from me."

Renee still had her arms wrapped around herself. Her fingers dug into the flesh of her arms.

"Why did we have sex if you were only planning on dumping me?" she blurted, and then was furious at herself for betraying so much. It was a pathetic thing to say to someone who had made it abundantly clear he didn't give a shit about her feelings. She wouldn't have said it if she wasn't so off-balance.

Jason looked pensive, his eyes distant and melancholy. Renee recognised his expression: it was the exact same one he had worn in his recent campaign for Celine. She'd passed a blown-up version in half the MTR stations and shopping malls of Hong Kong on her last trip there. This somewhat undermined its impact now.

"I should have said something last night," he admitted. "But it was so good to see you again. And you were so excited. I didn't want to, you know, ruin the vibes."

Renee's jaw was starting to ache. "You could've thought more about my feelings and less about the *vibes*."

"This isn't easy for me either," said Jason. "But we've got to face facts. What future do we have? My career's back in Asia. If there was a plan for you to move back to Singapore eventually, maybe we could have worked things out. But you say you like it here. You don't want to go back."

"You know what it was like for me there." Renee's mouth was dry. She had to swallow before she could get the next words out. "With my family."

"I get it." Jason was transparently keen to steer clear of her family, a topic liable to upset Renee at the best of times. "But this isn't sustainable. You see that, right? We've been drifting apart for a while anyway."

"I've been trying," Renee said, hating the self-pitying wobble in her voice but unable to stop it. "It wasn't easy to make the time for this vacation, with the new launch for Virtu coming up. But I cleared my diary for you."

Jason hated it when girls cried. Renee had thought it was cute when he'd told her this on their third date. It hadn't occurred to her then to wonder how many girls had cried in front of him, and why.

"Oh yeah, your launch," he said, in an ill-advised attempt to redirect the conversation. "What is it, your fall/winter collection?"

It was October, far too late to start marketing an autumn/ winter collection.

"It's our new homewares line," said Renee. She'd talked incessantly about Virtu at Home on their calls. But why should Jason have any recollection of that? It was only the thing that had consumed her life for the past eight months. "I've been planning to expand the brand beyond womenswear for a while. I showed you the samples. Your mom liked the bowls, remember? I was going to send her some."

Jason had the grace to look embarrassed. "Sorry. I've been busy."

Renee softened. "I know you are. I know what it's like. I find it hard to let go of work, too."

It was a bad idea to let her guard down. She kept forgetting she and Jason were no longer on the same side.

"And I've always admired your passion for your business," he said smoothly. "But let's be real, Renee. You can't afford two big careers in a relationship. I need someone who will be with me, who'll put me first. Can you honestly say you're willing to do that?"

His face was blurry, famously perfect cheekbones and all. Renee wiped her tears off on her arm, furious at her dumb eyeballs for betraying her. "It's not like you've put me before your job. Or are you the only one who gets to expect that?"

"Let's not do this." Jason got up, to make it clear he, at least, was done with the conversation.

"I'll always care about you," he said. "I'm just not in love with you anymore."

Renee registered the authenticity, the gentleness with which Jason charmed interviewers and fans alike. It wasn't working on her this time, but that didn't matter. She didn't matter to him anymore, except as a problem to get rid of.

2

*R*enee *decided to* walk back to her flat instead of getting a cab. It wasn't that far. She could go through Hyde Park. The fresh air might help clear her head. And it would be slightly less humiliating to be sobbing in a public park, surrounded by Londoners averting their eyes, than in the back seat of a taxi with the driver right there.

She'd always loved her proximity to the vast green oasis of the park. Its very scale was settling, dwarfing the red buses and tourist coaches stopping and starting along the busy roads bordering its perimeter.

But for once the place's magic failed her. Renee trudged past stately trees decked in autumn colours and tourists arguing over directions, dragging the suitcase she'd filled with date-night dresses and lingerie behind her.

With typical caprice, the weather had turned. The sun had gone in and the sky was a glowing off-white. The light, reflecting off the ruffled slate-grey surface of the Serpentine, made the grass look greener than ever.

The park wasn't as busy as it would have been on a weekend, but there were people around, as always in London. Families were feeding the ducks while trying to dodge the geese. Couples were out walking their dogs. Roller skaters skimmed along the broad, even paths. Renee felt like the only lonely person in the world.

Tears kept rising to her eyes despite herself. She wiped them away on her sleeve, sick of herself and her stupid feelings. She couldn't think of that morning without cringing right down to her soul.

Surely she could have foreseen how things would turn out. The signs were all there, in retrospect—Jason's reluctance to commit, his growing disinterest.

Anyway, wasn't this always happening to her? Chasing a man's approval, only to be discarded when it turned out she wasn't willing to give up enough of herself. Renee had let down pretty much every man in her life in this way, starting with her father.

With one exception. But *that* had been a bigger disaster than all the rest.

Ten years had passed since then. It seemed she hadn't learnt anything from the experience.

"You're back early from your holiday, Miss Goh," said the concierge, as Renee entered her building.

Renee didn't respond. Dragan took one look at her face, then discovered something on his computer screen that required urgent attention.

Renee lived in an apartment complex on the southwestern edge of Hyde Park, a severe-looking structure of white stone, black metal, and glass. Inside, the ambience was that of an upscale hotel someone had, for reasons best known to themselves, set up in a warehouse. A good fifty percent of the flats were unoccupied for most of the year, purchased by Russian oligarchs and Middle Eastern oil barons as pieds-à-terre.

It wasn't exactly where she would have chosen to live despite its amenities—a private gym, swimming pool, and health spa, as well as the right to claim Kensington Palace as a near neighbour. But she knew she was lucky. Though the business was doing well, she could never have afforded somewhere like this on the salary she paid herself.

And she loved her flat itself. The rooms were airy and light-filled, ridiculously spacious by both London and Singaporean standards, with large windows looking out on quiet residential streets. The flat had been a princely graduation gift from her great-aunt, bestowed partly for affection, but mostly as a blow in her baroque years-long quarrel with Renee's parents.

Over the years Renee had made the place her own, decorating it with vivid batik fabrics sourced from Indonesia, tropical plants whose carbon footprint equalled that of most celebrities, and rattan chairs that sent her Instagram following into joyful spasms of nostalgia. The fact she didn't spend all that much time in the flat was beside the point. She liked knowing it was there and beautiful, a haven when she needed it.

Right now, though, the flat seemed abandoned, the light filtering through the windows grey and deadening. Renee poured herself a glass of water and drank it standing at the kitchen counter, shivering. She'd told the smart thermostat she wouldn't be home for two weeks.

By the time she set her glass down on the counter, her mind was made up. She unzipped her suitcase, grabbing her toiletries bag without looking at the sad, hopeful collection of clothes folded under it.

Her face was a mess. Her eyes were puffy, dried tear-tracks tacky on her cheeks, and her nose was an auspicious, but not especially attractive, shade of bright red.

Jason was probably relaxing in his suite, relieved to have got an awkward conversation over with. Renee snatched up a facecloth, burning with humiliation, and set about repairing the damage.

She took a keen professional interest in her appearance. She worked in fashion; it made good business sense to be beautiful. Her features were all right—apart from her jaw, which was becoming as square as her father's. But getting her skin under control required the help of a dermatologist, as well as the daily application of an elaborate multistep regime, arrived at after years of painstaking experimentation. The regime was nonetheless vulnerable to being undermined at any moment by hormonal variations, atmospheric humidity, pollution, stress, or the random vagaries of fate.

Her skin was a bloody metaphor for her life, Renee thought ruefully. On paper, her life looked perfect—at least, until this morning. But even before then, had she been happy with Jason? How could you be happy with a boyfriend who lived thousands of miles away; who refused to be pinned down for regular calls; who left your messages on read while plastering selfies with gorgeous starlets all over social media?

She'd kept working at their relationship, because everyone knew that was what relationships needed—hard work. Renee had never lost out on anything for lack of trying. And yet here she was.

It would probably be some comfort to the randos who left mean-spirited comments on her Instagram if they knew how miserable she felt. The thought prompted Renee to take a sparkling selfie when she was done with her face and post it.

> Can't WAIT to share what I've got in store for you guys. Just one final push from all of us at @VirtuLabel!

And then she went to work.

Louise looked up, startled, with the expression of a PA who was definitely browsing Vinted.

"Oh hey, Renee," she said. "Did you forget something?"

Renee didn't talk much about her personal life in the office. Secrecy outside their immediate family circles had been a precondition of her relationship with Jason. Even though most British people had no idea who he was, Louise talked about watching East Asian dramas, and Renee suspected her of being BTS ARMY.

But Renee *had* said she was going on holiday with her boyfriend and would only be available in the event of an emergency. Her reappearance called for explanation.

"Plans have changed," she said brightly. "We've broken up."

Louise looked as though she couldn't decide whether to be more worried or intrigued. "Oh no! Are you OK?"

Renee had to be OK. It was Louise's job to manage her diary, not her feelings. Besides, she had things to do: bowls to launch, collections to develop. She'd been so preoccupied with Virtu at Home that their Chinese New Year collection was running behind schedule, and that was their biggest season, when people were buying new clothes to visit their families in, generating the bulk of their annual revenue.

"It's fine. It was mutual," lied Renee. "I thought I'd take the chance to catch up on stuff, since my diary's empty for two weeks. Maybe we'll even be able to roll out Virtu at Home early."

This summoned up a hollow rictus on Louise's face. The team were all feeling the strain of gearing up for the launch. Renee reminded herself to give everyone a bonus. It was looking as though the figures would justify it this year.

"Joke," she added. But before she could escape to her office, Louise said:

"About your diary—are your evenings free now?"

Renee paused at the door to her office. "What is it?"

"You know the Dior exhibition at the V&A?" said Louise. "I know you said you couldn't make the private view, but the Selfridges buyer rang this morning to ask if you were going to be there. Her boss is attending and wants to meet you. I wasn't going to bother you about it, but since you're in . . ."

"Louise," said Renee sternly. "If something like that comes up in the future, I want you to text me. I don't care if I'm on a beach in the Maldives, or pushing out a baby, or whatever. I'll make it work."

Louise had wide eyes and freckles scattered across her light brown skin, which gave her an air of innocence. She raised her eyes to the ceiling. "What was it you said at last week's one-to-one? Something about burnout and the importance of taking breaks . . ."

"Going to a museum is like a break," said Renee.

Louise gave her a look. Renee said airily, "When's the event?"

Louise shook her head, but she only said, "Tonight. I'll send you a calendar invite with the details."

"You're a star," said Renee.

She went into her office, buoyed up. She'd figured the evening would major on bingeing kdramas in her pyjamas while eating Ben & Jerry's straight out of the tub. Instead, she was going to be out at the hottest exhibition in town, wearing something glamorous.

She knew what it should be, too—her treasured Dior trouser suit from the Raf Simons era, with its pared-back take on the classic hourglass-shaped Bar jacket. She'd bought it for an enormous sum from a dealer in pre-owned couture back in Singapore.

Renee saw herself in a high-ceilinged gallery, drinking champagne (well, probably prosecco) and pitching Virtu to a major retailer.

Take that, Jason. She didn't need him or anyone else.

Once she was at her desk, the hours flew by. That was the great consolation of her work. Renee might not have a boyfriend anymore. She might not have many friends, or a family in any meaningful sense, or hobbies, or a social life that extended beyond networking events. But she had Virtu.

She had founded Virtu in her teens, starting out by selling bespoke cheongsam to monied women twice her age. She'd grown the brand over the years, designing her own prints based on Chinese brocades and Indonesian batik, producing dresses and suits modelled on traditional Asian attire—from cheongsam to salwar kameez, kimono to baju kebaya.

Dad had provided the capital, though he'd grumbled about it. No one would pay that much for a local brand, he said. They'd shell out for Louis Vuitton or Ralph Lauren, but not for anything made by someone called Renee Goh.

He'd scoffed when Renee reminded him of the existence of Jimmy Choo. But she'd refused to be put off. She had known there was a market for her work out there; she was only making clothes she wanted to wear herself. Over time she'd built a loyal following of women who recognised in her design aesthetic, with its mix of heritage and modernity, something they hadn't known they'd been looking for.

Now, besides the two Virtu boutiques in Singapore, the brand was stocked in high-end department stores in Malaysia and Thailand. It hadn't originally been her plan to tackle Europe so early on; the conquest of Asia would have occupied her for years. But since she was here now, the next goal was a London store.

They weren't there quite yet. The majority of their revenue came from their established markets in Southeast Asia. It was for those customers that the new homewares line was intended. But cracking London was the next thing on Renee's list, once she was able to raise the necessary funding.

It was possible her dedication to her business was a tad monomaniacal. Her therapist had had a lot to say about it. All Renee could say in her defence was that work was the only thing that had ever given her back what she put into it.

She spent the majority of her working time running the business rather than doing anything creative. A day free of meetings, like this one, was a luxury. She didn't mean to waste it.

She was deep in the details of a cheongsam—1920s inspired, with broad sleeves past the elbows—when her personal phone rang.

Tearing herself reluctantly from her sketches, Renee stabbed at the screen with a finger, meaning to cancel the call. It was probably some telemarketer . . . unless it was Jason?

It was neither.

"Su Ren." The voice on the line was male, resonant and authoritative, with a clipped Singaporean accent. It would have been immediately familiar to certain specific groups of people in Singapore and Malaysia: the business press, several politicians, a number of charities, and probably, most of the other people who regularly populated the pages of *Tatler Asia*.

Renee knew it well, too, of course. Her stomach clenched. "Dad. What's up?"

She hadn't spoken to her father in a while. She'd rung him in February to wish him a happy Chinese New Year. Dad had told her to come home and Renee had hung up. That was how their conversations usually went.

"Did something happen?" said Renee. "Is everyone OK?" She thought of her brothers, her mind skating uncomfortably over how she might feel if something bad happened to either of them. Her mind went on to her mom, and her nieces and nephews. A chill struck her heart.

Thank goodness. At least she wasn't a completely terrible human being.

"What if they're not OK?" said Dad. "There's nothing you can do over there, isn't it?"

Renee stayed silent, which was what she should have done in the first place. She should have learnt by now that there was nothing she could say or do that couldn't somehow be weaponised by her family against her. That was why she'd stopped talking to them.

"I'm calling about business," said her father. "I'm planning to step down."

Renee froze. "What?"

Of all the things she'd have guessed Dad might say, that wasn't on the list. Her father had *been* the family business, her whole life. Chahaya Group was synonymous with Goh Kheng Tat.

"I told your brothers this morning," said Dad. "I'm getting old. It's time for me to stop working so hard. At this age, I should be enjoying life. Spending time with my family, playing with my grandchildren."

This was pointed. It was Renee's parents' view that at her age, only a couple of months short of thirty-one, Renee was overdue providing them with grandchildren, even though they already had six from her brothers.

"Someone is going to have to take charge of the group," said Dad. "A business like Chahaya, it's not easy to hand over."

The joke about Chahaya was that it owned half of Singapore and had built the other half. It wasn't much of a joke, because it wasn't far from the truth.

Both of Renee's brothers and their wives were employed by Chahaya Group, as were innumerable uncles, aunts and cousins, her parents' many godchildren, and various others more tenuously connected to the family. It could have absorbed a lot more people—including Renee, as her dad had mostly given up on reminding her.

"I can't simply pass it on to anybody," Dad went on. "The company needs someone who can do the job. But I worked so long to build it up. It should stay in the family." He paused. "Can you hear me?"

Renee was clutching the phone so hard her hand hurt. She made herself relax her grip.

"Yes," she said.

"What would you say," said Dad, "if I asked you to take over Chahaya?"

3

It took Ket Siong a while to realise he'd misplaced his date for the evening.

He hadn't come for Alicia's company, any more than he'd come for the exhibition itself. The name Dior meant as little to him as, he supposed, Shostakovich or Britten would to someone who didn't care about classical music.

But he felt a twinge of guilt at his inattention. He wouldn't have been able to attend the private view if not for Alicia Tan. Only current or potential patrons of the museum had been invited—as well as celebrities and socialites whose borrowed glamour might tempt the monied but less famous to dip into their pockets. Alicia had an invite because her father was managing partner of a magic circle firm who occasionally indulged in being a patron of the arts.

Ket Siong was in his best suit, a relic of his performing days. His mother had taken him to his father's old tailor years ago to have it made up, in a small, unassuming lot that smelt of mothballs, tucked away in a corner of a Kuala Lumpur shopping mall. Mr. Loke had turned out an unexpected masterpiece, though when Ket Siong's mother had thanked him, the old man said dismissively, "Didn't do much. If everybody was shaped like your boy, I'd have an easy life."

Despite the armour of Mr. Loke's impeccable cut, Ket Siong felt out of place, adrift in a sea of elegant people smelling of designer perfume and champagne. Even the waitstaff were intimidatingly smart in monochrome suits, wafting past with trays of outlandish canapés: tiny glasses of smoked eel suspended in saffron jelly; garlicky curls of octopus nestled in mini charcoal brioche buns; teardrop-shaped dollops of ricotta coated with truffle dust.

Ket Siong conscientiously ate everything offered to him so he could report back to his family, but he wasn't in a mood to relish the spread. Upscale parties had never really been his scene, and he was out of practice now. He'd declined at first when Alicia asked him to come, but she'd kept pushing.

"I'd feel silly going by myself, and all my friends are busy." She'd handed Ket Siong the invitation to the event. "Come on, Ket." Ket Siong went by his generation name with Westerners, to save them having two syllables to butcher, and despite her Malaysian Chinese grandfather, for these purposes Alicia counted as a Westerner. "It'll be fun."

The invite bore the Victoria and Albert Museum's logo on the front, the stark black letters embossed on thick, glossy card stock. The card fell open in Ket Siong's hand, revealing images of women dressed in bold hues of green and yellow and blue.

"There'll be free drinks," said Alicia. "And hors d'oeuvres. We don't have to stay the whole evening."

"I'm not sure it's a good idea," Ket Siong began. Then he turned the invitation over and saw the list of major donors on the other side, printed in a grey so discreet it was nearly illegible. One name leapt out at him.

He told his brother about the event, but not about the name he'd seen in the list of donors.

"Are you interested in the exhibition, or the girl?" said Ket Hau.

Ket Siong blinked. "Alicia? She only graduated a couple of years ago. Too young for me."

"You're only thirty-one. It's not that big a gap," said Ket Hau. "She must not think it is, if she invited you."

Ket Siong shook his head. He wasn't sure why Alicia had chosen to invite him, but it wasn't that. "Do you think it's inappropriate to accept an invitation like that from the sister of a student?"

The female relatives of the kids whom Ket Siong taught piano had a disconcerting tendency to hover during his lessons. He wasn't sure what they wanted from him, but he had a feeling he shouldn't encourage them.

"She's not the one you're teaching," said Ket Hau. "But if you don't like the girl, should you go? You don't want to give her the wrong idea."

"I don't think I would," said Ket Siong. "Alicia was very clear it wasn't a date." She had placed so much emphasis on this point that it might have been offensive, if not for the fact that Ket Siong wanted it to be a date even less than Alicia did.

Ket Hau gave him a look. "What's the draw, if it's not the girl? I didn't know you were into fashion."

Ket Siong shrugged, but he'd known his brother would ask. After a moment he said, "She was so insistent, it was hard to say no. And it'd be something different. It's been a while since I've done anything like this."

"Had fun, you mean," said Ket Hau.

It was true their life in London over the past three years had held little space for fun. They had not come here via the usual pathways of schooling or work or marriage. They hadn't originally been planning on leaving Malaysia at all. It had been hard to believe that flight would be necessary, until the fact was forced upon them.

As a result, they'd had to start from scratch, with very little preparation, practical or emotional, for what proved to be a new life in the UK. Navigating the bureaucratic complexities of the immigration system, gaining employment, and finding a place to live had absorbed all their energy at first.

It had taken years to achieve the relative stability they enjoyed now. But Ket Hau had yearnings for more.

Not for himself. He claimed to be content with his job as a

paralegal at a City law firm, spending his days putting together court bundles and reviewing stupefyingly boring documents.

"You forget the conditions I worked in back home," he told Ket Siong. "I kept asking for a new office chair because mine was killing my back and they kept saying, no budget. Now I can have as many Herman Miller Aerons as I can sit on. I could line up three and sleep on them if I wanted."

Admittedly, paralegalling didn't pay much relative to the cost of living in London. Ket Hau earned just enough to enable them to live in a cramped flat and feel constantly stressed about it. But he was studying to pass the SQE, and his earning power would be improved once he qualified as a solicitor. The fact that he hated what he was doing was, he said, irrelevant.

For Ket Siong, though, Ket Hau demanded more than a decent job with as many expensive office chairs as his heart could desire. He wanted nothing less than that Ket Siong should be happy.

That wasn't something Ket Siong had been able to give his brother for some years now.

"I don't see why you shouldn't go," said Ket Hau. "How much would it cost if you had to buy a ticket, twenty quid? Do it, Siong. You can come back and tell us about the canapés."

So here Ket Siong was, with that name on the list of donors burnt into the back of his mind.

Alicia had been next to him during the speeches, nursing her glass of champagne and eyeing up the other guests. She must have wandered off after.

Looking for her, he passed mannequins in wasp-waisted cocktail dresses, extravagant satin evening gowns, and impeccably tailored coats. One room recalled the grandeur of a stately home, with mannequins posed in various attitudes in a Grecian gazebo. Another room was overhung with a profusion of trailing artificial foliage, illuminated by shifting multicoloured lights. The dresses on display shimmered and glowed.

It was all somewhat lost on Ket Siong. It was the people there who interested him, not the exhibits. It wasn't just Alicia he was looking out for.

He rounded the corner into another gallery—a relatively small room, dominated by a ballgown in a column of glass in the centre. Scanning the crowd, Ket Siong's eyes caught on a man's profile.

It was as though someone had poured freezing water down his back. He stiffened.

The man was talking to a white woman. From this distance, Ket Siong could only make out a few distinguishing features. A stout, prosperous figure, shorter than most of the other men there, with salt-and-pepper hair. He was in a dark suit—nothing particularly fashionable, to Ket Siong's untrained eye. He could have been anyone.

But then the woman moved away and the man turned. Ket Siong saw his face. The skin on his forearms prickled, excitement sour in his gut.

Ket Siong had never met the man before, but he knew who he was. Tan Sri Low Teck Wee, chairman of Freshview Industries.

Low was no celebrity. He only happened to control vast swathes of the state of Sarawak in Malaysia, through the conglomerate his father had founded and he had piloted to its present dominance.

Ket Siong had never particularly followed business news. Five years ago, he wouldn't have known to distinguish Low Teck Wee from any other middle-aged Chinese man. But he'd spent the night before reading articles about Low, and he recognised the face from the photos—a round, weathered, bespectacled face, deceptively jovial, with shrewdness lurking in the narrow eyes.

"Tan Sri," said Ket Siong.

Low Teck Wee was looking at his phone. He started.

"I'm surprised to see you here," said Ket Siong. He could feel his pulse fluttering in his throat. His face felt stiff, but he was glad to hear his voice was even.

He glanced at the exhibits ranked behind Low: faceless mannequins in gowns of red and cream and black, trapped behind glass. "Are you a fan of Dior?"

Low laughed. "No, no. My daughter wanted to come. She's here somewhere." The way the man spoke—the rise and fall on each syllable so different from the British accent—gave Ket Siong an unexpected pang. It was an accent he associated with home. He didn't hear it much these days, outside the confines of the flat where he lived with his family.

Low had identified a fellow countryman in Ket Siong, too. He peered at Ket Siong above his glasses. "You're Charmaine's friend? You must forgive me. I am getting old, cannot remember names already."

"You don't know me, Tan Sri," said Ket Siong. "But most people have heard of Freshview. I saw *The Edge* reported record profits for the company this year."

Low nodded. "You're from Malaysia? Interested in business?" He didn't seem surprised at having a stranger accost him. Perhaps he was used to being approached by young men on the make.

"The Ensengei venture must have been lucrative," said Ket Siong. He'd curled his hand into a fist, his fingernails digging into his palm. He loosened his grip with an effort.

"Management must have been pleased about the Court of Appeal ruling," he continued. "Didn't the first instance judge find the area was native customary land? Of course, I hear Freshview continued logging even after that judgment. Perhaps you knew you would be vindicated on appeal?"

The slightly sozzled friendliness evaporated from Low's face. "Are you a reporter or what?"

"An interested citizen," said Ket Siong. He did still have a Malaysian passport, though he wasn't going back anytime soon.

"You shouldn't believe everything you read online, young man," said Low. All warmth had fled from his voice. "At Freshview, we do things by the book. Everything above board. Why do you think the appeal court ruled in our favour?"

As though conscious that a defence premised on the irreproachable integrity of the Malaysian judiciary was perhaps not the most robust, he hurried on:

"All these bloggers and so-called journalists like to complain about development. But what would they do without their handphones and their Wi-Fi? If we were all like them, sitting around complaining only, the country would be going nowhere."

He seemed sincerely outraged. Face meant a great deal to such men, but Ket Siong thought that to Low Teck Wee, *being* in the right mattered as much as appearing to be right. There might be a way in there.

"Tan Sri," said Ket Siong. "Do you know what happened to Stephen Jembu?"

Low looked at him, his face wiped blank of expression. He did not say anything. After a moment, he turned on his heel and walked away.

His back radiated defensiveness, as though he expected Ket Siong to pounce at any moment. But Ket Siong made no move to stop him. He stayed where he was, watching as Low was swallowed up in the crowd.

Ket Siong was shaking. He only realised this when an attendant offered him drinks. Reaching out for a glass of orange juice, he saw that his hand was trembling.

Not with fear, but anger. He'd thought he had accepted what had happened, or at least that he had become used to the idea, as one grows inured to horror over time.

Evidently he wasn't used to it. He felt enraged, but also foolish, scaldingly ashamed of his naïveté. As ashamed as he had felt when he'd first heard the news about Stephen.

He ended up in front of the glass case in the centre of the

room, enclosing a mannequin in a ballgown. He stared at it, unseeing, his heart pounding dully in his chest.

He took a deep breath, held it, and let it out, counting to eight, as he'd learnt to do at yoga class. Stephen had had a hot yoga phase, had dragged Ket Siong and his brother to excruciating sessions in a Mont Kiara studio frequented by sinewy expats, until Ket Hau revolted: "I'm sweating my ass off every day in this country and you're making me do this. If you want to pay hundreds of ringgit to fold yourself into origami, that's your business. But leave me and Siong out of it. It's against our religion."

"Being lazy is a religion now?" Stephen jeered. But he'd come with them for a reparative iced lime juice, and even wangled a refund from the studio for the classes they were no longer doing. Ket Siong saw his face, flushed with triumph, as he held the cash out to Ket Hau.

The vividness of the image was a blessing. Ket Siong could no longer recall the precise timbre of Stephen's voice.

The adrenaline drained away. With it went his anger, leaving only grief. But grief was a familiar companion by now; it should be easy to bear.

As his mind quieted down and his heartbeat slowed, he found himself following the lines of the ballgown with his gaze, from the bodice down to the skirt, along the train and up again.

The gown was an explosion of ivory tulle, turned gold in the warm lighting of the gallery. The kind of thing a Disney princess might wear, but it had an architectural rigour that even Ket Siong, unused to looking at women's fashion with any kind of attention, could discern. He wondered what marvels of construction and design an expert might see in the gown. He should have done some reading before coming. The caption only told him that the gown had been designed by Christian Dior for Princess Margaret, to be worn on her twenty-first birthday.

Calm settled on Ket Siong, and he remembered Alicia. He should go find her.

But someone had joined him by the display case. A woman, gazing raptly at the ballgown.

"Isn't it amazing?" she said. "There's so much to see here, I feel like my brain is going to explode. Look at that embroidery!"

Ket Siong was not infrequently addressed by strangers in public spaces—mostly women, but sometimes men. He didn't think he invited it, exactly, but Ket Hau said, "You can't blame them for trying."

He was about to give a polite nod and move away, but something about the woman's voice caught his attention. The accent was unusual—vaguely but not quite American—and it was familiar. But he didn't really know anyone in London, except for his students.

He looked away from the exhibit. He had no preparation, so the sight of Renee Goh hit him between the eyes like a brick.

The immediacy with which he knew her shocked him. It had been ten years since he'd last seen her, but apparently his brain had stored his memories of Renee in a special compartment, ready to throw them up at the right moment, as fresh as ever. It was as though no time had passed at all.

He'd thought of her, when his family first cast up in London. But as far as he knew, Renee had returned to Singapore after finishing her degree. After so long, it was easy to resist the temptation to look her up online. That chapter of his life was not one he relished looking back on.

Renee's face had lost some of its softness, the squarish lines of her jaw more evident than they had been before. She'd always been self-conscious about her jaw, but she was no less lovely now—more so, if anything.

Her eyes were exactly the same. Beautiful eyes, shaped like half-moons and shaded by absurdly long lashes, but the most beautiful thing about them had always been their expression, how transparently they conveyed her every emotion.

She did not recognise him. She gave him a discreet once-over. Ket Siong registered, with a sense of unreality, that she was checking him out.

There was a slight trace of uncertainty in her eyes. It struck him that she might be trying to work out whether any interest she expressed had a chance of being reciprocated. Ket Siong probably wasn't the only straight man at the exhibition, but he was definitely outnumbered.

Whatever Renee gathered from her inspection, it seemed to give her confidence. She smiled. "My name's Renee."

"I know," said Ket Siong. He wondered if Renee often chatted men up at parties. She was wearing several rings, but the fourth finger of her left hand was bare.

"You do?" she said, her smile fading.

"It's Yap Ket Siong," he said quickly, as if he was a telemarketer at risk of being hung up on. "Maybe you don't remember . . ."

Renee's eyes widened. "Yap Ket Siong?"

Ket Siong felt a kick of apprehension in his stomach. He dreaded seeing her face close down. They hadn't parted on good terms.

Renee looked him over, this time not bothering to hide her scrutiny.

"Oh my God, it's really you," she said. "You've grown up!"

Her face came alive, her expression worlds away from what it had been when she thought she was flirting with a stranger. The smile that broke across her face now was a Renee classic, spontaneous and unguarded, a dimple appearing in her left cheek.

Ket Siong remembered the dimple. It had caused him considerable difficulty back in the day. It had seemed to him that it would be a lot easier being in love with her and having to hide it, if not for that dimple.

Relieved, he smiled back, only realising once it happened how unfamiliar the expression felt on his face. "So have you."

"But this is amazing! I never thought I'd see you again." Renee took a step closer to him, her hand hovering as if to touch him, confirm he was really there. She flushed and drew her hand back, pushing her hair behind her ear. Ket Siong felt a small, unwarranted stab of disappointment.

"Are you here on holiday?" said Renee.

She seemed genuinely pleased. It was generous of her, given what he'd done the last time they'd seen each other.

It had been a long time, Ket Siong reminded himself. What had passed between them back then meant less to Renee, probably, than it meant to him. She'd had numerous boyfriends before him, and no doubt boyfriends after.

He felt a glow of warmth nonetheless. "I live in London now."

"Me too." Renee laughed. "Funny how things work out. I guess everyone comes to London in the end. How have you been?"

Ket Siong's first thought was of Stephen. He felt his face stiffen, a sick lurching in his stomach. It was Stephen his brother meant when Ket Hau said, "The important thing is, we're safe, we're together. Everything else, we can handle."

"Fine," said Ket Siong. "What about you?"

"Oh, I can't even begin to tell you," said Renee, with feeling. "There's so much." She glanced around the room.

The gallery was shadowy, most of the light coming from the spotlights trained on the displays. This threw the gowns into sharp relief, so that they glowed against the velvety black backdrop like jewels, but it also gave the space a deceptive sense of intimacy.

Of course, they were not actually alone. There were a couple of other people there, older women with beautifully coiffed white hair and clothes so deliberately shapeless they had to be the extreme of fashion. They were talking in low voices by a glass case full of sketches, gesturing with their champagne flutes as they pointed out details to each other.

"Do you want to go for a drink?" said Renee, her eyes on the women.

Ket Siong hesitated for slightly too long. The light in Renee's face dimmed.

"You've probably got plans," she said, so easily Ket Siong wondered if he'd imagined her disappointment. "But we should catch up sometime. I'll see you around?"

If Ket Siong let her go now, he might never see her again.

"A drink would be great," he said. "But I came with someone. I should let her know."

Renee's expression flickered.

"Oh, you should bring her along," she said. "Is it your girlfriend?"

"No!" Ket Siong cleared his throat. "No. A friend. Let me just—I'll go tell her."

"OK," said Renee. "Ask her to join us. Will you come back here, or . . . ?"

Ket Siong nodded. "I won't be long."

4

K et Siong allowed himself a backward glance as he was leaving the room. Renee had wandered over to look at the sketches, her hair falling across her face as she bent her head. She was obviously eavesdropping on the fashionable white-haired women's conversation. She bit her lip to suppress a smile, that dimple coming and going in her cheek.

Renee had always been like this: alive to the people around her, perpetually ready to delight in their idiosyncrasies. He had to force himself to turn away.

He managed to track Alicia down in a stark white room. Glass compartments covered the walls from floor to ceiling, containing headless mannequins arrayed in white. Alicia was talking to a woman, a very trendy young person with pink hair.

Whatever they were talking about, it was clear it was important to Alicia. She kept glancing sideways at her companion, her hands flying periodically to her hair—twirling a strand around her finger, tucking it behind her ear.

This made Ket Siong feel a little better about his intention to abandon her. He attempted to catch her attention.

This proved more difficult than expected. Staring at her while walking past faux-casually did not work, though Ket Siong passed Alicia twice without looking away from her. He would have done it a third time, except a middle-aged woman in a floral dress noticed him. She gave him a flattening look of disapproval.

It wasn't part of Ket Siong's plan to have security called on him. He waited till the watchful floral woman had moved away, then tried his luck hissing and jerking his head—agonisingly aware, all the while, of the fact Renee was waiting by that ivory ballgown, all too capable of inviting the next attractive man she saw out for a drink, or being so invited.

It was evident that Alicia had spotted him, but was determined not to respond. She continued to pretend she didn't see him even when he approached close enough that he was right behind her interlocutor.

"You all right, Alicia?" said the pink-haired girl.

"Yes! Fine!" said Alicia. "Just got distracted by that gorgeous jacket—*no, not behind you.* Right here!"

She put a hand on the girl's shoulder, steering her to look at the display. While the girl was busy inspecting it, Alicia made a vigorous shooing motion at Ket Siong behind her back.

Loath as he was to intrude, Ket Siong felt it necessary to draw a line. He was not accustomed to being treated like a wayward chicken, especially by someone so much younger.

"Alicia, have you got a moment?" he said.

Alicia's friend jumped, understandably startled to realise he was there. Alicia glared at him.

"I'll be back in a sec," she told her friend.

"What's wrong?" said Ket Siong, when he'd finally succeeded in pulling Alicia aside.

"Ket," she said, "do you know what 'cockblocking' means?"

"Oh," said Ket Siong.

Fortunately, Alicia simmered down upon hearing his news. He did not mention Renee's invitation for her to join them.

"Who is this person you've run into?" said Alicia, intrigued. "Is it a woman?" She glanced back at her friend, adding, "Or a man? Or other? I mean . . ."

"An old friend," said Ket Siong, who knew perfectly well what she meant. "Will you be OK getting home?"

"Yes." But Alicia was avoiding his eyes in a way that suggested home might not be her destination that evening.

It was her brother who was Ket Siong's student, not Alicia. Still, he'd escorted her here. That gave him some responsibility for her.

"Do you know her well?" he said, glancing at the girl she'd been speaking to. The girl was eyeing Ket Siong suspiciously. "You've got my number. Text me if you need anything."

"I'll be *fine*," said Alicia. "You go. Have fun."

Renee kept browsing through the displays while Ket Siong was gone. The exhibition was staggering, wonderful. She was glad she'd come, even if nothing came of the encouraging chat she'd had with the Selfridges buying manager. Here were sketches from the hand of Christian Dior himself, right beneath her nose. It was a once-in-a-lifetime opportunity to look into the mind of one of the greatest designers of all time.

Yet she was finding it difficult to focus, her mind wandering after Ket Siong. Would he come back alone, or with his friend?

"Friend" covered a lot of ground. Renee had been friends with Ket Siong, once upon a time.

If he brought his friend along, Renee would be able to tell what the precise nature of their relationship was. Not that it was any of her business. But it was the sort of thing that would interest her best friend, Nathalie.

"Eh, hello, hello!" said a voice behind her, making her jump. "I didn't know you're here."

An older Chinese man in a moderately ill-fitting suit beamed at Renee, a glass of bubbly in his hand. She recognised him at once, but it took her a moment before his name came to her.

Low Teck Wee of Freshview Industries, of course. The last time she'd seen him was years ago, when they were sat at the same table at the wedding of the son of an Indonesian magnate.

Dad had taken Renee along because Low had two daughters, but Dad's attempt at multigenerational networking had flopped. A black cloud hung over the Low party; there had evidently been some family quarrel. Despite Renee's overtures, Clarissa and Charmaine Low had spent the entire dinner absorbed in their phones, pointedly ignoring everyone else.

The last time Dad had mentioned Freshview to her was this morning, when he'd rung to talk about stepping down from Chahaya.

"Low Teck Wee's company is investing in a project in London. Converting a factory site into housing and commercial units," Dad said. "Big development. Did you hear of it? We want to get involved. Maybe you can help."

What a coincidence. Fate seemed to be working overtime on Renee's case today.

"Su—Su—you're called what again?" said Low Teck Wee. "Su Yin?"

"Su Ren," said Renee. "How are you, Uncle Low?"

"Good," said Low. His face was already magenta, though the glass he held was only half-empty. "How is your father? I went golfing with him, must be two months ago now. After that, came to UK to see my daughters and do some business. I'm going back to Malaysia next week."

"He's well," said Renee. "Busy as always." Her father wasn't planning on announcing his retirement until he'd decided who was taking over from him. "Are you enjoying the evening?"

"Ah, this kind of thing is not for old men like me," said Low. "Charmaine is interested, so I came. Otherwise, who knows, she will be bringing some young man along, isn't it?" He twinkled at her. "What about you? You're here by yourself, or you have a friend?"

Renee knew what was coming next. She tensed.

Sure enough, Low added, "You know, Andrew got married last year. To the girl—can't remember her name—the Delima Corp daughter. You remember my nephew Andrew?"

Even without that call with Dad, Renee would have been reluctant to offend Low. He'd always been kind to her and was not to be held accountable for anything his relatives did.

But it took an effort to muster a smile. She could feel how tight it was.

"Of course," she said. "I heard he married Felicia Handoko. They seem like a great match."

"Felicia, correct," said Low. "Very nice girl. Not so pretty as you, of course. So when is your turn?"

Why were older Chinese people so nosy? Was Renee going to start interrogating all the younger people she vaguely knew about their relationship status the moment she hit fifty?

She'd better not let him see Ket Siong. The first thing Uncle Low would do would be to tell her father. Maybe Dad would assume it was Jason Uncle Low had seen her with, but he didn't approve of Jason, believing he was not the kind of man to settle down and have a family.

Turned out Dad was right on that count. Renee hadn't mentioned the breakup to him. She hadn't wanted to divert him from what he'd rung to talk about—matters far more important than the fact her jerk boyfriend had dumped her that morning.

"I'm here on business," she said. "You know I run a fashion company."

Low had obviously forgotten, if he'd ever known, but he brightened at the reminder. "Yes, yes. I must ask Charmaine to talk to you. She's studying business management at Westminster University, but she also wants to go into this area." He waved at the exquisitely gowned mannequins staring facelessly down at them. "You have WhatsApp? What's your number?"

Renee readily surrendered her digits and asked for Charmaine Low's number in return, promising she'd get in touch. She would have done this in any case—she was all for supporting aspiring female entrepreneurs, even if they had been somewhat uncouth at a wedding banquet when they were fifteen. But any opportunity to get in Low Teck Wee's good books was doubly valuable at the moment.

Nevertheless, she was relieved to see him off before Ket Siong reappeared. Ket Siong looked a little flustered. He was unaccompanied.

"Sorry I made you wait," he said.

"Oh, don't worry. I was chatting to someone else, so I didn't notice the time," said Renee. That was half-true, which was not as bad as a *complete* lie. "Is your friend not coming?"

"She has other plans," said Ket Siong.

Probably she was no more than a friend, then. That meant less gossip to convey to Nathalie. She would be disappointed—or no, she would be pleased, given the circumstances in which Renee and Ket Siong had parted ten years ago. Renee could imagine Nathalie sniffing, *Of course he does not have a girlfriend. I cursed him to be alone forever.*

Renee found that she was a little pleased Ket Siong's friend wasn't coming for drinks. It wasn't that she cared whether he had a girlfriend or not. It had all been so long ago, and so much had happened since. But it would be nice to be able to catch up, just the two of them.

Renee kept up a steady patter of small talk as they moved through the remaining rooms of the exhibition, making their way to the exit. But she was a little distracted, glancing around every other moment for Low Teck Wee. The event was approaching its close; there were fewer people to hide among.

She relaxed once they were out on the broad, tree-lined pavement, the entrance to the museum well behind them. She hadn't spotted Low on the way out, and the likelihood they'd run into him now they'd left the building was low. He wouldn't be walking. He'd either have a private car complete with chauffeur, or he'd get a taxi.

"Can you give me a sec?" she said to Ket Siong. She whipped a pair of ballet flats out of her bag, set them on the ground and reached down to take off her black patent heels, wobbling on one leg. "My place isn't that far from here. Couldn't bring myself to pay for a cab just so I could wear my Louboutins."

She should have found a wall to steady herself against, or a bike stand. With her trench coat and Prada tote slung over one arm, it was hard to keep her balance. But before she could tip over, Ket Siong took her hand, relieving her of her bag and coat at the same time.

The touch of his hand, warm and dry, sent an electric shock up her spine. She jerked back, but he was already letting go, now she had both feet on the ground.

She completed the changeover from heels to flats with her head bowed, her face burning. At least it was dark, both of them bathed in the orange glow from the streetlights.

When she stole a glance at him, she was startled for a moment at the new distance between them—he loomed over her.

Ket Siong was gazing down at his hand, as if it had surprised him. He stepped back, clearing his throat.

"You're still staying at your great-aunt's flat?" he said.

Of course, Ket Siong had been to the flat before. "Same one, yeah." Renee glanced along the road. It was an unexpectedly balmy night, the kind you got sometimes in the autumn. The evening breeze on her face was soft, a last breath of summer. "We'll end up at Gloucester Road if we keep walking in this direction. Is that OK for you? Where do you live?"

"Edmonton."

"Oh." Renee was pretty sure she'd seen the name "Edmonton" on the front of a bus before, but that was as far as her knowledge went.

Ket Siong smiled slightly. "Either way is fine."

His fingers brushed hers when he gave her back her coat and bag, but Renee was braced for contact this time. It only made her feel a little shivery.

Ket Siong flexed his hand and slipped it into his pocket, throwing a look over his shoulder at the museum. "Is everything all right?"

What Ket Siong said was always a lot less than what he meant. Renee grimaced. "I was being weird, right? Sorry about that. I bumped into a friend of my dad's in there." She hesitated.

Andrew Yeoh's uncle, she could say. Ket Siong would remember Andrew. But she didn't feel inclined to bring him up. That came with too many associations with the day they'd last seen each other—even now, probably the worst day of her life.

"He's from Sarawak, too," she said instead. "Or maybe Sabah? His name's Low Teck Wee, he's this timber tycoon."

Ket Siong was quiet for a moment. Renee had forgotten how he did this—paused to think before he spoke, sometimes for long enough that you thought perhaps he hadn't heard you. He was the only person she'd ever known to do that.

"I've heard of him," he said.

"I didn't want him to see me leaving with a strange man," said Renee. They started walking again. She was absurdly conscious of him, despite the decorous distance between them. "Next thing you know, Uncle Low will be mentioning it to my dad over golf, and Dad'll be on the phone wanting to know why I haven't brought you to dinner." She rolled her eyes. "Asian parents. *You* know."

"But I'm not a strange man," objected Ket Siong.

That made Renee smile.

It should have been awkward running into Ket Siong again, after everything that had passed between them. But it was surprisingly easy to fall back into their old rhythm, as though they'd never fallen out of touch and Ket Siong was still one of her best friends.

The call with Dad had helped, taking the sting out of her breakup with Jason. Finding out she was in the running to take over the family business was big enough news to overshadow almost anything else that could happen. Renee was already thinking of her life as divided into *before* and *after* Dad's revelation, the humiliation of the morning comfortingly sealed away behind the excitement of his call.

Her father had made no promises, and he hadn't tried to flatter her.

"You've done well, but your company cannot compare to something like Chahaya," he'd said on the phone, earlier that day. "People will look at you and think, who is this young girl trying to come in and give orders? If Su Beng and Su Khoon knew how to behave themselves, I wouldn't be looking elsewhere. But your brothers . . ."

Dad let out a breath, not quite a sigh. "Their lives have been too easy. At least you don't take things for granted. And you are also my child. It's only fair I give all three of you a chance. It's whether you want to or not."

There had been no doubt in his voice that Renee *would* want to.

And she did. To take over Chahaya would be a challenge on a new scale, a huge level-up in terms of money, influence, and visibility. Renee knew her dad was right that most people would assume she wasn't up to the job—and she knew she could do it, tough as it would be. She would never have a better chance to prove her mettle to everyone who had ever doubted her. Including, most importantly, her family.

Ket Siong's voice brought her back to the present. "Renee?"

They were passing the Natural History Museum now, its grand pointy Victorian façade lit up in the night. The gilt details on the ornate railings surrounding the museum gleamed under the street lamps. On Renee's other side—where Ket Siong had taken up position, with unfussy courtesy—the road was busy with traffic, cars grunting and roaring bad-temperedly along its length. An electric bus hummed as it heaved its bulk away from the stop.

There was something so familiar about this, strolling along a London street in the evening with Ket Siong by her side. He'd always insisted on walking her home if they were out after dark.

She glanced up at him. He looked a little anxious.

"You're not a strange man," said Renee gently. The connection they'd had, and the way it had ended, seemed both very close and far away.

At the time Renee had blamed herself for misreading the signs, overstepping the boundaries of their friendship. It was easier, then, than thinking ill of Ket Siong.

Looking back now, she felt a surge of compassion for both of them, Ket Siong as well as herself. Sure, he'd broken her heart, but girls were always falling for Ket Siong back then and he'd never known how to handle it. Why should she have been any different?

She *had* wondered over the years if he was gay and that was why things had gone wrong when she'd fallen for him. But she wasn't wearing a blouse under her jacket, and there was something about the way Ket Siong's eyes were carefully avoiding her neckline that made her think that wasn't it.

Was he with anyone now? It seemed impossible he could be single. As far as Renee could tell, he hadn't changed in the past ten years, except to grow into himself.

As a boy, he had been coltish and beautiful. As a man . . . well. He'd broadened out surprisingly, but what made him so attractive was something more than that—a quiet confidence in the way he moved in the world, free of swagger. A certainty of his own power that made his gentleness all the more compelling.

Ket Siong raised his eyebrows. She was staring. Renee looked away, heat rising in her cheeks.

Let's not make a fool of yourself again, *Renee.*

"But Uncle Low doesn't know that," she continued. "Best to be careful."

"Is he close to your family?"

"Not really," said Renee. "But the business community back home is pretty small. Everyone knows everyone. You know how it is. I have to keep my nose clean. No salacious rumours about me picking up men at galleries. There's a lot going on with my family right now."

She laughed, though the back of her neck prickled with an unpleasant sense of exposure. Talking about her family was like picking at a fresh scab. The old tangle of ugly feeling knotted in her stomach, anxiety and resentment and self-loathing twisting together.

Ket Siong said, "Yes?"

An invitation to elaborate, if she wanted to, but not a demand.

Renee hesitated, but Ket Siong knew what her family was like. She used to tell him everything. Even if their friendship was a thing of the past, she knew she could trust him to keep her secrets.

"I can tell you about it once we're settled somewhere," she said.

Worry carved lines into Ket Siong's forehead, but he didn't say anything. Only nodded.

In one regard, Ket Siong hadn't changed. For all his quietness, he was so much more *present* than anyone else. When his intent gaze rested on you, you felt like you were the only person in the world.

But he was like that with everyone, Renee reminded herself. It was just how he was. If only she had realised that back then, she could have saved herself some considerable heartache.

And yet, would it have helped? It wasn't like she'd fallen for Ket Siong because she thought he liked her back. She'd loved him because he wasn't like anyone else she knew.

It was a good thing Renee had long since decided there were better things for her than love. Better, not because they were more important, but because they were attainable. What had happened that morning with Jason had confirmed that fact.

Perhaps this time she could be the friend Ket Siong wanted, and no more. It wasn't like he'd ever demanded anything of her. He was the only person she'd ever loved of whom this was true. It was the greatest gift he'd given her—and the worst blow he'd dealt.

Then

Nathalie insisted Renee come to her party.

"You can't stay in the studio stressing out twenty-four seven," said Nathalie. "You're starting to grow moss."

Renee was in her final year of a BA in fashion at Central Saint Martins and she was haunted by the looming spectre of her graduate collection.

"I am not growing moss," she protested. "I just don't want to humiliate myself."

Nathalie rolled her eyes.

Renee had first met Nathalie, a glamorous Parisienne of mixed French and Vietnamese heritage, in an online group for young women interested in starting their own business, a couple of years back. They'd bonded over a shared love of Asian food and scurrilous gossip, as well as the fact neither was doing what her family wanted of her. Renee's father had thought she was going to London to study economics, and had not been happy to be disabused of the notion. Meanwhile, Nathalie was planning to abandon a family-mandated lifetime's worth of classical violin training in favour of something else. She thought she might design textiles, or found a cosmetics brand.

"You cannot create without living," she said now. "Come and get some inspiration. You might meet someone and fall in love, that's very inspiring. And it would help you to forget your ex."

Renee frowned. "I wouldn't have a problem forgetting Andrew if he'd get over me."

"He is kind of a stalker," Nathalie admitted. "Maybe if you had a new guy, he'd take the hint. You might like my friend Ket.

He's super cute, a third-year pianist. If it wasn't for Mihai, I'd date him myself." Nathalie was pining after a Romanian computer scientist she'd chatted up at a bus stop, who seemed perplexed at the idea that he might choose to hang out with a girl instead of spending all his free time playing video games. "Ket is from Malaysia. Don't you have family in Malaysia?"

"I am not looking for a new boyfriend," said Renee firmly. "I haven't even gotten rid of the old one yet."

But she went to the party, in the tiny lounge-cum-kitchen of Nathalie's Bloomsbury garden flat, with her battered old workhorse of a piano in one corner and prints of twentieth-century Vietnamese art on the walls. The room was crammed with a surprising number of people, including—from the look of it—every single Asian student currently at the Royal Academy of Music.

Renee found she was enjoying herself. Nathalie chose her friends with more discrimination than her crushes, and the refreshments were notably good. The wine was served in plastic cups, but—Nathalie being French—it was quality wine. Plates of cheese and crackers and Vietnamese spring rolls were set out on the small white dining table.

Renee felt vaguely sorry for the cheese platter. The spring rolls were going a lot faster, given the demographic. She was reaching out to help herself to some brie when a large, warm body collided with hers.

For a moment Renee was crushed against the table, the edge digging painfully into her side. She was mostly preoccupied with trying not to send the cheese platter flying, but she did notice that the heavy weight squashing the breath out of her smelt nice.

"Sorry!" The guy had been shoved into her by someone else passing by. He righted himself, freeing Renee, his ears red. "Are you OK?"

"I'm fine." Fortunately Renee had put her plastic cup of Beaujolais down somewhere else and forgotten it, so her silky grey vintage dress was safe.

The guy looked down at her and went even redder. This was not an unusual thing for boys to do around Renee, but on this occasion, it did seem to be because he felt bad. "I'm so sorry."

"There's not a lot of space. I'm amazed Nathalie managed to fit so many people in here." Renee smiled up at him. He was tall for a Chinese guy, six foot, with the slightly hunched shoulders of someone who felt he was taking up more space than was quite polite. "I'm Renee. How do you know Nathalie?"

"I'm studying at the Academy. I'm Ket."

"Oh, you're Ket?" said Renee. "I've heard so much about you."

"Nathalie's told me about you, too." Nathalie's friend had a nice voice, and a nice way of talking—quiet, but not nervous. His accent reminded Renee of home. And he was, as Nathalie had said—for Nathalie was a connoisseur in such matters—super cute.

He looked down at the plastic cup he was holding, looking oppressed. Renee guessed he wasn't used to introducing himself to girls by crashing into them at parties.

Renee *wasn't* looking to date. But Ket seemed nice. She wanted to cheer him up.

"Whereabouts are you from in Malaysia?" she said, to try to take his mind off his faux pas. "Sarawak? Are you from Kuching? Good, it's the only place in Sarawak I can name. My dad goes there on business sometimes. He's from Malaysia originally, but he moved to Singapore when he was young. Is Ket short for something? Oh, so I should really be calling you Ket Siong? I grew up in Singapore, but I have this weird accent because my parents sent me to international school. I'm a total banana, it's embarrassing. I have to pretend to be Korean when I go to China-town. Do you speak Chinese? And dialect, too? Wow."

Ket Siong looked slightly dazed by the flow of talk. Renee needed to adapt her strategy. She glanced around the room, her eyes falling on Nathalie's piano.

"You're a pianist, right?" she said. "Nathalie said. Will you play something for me?"

Ket Siong didn't answer at first. She must have put him off. Her brothers always said she talked too much.

But then he said, "What do you want to hear?" and Renee saw he'd only been thinking about her request.

"Something beautiful I could learn," she said. In her relief she added, "I'm pretty good, you know. I got up to Grade Five ABRSM on pure talent. After that, they could tell I never practised, so my teacher fired me."

Renee was to learn later that Ket Siong had won multiple music competitions and performed for the queen before she died—the actual British queen, the one everyone had heard of. But he gave no indication of this; only nodded, thoughtful.

"How about the 'Sonata facile'?" he said.

Renee narrowed her eyes. "Doesn't that mean 'easy sonata'?"

Ket Siong didn't bother denying it. "It's by Mozart."

"Oh, I love Mozart," said Renee, thawing out. "Is that a really basic thing to say if you know anything about classical music? Is it like loving pumpkin spice lattes?"

"It's like loving sunshine," said Ket Siong. He sat down at Nathalie's piano and played for her. By the end of the sonata, they were friends.

5

Now

Ket Siong and Renee ended up wandering for a while after leaving the V&A. They eventually cast up at what Renee called an "old man pub," an establishment with a wooden façade in peeling black paint and the name THE WHITE HART in gold letters above. The sign bore a spindly white deer with a gold collar around its neck, sitting with its limbs primly folded.

Inside, the pub was wood-panelled and warm, smelling of stale beer. Illuminated gaming machines burbled and hissed in a corner. A slight stickiness adhered to everything, from the coasters on the tables to the floors. Unusually for London, they seemed to be the only people there who were below fifty and not white.

Renee ordered their drinks with unfussy efficiency, impossible to contest.

"You can get the next round," she said, when Ket Siong protested.

She would have let him buy her a drink in the old days. They had both enjoyed his performance of small chivalries then.

They sat at a small wobbly table that threatened to tip their drinks over them at any moment. Renee smiled as she slid his pint of beer over to him. She was wearing a black trouser suit. From certain angles, glimpses of her bra could be caught under her jacket—flashes of pale green satin over golden skin. The effect was glamorous, sexy but untouchable.

The past decade had changed her. Ket Siong saw this in the set of her shoulders, the bland reserve of the smile she'd first turned on him at the museum, the practised and impartial quality of her charm.

The Renee he'd known before was someone who knew she'd have to fight for what she wanted out of life. This Renee knew what it was to win.

And yet there was no fundamental change. In the most important respects, she was the same person Ket Siong had fallen in love with, all those years ago.

If he'd been asked even a few hours earlier, he would have said he had more or less forgotten Renee. Now he realised that would have been a lie. He'd retained almost everything about her. But time had softened the intensity of the emotions associated with her, removing the sting and leaving only the pleasure of remembering. Ket Siong could feel himself slipping into a different self, a version of the boy he had been when he was Renee's friend.

He had almost forgotten that boy. It was strange being reacquainted with him. Strange, but good.

"What are you doing these days?" said Renee. "Did you come to the UK for work?"

This was a natural guess, if Renee thought Ket Siong was still on the path he'd been on when they'd known each other before, headed for a promising career as a concert pianist.

He said, "I teach music. Mostly to children."

When he had first moved to London with his family, it had seemed obvious that he could not continue to pursue a performing career, like the one he used to have back in KL. Most classical pianists, however lauded, enjoyed a relatively limited form of fame. But it wasn't the sort of job you did if you were trying to escape notice, as they were.

Ket Siong had minded this less than he might have expected,

given he had devoted his entire life before then to pursuing that job. Something vital had gone out of music. He wouldn't have been able to say why, or pin down the precise moment it had happened—whether it was when they heard about Stephen, or when they decided to leave Malaysia.

Three years on from the move, Ma and Ket Hau seemed to have lost some of their sense of being in ever-present danger— enough, at least, to think Ket Siong having a performing career wouldn't be antithetical to their safety. They'd started sending him links to auditions, and wondering aloud about whether it might be worth getting in touch with his teachers from the Royal Academy of Music.

He didn't like to tell them it was no good. Music was like a language he'd once been able to speak. He retained the grammar and vocabulary, could still understand it. But when he opened his mouth, the words wouldn't come.

He hadn't thought that was possible, before.

He could see the rapid recalculation behind Renee's eyes, as she adjusted her assumptions.

She said, without any change in tone or manner, "That sounds fun. Do you like it?"

The old Renee might have asked if he'd stopped performing, and if so, why. But neither of them was the person they used to be.

"Yes." To change the subject, Ket Siong said, "Are you in touch with your friends from uni?" He searched his memory for examples. "Derek Lim?"

It was only after he said the name that he recollected Renee had ended up dating Derek. That was after they had parted ways. He should have chosen someone else to mention.

But Renee said, unembarrassed, "Oh, Derek! Such a sweet guy. We were together for a while after uni, did you know that? It didn't last, but we stayed friends. He's married now, to a guy he met when he was doing his MBA in New York."

"Oh," said Ket Siong.

Renee darted a glance at him. She'd looked at Ket Siong the same way at the museum, before recognition hit—as though she was trying to unpack something about him.

There was no normal way to say, *I'm straight, in case you were wondering. You probably aren't, but just in case.* Maybe he should mention his ex-girlfriend? Would the fact he only had one ex-girlfriend to mention seem suspicious?

"It surprised me, too," said Renee, before he could try it out. "But they make a cute couple. I follow him on Instagram. How about you? Have you kept in touch with your friends from the Academy?"

Ket Siong shook his head. He'd dropped contact with his university friends upon returning to Malaysia. Everything associated with London—and by extension, Renee—had been too painful.

It was not possible to say this. He said instead, "I'm not on social media."

Renee nodded sagely. "I remember. You didn't even have a smartphone. I was so amazed by your old Nokia. You're not still using that, are you?"

"It died a while ago." Ket Siong showed her his Motorola phone in its peeling case. "My brother got me this as a replacement. He said it was too inconvenient not having me on WhatsApp."

"I can imagine."

That dimple again. Did Renee know how enchanting that look of delight was? She'd always been well aware of her appeal, ready to deploy it as necessary, but Ket Siong thought she wasn't consciously seeking to charm on this occasion.

She tucked a glossy lock of hair behind her ear and looked up at him, bright-eyed. He had a feeling she didn't often get the chance to let her guard down.

"I haven't really kept up with people, either," said Renee. "The only one I talk to is Nathalie. You remember Nathalie? She was working for Shiseido in Tokyo for a while, she'd ring me up when she was coming to Singapore. I went to her wedding a couple of years ago. It was in the most beautiful château in the south of France. Her husband's a Flemish software engineer and they've got a kid. Three years old and he speaks four languages! They've only just moved to London.

"She mentioned you the last time we spoke," Renee added. "We were reminiscing about our youth, talking about men—you know how it is. Nathalie was saying how beautiful you were, back then."

Renee looked at him, considering. "It's a good thing she hasn't seen you now. Jeroen's started balding, he can be a bit insecure."

Ket Siong's cheeks warmed. This, in contrast with the dimple, was a calculated move. If he'd thought twenty-year-old Renee's attempts at flirtation were charming, she was devastating now.

"I'm honoured," he said, as lightly as he could. "Nathalie has high standards."

"Only the best for my girl," Renee agreed.

He was struck by the unconcern with which she spoke of the past, how easily she sidestepped the disastrous end to their friendship. But Renee had always been good at navigating emotional minefields, shaking off hurt that would weigh down anyone else. It was partly bravado, but that wasn't all it was. It was pretence, but it was personality, too—a refusal to carry the burdens others placed on her.

"Where did I come in your rankings?" he said, taking his cue from her. "There was a lot of competition, as I recall." Renee had had a veritable harem of suitors at university.

"My rankings?" Renee looked rueful. "I mean, I liked everything about you. Your looks wouldn't even have made the top five of things I liked about you." She gave him an assessing look, a smile flickering over her face. "Top ten, maybe."

Ket Siong's heart turned over. He saw Renee's face when he'd told her he didn't want to see her anymore, ten years ago. The lips bloodless; the eyes stunned, like a struck child's. But she'd lifted her chin and smiled, with the gallantry he'd loved in her.

He looked down at his drink, breathing through the memory. There was no way to respond. The ability to say things like that without killing the conversation dead was peculiar to Renee. She changed the subject, moving on.

The pub was stuffy, the heating turned up too high for the mild night. Ket Siong had taken off his suit jacket and pushed up his shirtsleeves, revealing a distracting expanse of forearm, dusted with fine hairs. His long-fingered hands loosely cradled his beer.

Renee realised he was looking at her, his expression inquiring. She didn't want to think about what hers must have been. Hopefully her tongue hadn't actually rolled out of her mouth.

She replayed the last few seconds of the conversation. Ket Siong had asked after her family.

"They're OK, I guess," she said.

It was strangely easy, talking to him—in a way, even easier than it had been back when they'd been friends and spoken every day. There were no longer any stakes, nothing to risk or lose.

"My eldest brother ended up in the papers last year for getting a college student pregnant," she went on. "But I haven't heard about a divorce, so his wife's probably forgiven him. My second brother lost a huge amount of money in a cryptocurrency scam. That's not public, though—my dad told me that. I haven't seen any of them since I moved to London."

Remembering the conversation with her father earlier that day, Renee shivered. She hadn't mentioned it to anyone yet. There wasn't really anybody in her life she could talk to about that kind of thing, now she was no longer in therapy. Maybe Nathalie, but it was hard to vent to Nathalie about her problems, these days. Nathalie had enough to worry about, what with her kid and her husband and her job.

Even Jason had never heard that much about Renee's family.

She'd had a clear sense of what he wanted from her, and her family baggage was decidedly not included in that.

"You managed to persuade your father, in the end," Ket Siong said.

She'd told him all about her dreams to leave the family home and seek out wider horizons beyond Singapore. It was nice he remembered.

"No," said Renee.

Even thinking about the circumstances of her move made her stomach hurt, bitterness spreading on her tongue. She had never talked about them before, except to her therapist. She heard herself say:

"I got accused of ripping off my designs for Virtu. That's how it began. This art student said I cheated her, took her work and didn't pay her. It was all over social media. The press picked up on it, and then the other allegations started coming. They said I underpaid my staff, cut corners. A model claimed she got sexually harassed on a shoot for Virtu and I told her if she talked about it, she'd never work again.

"It was a very well-judged character assassination," said Renee. "My brand is all about empowerment and equity. Our customers tend to be socially aware, they're willing to pay a premium for a business that shares their values. I lawyered up, hired enquiry agents. It was only when I told my brothers I was going to take legal action that my dad stepped in and got them to stop."

She rubbed her temple. "The most incredible part is that my brothers even understood Virtu well enough to take it down. That's why it took me so long to believe they were behind it. It was probably their wives who came up with the accusations. They're pretty smart."

Ket Siong said, "Why . . ." before he thought better of the question, trailing off.

Renee didn't mind being asked. She'd given the matter a lot of thought over the years.

"They were already pissed off at me," she said. "Virtu was starting to take off. I was going to therapy and challenging some of the dynamics in my family. But the trigger was my flat—my great-aunt's flat, I mean. You know the one."

Ket Siong nodded.

"Auntie Mindy gave it to me when I graduated," said Renee. "She was always beefing with my parents, that was probably why. It caused some ill feeling at the time, but then Auntie Mindy passed and it turned out she'd willed all she had to charity. Causes calculated to annoy my dad—LGBT rights groups, modern art galleries, animal shelters." Renee laughed. "There's a donkey sanctuary in Sussex that got a huge bequest. I went to visit a couple of years ago. You've never seen such spoilt donkeys in your life.

"My dad and brothers challenged the will. And they included the flat. The proceedings dragged on for years."

She paused. Ket Siong's eyes were on her, his gaze steady and kind. It felt safe to speak, safe to go on.

"I'm not saying I deserved the flat," said Renee. "I know Auntie Mindy was mostly trolling my dad when she left it to me. But that wasn't all it was. We always got along. She was the only one in my family who supported me over going to Central Saint Martins. And the flat was valued at three million pounds. Obviously, that's a lot of money, but compared to the rest of the estate?"

Renee shook her head. "They didn't need to do that. It was because my brothers couldn't stand the idea of me having something they didn't. When the court ruled in my favour, they weren't happy. A few months after that, they launched their campaign against Virtu.

"Dad made them fix things. They got the press to print corrections. The model withdrew her allegations. But the damage was done by then. So I packed up and came here." She smiled faintly. "To my flat."

"I'm sorry," said Ket Siong.

Renee shrugged. If she looked at him, there was a real risk she would cry, so she took a slug of beer instead. They'd been sitting there for long enough that it was warm.

"I was lucky. It didn't affect our markets outside of Singapore. I've been wanting to build up the brand in the West anyway. That will help with cracking China. It's taken a while, but we're finally getting some traction. We need funding to really level up, that's the next thing on the list."

Focusing on work calmed her, as it always did. She raised her eyes to Ket Siong's, now they were no longer stinging.

But there was something uncomfortable about meeting his gaze. Ket Siong had always seen a little too much about her. The warmth in his eyes now was both reassuring and a little frightening.

Renee looked away.

"It's a long list," she said brightly.

"I can imagine." Ket Siong paused. "You're still in touch with your father."

Renee nodded. "He called me today, actually."

Now she'd started talking about her family, it was hard to stop. She told Ket Siong about the call with Dad, her shoulders loosening as the words flowed out.

"We're all in the running—me, Su Beng, and Su Khoon. Dad's giving himself till the end of the year to decide. Nothing's set in stone, but the fact he's even considering putting me forward as CEO of Chahaya . . ." Renee let out a breath. "I never even dreamt of anything like this. My brothers are older, they've been working for the company for years, and—they're his sons."

"You're his daughter."

"Right, only a daughter. Not even a good one. Dad was so mad when I left home." Renee tried to smile, but she could feel it had come out wrong, so she stopped. "He said all these things, when we spoke this morning—things he's never said before. He told me I've shown I can make it in business. I have good judgment and I know how to work hard. But I'm too stubborn, he says. He wants to see if I can work with my brothers."

Ket Siong raised his eyebrows. "These are the same brothers who tried to sabotage your business."

Renee shrugged. "Dad's got a point. My brothers are going to remain involved in Chahaya one way or another. If I took over, I'd have to make it work with them. The company's pitching for a big job at the moment, to do with a development here."

She paused, wondering whether to mention Low Teck Wee's involvement in the project. No, better to avoid it. She didn't want to slip up and talk about something she shouldn't—a lot of the detail was commercially sensitive. Besides, why would Ket Siong care?

"My second brother, Su Khoon, is coming over to the UK for a few months to try to seal the deal," she continued. "Dad's asked me to help him. That'll be my test."

"Su Khoon's test is to win the deal?" said Ket Siong. "And your eldest brother?"

"We're—Chahaya's divesting its retail interests," said Renee. Warmth rose in her face. It had been a long time since her family and Chahaya had been "us" rather than "them." "Su Beng's in charge of that."

If Ket Siong noticed her gaffe, he didn't mention it. He took a sip of his beer. Renee could practically hear him processing what she'd told him.

"This is something you want," he said.

"Yes," said Renee. Even thinking about the possibility of taking over from her father made her chest clench, with anticipation and terror mixed together. "It's not only getting to be in charge of one of the most successful companies in Southeast Asia. Chahaya is my dad's life work. I can't tell you how much it means."

Renee could pinpoint the precise moment when she'd realised what Chahaya Group meant. She had always known of it, of course, as the thing that took her dad away from home, had bought them their houses and cars, paid the servants and her school fees. But it was more than that.

Aged twelve, home from school and bored, she had come across a business magazine on the dining table, left open at a feature analysing Chahaya. She read the article over dinner, for lack of anything better to do. Renee had most of her meals alone, since her nanny had gone back to the Philippines.

It took a while to work through the piece, with its arcane references to "adjusted EBITDA" and "operating leverage." But she had no difficulty understanding that it was talking about the most important thing in the world—money.

That evening, she waited up in the nice living room by the main entrance, with the Austrian-crystal chandelier and glass sliding doors looking out onto the swimming pool. The family only used the room when they had guests, so no one noticed her. One of the maids even turned off the air-conditioning without realising she was there.

Renee lay on a leather sofa, getting stickier and stickier as the cool air turned warm, entertaining herself by pressing her foot against the marble floor to feel its chill before jerking it up again.

It was technically past her bedtime by the time she heard the bustle at the door heralding her father's return, but he wouldn't remember a minor detail like that. She popped up over the sofa before he could disappear into his study or bedroom and said:

"Dad, can I ask you something?"

Dad had been out at a function. His navy blue mandarin-collar shirt was creased, the sleeves rolled up. He barely glanced at her as he took off his shoes, the smell of alcohol and cologne wafting from him. "If you're having problems with homework, better ask your teachers."

"Was the SB Permata acquisition really a bad idea?" said Renee. She held up the magazine. "I looked them up online and they sound like a good investment. But this says nobody's going to want to go to all the malls they've built. Is that true? Should Chahaya not have bought the company?"

Dad put his shoes on the rack by the door and looked her in the face for the first time. "You researched it online?"

Renee felt abashed. "I wanted to find out more. I didn't know if this guy was right, or if he was making stuff up."

Dad kept looking at her. It was already the longest conversation they'd had that week. Renee became conscious that she was sweaty, her T-shirt sticking damply to her back.

Her parents expected her to be presentable. She should have taken a shower and changed, but she'd been worried about missing her father.

Dad let out an amused puff of breath.

"That's the right attitude," he said. He lumbered to his feet. "Come."

Renee followed him to his study and he explained the SB Permata deal, taking her through the figures and strategy. Talking to her like she was a person, someone he respected.

It was hard to explain all this, even to Ket Siong.

"It shows Dad takes me seriously," she said finally. "That everything I've done matters."

Ket Siong's voice was very gentle when he said, "You'd do a great job."

"Thanks," said Renee. She found herself glad of the bad lighting. He probably couldn't see her blush.

Ket Siong held up his pint glass, and she clinked hers against it.

6

The evening went by quickly. It was only when a staff member came round to tell them they were closing up that it struck Ket Siong that his family might be wondering where he was.

He checked his phone, but it was dead.

"Wow, it's almost eleven," said Renee, blinking like she was waking up from a dream. "I didn't realise it was so late. Is someone waiting for you?"

"My family," said Ket Siong, putting his phone away. "My mother and brother." The clarification felt important, though it wasn't like it mattered if Renee thought he was married.

She swayed a little as she got up. Ket Siong put a hand under her elbow, steadying her.

"How are you getting home?" he said. He would have guessed they were at least half an hour's walk from her flat. He hadn't been paying attention to where they were going earlier, or he might have insisted on staying closer to her place.

Renee yawned—delicately, like a cat. "Cab."

Ket Siong hesitated. "It's late to be going back on your own. Let me see you home. I can get the Tube from High Street Ken."

"I haven't had that much to drink," said Renee, amused. "It's tiredness, not alcohol."

He shouldn't insist. Renee was an adult, and London was

relatively safe. Broadly. Most women got home unmolested from a night out.

Just as most people lived out their lives with nothing too bad happening to them, no unexpected tragedy snatching them away from their loved ones. Ket Siong thought of Stephen, heading out to work in his ratty old Myvi, on the last morning he had been seen alive. Ket Siong's own father, who had died in a road accident when Ket Siong was two.

"It's late," he repeated.

At least Renee wasn't offended at his persistence. She smiled, her eyes sleepy. "OK. We can tell the driver to do a second drop-off. Save you a walk to the Tube station, if you think home's too far," she added, when Ket Siong started to protest.

He couldn't have afforded the taxi fare home, but arguing over the five-minute ride between Renee's flat and the Tube station would have been as ungracious as letting her send him back to Edmonton by black cab. He shut up.

They were quiet in the taxi. Renee was a million miles away, gazing out of the window. Ket Siong wondered what she was thinking.

Beyond this, he did not engage in much thinking himself. Images from the evening flitted through his mind. Low Teck Wee's face when he was asked about Stephen; that spangled ballgown behind the glass; Alicia saying, *Have fun.*

Beneath these impressions sat the fact that Ket Siong might well not see Renee again after tonight. So he did not ask himself what the evening had meant, or what might come after. For now, he was simply existing in the moment, looking neither to the future nor the past.

He got out of the taxi when they arrived at Renee's place, partly to help her out of the car and partly to say a proper goodbye, out of the driver's hearing. Not that they said anything anyone could not have heard.

Ket Siong watched Renee walk up to the entrance to her building. She pushed open the glass door, then paused.

I probably shouldn't do this, thought Renee.

But it had been a long day. She was so tired everything had taken on a sparkling clarity, and she hadn't eaten quite enough to soak up the couple of drinks she'd had.

In this floating, light-headed state, it was hard to recover her daytime inhibitions. The Renee of this evening was perilously close to the Renee of ten years ago, around Ket Siong—her guard lowered, longing to touch. She wanted to run her hands over his forearms, feel the muscle shifting under smooth, warm skin.

If she was being sensible, Renee would accept this reunion as the gift it was. Let it slip through her fingers, fleeting and lovely.

But it was the self underneath her defences who was in charge right now. The lonely girl, yearning for something straightforward and sweet. She thought, *If you walk through this door, you're never going to see him again.*

Renee turned around.

Ket Siong was standing by the black cab, looking woebegone. Renee was reminded absurdly of a dog waiting outside a supermarket, patient and consciously good, but just a little worried that its owner might never emerge.

The mental image made it easier to say, "Do you want to come in for a coffee?"

"I don't take coffee in the evening," said Ket Siong.

The sting of the rebuff hardly had time to make itself felt when he blurted, "But I could do with some water."

He looked uncharacteristically flustered. This made Renee feel a little better, but she couldn't bring herself to meet his eyes.

The cabbie rolled down the window. "Not to rush you, but metre's running, just so you know."

"It's OK," said Renee. She could barely hear herself over the blood thumping in her ears, but what she could hear sounded surprisingly insouciant. It was as though her voice belonged to someone else. "My friend's staying. How much does it come to? You might as well round it up. No worries. Have a good one."

She watched as the taxi drove off, trepidation and excitement uncoiling inside her. When she turned back to Ket Siong, his eyes were fixed on her, as if he was trying to record every detail.

"Come on," said Renee. "Let's get you that water."

Renee's place was instantly familiar, though Ket Siong hadn't seen it in ten years. The hallway was the same, with its walls panelled in honey-coloured wood, and the shining parquet floor necessitating the immediate removal of shoes ("Auntie Mindy will kill me if it gets scratched"). The air had the same faint, sweet floral smell, too—a scent he associated with Renee.

Some things had changed. Renee's aunt had originally paid an interior decorating service to kit the flat out with a full set of furniture. The effect had been luxurious but neutral, everything in shades of taupe, beige, and grey. It had been almost oppressively free of personality, except for the occasional eccentric touch where the interior decorator had ventured to express themselves.

"You've kept the monkey," said Ket Siong.

The monkey was about the size of a human baby and covered in an aggressively ugly hard-wearing paisley fabric. It sat eyelessly on a rattan console table in the hallway, facing the door. They had never been able to identify any useful purpose it might serve.

"I thought of getting rid of it, but I felt it would be disrespectful to Auntie Mindy," said Renee. "It's probably good feng shui. Scaring off the bad spirits." She patted the monkey on the head.

Respect for her aunt had governed Renee's approach to decoration when she lived here as a student. Conscious of her status as a guest, she'd never so much as Blu-Tacked a poster to the walls.

But she was a guest no longer. Through the door to the living room could be seen a pink velvet art deco–style sofa, draped with a leaf-patterned throw, rattan chairs on either side. The sofa's predecessor had been oatmeal coloured and weirdly shiny, heaped with fussy cushions that poked you in the back.

Renee had indulged her own taste, too, in the matter of art on the walls. As Ket Siong followed her into the kitchen, he passed a striking photograph of a woman in a cheongsam, the wall behind her divided into stark triangles of light and shade; a couple of Egon Schiele pieces; a nude of a Chinese woman with her back to the viewer, her face in profile haughty and remote; and a black ink painting of a crevasse between gargantuan mountains.

The kitchen used to be all white, a vaguely clinical room. It had been impossible to imagine making a spaghetti Bolognese there. Now the cabinets were a friendly sage green, with bronze handles. Half of one wall was covered with a large framed piece of green-and-pink batik, adorned with flowers and swallows on a latticework background.

"Javanese batik tulis," said Renee, when she saw him looking at it. "The pattern's hand-drawn." Then, when he started to grin, "Don't laugh at me! I didn't grow up speaking Malay."

"I wasn't saying anything," said Ket Siong mildly. He tapped the dining table, a round marble-topped piece in dark hardwood, with matching chairs. "My grandmother had a table like this."

"I bought the set secondhand in Singapore," said Renee. "Don't ask me how much it cost to ship here, your grandmother would be ashamed of me. It reminds me of home. And," she added, turning to the fridge, "my Instagram followers go crazy for it."

It was a good thing Ket Siong had asked for water and not any other form of refreshment. Renee's fridge was pristine, empty save for a row of bottles of mineral water in the fridge door.

Ket Siong made no comment, but Renee seemed conscious this was weird.

"I'm not home for meals much," she said. "I have someone come in to do the housekeeping. Is Evian OK?"

She spilt some water on the counter as she was filling the glass. Ket Siong found a tea towel and mopped it up. The cloth was crisp, with an attractive graphic print of tigers on it. He wondered how much it cost, and if it had ever been used before.

"Thanks," said Renee. "Maybe I am a little drunk."

If she was inebriated, it wasn't obvious. What was clear was that she was nervous. This made Ket Siong feel a little better about the adrenaline racing through his veins, but unfortunately it did nothing to calm him down.

Renee raised a hand to push her hair out of her face, looking self-conscious. "How about you?"

Ket Siong drank his water. It was fizzy, which he hadn't expected, but he managed not to cough. "A bit."

He realised Renee was watching him swallow. She noticed he was looking, and cast her eyes down, a pink flush rising in her cheeks.

"You should know I never do this," she said, after a moment.

Ket Siong had been circling around the reason she'd invited him in, not daring to speculate on what it might be. So long as he didn't think about it, he couldn't be wrong, and disappointment couldn't get any purchase on him.

Renee was making it hard to keep up this obvious and rational approach, however.

"Yap Ket Siong." Her gaze was wistful. A wisp of hair had escaped from where she'd tucked it behind her ear. It made Ket Siong's fingers itch.

"It must be destiny, us meeting again like this," said Renee. "You know, you broke my heart."

In this evening's chance encounter with Renee, Ket Siong recognised a gift from the universe—the workings of an unexpectedly generous fate, beyond predicting or outmanoeuvring. If he did or said anything, he might shatter the magic, set the moment to flight.

But this was too much to endure in silence.

"Renee, I never meant to . . ."

She put a finger on his lips. He felt the touch all through his body, like the vibrations of a struck bell.

"It's OK." Renee smiled up at him. "I'm not a girl anymore. You don't have to worry about me taking this too seriously. I'll take it for what it is."

There were questions Ket Siong should be asking, things that needed to be understood between them. He should clarify what *this* was, that she wasn't going to take too seriously. He owed her an explanation of the reason he'd hurt her all those years ago. And though he was scarcely entitled to it, confirmation of the current status of her heart—engaged or otherwise—would have been welcome.

But these were all the demands of his brain, which was decidedly behindhand with events. His body was ahead of him; it knew the game. His arms were already sliding around Renee, his head bending.

Renee raised her face, her lashes veiling her eyes. He'd forgotten how small she was. She was as fine-boned as a bird in his arms. But there was nothing delicate about the way she met his kiss.

She put an arm around the back of his neck, pressing herself against him, her mouth bold against his. Her body locked perfectly into his, all softness and strength.

Amazing as this was, his neck was starting to ache from the angle. He gathered her up, hoisting her up onto the kitchen island without breaking the kiss.

Ket Siong was busy trying to get Renee's jacket off her without allowing any distance between them when it struck him that he should probably check that that was OK. He pulled back.

Renee was breathing hard, her lips red. She didn't seem inclined to talk. She drew him back in, wrapping her legs around him, and Ket Siong's body told his brain in no uncertain terms to check out and come back later.

There seemed nothing for it but to comply.

Then

"I don't know what to do," said Renee.

They were in Ket Siong's room at halls, on a chilly November evening. Renee had come by from a cookout with friends, bearing a plastic container of fried rice.

"Derek made it," she'd said. "He insisted I take it home, but there's no way I'm going to finish it all. I thought you could have it. You're so tall, you can't tell me instant noodles are enough to keep you going."

Derek Lim was one of the various boys who orbited Renee. There was an Italian personal trainer who texted her photos of himself after workouts, gleaming and minimally dressed; a Chinese Ph.D. student in Glasgow, the son of a CCP bigwig, who sent her iPhones and Tiffany bracelets she either donated to less-monied friends or returned in the post; and Derek. He was a Singaporean studying engineering at Imperial who teased Renee about her international school–accented Singlish and made her regular offerings of home-cooked chicken rice and curry laksa. Ket Siong cordially disliked him.

But all of these boys combined worried Renee less than her ex.

"Andrew keeps messaging me," she said. "I don't reply, but he gets so worked up. But I can't block or report him, because of my family."

She was sitting on the floor with her back against the wall, her legs stretched out in front of her. She was a little drunk.

Ket Siong didn't usually like the smell of alcohol on people, but it was like Renee processed it differently, or something. A clean, sweetish smell rose from her, like the aroma of a good sake.

He was at his desk, eating Derek Lim's under-seasoned fried rice, because Renee had said she would throw it away otherwise.

"Your family don't care that Andrew was messaging that girl?" he said. Renee had told Ket Siong about breaking up with Andrew over the summer, when Andrew had sent her an R-rated text obviously intended for another girl.

"I haven't actually told them we broke up," admitted Renee. "They'd kick up a huge fuss. Dad loves Andrew. His grandfather founded this big property empire in Malaysia. Dad's hoping we'll get married. It would be a big win for Chahaya."

"Isn't your father rich enough already?"

That startled a laugh out of Renee. She had a pretty laugh, an intensely delighted gurgle that made it impossible not to smile along. "In Dad's world, there's no such thing as having enough money." She drew her feet in, hugging her knees. "Is everyone's family like this?"

They were less than two months into their friendship, but Ket Siong had already heard all about Renee's family. She dropped casual references to them into conversation, almost all appalling. Her parents lived on different floors of a good class bungalow in Singapore, communicating exclusively via messages conveyed by the servants. Her father had not spoken to Renee for a year after she started her degree at Central Saint Martins. When she was little, she used to run to her nanny's room and hide under the bed when she heard her brothers coming back from school.

Ket Siong could not give his real opinion, which was that Renee's family struck him as cruel and unnatural, more like villains in a drama than actual people you might meet in real life. He settled for saying, "You're not much like the rest of your family."

"I guess not." Renee tilted her head back against the wall, reflecting. There was something pleasingly neat about her: the sweep of her hair over her forehead; the shape of her legs and feet in their black tights; the short polished nails on her fingers.

"I didn't see a lot of my parents, growing up," she said. "And my brothers are so much older, you know. And they're boys, that makes a big difference in my family. At meals, my dad and brothers get served first, then Mom and me after. There's a hierarchy."

Ket Siong chewed on a prawn. Derek might have been stingy with the salt, but he'd gone all out with the other ingredients. Ket Siong had not seen so many king prawns in one place since he was last home. "It was your nanny who looked after you?"

"That's right. Auntie Francesca." Renee brightened. "She was really the one who brought me up. She went back to the Philippines when I was twelve. We chat on Facebook sometimes, but she's super busy. She has eight grandkids and runs a restaurant." She looked over at him. "What's your family like?"

It took Ket Siong a moment to answer. The picture Renee had painted of her childhood was so bleak, he was struggling against an uncharacteristic desire to say something, though he hardly knew what.

He looked at her shining dark hair, with the subtle tint of red winding through its waves (both colour and curl courtesy of an expensive Japanese salon off Tottenham Court Road). Ket Siong knew suddenly that he should not say or do any of the things that were trying to break out of him. His family was a safer topic.

"There's just the three of us," he said. "My grandmother passed a few years ago. And my father died when I was young."

Renee's eyes were soft. "I'm sorry."

Ket Siong shrugged. "I don't remember much about him."

His grandmother was a different matter. Ah Poh had looked after Ket Siong and his brother while Ma was getting back on her feet, after their father died. There was a picture of her pinned on his noticeboard. Ah Poh looked severe, with her faded samfu and iron-grey curls, but her hands rested on the young Ket Hau and Ket Siong's shoulders, protective.

"That's a lot of loss," said Renee.

Ket Siong had never thought of it that way before. Renee had a knack for casting a fresh light on the world, making him see it anew.

"We've learnt to rely on each other," he said, after a pause.

"My mother used to work in human rights, but she switched to corporate law so she could support us."

"Wow," said Renee. "Does she miss it? What she used to do, I mean."

Ma never talked about her career change, much less how she felt about it. Ket Siong had been young enough when it had happened that he only knew about it because his grandmother had told him. Ah Poh had approved of the change: Ma earned significantly more now than she used to.

"She doesn't talk about it. But it's not easy." He paused, but there couldn't be any harm in telling Renee. It wasn't like she knew any of the involved parties, or would tell anyone else. "Right now, her firm's representing this company, she thinks it might be involved in money laundering. She reported it to the managing partner. But the company's a big client for the firm, and the founder is well-connected. She's not sure what's going to happen."

"It's brave of her to speak up," said Renee. "It explains a lot about you, actually." At Ket Siong's expression, she added, "How you care about doing the right thing. You care more than most people. That must come from your mom."

Ket Siong looked down under her gaze. It was easier to talk about his mother than himself, so he said:

"Her job makes it difficult, sometimes. But it would be tough for us, without it. Even with my bursary . . . My brother's helping to pay for this as well. We couldn't make it work, otherwise." He waved at his room, encompassing in the gesture his presence in one of the most expensive cities in the world, pursuing what most people he knew back home considered a wildly impractical career.

Ket Hau and Ma never mentioned the sacrifices they'd made so Ket Siong could do what he was doing. He would never hear from them what small luxuries they denied themselves, what opportunities they might have pursued if they could. But he knew his freedom came at a cost, paid by the people he loved best.

"I couldn't be here if not for them," he said.

"That's true of all of us, I guess," said Renee. "I should be grateful."

Ket Siong did not think Renee owed it to her terrible family to be grateful. He was trying to think of a polite way to say this when she said:

"Do you know why my family hates me?"

She was picking at the hem of her dress—a very un-Renee-ish thing to do. The weight of a revelation hung over her.

Ket Siong did not try to argue that Renee's family did not hate her. He shook his head.

Renee was finding it hard to speak, for once. Ket Siong kept eating, even though he was no longer really tasting the rice, because he had a sense that would make it easier for her.

"I only remember my dad punishing my brothers once, when we were kids," she said finally. "They were so naughty, you can't imagine. But Dad would lecture them and let it go. Mom didn't like him punishing them, she even objected to the lectures. They used to fight over it.

"But there was one time. My second brother used to tease me, say I was adopted, I didn't belong to the family. One day he said there was this big secret about me, everybody knew except me. He made this big deal out of it, swore me to secrecy and everything. Finally he said, 'You know why you're so dark, when we're all fair? Your real mother was a maid. She couldn't look after you, so she left you here.'"

Ket Siong thought the golden-brown shade of Renee's skin was pretty, but he would have died rather than say so. In any case, compliments weren't what she needed just then. "Did you believe him?"

Renee looked up at him, her eyes huge. "Well, yeah. It made sense to me. I was just a kid. I got so stressed about it I told Auntie Francesca. She mentioned it to Dad, and he took my brother and *walloped* him. He'd never done anything like that before. I always remembered it." She swallowed.

"I only found out why when I was a teenager," she said. "It turned out my dad had an affair with a maid while Mom was pregnant with me. It was too late for her to have an abortion by the time she found out, or she would have done it."

Ket Siong put down his spoon. "How do you know that?"

"Mom told me." Renee wiped her eyes on her sleeve. "That's why my parents fight all the time. Because of me. My brothers are jerks, but you can't blame them, in a way. Everything was fine until I came along."

Her voice broke. It made Ket Siong's heart ache.

"It's not your fault," he said. "You didn't do anything wrong."

"Maybe," said Renee. "But Mom wishes she never had me. She told me that, too. I can't forget it."

She bowed her head, gulping. Ket Siong looked out of the window, though there was never much to see—the blind walls of the building next door and a blank sky above. Without ever having discussed it with Renee, he knew she hated anyone seeing her cry.

It was a while before Renee looked up again. There were tears on her lashes.

"I've never told anyone this before," she said. "It's a huge secret. Even my grandparents never knew."

"I won't tell anyone," said Ket Siong unnecessarily.

He wanted to do something for her, so he said, "I'm going to make myself tea. Do you want some?"

Renee let him make her a mug of rooibos. She folded her hands around it, smiling a little.

"Yap Ket Siong." She made the syllables sound sweet. "I can't believe we only met a couple of months ago. You're one of my best friends."

Ket Siong stared, appalled.

The correct response would have been, *You're one of my best friends, too.* If Ket Siong had been foolish enough to open his mouth, what he actually would have said was, *I adore you.*

He'd been silent for too long. Renee hunched over her mug.

"I don't have that many friends," she said, piqued. "So it's not a big deal."

"That's not—" said Ket Siong. *I like you, too,* he was about to add. But there was no way he could say *that* without Renee knowing what he really meant.

"I don't have many friends, either," he said feebly.

He would have known this was a bad idea if he hadn't been reeling from what he'd just discovered about himself. It always fired Renee up when anyone suggested Ket Siong was unsociable, even if the suggestion was coming from Ket Siong himself.

"That's not true," she said. "What about Nathalie? Radost? Haresh?"

"OK, then, you have friends, too," said Ket Siong. "Derek, Giuseppe, Yingji, Andrew . . ."

Renee gave him a look that said he was being disappointing. "*He* is definitely not my friend."

"No," said Ket Siong. "I'm sorry."

Renee pursed her lips. There was a grain of rice stuck to the side of her mouth. If Ket Siong were her boyfriend, he'd be allowed to brush it away. He curled his fingers into his palm.

"It's OK." Renee sighed. "I've made things weird now, right? I shouldn't have talked about feelings. Boys hate that kind of thing." She peered at him. "What do you all do with your feelings? I assume you have them. Do you just bottle them up?"

Ket Siong nodded, because if he had spoken, he would have been compelled to point out that he, personally, had a lot of feelings he was all too capable of sharing. Almost all of those feelings were about Renee, because he saw now that she had somehow become part of everything good in the world—music, the first flowers of spring, the smell of coffee in the morning, small babies in sunhats, cats.

Renee was intertwined with all of these things. He would never see or hear or smell any of them again without thinking of her.

Talk about making things weird. Renee had said he was one

of her best friends. That was what she needed—a friend. Not yet another man who wanted something from her she wasn't able to give.

"You've got, um . . ." Ket Siong gestured at his own mouth.

Renee touched her face and found the stray grain of rice. "Oh God. That's so embarrassing." She held up the grain of rice between her fingers.

"Let this be added to Derek Lim's sins," she announced, and popped it in her mouth.

7

Now

Renee woke to the pale light of London shining through the blinds into her bedroom, and the smell of coffee. The bedroom door was shut, but through it came the sounds of someone trying to be quiet in her flat.

She was alone in her bed. When she sat up, pushing the duvet down, a scent rose from the sheets, of Ket Siong, and what they'd done together the night before. Heat flooded her face.

That was a first for her. Not having sex—*that* she'd done, obviously—but she'd never previously slept with anyone she wasn't already in a relationship with. It was the kind of thing white people did in movies.

Examining herself, Renee found she didn't regret it. She felt a little surprised, but also energised, the way one did when trying something new, discovering unsuspected capacities in oneself.

She could see why people had hookups, if it was always like *that*. Whatever the problem had been between her and Ket Siong, it definitely wasn't lack of chemistry.

That was "have a one-night stand" ticked off her bucket list. It was a good time to have done it, if she was ever going to. If everything worked out with her dad and Chahaya, Renee might soon have a lot less freedom to have liaisons with guys she fancied.

Next time she wanted to feel refreshed, she'd have to go skydiving or something.

She rolled out of bed, pulling on a sweatshirt and shorts. She smelt of Ket Siong. It was both hot and weird.

She should shower, brush her teeth, and do something about her hair. But she was drawn to the living room by that smell of coffee.

Ket Siong was sitting at the Peranakan marble-topped dining table she'd paid way too much for. He was in his suit, limned in morning light, eating something.

The scene was like something out of a magazine shoot. Ket Siong looked like an actual dream, a fantasy boyfriend Renee's fevered brain had concocted out of lust and loneliness.

Whoa, girl. Renee didn't want a boyfriend—not right now, anyway. It wasn't like Jason had been much of an advertisement for the species. She needed to focus on herself for a while, figure out why she was always going for unavailable men.

Which was *not* what was happening here, she told herself. Sure, Ket Siong had rejected her years ago, but she was long over that. The whole reason she'd invited him in was that she'd known nothing serious would come of it. He'd probably agreed for the same reason.

This sudden longing was no doubt partly chemical—a product of the hormones generated by a night's admittedly great sex—and partly psychological, proceeding from a retrograde part of her brain, convinced she needed a boyfriend to matter and desperate to find one to replace Jason ASAP.

"You're up." Ket Siong looked relieved. She supposed he hadn't wanted to slip out while she was asleep. That was nice of him.

Renee looked at the table so as not to stare at Ket Siong and his offensively great skin. She'd bet he splashed some water on his face every morning and called it a day. God was so unfair.

Baked goods were spread out on Emma Bridgewater plates on the table. Seeing the plates, with their cheery pattern of wildflowers, gave Renee a little shock. They were Auntie Mindy's, and Renee hadn't seen them in years. It was like being thrown back in time.

She couldn't remember the last time she'd had friends over to the flat. Ket Siong must have unearthed the plates in the kitchen cabinets.

He'd also presumably acquired the baked goods. There were pastries, buns of various kinds, and . . .

"Is that coffee for me?" said Renee, brightening.

Ket Siong pushed the cup across the marble surface towards her.

"That's a cinnamon bun, and that one's cardamom," he said. "This one has a custard-and-coconut filling. You should eat them now. They're freshly baked."

"You've been busy." The natural thing to do would be to sit down. After a moment's hesitation, Renee slid into a chair one seat over from Ket Siong, scooping up her coffee. That left a polite amount of space between them—not so distant as to be offensive, but not so close as to be weird.

He'd got her an Americano. Funny that Ket Siong should have remembered her coffee order after all these years.

"Where did you get these from?" she said.

Ket Siong jerked his head at his phone, charging in a corner. "There's a Scandinavian café nearby. They deliver. I borrowed a charger," he added. "I hope that's OK."

"Of course." Renee was smiling helplessly. "I love this kind of thing." She took a bite out of the cardamom bun, closing her eyes briefly in bliss. "Sweet buns, they're all I'd eat in heaven."

Ket Siong was watching her. Renee remembered, suddenly, dragging him into a Chinatown bakery once when they were students. She'd insisted on buying one of every bun. They'd sat in Leicester Square and eaten them together, watching the tourists.

She cast her eyes down. "It's really good. You're bringing some home for your family, right?"

"You eat first," said Ket Siong.

Renee cleared her throat. "Got anything planned for the day?" She glanced at the clock. It was quarter to eight, early for a Saturday. She tended to sleep in on the weekend.

"I've got a few classes. You?"

"Got some work stuff to catch up on. There's never enough time during the week."

Ket Siong would want to get going. He taught kids music; the weekend was probably his busiest time. It had been sweet of him to buy breakfast.

"This has been nice," said Renee. "I've enjoyed . . . this." She flicked her hand in a gesture meaning him, the table laden with coffee and pastries, and the night they'd spent together.

She was a little startled, looking up, to catch Ket Siong looking at her. His face was set, like he was bracing himself for something.

He didn't need to worry. Renee wasn't going to angle for another meetup, or ask for his number. She knew that, in the nicest way, the only reason he'd slept with her was because they didn't have a friendship to ruin anymore.

She opened her mouth, intending to make it clear he wasn't about to hurt her feelings, because she'd never invested any in their encounter in the first place. But Ket Siong spoke first.

"Yes," he said. "I'd like to see you again."

Renee blinked. "Oh."

It was flattering to be asked. There was no reason it should send a thrill of terror down her spine. She took another bite of the cardamom bun to disguise her reaction, trying to ignore the twisting in her stomach.

An enjoyable hookup with someone she could trust to be discreet was one thing. She couldn't afford anything more complicated. She had too much going on in her life as it was.

The narrative slotted in place in her head, her heart rate slowing. It sounded good. It held together. It was significantly less embarrassing than the conviction running underneath it, that she couldn't let Ket Siong keep looking at her the way he was doing now, because one day he might decide to stop.

She didn't want to imagine what that would feel like. It had hurt enough the first time around.

This was getting way too close to memories and feelings Renee did not want to look at. The whole point of last night had been to have something nice and affirming after the shitshow of her morning with Jason. She needed to keep this clean, manageable. Under control.

"The thing is," said Renee, "I told you what's going on with my family."

Ket Siong nodded. "Your father is choosing his successor to run the family business."

Renee leaned forward, anxious to impress the significance of the opportunity on him. "I really think I've got a fighting chance. My brothers are approaching their forties and showing no signs of growing up. Dad's getting fed up. Meanwhile, my business is doing well . . . but you know what my family's like. I can't give anyone any dirt on me. My family still think I'm with Ja—with my boyfriend."

Ket Siong's expression flickered. "Your boyfriend?"

"Ex," said Renee. Even though it was none of his business, she didn't want Ket Siong to know how recently it was that Jason had gone from boyfriend to ex.

"I don't want you to think—it's not that you aren't—" Renee felt a flush rise under her skin. She wanted to be careful of Ket Siong's feelings, but she also didn't want to give away too much of her own.

"It's never been easy for me to make friends," she said finally. "Your friendship meant so much to me, back then. You're a great guy. I'm just not looking for anything serious right now."

The silence that followed was awful. Renee wrapped her arms around herself, wishing she hadn't opted for shorts. Growing up in the tropics meant they were her automatic choice for lounging around in at home, but the underfloor heating wasn't doing quite enough to set off the morning's autumnal chill. She felt exposed, in more ways than one.

Though it wasn't like Ket Siong was staring. He was looking down, toying with his cup of coffee. Renee couldn't make out his expression.

"I understand," he said.

Renee sighed.

"Do you think I'm a huge slut?" she said plaintively.

That succeeded in making Ket Siong raise his head. He looked taken aback. "No."

"Good. Obviously it's fine if casual sex is your thing," Renee added conscientiously, thinking of Nathalie, whose amorous adventures prior to marriage Renee had always regarded with respectful admiration. "But I don't usually—last night was the first time I've ever taken a guy home like that." She smiled. "As you said, you're not just any guy."

Ket Siong reflected her smile back at her, but she seemed to have made him more depressed than anything else.

He said, "Back then . . . it didn't end well between us."

Maybe it had been a mistake to refer to their shared past.

"No," said Renee.

"I've always been sorry for that."

Renee didn't want to go over that old ground.

"It's fine," she said quickly. "Ancient history."

Ket Siong shook his head. "I didn't handle it well." He didn't seem comfortable talking about how they'd parted, either, but it was clear this was important to him.

"It's not how I wanted things to go," he said, with an effort. "I felt I didn't have a choice."

"Because you were leaving London," said Renee, who desperately wanted this part of the conversation to be over.

Ket Siong hesitated. "That was part of it."

Renee could have asked what the other part was, but she knew the answer. She'd spent enough time brooding on the ill-starred evening that had ended their friendship.

She'd pushed things too far, dragged Ket Siong into something he'd later realised he didn't want. It would have hurt less if Ket Siong had pretended he wanted to stay friends after. But the fact was, he hadn't trusted her not to make things weird again.

And he was probably right. Renee had been head over heels for him, and she wasn't used to being into a boy without him returning her feelings. The guys she'd dated at that age might not have treated her well, or turned up on time for dates, or valued her achievements. But she'd never had any difficulty getting them to *date* her. She wouldn't have been great at keeping things platonic with Ket Siong.

He'd had to leave the country anyway. From his point of view, there had been no reason to maintain the connection.

"I get why you did it," said Renee. "I'm not going to pretend it didn't upset me at the time. But it was a long time ago, Ket Siong. We were both so young. There's no need to dwell on the past."

Ket Siong was turning his cup over and over in his hands. He put it down.

"I understand you're not interested in . . . that now's not the right time for a relationship," he said. "But I meant what I said. I'd like to keep in touch."

"Keep in touch," echoed Renee.

"It was good, when we were friends," said Ket Siong. "Wasn't it?"

That, Renee couldn't deny.

If this was a guy Renee had pulled at a club, or even an old acquaintance from uni, it would have been easy to decline further contact. But Ket Siong was different. She knew he only ever said what he meant. She could trust him to respect the boundaries she'd drawn.

And it wasn't like Renee had loads of friends. It had been exciting when Nathalie announced she was moving to London, but they hadn't seen all that much of each other since she'd arrived with her family a few months ago. With a big job, a small child, and a husband, Nathalie was never quite as available for cocktails and gossip as they both would have liked.

Renee was busy, too, of course. Even though Nathalie was the only close friend she had in London—the one person she might ring up in an emergency, or suggest lunch to for no particular reason—she barely noticed her isolation, day to day. It wasn't like she'd had many friends she could rely on in Singapore, either. She was used to being on her own.

That didn't mean she didn't know it was a problem. Her therapist used to suggest it might be an idea for Renee to be less guarded with others, allow people to get close to her. Or rather, she'd listened and asked questions until Renee herself came to that conclusion. But it was one thing to recognise that something might be a good thing in theory, another to execute.

Here was an opportunity.

"It was good," said Renee. "Is that what you want? To be friends?"

Ket Siong met her eyes. "I've missed you."

Renee's treacherous heart gave a thump. A small voice at the back of her head said, *Maybe this isn't a good idea.*

But it would be a pity to lose touch with Ket Siong again. There was no need to let her baggage get in the way. She wasn't in love with him anymore. Perhaps that meant they could actually be friends, this time.

"I missed you, too," she said. "You're on WhatsApp, right? What's your number?"

Ket Siong had more concrete ideas. As he saved Renee's number to his phone, he said, "There's a retrospective of Rembrandt's works on at the National Gallery. I was thinking of going. Would you be interested?"

Renee was always forming resolutions to make more of the

city's galleries and theatres, and never doing it. She hadn't been to a museum in months, other than the reception the night before.

"That sounds good," she said. She smiled, a little nervous, and was rewarded when Ket Siong smiled back—his rare, sweet smile. It lit up his face, giving it a totally different cast.

Maybe this was going to work.

"Let's do it," said Renee.

8

It was quiet when Ket Siong let himself into the house where he lived with his family.

Maybe Ma and Ket Hau were out. Ket Hau often took their mother out on the weekends, for a meal and a wander around London. Otherwise, he said, she'd never leave the house.

Or they might be having a lie-in. Ket Siong took off his shoes before climbing the stairs that led from the front door up to their first-floor flat, wincing at every creak.

He was tiptoeing towards the bedroom he shared with his brother when Ket Hau said:

"Where have you *been*?"

Ket Siong let out a strangled yelp. His brother surged out of the shadows like a vengeful ghost, grabbed him by the arm, and rushed him into their room, kicking the door shut behind them.

"Shh! I don't want to wake Ma," said Ket Hau. "She was so worried, she would have stayed up all night if I didn't make her go to bed. What happened to you?"

His face had relaxed upon seeing Ket Siong, but Ket Siong could see the marks of a night's worry scored across it.

Ket Siong hadn't been thinking about anything except Renee till now. Guilt twisted in his chest. "My phone died."

"Yeah, I told Ma that must have happened," said Ket Hau. "Probably you lost your wallet and couldn't get back home, so you had to stay over at your student's place. And you couldn't remember our numbers, so you couldn't borrow a phone to tell us. All kinds of nonsense. I had to say something. Ma was terrified, she thought . . . I was thinking the same things. Couldn't make up my mind whether to call the police or not. Are you OK?"

Ket Siong could well imagine what they had been thinking. The same horrors would have been parading before his mind's eye, had either of them gone missing. After what had happened to Stephen, his family had lost all faith in the safety or predictability of the universe.

How could he have forgotten them? He could have borrowed Renee's phone to give them a call. Though if they knew the full story of what he had been up to, they would scarcely have found it comforting.

Ket Siong's encounter with Low Teck Wee at the V&A had been overshadowed by what subsequently happened, but it came back to him now.

"I'm fine," he said, suppressing a wince. Could he get away with not telling his brother about confronting Low Teck Wee? If Ket Hau was disappointed in him now, that was nothing to the reaction *that* would elicit. "I'm sorry I didn't let you know."

"Where were you last night?" said Ket Hau. He looked Ket Siong over.

Ket Siong was acutely conscious of every crease in his suit. They hadn't been particularly careful about taking it off the night before. Warmth flooded his cheeks.

"Did you go on a bender or something?" said Ket Hau, disbelieving. A more plausible scenario struck him. "Did somebody slip something into your drink?"

"No, I . . ." Ket Siong cleared his throat. "I started talking to someone at the reception. We went for a drink and it got late, so I saw them back to their place and, um . . . and then it was too late to come home."

This sounded infinitely worse, spoken out loud, than it had felt inside his head. He wished he'd come up with a lie instead.

"Ket Siong," said his brother, in an awed whisper, "are you saying you went home with a woman?"

Ket Siong hung his head.

"I forget you're not a kid anymore," said Ket Hau. He let out an exhale, at a loss. "Should you be doing that kind of thing with the sister of a student?"

"What? No, it—it wasn't her," said Ket Siong.

"That's something. Wait," said Ket Hau, with growing incredulity, "you mean you really went home with someone you met at the event? A stranger?"

Ket Siong did *not* want to tell his brother about Renee. Ket Hau might ask why, exactly, Ket Siong had revived a connection he'd cut off ten years ago for good reason; whether friendship was all he wanted from Renee; and where, at the end of the day, he thought he was going with everything he'd said and done in the past twelve hours.

They were reasonable questions. Ket Siong did not feel ready to answer any of them, even to himself.

"You used, uh—you were safe, right?" said Ket Hau, with the expression of a man seriously weighing up the possibility that he might need to give his thirty-one-year-old brother an explanation of the facts of life.

Telling him about Low Teck Wee was appearing more attractive by the minute.

"There's something else," said Ket Siong. "I saw Low Teck Wee at the museum. Chairman of Freshview Industries."

The clarification was unnecessary. Ket Hau was not likely to have forgotten Low Teck Wee, or anyone else connected to the Ensengei debacle. His face changed. "What do you mean, you saw him?"

"I talked to him," Ket Siong admitted.

Ket Hau took a deep breath and let it out. "OK."

Ket Hau was rarely genuinely angry with Ket Siong, but then

again, this was a day of rare and unusual events. Ket Siong could practically hear his brother counting to ten in his head.

There wasn't much space to move around in, with both of them in the room. It was a decent-sized bedroom for two to share, by London standards, but it held too much furniture, which the landlady had declined to remove. Besides their two single beds, there was a built-in wardrobe covering one wall, a desk, a chest of drawers on wheels under the desk that had an unpleasant habit of rolling over one's feet without warning, and a large metal shelving unit.

Ket Hau sank onto his bed, avoiding banging his head on the shelving unit with the ease of practice.

Ket Siong sat on his own bed opposite. He could always be sure that he would have mercy over justice from his brother, but sometimes that was worse, somehow.

"So that's why you wanted to go," said Ket Hau. "I thought it was the girl."

Ket Siong shook his head, thinking of Alicia's pink-haired amour. "I told you she's not interested in me."

In other circumstances, Ket Hau wouldn't have been able to resist interrogating him about the stranger who *had* been interested. Now, he merely nodded.

"You said." He paused. "What was Low Teck Wee doing at the V&A? Don't tell me Freshview is expanding into fashion. Hardly fits with the core timber business."

Ket Siong thought back to his conversation with the man. "Low mentioned his daughter Charmaine. The company's a donor to the V&A."

"That makes sense," said Ket Hau. "That's the other kind of money laundering. Where you use your money to wash yourself clean, buy face . . . What did you say to Low Teck Wee?"

He had to have some idea. Ket Siong had had nothing to do with the grassroots campaign against Freshview Industries' logging activities on native customary land in Ensengei, Sarawak. Ket Siong had only been aware of it as one of Stephen's causes— *the* cause, the one closest to his heart.

Ket Hau had been involved in the campaign, too, but unlike Stephen, he wasn't from Ensengei. The fight was, for him, more work than vocation.

Still, anything that mattered to Stephen was important to Ket Hau. They'd been best friends ever since Ket Hau had joined the NGO they both worked at. Stephen was a few years older, but they'd bonded over being Sarawakians in Kuala Lumpur, having been raised Catholic, and supporting Liverpool FC.

The first time Stephen had visited Ket Hau at home, he'd come laden with gifts for the family—Oreo layer cake and Sarawak pepper, sourced on a recent trip back east. After lunch he'd sat down with them in the living room for a cup of Nescafé, while Ma put her latest kdrama on. Stephen started by heckling the cast for their preternatural beauty ("In Korea there's no such thing as a pimple, hah?") and ended up staying five hours and sobbing at the finale. From then on, he'd been family.

There was only one thing Ket Siong wanted to know that Low Teck Wee might be able to tell him.

"I asked him if he knew what happened to Stephen," said Ket Siong.

Ket Hau's head whipped around. "You did *what*?"

So much for counting to ten. Ket Siong hunched his shoulders, curling in on himself.

"What were you thinking?" said Ket Hau. "We know what happened to Stephen. They got rid of him! What, you want the same thing to happen to you?"

"No," said Ket Siong. "But we're in the UK—"

"Where we only came because those bastards murdered Stephen!"

"They never found a body," said Ket Siong. "Ko, don't you want to know what really happened?"

Ket Hau had always looked young for his age, but this had changed after their move to the UK. Now, three years after Stephen had stepped into his car and never come back again, there was silver hair at Ket Hau's temples, wrinkles around his eyes and mouth.

"Don't I want to know what happened?" he echoed. He sounded old, too. "I wish I knew less. Siong, learn from my mistakes. Hasn't Ma been through enough? Because I got involved in that dodgy business, she lost her home. She's spending her old age in this shitty flat thousands of miles away from her work, her relatives, everything she cares about."

"It's not your fault," said Ket Siong.

But Ket Hau shook his head. "The fact is, if I took a decent job at some law firm when I graduated, none of this would have happened. We'd be in Malaysia. You'd be performing with the MPO. Ma would be gardening, playing mahjong with her friends, volunteering with her church . . ."

"You were trying to make a difference."

"Well." Ket Hau blew out a breath. "I did that."

"If Stephen's family had a chance to talk to Low Teck Wee," said Ket Siong. "If they could ask . . ."

But mentioning Stephen's family was a bad move. Stephen hadn't got along with his family. They'd been more or less estranged by the time Ket Hau had met him. The family had been vocal about the inadequacies of the police investigation of his disappearance, but even that hadn't inclined his friends to forgive them.

"I'm sure they'd love to question Low Teck Wee. They'd be the first to call a press conference, ask everybody to take photos," said Ket Hau. "Pity they couldn't be bothered to talk to Stephen when he was alive."

"Ko . . ."

"Stephen's family is not my business," said Ket Hau. "If they want to pester Low Teck Wee, they can ambush him at his golf course. We have to look after ourselves. How do you think Ma would feel if she knew what you did?"

Despite the reproach, the tension in Ket Siong's chest eased. If Ket Hau was asking the question, that meant he hadn't decided to tell Ma.

"It's not like I could actually make trouble for Low Teck Wee," said Ket Siong. "Freshview won their case. And he doesn't know who I am. I didn't say my name."

"You think it'd be hard for him to find out?" said Ket Hau. "What were you trying to achieve?"

Ket Siong stared at his feet. It was true confronting Low Teck Wee was never likely to result in any clarity about Stephen's fate. It had simply seemed, when Ket Siong had seen "Freshview Industries" in that list of donors on the invitation, that he was meant to do something about it.

"I wanted to see what he looked like," he muttered. "Hear what he said."

"What did he say?"

"Nothing. He walked off."

Ket Hau scrubbed his face, sighing, but he seemed to be calming down.

"Do you think Low Teck Wee was involved?" said Ket Siong.

He wasn't sure if his brother would engage, or if he'd get up and storm off. There was a long, fraught silence.

Finally, Ket Hau shrugged.

"Who knows?" he said. "He could have hired the guys who did it. Or it could have been a 'don't ask, don't tell' situation. The order came from the politicians, and Low looked the other way. One way or another, there's no way he didn't know. He's complicit. That means he's dangerous."

He looked Ket Siong in the eye, serious as he rarely ever was. "We came here to get away from all that stuff. You should know better than to get mixed up in it again."

"I'm not mixed up in anything," said Ket Siong. "Nothing came of it."

"So far," said Ket Hau, but he did seem mollified by the anticlimactic ending to Ket Siong's story. "Leave it, OK? There's nothing we can do about what happened."

Ket Siong had accepted this as the truth when they'd first found out about Stephen and decided they needed to leave Malaysia. For the first time, he found himself doubting it.

There was, perhaps, nothing to be done about the forests of Ensengei. Much of the land had been cleared, to be planted with oil palm. The villagers were suing for compensation, supported by the NGO that had formerly employed Ket Hau and Stephen.

But Stephen himself . . . he had been kidnapped in broad daylight, out of the decrepit Myvi he used to drive everywhere. There was a reason whoever had arranged his disappearance hadn't been more discreet. They wanted people to know what happened. They wanted Stephen's associates—people fighting, like him, to thwart the exploitation of the land for the benefit of a narrow elite—to be afraid.

It had worked, on Ket Siong's family, at least. But that very lack of discretion, that indifference to publicity with which the atrocity had been committed, meant that multiple parties must have been involved. Someone had to know what had become of Stephen.

Probably he was dead. But if so, why had his body never been found? They could have had the police discover his body and invented a story—said that Stephen had borrowed money from loan sharks and suffered the consequences, or something like that. Similar cover-ups had been effective with other such murders.

Ket Siong felt like he'd been sleepwalking for years—in shock, alienated from himself and the world—ever since they'd left Malaysia. But whether it was seeing Low Teck Wee in the flesh, or that run-in with Renee, bringing something of Ket Siong's old self back to life, now he was awake.

And it seemed to him there might still be something to be done about Stephen. Just to *know* what had happened would be more than they had now.

Ket Siong's family no longer lived in Malaysia. They had distant relatives there, but nobody closely connected enough to be at risk of retaliation. On one view, he couldn't be better placed for looking into the matter.

"They've stripped the land bare," Ket Hau was saying. "I send some money for the villagers' case for compensation. But apart from that, what can we do? We're over here. We've got our own problems."

"You send money?"

Ket Hau shrugged, a little embarrassed. "When I can." He leaned back, propping himself up on his palms on the lumpy mattress. The bedsheet under his brown hands was a cheap one from Primark, faded from many washes to an indeterminate yellowy-grey. "Stephen was a practical guy, you know. You remember, when you came over here to study, he said, 'Tell Siong, better not come back. Who wants to stay in this country if they can get out?'"

Ket Siong thought about this. "*He* wasn't planning on leaving."

"He wouldn't." Ket Hau snorted. "Even Kuching was too far. He wanted to move back to Ensengei and start a Sarawak pepper-export business."

"Do you . . ." *Miss him,* Ket Siong had been about to say, but that was a stupid question.

He stole a glance at his brother. Ket Hau's eyes were fixed on the window by his bed, his expression uncharacteristically sombre.

They were all agreed that one of the great benefits of their location on the outskirts of London was that they could see trees out of the window. They lived on the converted first floor of a narrow terrace house—what estate agents referred to, grandiosely, as a maisonette. The landlady, who owned the house, lived downstairs. In theory they had access to part of the garden, but she got a little funny about any of them being in it for too long.

Watching his brother gaze out at the trees, Ket Siong wondered, not for the first time, what it was that Stephen had meant to him. Colleague and best friend, yes. But whether there was anything more to their connection had never been said out loud.

They were not the sort of family that discussed such matters. It might have been possible to ask, sometime, if things had stayed as they were—as they were meant to be. But Stephen's loss had put certain topics out of bounds, made certain conversations verboten. Ket Hau as he was now, weathered by grief, was not as easy to talk to as he had once been.

It didn't matter, anyway. It was enough that Ket Siong knew they had been a refuge for Stephen, and Stephen had been a refuge for his brother.

"Do you think about him?" said Ket Siong.

"I try not to," said Ket Hau. "We have to move on."

"I think about him a lot," said Ket Siong, because it was true, and he knew it would comfort Ket Hau.

They sat in silence.

After a while, Ket Hau passed a hand over his face and looked up, as though he was returning to the present day from another time. "Don't you have teaching to do?"

Ket Siong's classes had gone clean out of his mind. He glanced at the clock and leapt off the bed. "I need to change."

It was a good thing he'd showered at Renee's place while waiting for her to wake up. Even if it meant he kept catching evocative nosefuls of her scent—a delicate floral fragrance, for which Ket Hau had fortunately not yet mocked him.

"I'll get out," said his brother. He paused at the door while Ket Siong was pulling clothes out of the chest of drawers.

"I know it's not always easy," said Ket Hau, "but we've got a good thing going here. We've been lucky. Don't forget that."

"I know," said Ket Siong. He didn't look up, for fear of what his brother might read in his face.

The next day was a Sunday. Ma had gone out to the supermarket, and Ket Hau was studying for his exam. He'd taken over the living room with his books and papers, so nobody would wonder at Ket Siong retreating to the bedroom.

Investigating an enforced disappearance wasn't exactly something Ket Siong had been trained to do. But he was motivated, he had connections, and he had the Internet.

His Google search turned up the usual reports about Stephen, old articles he'd read before. There had been a fair bit of noise in the immediate aftermath of the disappearance. Stephen's family had conducted rallies, written to the newspapers, petitioned the government. But they had gone quiet after a while. ("Police kept calling them in for questioning," said Ket Hau. "Told them to 'look after themselves.' Well, they knew what that meant.")

There were a couple of new pieces. The first was a Facebook post by the author of the famously obstreperous political blog the *Hornbill Gazette*, commenting on the recent announcement of Freshview Industries' splashy investment in London. The post called on the Malaysian government to clarify the details of its involvement in the development—particularly the funding arrangements.

It was not obvious what any of this had to do with Stephen. But the blogger went on to refer to Freshview's history in Ensengei:

> Stephen Jembu was the most prominent of the staunch activists and villagers who resisted the destruction of Ensengei's ancient rainforest (and a lovely man this reporter had the pleasure to meet several times). Where is he now?
>
> We don't know. But we know the premier's daughter was a director of Freshview Industries

*for several years. We also know her husband held
responsibility for granting logging concessions, at
least for a time.*
  *These tangled connections call for explanation.
The question we have is: What did Stephen know?*

The other new search result was a recent article in one of the
online Malaysian news outlets, about a vigil hosted by a civil society alliance in Kuala Lumpur, in memory of Stephen and other
disappeared persons.

Ket Siong scrolled past pictures of the bereaved families. They
looked less sad than angry—people who knew they had been
cheated. Stephen's family wasn't there.

He tabbed back to the *Hornbill Gazette*'s Facebook post and
gazed at it, running his thumbnail over his bottom lip.

What was the difference between the *Hornbill Gazette* and
Yap Ket Siong? They both had strong bonds to Malaysia, but
lived in the UK. They had both known Stephen Jembu, been
grieved by the horrific circumstances in which he was lost, and
wanted to know what had become of him.

Ket Hau might point out that the author of the *Hornbill Gazette*,
a well-connected British woman, was shielded by her privileges of
nationality, race, and class, as well as her political ties. But that
wasn't all it was. The fundamental difference was that she was
brave enough to speak up, to try to do something.

Renee had once described Ket Siong as someone who cared
about doing the right thing. He wasn't sure there had been much
evidence of that, in recent years.

Ket Siong wasn't active on social media, but he did have a
Facebook account. It was in fact Renee who had set it up for him,
during their university days.

"You need it for your career," she'd said. "You want people to
be able to go online and see how amazing you are."

She'd registered accounts for him on YouTube, Instagram, and
Twitter, too. But they hadn't really taken.

He'd forgotten his Facebook log-in, but it wasn't too difficult to get back in. He was confronted by a backlog of friend requests: university acquaintances, people he'd known through work back home, parents of the kids he taught in London.

He ignored these, navigating back to the *Hornbill Gazette*'s page.

He kept his message simple.

Hi, this is Yap Ket Siong. Could I talk to you about Stephen Jembu?

He didn't know the *Hornbill Gazette* personally, but if the author had met Stephen, she would almost certainly know of Ket Hau and possibly of their mother. If not, she'd figure it out. Malaysian civil society was a small world.

"Siong, have you seen the nail clipper?" said Ket Hau, coming into the bedroom. Ket Siong hastily closed the message thread. "I thought I put it down on the dining table—is that *Facebook?*"

"Uh," said Ket Siong. His heart was hammering against his ribs, but the screen showed nothing more incriminating than his Facebook feed—pictures of a secondary school classmate's baby; an advert for water bottles. He cleared his throat. "It's in the bathroom. I'll go get it—"

"Didn't even know you had a Facebook account," Ket Hau marvelled. His eyes widened. "Wait. Are you stalking that woman, the one you met at the V&A?"

Ket Siong opened his mouth to issue an indignant denial. But his being on Facebook was sufficiently out of character that it demanded an explanation, and the real reason wasn't one he wanted to share with his family.

He shut his mouth.

Ket Hau took this as a yes. He sat down on his bed, nail care and legal studies alike forgotten. "Find anything interesting?"

"No," said Ket Siong firmly. He shut his laptop. "It doesn't look like she's active."

"How old is she? Around your age? Younger?" When Ket Siong refused to be drawn on this, Ket Hau said, sagely, "Try Instagram. Facebook's for old farts like me."

After he left, Ket Siong reopened his laptop and looked up Renee's Instagram.

He tried to ignore the voice of his conscience, pointing out he was overstepping a boundary. Renee had made it clear she wanted to be friends, nothing more. She'd drawn a line. He should respect it.

The voice of his conscience spoke in vain.

Renee's Instagram was an attractive collection of selfies, images and videos of food and places of interest around London, and Virtu hype.

Ket Siong paused on a recent selfie. The timestamp said the image had been shared the day of their encounter at the V&A.

Renee was wearing something pale blue that she must have changed out of for the evening. She was illuminated by morning light, smiling. She looked beautiful, but there was something distant about her expression, her true self guarded behind it. It was similar to the smile she'd given Ket Siong at the museum, before she'd realised who he was. The face she showed the world at large.

That he got to see anything else was precious. He couldn't risk that. This time, he needed to make sure he was what Renee needed—no more and no less.

But he kept staring at the photo. Renee's hair coiled over her collarbones, the tender hollow of her throat. Ket Siong was hijacked by a sudden sense-memory, extraordinarily vivid, of leaning into Renee, pressing his lips to her throat and hearing her sigh.

Arousal whiplashed through him. He jolted upright and closed the browser.

9

*Y*ou *agreed to* do *what?*" said Nathalie.

It was the middle of the week, a few days after the V&A private view. Renee hadn't originally been expecting to see Nathalie. Their meetups these days were either crowbarred at short notice into gaps in their packed schedules, or else they required all the planning of a military operation, months in advance.

This one fell into the first category. Nathalie happened to be in South Kensington for a meeting that was cancelled at the last minute. Instead of heading back to the office, she'd texted Renee to ask if she was free for a coffee.

Now they were holed up in a cosy Lebanese café, perched on a bench covered with a worn red rug and sharing a couple of baklawa between them—small crisp pastries, dense with nuts and fragrant with orange blossom water. Renee was having a black coffee, Nathalie a beetroot latte because she could never resist ordering whatever novelty drink happened to be on the menu.

"Not as bad as turmeric," was her conclusion, but she wasn't making great progress on finishing her drink.

Their conversation had so far majored on Nathalie's work woes. Nathalie had returned to Europe for a dream job, a role as creative director for a luxury cosmetics brand, but the dream was not without its challenges. It transpired that a long-standing employee in her team had applied for the job, too. Her working life now consisted of incessant warfare—passive-aggressive email chains, shady business with Outlook scheduling, sniping over team lunches.

Nathalie seemed to value Renee's insights into the situation, but she'd yet to take Renee's advice to turn her nemesis into an ally by the determined application of flattery. "That might work for you, Miss Charisma, but *I* don't have the ability to make everyone like me."

Renee rolled her eyes. "Because I'm so popular. You're the only person I hang out with who isn't paid to be around me." She thought of Ket Siong and blushed. "I mean, pretty much the only person."

"Yeah, right. What about Jason?" Nathalie waggled her eyebrows. "Is he waiting for you back at the suite? I'm surprised he let you out to see me."

She looked at Renee's face and said, "Don't tell me. He stood you up?"

"He broke up with me," Renee admitted. "The day after he arrived in London."

Nathalie said, with gratifying energy, "That motherfucker!"

"I was going to tell you," said Renee. "It's just been so busy . . ."

And if she'd texted Nathalie about Jason, she would have been bound by the laws of their friendship to tell her about Ket Siong as well.

Renee wasn't sure she felt like telling anyone about that reunion, especially not someone who knew as much about her history with Ket Siong as Nathalie. It was Nathalie who'd picked up the pieces when Ket Siong had rejected her, all those years ago—her shoulder Renee had sobbed on afterwards.

Which meant, of course, that Nathalie was best placed to extract the details of what had happened from Renee. She set about this with characteristic efficiency, only interrupting to exclaim, "I can't believe you let me go on about Annalisa at work when you had actual news!"

She listened to Renee's account of the day Jason had broken

up with her—and the night that followed—with admirable restraint. It was only when Renee said she had fixed a day with Ket Siong to go to the National Gallery together that Nathalie had her outburst.

"What's wrong with that?" said Renee. "We said we'd be friends."

"Then why are you going on a date with him?"

"It's not a date. I've been meaning to do more arts and culture stuff. The only London thing I do is hit the sales at Liberty."

Nathalie ignored this. "Everyone knows when people say, 'Let's be friends,' what they mean is they're never going to see each other again."

"Right, but this isn't some guy off Tinder—"

"No," said Nathalie. "It's Ket Yap, whose name is mud. We agreed his name was mud! Remember the exorcism?"

Renee grimaced. The exorcism had been Nathalie's idea. Nathalie had proposed it when, several months after Ket Siong had stopped talking to Renee, she was still crying herself to sleep every night.

Ket Siong had returned to Malaysia by then. They were not in contact; because he wasn't on Facebook, Renee couldn't even stalk him online. It was, Nathalie declared, becoming an unhealthy obsession.

"It's time to get over him," she decreed. "We need to cleanse your spirit."

She officiated at the ceremony, watching sternly as Renee burnt photos of herself and Ket Siong together, printed off from her phone for the purpose.

"This is crazy. Why am I doing this?" Renee grumbled, but Nathalie was justified by the results. Three weeks later Derek Lim had asked Renee out, and they'd ended up dating for almost two years. They'd only broken up in the end because Derek wanted to further his studies in New York and neither of them was up for a long-distance relationship.

"I can't believe you got me to do that," said Renee now, shaking her head.

"I thought it worked. But clearly it has not," said Nathalie. "Because not only has Ket returned, you took him home and slept with him—"

"Shh!" Renee glanced around the café. Her Instagram follower base was mostly Southeast Asian, but there were times people recognised her in public, even in London. She said, in a low voice, "You're always saying a rebound is the best way to get over an ex."

"Not a rebound with your first love! Your first love who dumped you in the worst way possible!"

"I thought you'd approve. It's a flex, if you think about it," argued Renee. "Twenty-year-old me would be freaking out."

"Twenty-year-old you would be pinning wedding inspo," said Nathalie. "No, I do not approve. If you had left it at the hookup—yes, fine. I assume he is hot and not, like, portly with a receding hairline."

Renee nodded, though she felt she was being a true friend in refraining from pointing out that "portly with a receding hairline" was not an inaccurate description of Nathalie's husband, with whom Nathalie had as passionate a sex life as two sixty-hour-a-week jobs and a three-year-old allowed for.

"You know how you were saying how beautiful Ket Siong was back then?" Renee smiled reminiscently. "You should see him now."

Jason was pretty, and worked out in accordance with the demands of his job, but his audience favoured the ethereal look. Ket Siong, too, had been on the slender-brooding-artist side of attractive ten years ago, but that had changed. He'd always been tall; now he was broad in proportion.

"I think he must have gotten into the gym since uni," added Renee.

"I have changed my mind. He was not beautiful. He was a dick. A poop emoji with hair," said Nathalie.

But as Renee expected, she couldn't resist. After a moment she said, "Do you have photos? You didn't take a selfie with him? Oh, and of course he is not on social media."

She let out a sigh of thwarted nosiness. "I'll take your word for it that he is not ugly. That is good, so far as it goes. But this see-ing him again, being 'friends'"—Renee could hear the quotation marks in Nathalie's voice—"that is much further than it should go. You can't be friends."

"Why, because I'm a straight woman and he's a straight man? Well, a man attracted to women," Renee amended conscien-tiously, thinking of Derek. "He might be bisexual."

"No. Because it's *Ket*," said Nathalie. She was so cross she downed the remainder of her beetroot latte without even grimac-ing. She patted her mouth with a napkin, continuing, "He broke your heart! Do you think that's a good foundation for friend-ship?"

Renee had known she would come in for a telling-off when Nathalie heard about Ket Siong, but she felt injured. Did Nath-alie think she hadn't changed at all from the naive twenty-year-old who'd had her heart broken?

Sure, thinking about that night with Ket Siong made her giddy and warm and smug. But who wouldn't feel like that about getting off with a hot guy? It didn't have to mean anything. It *didn't* mean anything. Renee was one hundred percent in control of the situation.

"That was a long time ago," she said. "We're both adults now. There's no reason we can't decide to let go of all that baggage."

"Ket only came up with that line about being friends when you said you weren't up for a relationship," said Nathalie. "I thought you learnt your lesson about being friends with guys who only want to sleep with you."

That was a hit. Renee winced. She wasn't proud of that phase of her late teens and early twenties, before she'd grown out of appreciating the perverse validation of men feeling entitled to her body, and pruned guys like that out of her social circle.

Nathalie pursued her advantage. "Remember all the whining about friend zones?"

"Ket Siong isn't like that," said Renee weakly.

"Only because you liked him! And you still have a big old crush on him. Admit it."

"No, I don't," said Renee, but she didn't sound convinced, even to herself.

Maybe she did have a tiny crush on Ket Siong. It would explain the way her heart skipped whenever she thought about their upcoming non-date.

But even if that was true, it was no big deal. It wasn't like she was in *love* with Ket Siong. This was probably just her psyche's way of distracting her while her ego recovered from the Jason breakup.

"Anyway," said Renee, "so what if I do? I'm allowed crushes."

Nathalie shook her head. "Your terrible taste in men . . ."

"You *liked* Ket Siong. You kept telling me to go after him, back then!"

"He was so soft-spoken he fooled me," said Nathalie. "Then he messed you around and I realised he was no different from all the other jerks."

"We were just kids. We both made mistakes," said Renee. She remembered what Ket Siong had said. "But we were good as friends. That part worked."

Nathalie leaned back in her adorable but uncomfortable wooden chair, which looked like it had done duty in a primary school in a previous life. She crossed her arms, dissatisfied. "You will not listen to me."

"It's a morning at a museum. What's the worst that could happen?"

"He could break your heart again. I deal with enough bodily

fluids from Thomas, I don't need you sobbing all over my clothes, too." Nathalie sighed. "Thomas wiped his nose on my red DVF dress the other day. You know the new one, with the flowers?"

"And the cute flared sleeves," confirmed Renee, adding, with feeling, "That's horrific. How much was the dress?"

"Too much," said Nathalie darkly. "Thomas is lucky he's so cute."

Renee considered her options. She wasn't about to persuade Nathalie that hanging out with Ket Siong was a good idea. But there must be some way to reassure her best friend that her decision-making skills could be trusted—more, at least, than those of a three-year-old with no respect for fashion.

Renee had fallen in love with Ket Siong once before and suffered the consequences. What better inoculation could there be against her developing feelings again? Looked at that way, Ket Siong was the safest guy she could be spending time with right now.

"You don't need to worry," she told Nathalie. "I'm not going to break my heart. I didn't even cry on your shoulder when Jason broke up with me."

Nathalie sat up. "Yes, why didn't you? You should have told me. I could have taken you out to get smashed."

"I was busy," Renee reminded her. Despite herself, she felt a little smile curve her lips at the recollection of what she'd been busy with.

Her mind threw up an image of Ket Siong from that night: shirtless, looking up at her from between her knees with that breathtaking intensity peculiar to him. Her cheeks warmed.

Nathalie did not miss this. She looked forbidding. Then— even more alarmingly—she brightened.

"When is it you are seeing Ket again?" she said. "Saturday? Great. I'll come."

Renee stared. "What?"

"I like Rembrandt. All those cute little old men in hats." Nathalie started tapping at her phone, pulling up the exhibition web page.

"But you hate museums," said Renee. "You say it's like going to an art zoo."

"Let's have lunch after," said Nathalie. "What about Roka? I've been craving Japanese. I can book. Is Ket coming, or can we ditch him?"

"Who's going to look after Thomas?" tried Renee, though she was conscious the note of desperation in her voice was far from dignified.

"He's got two parents," said Nathalie, mildly surprised. "Jeroen doesn't have any plans this weekend." She pinned Renee with a penetrating look. "There's no reason I can't come, is there? I was friends with Ket, too, before he turned out to be a cad. Of course, if it was a date, I would not dream of intruding."

In spite of Renee's exasperation, Nathalie's dogged support warmed her. After all, Nathalie had been friends with Ket Siong, too, originally. Renee tended to forget.

She'd definitely got Nathalie in the breakup, if you could even call it a breakup. It wasn't like she and Ket Siong had ever actually dated.

She could see why Nathalie was concerned, to be fair. Renee's record with Ket Siong was not such as to fill her friend with confidence that she wouldn't get overinvested.

"You become more of a terrible Asian auntie by the day," said Renee, giving up. "You'll have to buy your own tickets. Ket Siong's already booked for the ten-thirty entry."

Nathalie might fulminate all she liked, but she could be trusted to be civil to Ket Siong in person. And maybe she was right. Having her there would take the meetup further away from any possible date vibes—establish it on the right footing, as a platonic hangout between people who liked each other but had no plans to sleep with each other (again).

"Thank you," said Nathalie placidly. "I will."

Then

Ket Siong tried to be Renee's friend and nothing more. He might have succeeded, if not for Renee's ex.

It was a pity Ket Siong wasn't there when Andrew Yeoh came to her flat. Fortunately, a neighbour heard the shouting and knocked on the door. Renee got to the door first and managed to flee, leaving the neighbour to deal with Andrew.

Ket Siong would have liked to deal with Andrew. It might have worked off some of the inhuman energy that had bedevilled him ever since he'd realised he was in love. He had been jittery and on edge since then, feeling simultaneously as though he could write a dozen symphonies and as though he'd explode unless he did something drastic, like throw himself in front of a speeding train for Renee. Or kiss her.

His teachers had noticed: "It'll be good for your music," said his favourite, a chain-smoking Lithuanian who loved Rachmaninoff.

So had Nathalie.

"Why don't you ask her out?" she said.

Ket Siong froze. "Who?"

Nathalie looked patient, though she might as well have rolled her eyes—her expression had much the same effect. "Renee, obviously. You like her, don't you?"

They were perched by the window of a Pret, where Renee met with Nathalie every morning for a companionable coffee. Ket Siong had started joining them at Renee's invitation, though he didn't order anything himself. He seemed to be the only one of the three who was subject to a student's usual budget constraints.

He stared out at the street, hoping his face wasn't doing anything unhelpful.

The thing was to act natural.

"Of course," he said. "We're friends."

This time Nathalie actually rolled her eyes. "You're both hopeless. Look, no matter what, Renee's never going to make the first move. She always expects people to screw her over, because of her family. It would be nice for her to have a boyfriend who treated her like a person, instead of a trophy. More importantly," said Nathalie, "it would be nice for me, her best friend."

"She said I was her best friend," said Ket Siong, without thinking. It took him a moment to realise how that might sound. "I mean . . ."

But Nathalie only laughed. "*You're* not her best friend. You're something else. Think about it, all right? You might be surprised."

Ket Siong said, "Nathalie. Are you saying . . ."

It was astonishingly difficult to put the question into words. He tried again. "Do you mean—has Renee said—"

Nathalie was getting up, coffee in hand.

"I've said as much as I can," she said, adding mysteriously, "Girl code. The rest is up to you."

He was thinking about this conversation with Nathalie while trying to study in his room when the intercom buzzed. He started guiltily. It could only be Renee. She was the main person who visited him at halls.

Renee was crying. She'd walked all the way in her socks.

"I didn't have time to put my shoes on," she said. Despite the tears trickling down her face, she was composed, flinty as Ket Siong had never seen her. "Andrew threw my phone out of the window. He said there was no point in me having it, since I never answer my messages. Wait . . ." Renee's composure wavered. "Where are you going?"

Ket Siong was putting on his coat. He looked up, puzzled Renee had to ask. "I'm going to kill him."

"Don't be stupid," said Renee. "My neighbour called the cops before she even knocked. Andrew's probably in the back of a police car getting screamed at by his father right now, if they even let him make the call."

Despite her reproof, Ket Siong must have done something right. Renee had lost her unearthly calm. She was sobbing properly now, her voice breaking.

"I c-came here because you have my shoes," she said. "My Converse? I left them here the other day."

"Those hurt your feet," said Ket Siong. Renee had dropped by after dim sum with friends, complaining that her shoes chafed. She'd kicked off her Converse and refused to put them on again. He'd gone to her flat and got her another pair of shoes so she could go straight to her next tutorial from his place.

"It doesn't matter. My feet already hurt," said Renee. She put her face in her hands.

Ket Siong knelt and peeled her socks off her feet, as gently as he could. Her feet were rubbed raw. She must have been limping for the last part of the walk.

"You can get blister plasters," he said. "I'll go to Boots. Do you have your keys?" She didn't. He handed Renee his phone. "Tell your concierge I'm coming. It's those black Adidas trainers you like, right?"

"You're not going now?"

Ket Siong paused while pulling on his shoes. "Do you need anything else?" It *was* coming on to dinnertime. "I could get a takeaway?"

Renee shook her head. "I don't want food." She paused, then said, in a small voice, "I want a hug."

Ket Siong stopped. Renee wouldn't meet his eyes. She was curled in on herself, her shoulders hunched. It wasn't how he was used to seeing her. There was no sign of her characteristic happy confidence, like that of a delightful baby charmed with all the world.

He took off his shoes and, slowly, his coat. Renee was sitting on his bed. She'd never done that before. Neither of them had noticed, what with everything going on.

He sat down on the bed and put an arm around her. Renee turned in towards him at once, burying her face in his shoulder, and then it was surprisingly easy to put his other arm around her. It felt natural to hold her close, as though he had nothing to hide.

For a while they were quiet. Ket Siong thought, *I'll remember this for the rest of my life.*

It was Renee who broke the silence.

"Your heart's beating so fast." Her voice was a near whisper.

Ket Siong had been hoping she wouldn't notice. It was typical of Renee to have pointed it out, instead of politely pretending nothing was happening.

It was also like Renee not to leave it there.

"Ket Siong," she said, in wonder. "Do you *like* me?"

Now it came to it, it was impossible to lie. Ket Siong nodded.

"Nathalie said so, but . . ."

Ket Siong's head came up. "What did she say?"

"She said no boy does the stuff you do for me unless they—you know," said Renee. "I told her, Ket Siong's just being nice. We're friends. She laughed at me," she added, with a hint of petulance.

"I am your friend," said Ket Siong, because it was important that she understand that was still true.

"Why didn't you say anything?"

Ket Siong thought of Andrew Yeoh, shoving his way into Renee's home. "I didn't want to be like the others."

"You couldn't be," whispered Renee. "There's never been anyone else like you."

Something in her voice gave him the courage to meet her eyes. Suddenly Ket Siong knew that, incredible as it seemed, Renee wanted him to kiss her—would be disappointed if he didn't lean in and press his lips to hers.

He'd never yet been able to resist giving Renee anything she wanted.

Their first kiss was everything he had imagined it might be.

Even so, it was rapidly overshadowed by the kisses that followed. Renee pressed herself against him, her mouth hungry, as though she had been thinking about this too, had been wanting it just as much.

To the extent thought was guiding him, he was trying to be respectful. It was Renee who lay back, pulling him down onto the bed, Renee who slid her hands under his shirt. She stroked his waist, her touch tentative, then—growing bolder—explored the dip in his lower back. Her clever fingers skimmed up his spine, finding his shoulder blades.

It was starting to feel almost rude keeping his hands to himself. Ket Siong tried putting a hand up under Renee's blouse and was encouraged by her receptive wriggle. He felt the lace of her bra under his fingertips and reached under it, cupping her breast. The nipple was soft against his palm, but it stiffened as he rolled it between his fingers.

He was lying sideways, so only his top half was pressed against her. Renee tried to tug him closer, but Ket Siong held back, conscious of his erection digging into the mattress. He had a feeling things might be over a little too soon if he got too close, and there were things he wanted to do first. He pushed the fabric of Renee's blouse out of the way, fumbling with her bra.

He had no experience of taking anyone's bra off, and figuring it out took an embarrassingly long time. They both started getting distracted, till Renee sat up and took off her blouse, undoing her bra one-handed. Fortunately, she only had to stop kissing him briefly in order to do this.

Ket Siong was vaguely aware he should take his shirt and jumper off—it was what they both wanted—but kissing Renee was taking up all his attention.

Wasn't there something else he was going to do as well? Something important.

It was bothering him enough that he pulled away from her so he could remember. She looked adorably rumpled, her hair tousled and her cheeks flushed.

He hadn't done anything yet about the fact she'd taken off her bra. That was what he'd forgotten.

She sighed when he lowered his face to her breasts. He took a nipple into his mouth, sucking it. Renee let out a stifled moan.

It was at this point that the phone rang.

Ket Hau had chosen Ket Siong's ringtone for him, in the hope of curing his inattention to his phone. It was like having a car alarm go off in the room. Renee started, kneeing Ket Siong in the chest. He fell off the bed, landing on the floor with a thud that knocked the air out of him.

As he was staring up at the ceiling, dazed, Renee's face hove into view.

"Oh my God, are you OK?" she said.

He had to strain to hear her over the phone ringing. It had to be a spam call. His family would have texted in advance if they wanted to speak, and it was late in Malaysia. Ma and Ket Hau would be asleep.

Ket Siong grabbed his phone off the desk and rejected the call. It was from a private number.

He collapsed back onto the floor. Renee looked down at him, pink and apologetic.

"Sorry," she said. "Did I hurt you?"

"I'm fine," said Ket Siong. "I need to change my ringtone."

Renee was still topless. He was struggling not to stare. But it didn't seem to occur to her to feel awkward.

"Why do you even have one of those?" she said, meaning his phone. "It looks like it should be in a museum. You can get a smartphone cheap nowadays." She paused. "Your birthday's in May, right?"

"I don't want a smartphone," said Ket Siong. "My phone does everything I need it to."

Despite his best efforts, his gaze had drifted downwards from her face. He only realised when Renee caught him looking. She smiled.

For a moment they gazed at each other, sheepish and delighted.

"Do you want to come back up here?" said Renee. She held out her arms.

With impeccable timing, her stomach let out a loud growl.

Ket Siong sat up. "When did you last eat?"

Renee sighed, slumping against the wall. "You're not going to interrogate me about my diet now? We could be *making out.*"

"Did you have lunch?" said Ket Siong, frowning. Renee had a bad habit of skipping meals.

Her shifty look was all the answer he needed. He rummaged around for his shoes, sitting on the bed next to Renee while he put them on.

"Ket Siong . . ."

"I'll get us dinner," said Ket Siong. "Takeaway from the Vietnamese place?"

Renee loved the Vietnamese place. She wavered visibly at the thought of their bún bowls.

"I can get that Thai canned drink you like," said Ket Siong. "Coconut? Aloe vera?"

"Can I have grass jelly?" said Renee, giving in. "I'll give you some money—oh, I don't have my purse. I'll pay you back."

Ket Siong shook his head. "I'll drop by your place and get your shoes. Do you want me to bring back anything else?"

"My purse?" said Renee, without much hope. Then, not meeting his eyes, "It might be good to have my pyjamas. And a change of clothes? If . . . I mean . . ."

"Oh," said Ket Siong. It was some comfort to know, first, that Renee wasn't looking at him, and second, that she was also blushing. "That's—that's a good idea."

On an impulse, he swooped down and kissed her. Renee moved at just the wrong time, so they bumped foreheads, and his kiss landed to the side of her mouth, instead of on her lips. But when Ket Siong pulled back, she was smiling.

"Don't be too long," she said.

"I won't," he promised.

10

Now

Renee was humming to herself as she entered the lobby of her office building, after her coffee with Nathalie. She was looking forward to the weekend, getting to see friends in a context that had nothing to do with work. It was like being in her twenties again and having a social life.

Now she'd had time to get used to the idea of Nathalie joining her visit to the National Gallery with Ket Siong, Renee decided it would be nice. She never got to do stuff like that with Nathalie anymore.

On reflection, she felt she'd pulled off something rather clever. Nathalie would have felt guilty about dumping childcare duties on her husband for most of a Saturday if not for the compelling excuse of having to avert romantic disaster.

So Renee was in a good mood, until she saw the man standing in the lobby.

He was inspecting a painting on the wall—a blotchy, half-hearted imitation of a Rothko, blandly corporate. His back was to her, but everything about him was instantly familiar: from the dark hair stiff with hair gel, to the discontented slope of the shoulders in the Ralph Lauren suit, down to the knobbly ankles emerging from the custom-made leather shoes. He'd put on some weight, but he carried it well: it made him look substantial, a man to be reckoned with.

Renee hadn't seen him in years. Perhaps that was one definition of family—a body of knowledge it was impossible to carve out of yourself, no matter how hard you tried.

Su Khoon turned, as though he'd sensed her watching him.

If not for that call from Dad at the beginning of the week, Renee would have kept on walking, pretending she hadn't seen her second brother. On leaving Singapore, she'd blocked her brothers' numbers, put them and their wives on restricted view across her social media accounts, and set up a filter on her inbox so any emails from them would go straight to Trash. As far as she knew, they hadn't tried to get in touch. They'd accomplished what they wanted, after all—got rid of her, cleared the field.

They must have been royally pissed to hear Renee was in the running to take over Chahaya. If that piece of news had surprised her, she could only imagine her brothers' reaction.

She suppressed a smile.

"Er Ge," she said. "I didn't know you were in London already."

"I messaged you," said Su Khoon. "But you didn't reply."

"Weird," said Renee blandly. "Are you sure you had the right number? I've changed it."

If she was going to have to work with Su Khoon, she'd have to update the filters on her inbox so she'd see emails from him, if not Su Beng. Maybe she could get a burner phone exclusively for fraternal communications.

"It was the number Dad gave me." Su Khoon glanced at the reception desk. The two women on it gave him a forbidding glare, as did the security guard by the barriers. Evidently there had already been some form of interaction, and it hadn't gone well.

"Must be some glitch, then," said Renee. "I'll have to check my phone settings." She directed a reassuring smile at the reception staff.

She could practically see the ill temper hovering over her brother, as if he were a cartoon character dogged by a storm cloud. He was fidgeting with his cuff links, a crease between his eyebrows.

At least it was her second brother she was dealing with, not Su Beng. Su Khoon could be trusted not to shout or get physical, no matter what shitty things he might say in that even voice.

The downside was that he was the smarter of her two brothers. That *should* mean he'd see the benefits of playing nice with her. What it would probably mean was he'd try to sabotage her, but with a better chance of success than if it was Su Beng doing it.

"We need to talk," said Su Khoon.

Renee knew how this was supposed to go. Her job, as the youngest sister, was to identify his displeasure and set about soothing it. *Yes, of course, Er Ge. I'll clear my schedule. Come up to my office and I'll get you some refreshments while you say whatever the hell you want to me.*

She glanced at her phone. "You're in luck. I've got a gap now, though we'll have to wrap up before four thirty."

Renee had never been good at managing her brothers' feelings for them. It was one of the many ways in which she was a failure as a daughter and a sister, by the standards of her family.

Su Khoon's face twitched. But he knew, just as Renee did, that their behaviour was under scrutiny. Neither could afford to lose points with their father, and they could trust that the other would not waste any advantage they gave away.

"It's about Chahaya," he said, with what for him amounted to patience. "We should talk in private." He cleared his throat. "Can we go to your office?"

For Su Khoon, even this courtesy—making a request of his younger sister, instead of commanding her—amounted to a loss of face. He'd see it as a strategic concession.

Renee decided to take it as a good omen. Maybe they were going to be able to work together, after all.

"Sure," she said. "Come on up."

Su Khoon looked around Renee's office with an expression of faint disgust.

"A little over the top, no?" he said.

This might have hurt Renee's feelings fifteen years ago, but the one nice thing about her brothers trying to ruin her reputation was that it had made her indifferent to their approval. Anyway, she knew what Su Khoon's office was like—a gleaming glass-walled room at the top of a skyscraper, with pictures of him shaking hands with various dignitaries and industry tycoons, looking like a dick.

Renee's office was much nicer, no contest. Virtu rented a serviced unit on the top floor of a restored Edwardian property, so there wasn't much she could do about the dimensions or layout of the space. But it had large windows, letting in ample natural light, and she'd painted the walls in muted pastels: mint green, blush pink, primrose yellow and hazy blue. Her room was furnished with vintage finds from antique markets and eBay, batik sarongs repurposed as wall hangings, nineteenth-century prints of Southeast Asian flora and fauna, and a thriving miniature grove of plants that was the bane of Louise's life.

What obviously annoyed Su Khoon the most was the display of framed articles and awards, including a blown-up image of the *Vogue Singapore* cover featuring Renee. She'd dithered over putting up the *Vogue* cover, worrying it might come off as narcissistic, but Su Khoon's jaundiced expression put doubt to rest. It was one hundred percent worth it.

"I'll get to the point," said Su Khoon crisply, turning so he couldn't see the cover. "Dad's getting old. If he was in his right mind he wouldn't be giving you ideas about running Chahaya."

"You don't want a drink, then?" said Renee. She poked her head out of the office. "Louise, could I have a green tea, please? Lovely, thanks."

"You don't need to think it's a compliment, what Dad's doing," said Su Khoon, when she'd got her green tea and shut the door. "He wants to test me and Su Beng, keep us guessing. After all these years, he's still hoping to get Da Ge to shape up." He looked down his nose at her, cold. "You're only useful because Da Ge's stupid enough to believe you're actually in the running."

Renee sat down behind her desk, not bothering to offer her brother a seat. He'd take one if he felt like it.

"That must be annoying for you," she said. "Having to go through this charade, if you think Dad's preselected Da Ge anyway."

"Dad has his preferred choice. He's traditional," said Su Khoon. "But he's not stupid. Da Ge's going to mess up. Then Dad will see there's only one person for the job."

Renee sipped her tea while she considered her response.

Dad would want her to be discreet and accommodating, not say things she knew would piss her brother off.

But being herself had always been her best asset in business, if not in her personal life. Which meant saying what she thought. It was not an approach her family had ever appreciated, but she had to set the terms on which she was willing to engage with them, if this exercise was to be sustainable in the long run.

"Yourself, you mean," she said. "That's why you're here. You're confident about beating Su Beng, but you're scared I'm real competition."

Su Khoon scoffed. "Don't be ridiculous. You think you can manage Chahaya? Your little fashion label's all very well. I assume you're not losing money if you can afford to fill your office with this crap."

He glanced around the room again to show what he thought of it. Renee bit her tongue so as not to say, *No, we aren't losing money. Unlike some other people I could name. What was the crypto-currency you invested in called again—IdiotCoin?*

Squabbling with her brothers always reverted her to about age twelve.

"But Chahaya's beyond you," Su Khoon was saying. "You can't take the stress. A little criticism in the newspapers and you ran away. The CEO of Chahaya has to be tougher than that."

He lowered himself to the sofa, leaning forward and meeting Renee's eyes.

"Look, I didn't come here to fight," he said. "You're a sensible girl. You need to be realistic about what's going to happen if you try to take over Chahaya. This isn't about you or whatever you want to prove. Chahaya is about the family. If you mess up, it's not only money or investments you're risking. It's our future— the kids' future. They deserve to benefit from everything Dad's worked so hard to build. True or not?"

This was a calculated blow beneath the belt, attempting to deploy Renee's nephews and nieces against her.

It might have worked better if she was insecure about her abilities.

"Of course," she said. "But deciding I'd mess up if I took over seems a big assumption to me. Do you think it's really justified by the evidence? I appreciate there's no reason you should have been following Virtu."

This was a deliberate jab. She knew Su Khoon and Su Beng had to have been watching Virtu closely in order to do what they did a few years back, and they knew she knew.

"But Dad has, and he thinks I could do the job," Renee continued. "We're going to have to work together on this pitch to Freshview for the construction contract. Why don't you give me a chance, see how I do? I might surprise you."

"Sure," said Su Khoon. "I should bring you to meet Low Teck Wee. Hope he doesn't remember you're the one who fucked things up with his nephew.

"Oh, you thought I didn't know?" he said, at Renee's expression. "Andrew Yeoh told me you called the cops on him back then, when he was only trying to apologise. Now Dad's saying you're going to help us strike a deal with his uncle's company." Su Khoon snorted. "I should get Dad tested for dementia."

Big talk from a man whose father pays his phone bill, Renee didn't say.

Her first instinct was to defend herself—explain that Andrew had stormed into her flat, screamed at her for daring to break up with him, and thrown her phone out of the window. She hadn't even involved the authorities, despite all of that; that was the neighbour's idea. But her flush of indignation was succeeded almost immediately by weariness.

If Su Khoon cared about what had really happened, he would have asked Renee. This was just another bid for leverage.

"Have you ever told Dad about that?" said Su Khoon.

"He hasn't raised it," said Renee. "But you've reminded me, I saw Uncle Low the other day. I'm going to meet up with his daughter, she's interested in getting into the fashion industry. I should mention it to Dad." She leaned back in her chair, watching her brother's face work.

"I wasn't the first woman to dump Andrew, or the last," she said. "I doubt Low Teck Wee is going to let that influence his business decisions. So how about it? Are you going to work with me, or not?"

Su Khoon had to have expected that she would put up some resistance to his negging campaign. But he'd never been any more patient than Su Beng, merely better at hiding it. His patience was visibly fraying now.

"Work with you?" he said. "Might as well torpedo the deal. I'll lay it out for you. You can tell Dad you're not the right person to run Chahaya, withdraw yourself from consideration. Or you can go ahead and destroy your relationship with the family for good. Take up Dad's offer, and you can forget about seeing the kids.

You won't have brothers anymore, or nieces and nephews. Mom will never talk to you again."

Renee had been prepared for this threat from the moment Su Khoon mentioned the kids.

It was probably no use pointing out that she had moved to London precisely so she *wouldn't* have to see her family. She was fond of her brothers' kids, but it wasn't like she kept sending them birthday and Christmas presents because not seeing them had left a void in her life. The pleasure of hanging out with the kids had always been balanced out by having to deal with their parents.

But she figured it was worth reminding the kids they had an aunt who cared about them, whether or not they met their parents' standards for satisfactory offspring. That was what Auntie Mindy had done for her.

"Dad's made his decision. He wants to consider all of us," said Renee. "It's not my intention to offend you and Da Ge, but it's an interesting opportunity for me. I'm not going to withdraw."

Su Khoon sighed. "Wasting my time. I knew you wouldn't listen, but you're my sister. I thought I should try to reason with you first."

He sat up, crossing his arms. Renee tensed. They were coming to what Su Khoon had really come here to say.

"I didn't want to do this, but you're forcing my hand," he said. "I've got photos of you from Jason Tsai. If you don't tell Dad you're pulling out, I'll release them to the press. It's your choice."

For a moment, Renee didn't feel anything. Then her brain caught up with her ears.

Here she was, telling herself the breakup with Jason hadn't bothered her much, she thought dully. It was true she'd never allowed herself to get too attached to Jason. A part of her had always held back, never quite sure how much she could rely on him. She probably hadn't been in love with him for a while, even before he dumped her.

But she had never thought he would do anything like this. It hurt astonishingly to find out she was wrong.

And Renee prided herself on her judgment of character. What a joke.

She must have betrayed too much emotion. Su Khoon couldn't resist the opportunity to rub it in. He put his elbows on his knees, looking grave and concerned.

"I understand Jason has video, too," he said. "I haven't been able to get his agreement to pass that to me yet, but we're in negotiations."

"You know, there are laws against this kind of thing," said Renee.

Su Khoon shrugged. "Sue me if you want. Once the images are out there, they can't be taken back. Stupid thing to do," he added, in a tone of fraternal reproof, "sharing that kind of thing with a man."

A freezing calm descended on Renee, numbing emotion. Su Khoon's condescension didn't register as more than a pinprick, incapable of causing any real sensation.

"You're right," she said. "I should have learnt from my family that men can't be trusted." She rose to her feet. "I assume that's all? Don't let me keep you. I've got a call I need to prepare for."

This took Su Khoon aback, though he covered it up well after the first moment of surprise.

"What's your answer to my offer?" he said.

Renee allowed her lips to curve in an incredulous smile.

"That wasn't an offer. That's what's usually known as blackmail," she said. "It's interesting you thought the first people I'd call were my lawyers. I would've thought of the police."

Su Khoon rolled his eyes. "You're not going to report me. Dad won't be impressed if you set the police on your own brother."

He was right. Renee wasn't going to report him—or Jason, though that would be tempting, if it weren't for the fact there was no way she'd be able to keep her family out of it.

But there was no harm in planting a seed of doubt in Su Khoon's mind. Her brothers found her unpredictable, because she operated by rules they either couldn't or wouldn't understand—she'd never quite worked out which it was.

"Do you know your way out, or would you like me to get someone to show you?" she said.

"I'll manage." Su Khoon got up, his expression ugly. "You've had fair warning. It's up to you to resolve this in a way that works for everybody. You can't say I didn't give you a chance."

Renee made no reply. She didn't take her eyes off him, but stood, rigid, behind her desk, while he slunk out of her office. Her staff feigned obliviousness as he passed by.

She only relaxed once the lift doors closed on him.

Louise was staring at her through the glass panel that divided her office from the open-plan workspace. Louise jerked her gaze away when Renee met her eyes.

Renee sat down.

She didn't know how much time had passed when the knock came at the door. She had to try twice before her voice came out, clear and steadier than she felt: "Come in."

It was Louise. She hovered by the entrance, her freckled face full of worry.

"Are you OK?" she said tentatively.

Renee could pretend there was nothing to be upset about, ask why she wouldn't be OK.

She said, "Yes."

It was true, more or less. Su Khoon was behind the times. There was no need for him to come to her office to tell Renee she would no longer have a family if she took over Chahaya. She had known she didn't have a family for years.

That was nothing to get worked up about. She should be used to it by now.

"Thank you," she added.

Louise's gaze lit upon the mug of green tea she'd brought in earlier. She brightened.

"Your tea'll have gone cold," she said, with the relief of a Brit who had found something definitely appropriate to do at a time of crisis. "I'll get you another." She hesitated. "Would you like me to cancel your four thirty?"

Renee glanced at her computer screen. Fifteen minutes to go. That was ample time to get her head back in the game.

"No." She managed a smile. "I'll be fine."

As Louise left to refill her cup of tea, Renee opened her inbox to track down the email chains she needed for the call. But then a thought struck her. She picked up her phone and tapped out a text:

Jason, we need to talk.

She paused, looking down at the words. She had much more to say to him, but that would do as a start.

She hit send.

11

By the time Renee got up from her desk to head home, it was ten o'clock, her room an island of light in the darkness of the office. Her neck ached, her shoulders were stiff, and every time she thought of her exchange with her brother, she felt dirty and gross and ashamed.

So instead of thinking, she put plans in motion. By the next morning her lawyer had confirmed receipt of instructions to draft a formal letter to Jason, and she had a crisis PR consultant on board. The PR consultant set up a press search and a Google Alert, and would let her know as soon as any pictures were released.

Jason hadn't responded to her text asking to speak, which was no surprise. It had been meant as an opening volley, a chance for Jason to do the decent thing. But he'd never taken any of the chances she'd given him during their relationship, so why would he start now?

What made no sense was why Jason had decided to sell Renee's pictures to her brother. He was hardly hurting for money. And he'd dumped her, so it couldn't be about revenge.

Su Khoon must have offered a huge sum, combined with some light blackmail by way of incentive—threats to leak gossip about Jason's secret relationship with a Singaporean heiress, for example. Even something as unobjectionable as that would go down like a lead balloon with his audience, and there might be worse skeletons in Jason's closet. She knew he'd been something of a party animal at college.

But all of this was speculation, and not about to make any difference to her position. Having done what she could to protect herself, Renee tried not to worry about it. She didn't even know if Su Khoon had the images he claimed. She should have demanded proof, but she'd been so sickened all she could think of was getting him out of her space.

It was unlikely he'd been making empty threats. That would be too easy for her to discredit. But possibly he was more reluctant than he let on to pull the trigger on publishing the photos. It wasn't like disseminating revenge porn of his sister would make him look good in Dad's eyes—though that assumed she would be able to persuade their father Su Khoon was behind it.

The genius of the threat was its shittiness. Renee wouldn't have believed her brother capable of it until he'd said it. She should have recorded the conversation. She ought to know by now that no matter how low her expectations of her family were, they would find some way to disappoint her.

At least the biggest splash any photos were likely to make was in Singapore. Renee didn't have a public profile anywhere else—certainly no one in the UK would be interested. She was trying to build Virtu up in its other markets, though, and having nudes in public circulation wouldn't help there, given Asian standards for female virtue. But that was what the crisis PR consultant was for—to help her bury the pictures, to the extent she could.

Of course, if it was known Jason Tsai was involved, it would be a much bigger deal. But that was why Renee wasn't worried about Su Khoon getting any video footage out of Jason. There was only one video, so far as she knew, and Jason was identifiable in it.

She was very ready for the weekend when it came. She felt too fragile about the whole affair to want to tell Nathalie about it—not that Renee could talk about something like this in Ket Siong's presence, anyway. But hanging out with Nathalie always made her feel better, no matter what else was going on in her life.

It would be good to see Ket Siong, too. The prospect made her chest feel bubbly, as though she'd swallowed a bottle of sparkling water.

Possibly Nathalie had a point about her having a crush.

"Well, maybe that's what I want," Renee said defiantly to her reflection in the mirror, while she was putting her face on. "A nice crush on a nice guy. It's not going anywhere, it's not doing anything, except distracting me from all the shit I don't want to think about." She set her eyeliner pencil down on the dressing table with slightly more force than necessary. "Perfect, if you ask me."

Her possible tiny inconsequential crush *did* mean that Renee spent so long getting ready that she was too late to take public transport to the National Gallery and had to jump in a cab. She was wearing a deep brown velvet dress, belted at the waist, and pointy-toed gold slippers, each topped with a row of black satin bows.

She checked herself again in her compact while the cab set off. She looked fresh and natural. Not at all like she was trying too hard, even if the casual tumble of her hair had taken half an hour to achieve.

Nathalie agreed. "Those shoes are *too* cute," she said, hugging Renee.

Ket Siong made no comment on Renee's outfit, only looked at her. It was hard to read his expression. He turned away just as Renee was starting to blush.

"Shall we go in?" he said.

Renee could feel Nathalie's eyes boring into her.

"Sure. How much do I owe you for the ticket?" she said to Ket Siong, as they were waved through into the gallery.

Ket Siong shook his head, which Renee had been prepared for.

"I'll get lunch, then," she said, before remembering they hadn't talked about going for a meal. "You want to come for lunch after? Nathalie and I are going for Japanese. The restaurant's a bit fusion-y, but good."

Ket Siong hesitated. "I don't want to intrude."

"You wouldn't be intruding. Seriously, come. I think Nathalie booked for three anyway." Renee knew this for a fact, because she had insisted, over Nathalie's protests.

"How are we going to do a debrief if Ket's right there?" Nathalie had said.

"We won't need a debrief," said Renee patiently. "Because it's not a date."

Nathalie had grumbled, but done as she said.

Renee was vindicated; it didn't feel like a date. She wasn't getting to talk to Ket Siong much. The exhibition was popular and the gallery was bustling with people.

But it was nice—looking at art and gossiping discreetly with Nathalie about the other museumgoers. Renee felt herself relaxing, her shoulders coming down from around her ears.

It sucked about her brother and Jason, but they didn't matter. She had friends, people she could trust and be herself with.

In time, she cast up before a painting of a man and a woman, executed with extraordinary tenderness and delicacy. Renee had been drawn to the picture for the richness of their dress—the colours leapt off the canvas—but she lingered, struck by the couple's expressions. The man had a hand on the woman's bodice; her hand rested lightly on his, her rings gleaming.

She'd lost track of the others in the crowd, but Ket Siong joined her now. Renee didn't speak straight away. Ket Siong liked having time to process things.

"It's the hands I love," she said, after a while. "They're so beautiful."

But when she glanced away from the painting, Ket Siong was gazing at her.

There was that look in his eyes again—the same look as when Renee had first showed up. Except she was beginning to suspect the meaning of his expression wasn't that hard to decipher.

Flustered, she ducked her head.

"I wonder where Nathalie's got to," she said. Her voice sounded hurried and artificial. She turned to scan the crowd, and looked right in the face of international pop idol Jason Tsai.

Jason was wearing a baseball cap, sunglasses, and a face mask, but she'd seen him in this getup enough times that it only made him more recognisable. She did not recognise the younger woman hanging off his arm.

He hadn't spotted Renee yet. She had the advantage. And Renee wouldn't have got where she was today if she'd ever wasted an advantage.

She marched over to Jason, grabbed his free arm, and said pleasantly:

"We can talk, or I can make a scene. I've got a friend standing by with her phone and you know I've got a Weibo account. You decide, Jason."

Jason managed to suppress his yelp, but the girl didn't. Nathalie magically emerged from the crowd, took in the scene in a glance, and—bless her—whipped out her phone. It looked like she was recording.

Renee said dramatically, raising her voice and taking care to enunciate, "You were cheating on me all along?" She added in Mandarin, for good measure, "I trusted you!"

"I'll talk! I'll talk," said Jason. "Just, not here." He looked at his horrified companion. "Cherry, babe, give me a moment, OK? I can explain everything, I promise."

Renee was already turning away.

"Come on," she said.

On a Saturday morning there was not, in fact, anywhere in the National Gallery quiet enough for the kind of conversation Renee was planning to have with Jason.

Renee's mistake was turning her back on Jason as she confirmed this. She heard Nathalie shout, "Hey!" And then Jason shot past them, legging it for the exit.

His girl's expression as she watched her date leave her in the dust was a picture. It would have been funny if Renee wasn't so busy kicking herself. Stupid, *stupid*—

"Jason!" she shouted.

Jason didn't look back. They were on level two, a grand flight of stairs away from the ground floor entrance. He was heading down the stairs when Ket Siong barrelled past Renee, slid down the railing, and flung himself on Jason, knocking him off his feet.

Jason went down with a screech. The two men rolled down the stairs, catching up on a landing, Jason swearing all the way.

By the time Renee got to them, Ket Siong had Jason's arms pinned and a knee on Jason's back, holding him down.

"Oh my God, are you OK?" said Renee.

People were hurrying past them, giving them alarmed glances. Nathalie tripped down the stairs with her phone held aloft.

"Perfect!" she said brightly. "I think I caught all of that." She smiled at a disapproving middle-aged white couple passing by. "We're making a film. Amazing what you can do with phones nowadays."

"No, I am not OK!" said Jason, his voice strained. "Who the hell is this guy? Get him off me!"

He bucked. Ket Siong shoved him down again.

"I wasn't talking to you," said Renee. She looked at Ket Siong.

Ket Siong's hair was mussed and he was breathing fast, but he was otherwise remarkably composed for someone who'd just pulled a move out of a Jackie Chan film. "I'm fine."

"You won't be when I sue you for assault!" snarled Jason.

Renee didn't see what Ket Siong did, but Jason squeaked and shut up. She bent down to look him in the face.

"Let's try this again," she said. "You've got a few options here. You could have a sensible conversation with me. Or I could post that video we just took, with me accusing you of cheating on me. Or—here's an even better idea—I could ring the police and report you for distributing revenge porn. That would probably go viral, don't you think?"

A number of different expressions chased themselves across Jason's face in rapid succession.

"I don't know what you're talking about," he said sulkily. "If you're going to physically assault me, fine, I'll do whatever you want. It's not like I've got a choice. But get your bodyguard off me. He's hurting my back."

They took Jason outside, to the terrace by the grand portico entrance to the museum, overlooking Trafalgar Square.

The square was busy with tourists, as always, clambering over the lions around Nelson's Column and taking selfies in front of the fountains and the giant crochet dodo currently occupying the fourth plinth. There was a group of climate change protestors in one corner of the square, chanting slogans and handing out flyers. On the terrace, a busker with a guitar sang throaty renditions of songs from the early noughties. It wasn't exactly private, but one could be reasonably confident of not being overheard.

Renee made sure Jason had his back to the stone balustrade lining the terrace. If he tried to break free again, he'd have to get past her—and Ket Siong, who was hovering just out of hearing distance, positioned to intercept any attempt at escape.

His expression was inscrutable. Renee had no idea what he was thinking, but she couldn't afford to care about that right now.

Nathalie was standing farther along the terrace, chatting affably with Jason's date. The girl looked worried, but she would have needed to be several years older and possessed of significant strength of mind in order to disentangle herself from a Nathalie determined to hang onto her.

Jason opened his mouth, but Renee got in first.

"You're a disgusting piece of shit," she said. "I didn't think dumping me the day after you arrived was the nicest thing you've ever done. But selling my pictures to my brother? That's low, Jason."

Jason's forehead wrinkled. "Selling . . . you mean photos of us have been leaked?"

It wasn't convincing. He'd never been a good actor.

"Photos of me, you mean," said Renee. "Did my brother say he wouldn't tell me? I told you about my family. You should've known it was a bad idea to trust him."

"Look," said Jason, "I don't know what your brother's told you, but I haven't sold any pictures to anyone. I'm the last person in the world who'd want a scandal.

"That's the only reason I ran," he added. "I'm not here for drama."

He leaned back, looking pleased with himself, as if he thought she might actually buy that explanation of his behaviour.

Well. Renee hadn't dated him for his brains.

She was struggling to remember why, exactly, she had dated him—or agreed when he'd asked for nudes. But it had seemed a natural enough thing to do in a long-distance relationship. She'd even been flattered. She knew how many girls there were out there who would fall over themselves to send Jason anything he wanted.

"That's what makes it so stupid on your part," said Renee. "It's not like you needed the money. And I have images of you, too. With audio, remember? That was your idea.

"Nobody cares about me outside of Singapore. Hell, even in Singapore, who's Renee Goh? Some rich guy's daughter who sells clothes. But a sex tape of Jason Tsai?" Renee crossed her arms. "That's going to draw some interest."

Jason blanched. "You wouldn't."

"I wouldn't have, before my brother started threatening to publish the photos you gave him," said Renee. "What have I got to lose? The public might as well know who those photos were for."

"I didn't know he was going to—I would never have agreed if he wasn't your brother, Renee," said Jason. "You've got to believe me."

Renee felt a thrill of grim satisfaction, not unlike the exhilaration of nailing a deal, or having a breakthrough on a knotty point of design—the kind of inspiration that brought a piece or collection together. That this particular thrill was tainted by feeling like she was wading through mud was to be expected. This was what dealing with her family was like. She would have to get used to it, if she was going to take on Chahaya.

"I thought it was about protecting you," said Jason. "Your brother said he was worried. He'd heard rumours, someone told him I've got a bad reputation. Total bullshit, obviously, but that's what families do, right? They worry. I had no idea he was going to—he told you he's going to *publish* them?"

"So he did threaten you," said Renee. "I figured he must have gotten dirt on you."

Jason was at least smart enough not to confirm this, or to attempt a denial that would be as good as confirmation.

"I haven't sent him the images yet," he said. "Part of me must have sensed he was shady."

Renee stiffened, the back of her neck prickling. A chill ran down her spine. "He doesn't have the photos? Are you telling the truth? You're going to suffer if you lie to me now, Jason. I'm not kidding."

Jason's eyes skidded away from her. It took Renee a moment to clock that he was looking behind her.

At Ket Siong. Who was glaring at Jason, as much as to say, *I will murder you if you make a single wrong move.*

It wasn't a face Renee had seen on Ket Siong before. Combined with the way he'd bulked up in the past decade, it was startlingly effective. She'd always been drawn to his gentleness, but seeing this side of him made him even more attractive. She turned back to Jason, unsettled.

"Where did you find that guy?" said Jason in a hushed voice. "You've never had security before."

"I asked you a question," said Renee.

Jason tore his gaze away from Ket Siong. "I, uh, I'm not lying. I agreed to think about it, but I haven't done anything yet. It's not like I *wanted* to do it," he added, aggrieved. "It's not who I am. You should know that, Renee."

Renee stared at him. Incredibly, he seemed serious.

"I don't know who you are," she said. "I don't know anything about you. I would have said you would never do anything like this."

Jason coloured.

"If it's not who you are," said Renee, "why even do it? If you'd thought about it for one second, it must have been obvious the risk wasn't worth it."

Jason muttered, "I need the money." At her disbelieving look, he added, "It's true. You know my parents manage my money."

"I thought you had a good relationship with them."

"I do," said Jason, injured. "A great relationship. But I've had some expenses recently. They're not a big deal. We could afford it, wouldn't even make a dent. But Mom wouldn't understand . . ."

"What was it? Gambling, hookers, drugs?" said Renee.

All of the above, probably. Renee had bought into Jason's clean-shaven image, duped along with his fans. She'd been so charmed by the fact he was a mama's boy, spoke to his parents every day, shared—Renee thought—everything with them.

"You know what, I don't want to know," she said, stuffing down her feelings about having been made a fool of at least three times over. She'd deal with them some other time. "How much does it come to?"

Jason hesitated. "Why do you want to know?"

He wasn't *that* dense. This was him pushing for an explicit assurance about where this was going.

That, Renee was happy to give him. "I'm going to make you an offer. How much do you need?"

She winced inwardly when he named the amount. Jason's overall estate might not notice money like that, but Renee would. She didn't have much spare liquidity. Everything went into the business. Extracting the sum Jason wanted would set back her plans for Virtu by years. So much for her dreams of a London store.

But if she beat Su Khoon at his game—if she won Chahaya—that would no longer matter. She'd be able to raise all the capital she needed for Virtu, then.

"I don't have that much money," she said. "But I can give you—" She named a figure that was around sixty percent of the sum.

Jason frowned. "Your brother . . ."

"Wouldn't have offered more than that, because he's not an idiot," said Renee. Su Khoon wasn't wholly in control of his own money, either—especially, she imagined, after his cryptocurrency losses. Dad would be keeping an eye on him. There was only so far he would've been able to go.

She had a flash of insight. "That's why you haven't sent him the photos yet. You've been trying to get more money out of him."

Jason's expression confirmed this. Renee moved on before he could start up with denials.

"I have something extra to sweeten the deal," she said. "Give me the images, delete any copies you have, and I'll delete my copies of our video. Your face is perfectly clear in it, if you don't remember."

This time it was Jason who winced. But he said, "If I accept your offer, that still leaves me in the red. Don't get me wrong, Renee, I want to help—"

"And I want to help you," said Renee. "It shouldn't be too hard to cover the remainder. Tell your parents you paid for a fan's cancer treatment or something. But I can't go any higher. Even giving you that much is going to hurt Virtu."

Jason's lip curled. "Of course, Virtu. That's always been the most important thing to you."

"Virtu has never fucked me over the way you were planning to," said Renee sweetly. "Are you taking the offer or not? There are other ways I can raise capital. I'm not going to be struggling to find buyers for my material."

Jason flushed a dark red. "If this is how you do business with everyone . . ."

Renee should have been less angry, more coaxing. Jason, like any man, had always responded better to being humoured than having his hand forced.

But she was running out of patience. There was a throbbing ache behind her temples. She hadn't had breakfast that morning, which was normal for her, but proved a bad idea today: she was feeling light-headed and wobbly.

"This is not how I *do business*," said Renee. "This is me doing my best to deal with a shit situation, brought on by you and my fucking brother and my stupid belief that I could trust my boyfriend. I've made you the best offer I can. If you want to reject it, go ahead. But you should remember, Jason. I don't only have that video. I have your mother's phone number."

She wasn't proud of that last line. If she'd had the foresight to eat some granola and yoghurt that morning, maybe she wouldn't have said it. But it sealed the deal.

"Fine," said Jason, his lips white with fury. "I accept."

12

Renee insisted on going straight to Jason's hotel room, so he could surrender his devices to her there and then. She had no intention of letting him go off to screw a counteroffer out of Su Khoon.

Jason resisted, until Ket Siong got involved. He didn't *do* anything—just loomed, with an uncharacteristic lack of respect for Jason's personal space. But Jason caved with remarkable rapidity. Renee had a feeling he wouldn't be going out without his security detail again.

They all went to the hotel together, the whole posse packed into a black cab, Jason's girl included. She looked pale and abashed.

If Renee had had any spare emotional bandwidth, she might have felt sorry for the girl. She'd set out that morning, the lead in a rom-com with a hot celebrity love interest, only to end the day playing a bit part in a tawdry melodrama.

Renee might have been embarrassed about dragging Nathalie and Ket Siong into the affair, too. Well, maybe not Nathalie. Nathalie wouldn't have been anywhere else for the world. She was making the most of her ability to beam rays of hatred at Jason while sitting opposite him in the cab. He was visibly wilting under the pressure.

Ket Siong, though . . . helpful as he'd been, Renee would happily have done without him. He was sitting in the passenger seat next to the driver, so she couldn't watch him and obsess about what he must be thinking.

She'd freak out about that later. For now, she couldn't find it in herself to worry about anything except wrapping up this hideous business.

The scouring quality of Nathalie's scrutiny seemed to put Jason in a penitent mood. When they arrived at the hotel, he dropped back from the group. Renee paid the cabbie, so she was lagging a little behind everyone else.

"Today was the first time I met Cherry in person," Jason said abruptly. He glanced at the others, his gaze skipping over his new girlfriend to rest on Ket Siong and Nathalie. He seemed unsure which of the two terrified him more.

"I never cheated on you with her," he went on. "I know you think I'm the scum of the earth, Renee, but you can trust me on that. When we were together, I was all in."

There must be something incurably honest about Jason, after all; his phrasing was so revealing. Renee hadn't seen him "in person" in months when she sent him those accursed photos of herself. As for that telling "never cheated on you with *her*" . . .

"I really cared about you," said Jason. "But you and Virtu . . . it was like you were married to your business. *We* were never going to come first."

"I believe you," said Renee wearily, because it was less effort than explaining she didn't give a shit anymore.

She waited till he moved away to take out her phone and schedule a reminder to herself to get tested for STDs. They'd been safe the last time they slept together, but who the hell knew anymore?

The operation went off without a hitch. Jason didn't even get Renee's phone off her, though he tried.

"I'm not the one who was auctioning off nudes," Renee said. "You can tell me when your people want to come over and go through my devices, and we can set something up. *You* are not invited," she added.

It was afternoon by the time she, Nathalie, and Ket Siong emerged from the hotel. The longer they'd been in Jason's room, the less abashed and the more thunderous Cherry had looked. It was clear Jason's day of mortifications was far from over.

This would no doubt be gratifying some other time. Renee should probably be feeling triumphant, or violated, or *something*. But she was blank as a stone. All she wanted was to crawl into bed and sleep for a thousand years.

She started saying to the others, "Sorry about all of that. You guys will be wanting to get home."

But a wave of dizziness passed over her. She stumbled. Ket Siong caught her by the arm.

Nathalie said, "You need to have lunch. I cancelled the reservation at Roka—the Aldwych branch is closing soon anyway—but Mayfair's open. How about it?" She held her phone up to show them the location of the restaurant on Google Maps. "It's not far. Ten-minute walk, at most."

Renee was aware of Ket Siong's gaze on her. He said, "Do you feel up to it?"

"I can do a ten-minute walk," said Renee, with dignity. Ket Siong nodded, letting go of her arm.

She found herself regretting the loss of his warmth. Maybe she should have toned it down with the dignity.

The walk to the restaurant and the wait for a table felt interminable. Exhaustion weighed Renee down.

She should have insisted on going home. She wasn't hungry, and she was hardly going to be good company.

But that didn't seem to bother Nathalie and Ket Siong. They chatted quietly together, as though there had never been any animus between them. Neither made any effort to involve Renee in the conversation, or asked her questions, save to check that the menu they chose was fine with her. She might not have been there, for all the overt attention they gave her.

It wasn't how Renee had imagined this day might go. She'd been prepared to be the social linchpin, mediating between Nathalie and Ket Siong.

It took her a little while to understand that she was being looked after. It was a novel experience. She sank into it gratefully, if a little dubiously, like someone lowering themselves to a rickety chair they weren't sure could bear their weight.

She felt much more human once she'd got some black cod and green tea down her. Renee found herself telling them everything—Su Khoon's appearance at her office, his threats, her attempt to contact Jason.

Ket Siong listened with that stillness she'd never encountered in anyone else—a completeness of focus that was both soothing and a little unnerving.

Nathalie managed to contain herself while Renee was speaking, but she turned puce from the effort. Renee finally stopped because she was a little worried Nathalie might explode if she didn't get to express herself.

"That douchebag!" Nathalie burst out. "I always hated that motherfucker."

"Do you mean my brother, or Jason?" said Renee.

"Both of them," said Nathalie. "But especially Jason. No, especially your brother. Oh, I don't know who I hate more. I shouldn't have given up smoking. If I had a lighter, I could have set fire to that shit's hotel room."

It was a little funny how differently she and Ket Siong were taking it. Ket Siong's head was bowed. He was curling his right hand into a fist and uncurling it, over and over.

But when he looked up, his gaze was steady. He said, "Are you all right?"

"Yes," tried Renee. Then, because if she didn't say it, Nathalie would: "Not really. No."

"I'm sorry," said Ket Siong.

"It's fine," said Renee, though it wasn't. She looked down at her plate, tears filling her eyes. She cleared her throat and said, "What are Thomas and Jeroen up to today?"

Nathalie told them, transitioning from there to general anecdotes about her son. Renee was used to people being tedious about their children, but Nathalie, of course, was not like that. Laughing over a photo of the destruction Thomas had wrought with Nathalie's makeup stash, Renee suddenly realised she hadn't thought about Jason once in the past half hour.

Ket Siong said very little during the meal. He mostly looked, mostly at her.

It was comforting. Renee was not prepared to think about what any of this meant.

Nathalie was not standing for such wilful obliviousness. After they settled the bill (Nathalie won the fight), she said she'd wait with Renee for her Uber. The moment Ket Siong's tall figure disappeared down the street, Nathalie said to Renee:

"What is going on with that guy? He acts like he's crazy about you back at uni and then you make out and he dumps you. Now he turns up and acts like he's crazy about you again."

She'd evidently been mulling on the problem throughout lunch and was desperate to hash it out. "I was thinking, do you think he has a split personality? Maybe it was Hyde who was into you, but Jekyll who broke up with you. No, Hyde was the evil one. I mean, Jekyll who was into you, but Hyde . . ."

"I know what you mean," said Renee. "Ket Siong's just a friend."

"That is fake, though. You and Ket have made it up between you," said Nathalie. "I thought he wanted to sleep with you and that was why. But now I have seen you together and I see I got it wrong. Obviously, he wants to marry you. What I don't understand is why he didn't go for it back then."

"I don't really want to—"

"Maybe it's something to do with the family?" Nathalie chewed her lip, her brow furrowed. "But what could they even

THE FRIEND ZONE EXPERIMENT · 139

find to disapprove of? You are hot, you are successful, you are smart, you are even nice. It is the whole package. Are they racist against Singaporeans? Is that a thing?"

"*Nathalie,*" said Renee.

There must have been a note in her voice that warned Nathalie to lay off. She looked Renee in the face and went quiet.

Renee wasn't sure she'd be able to explain without embarrassing herself again. She was already maxed out on humiliation after the morning's shenanigans. But she owed Nathalie—for this day, and every other time Nathalie had come through for her.

"It meant a lot," Renee said, with difficulty. "Having you and Ket Siong with me today. Having your support. That's what I need right now. I need him to be a friend. Not a complication."

Not someone she'd be tempted to trust too much, who would become a vulnerability her family could exploit. That was all love had ever been for her.

But a lump had risen in her throat, preventing her from saying any more. Renee swallowed.

Nathalie got it, anyway.

"OK," she said. "OK." She put her arms around Renee. "I'm sorry."

After a moment, Renee relaxed into the hug. She buried her face in Nathalie's shoulder.

"Is that a new scent?" she said. "What happened to Chanel No. 5?"

Nathalie had already had a signature scent by the time Renee met her, at the advanced age of twenty-one. Renee remembered how impossibly cool she'd seemed then. That was one thing that hadn't changed.

"I'm branching out," said Nathalie. "This one's Citrus Noir by Molinard. Notes of calamansi and incense."

"It's nice," mumbled Renee. "You smell nice."

They started laughing and broke apart, wiping their eyes, and then Renee's Uber came, so that was where they left it.

Then

Ket Siong's phone started ringing again as he left the Vietnamese restaurant with the takeaway he'd promised Renee. The thought of her waiting for him in his room sent excitement shivering over his skin.

He'd already gone by her flat and picked up her things— her favourite trainers, jeans, a top and a jumper she often wore, sweatshirt and tracksuit bottoms for sleeping in. He fumbled in his coat pocket for his phone, trying not to drop anything.

It was a private number calling, again. Strange. Maybe it was important. Ket Siong accepted the call.

"Siong?" said his brother's voice. "You OK? You didn't pick up earlier."

Ket Siong blinked. "I didn't realise it was you. Did you change your number?"

"Oh. No, I just changed the settings," said Ket Hau. "Can you speak? Are you at home?"

"I'm walking back to my place," said Ket Siong. He checked his watch. It was two a.m. in Malaysia. There was a kick of worry low in his gut. "Is everything OK?"

There was a pause on the line.

"You probably shouldn't be on your phone if you're outside," said Ket Hau.

"No one would want my phone," said Ket Siong accurately. That was one of the chief benefits of having a phone whose most advanced feature was the game Snake.

But he stopped outside an off-licence, ducking under a canopy sheltering boxes of withered-looking fruit and veg.

"What's going on?" he said. "Is it Ma?"

"Ma's fine," said Ket Hau, too quickly. "Don't worry. I couldn't get to sleep, and I thought you'd be done with classes." He paused. "Ma's planning to call you tomorrow, but I wanted to speak to you first. She's pretty upset."

"What happened?"

"You know this issue Ma's been dealing with at work," said Ket Hau. "The dodgy client she reported for money laundering?"

"Yes."

"The firm's let her go."

Cans of grass jelly drink rattled as Ket Siong put his bags on the ground. "They fired her for whistleblowing?"

"They told her if she withdrew her report about the company, she could keep her job," said Ket Hau.

He didn't need to say how Ma had responded. Ket Siong had been raised by her, too.

He knew why his brother had called him, despite the late hour. He was braced for bad news, so it didn't surprise him when Ket Hau said:

"There's more. Ma doesn't want me to tell you this part. But I think you need to know."

It's fine, Ket Siong prepared himself to say, even as his hopes of finishing his degree crumbled into dust. No more Royal Academy, no more performing career in one of the greatest cities in the world.

Who was he to complain? To have got as far as he had was an unimaginable privilege. Part of him had always feared Fate wouldn't let him get away with chasing so selfish an ambition.

Ket Hau said, "Before the firm told her they were firing her, Ma got a call. Private ID, caller didn't give his name. He threatened Ma. Said if she tried to go public with her allegations, she'd face consequences. The caller mentioned Pa, talked about you and me. He knew a lot about us." Ket Hau paused. "Ma hasn't said it in so many words, but she thinks Goh Kheng Tat is behind it."

The name sounded familiar. "Goh Kheng Tat?"

"He's the guy who owns the dodgy company," said Ket Hau. "Only Ma would take on a guy like that. There have been whispers about Chahaya Group forever—not only whispers, there was that big lawsuit a few years back. But nobody's been able to make anything stick. Goh Kheng Tat is too entrenched. If he goes down, a lot of people will be in trouble."

It was cold, but Ket Siong had stopped noticing it. He stared at the street in front of him, unseeing.

It would be a big win for Chahaya, Renee had said, talking about why her father wanted her to marry Andrew. Meaning the company her father had founded.

Her father. Goh Kheng Tat.

"The client is Chahaya?" Ket Siong said, in the impossible hope that he had somehow misheard.

"A Malaysian subsidiary," said Ket Hau. "They're firing Ma to placate Goh Kheng Tat. He told them, 'Either you get rid of her, or you lose my business.'"

"He's that important?" Ket Siong had known Renee's family was wealthy, but he'd never really thought about what that meant. That they were powerful, that it would be a bad idea to cross them.

Ket Hau sighed. "The problem is, it's not just Goh Kheng Tat. It's whoever he's doing this for. Chahaya is doing well, there's no reason they need to dabble in this kind of shady business. Ma thinks he's doing it as a favour for one of his connections. He's got friends high up in government, people you don't want to piss off. That's why the firm's sacrificing Ma. She's the scapegoat."

Ket Siong felt a seizing in his chest, a precursor to the greater pain he could see bearing down on him. "She's only trying to do the right thing."

"It's broken her heart," said Ket Hau. "But the thing she's most upset about . . ." His voice trailed off. He was struggling to say this next bit.

"It may not be as bad as she thinks," he said finally. "You've got your bursary, and I've got some savings. Not much, but it should help. The Royal Academy has a hardship fund, I saw on their website. We could look into that. And there are loans we could apply for."

"We are not applying for loans," said Ket Siong. Money had been tight after his father's death, and Ma hadn't quite paid off the debt they'd accumulated then when his grandmother's health had started declining. When Ah Poh had passed, after a long illness, she'd left more bills to be settled. Ma had insisted on going private for her care, no expense spared.

"Siong . . ."

"I'll come back and finish my degree in Malaysia," said Ket Siong. "I've only got a year left. Then I can get a job."

Ket Hau must have rung to prepare him for this, so he would have got over the worst of his distress by the time Ma spoke to him. But now Ket Siong had accepted the inevitable, it was Ket Hau who seemed determined to resist.

"We can't give up so easily," he said. "You've worked so hard. I was looking at jobs just now. If I could get a government affairs role at a corporate, that would be a big jump in pay. That's basically what I do anyway, lobbying." He laughed.

"No," said Ket Siong firmly. "I'll come back. It's fine." He meant it.

Ten minutes ago, having to leave London without finishing his degree would have been the most devastating thing he could imagine, short of something happening to his mother and brother. Now, it barely registered.

He would feel it later, no doubt—the sudden collapse of the dream that had dominated his life. For now, though, he was possessed with the other thing he had to do. The harder thing, by far.

"I'll tell Ma I spoke to you," Ket Hau said. "She'll probably want to talk to you in the morning. Most likely it'll be around midnight your time, will you still be up?"

"Yes. No. It doesn't matter," said Ket Siong, hardly knowing what he was saying. "Ma can call whenever. Ko, I have to go."

He looked down at the collection of bags at his feet. Through the opening of a tote bag, he glimpsed the cream wool of the jumper he'd taken out of Renee's wardrobe. It felt like someone had kicked him in the stomach.

"I'm late," he said.

His voice sounded funny to him, but his brother didn't seem to notice.

"You go," said Ket Hau. "Siong, you'll know this, but you can't tell anybody about this mess. It's sickening having to keep these bastards' secrets, but if anybody finds out, Ma will be in even worse trouble."

"I know," said Ket Siong.

Ket Siong thought—half feared, half hoped—that what he'd learnt about Renee's father might somehow bleed into how he felt about her. That the anger and revulsion rising in his throat when he thought about how Ma had been treated might make it easier to do what he had to do. But then he opened the door to his room and Renee lifted her head, smiling.

She was sitting on his bed with her legs crossed, fully clothed, with one of his books—a text on Renaissance music—propped open in her lap. Ket Siong knew then that it didn't matter who her father was and never would.

To him. But his feelings weren't important.

Renee wasn't responsible for anything her father had done. She wouldn't know anything about it. But she was her father's daughter, as strained and thorny as that relationship was. Ket Siong was his mother's son. That was all there was to it.

"You took your time," said Renee, but she wasn't mad. Her eyes were mischievous, as if she knew how desperate he'd been to get back to her.

Up till now, Ket Siong had been preoccupied with how bad this was making him feel. For the first time, it came home to him how much it was going to hurt Renee—and that was going to be the worst part, the part that would stay with him for the rest of his life.

Ket Siong put down the stuff he was carrying, bending to unknot the takeaway bag. He'd give Renee her dinner and her things and send her away. He'd say something had come up. A last-minute deadline, or . . .

"What did you get?" said Renee. She was standing right by him.

When he straightened up, she raised her face as if for a kiss, the movement as natural and instinctive as that of a plant turning towards the sun. She checked herself, blushing.

Ket Siong's heart felt dead in his chest, but at this it gave an anguished thump.

Renee was smiling—shy, but wrenchingly sure of him. He saw her arrive at a decision. She reached up, but Ket Siong dodged before she could take her kiss.

He found his dinner and drink, extracted them from the plastic bag and set them on his desk. He held the takeaway bag with Renee's portion in it out to her. She took it from him.

The light had gone out of her face. He couldn't look at her.

"I got your keys from the concierge," said Ket Siong. "And your shoes." He nodded at the takeaway bag. "I ordered you the lemongrass pork. You can take it home."

"Ket Siong," said Renee. "What's wrong?"

There would be no giving of excuses, no letting her down gently.

"It was a mistake," said Ket Siong. "Earlier. We shouldn't have . . . I think it's better if you go home."

"I don't understand." Renee looked bewildered. "Did something happen?"

"I have to go back," Ket Siong blurted. "This summer."

"To Malaysia? What about your studies?"

Ket Siong didn't answer, busying himself with the bags containing Renee's stuff. When Renee said, "Did something happen with your family?" he only nodded.

He pulled her trainers out and laid them on the floor.

"I'm so sorry," said Renee. "I can't imagine how you must be feeling." She paused. "Is that why you've—why you think it was a mistake, when we—I thought you wanted to."

"You didn't do anything wrong," said Ket Siong quickly. "I just think it's better if we don't . . . if we leave it there."

"OK." Renee was pale. She said tentatively, "Do you want to talk about what happened with your family?"

"*No*," said Ket Siong.

She flinched as though he'd slapped her.

He was messing this up. It was impossible to think with Renee staring at him like that. He had to get her out of his room.

"I have things I've got to do," he said. "Do you mind . . . ?"

What he was most afraid of was that Renee would see through him. If she pressed, even a little, he might give way, regardless of all his resolutions to do the right thing.

Because this was the right thing for her as well as for him, even if it didn't feel like it. If her family thought Andrew Yeoh was a good prospect, they were not going to accept Yap Ket Siong as a substitute. He knew how much their opinion mattered to her. He might wish it mattered less, but how could things be otherwise?

For all that their families were polar opposites, at the end of the day, it was for Renee as it was for him. Family was a bond that could be stretched or twisted, resisted or negotiated, but it could not be severed.

She would make the same decision, if she knew the full story. But that didn't make Ket Siong feel any better. He couldn't tell her the full story. He'd promised his brother. He had to keep his family safe.

To his relief, Renee said, "I'll get out of your hair." She sounded lost, but when he glanced at her despite himself, she rallied, trying for a smile. "I'll see you tomorrow at Pret?"

Ket Siong recognised this as an out. A chance to pretend nothing had happened, to go back to how they were before.

It was more of an out than Renee realised. It would be straightforward to do a slow fade on her from there—stop turning up for meetups, ignore her texts. But she deserved better from him.

The idea was unbearable anyway. Ket Siong needed to make a clean break, so he could lick his wounds in peace.

"I don't think that's a good idea," he said.

If it were Renee saying these things to Ket Siong, after what had passed between them, he would have slunk home with his tail between his legs. He would have hung his head and never raised it again.

But Renee was made of stronger stuff. She said, her voice hardly trembling, "Why not? Do you not want to hang out anymore?"

Ket Siong repeated, "I don't think it's a good idea."

He sounded like a robot that had broken down and could only repeat the single line it had been programmed with. He felt like a broken-down robot. There must be more he could offer her, something he could do that would make this less awful, but his mind was blank.

"Right." Renee lifted her chin. "You can't blame a girl for asking."

Her tone was light, though there were tears in her eyes. Ket Siong had never loved her more.

"I'll get going," she said.

Ket Siong glanced at the window. It was dark outside. He knew he should keep his mouth shut, but he said, "I'll come with you."

"No," said Renee. Her voice was gentle, but she now seemed infinitely distant, removed. "Let's not do that."

"You should get a cab. Don't walk home."

Renee had put down the takeaway while she pulled on her trainers. Her face twisted.

If she cried, thought Ket Siong, he would have to hug her. No one could blame him for that.

But she didn't cry.

"Don't worry, Ket Siong," she said. "I'll sort myself out." She took her keys and her clothes and the bún bowl and the can of grass jelly drink he'd got her, and headed off alone into the night.

13

Now

The day after his visit to the Rembrandt exhibition, Ket Siong went to Richmond, to teach Alicia Tan's brother Jasper the piano.

Ket Siong was off his game, preoccupied. It took a particularly discordant muddling of chords to stir him from his reverie. He came to himself to see Jasper gazing at him, wide-eyed and penitent.

"Sorry," said Jasper.

Jasper was not one of his keener students. Jasper's mother, a former hedge fund manager who had quit to focus on her kid, worked off her considerable energy by endeavouring to cultivate genius in him. The piano lessons were part of this uphill effort. Jasper would rather have learnt to play the harmonica.

"It's all right," said Ket Siong, with a twinge of guilt. "Just needs more practice. Let's take it again from the top."

He hadn't slept well. He'd lain awake for a long time after going to bed, replaying the events of the day in his head. Imagining hauling off and punching Jason Tsai, as he'd so dearly wanted to do in reality. It was a natural next step to imagine Renee flinging herself in his arms, and from there his fantasies had devolved into scenes not at all suited to the platonic footing they'd agreed to be on.

Ket Siong often missed having his own room. He'd definitely felt the lack of privacy the night before.

Jasper—never the most focused student—was taking his cues from Ket Siong's distraction.

"Ket," he said, "did you want to be a piano teacher when you were a kid? Was that your dream?"

Jasper's current dream was to drive a Tube train and run a dim sum restaurant on the side, the two ruling passions of his life being the intricacies of the London Underground, and siu mai. Ket Siong and Jasper's mother had attempted to persuade him that being proficient at the piano would help him achieve these goals, but this had so far had no visible effect on Jasper.

"No," said Ket Siong, after a moment. "I like doing it, though."

Jasper wasn't buying this. "What was your dream?"

Ket Siong stared at the score propped on the piano. Petzold's Minuet in G major, commonly attributed to Bach. It was one of the earliest pieces he remembered learning as a child—an old friend, as familiar as the mole on the underside of his mother's chin. "I wanted to be a concert pianist."

"Like Lang Lang?" Jasper's mother occasionally suggested that he might like to be like Lang Lang when he grew up.

Ket Siong smiled. "A bit like Lang Lang."

Jasper was frowning, dissatisfied. "Why didn't you become a concert pianist?"

"I did," said Ket Siong.

He'd had a career in KL. Not exactly the career he'd dreamt of when he was studying at the Royal Academy of Music, but one he could be proud of nonetheless, combining performance, touring, and teaching at a somewhat higher level than he was doing now.

Jasper asked the obvious question. "Why'd you stop?"

I left home and it was too dangerous was one answer. It had served Ket Siong well for years. It had been useful to have an excuse that was true, so it could obscure the real answer: *I stopped caring.*

He'd assumed his indifference to music was a fixed principle of the nightmarish new world he lived in now. But for the first time, Ket Siong found himself wondering if that was correct. Gazing unseeing at Petzold's minuet, he saw in his mind's eye Renee, standing by Rembrandt's *The Jewish Bride*, her face alight.

With the image came music. It took him a moment to recognise it. Mozart, the second movement of the D minor concerto.

"Ket?" said Jasper.

Ket Siong cleared his throat, tapping the score. "Come on. Petzold."

Alicia ambushed Ket Siong after the lesson, coming down the stairs as he was putting his shoes on in the hall.

"How's Jasper doing?" she said.

"He'll pass if he practises," said Ket Siong.

"It's not looking good, you mean. I'm glad Maje's only my step-mum. She's great, but I would've been shit at being hothoused." Alicia leaned against the banister, giving him a sidelong glance. "So how did it go the other night? With your 'old friend'?" She did the quotes with her fingers.

Ket Siong undid his shoelaces so he could retie them, giving them more attention than had been necessary since he turned five. "Fine. Did you get home safe?"

"Yes," said Alicia, but there was something on her mind. "Ket . . ."

Ket Siong looked up at her, inquiring.

"My parents don't know about . . ." Alicia cleared her throat. "About the person I was with. I think Dad would be OK with it, but he'd feel he should tell Mum, and she's pretty conservative. I don't think she's ready."

It hadn't occurred to Ket Siong that Alicia might be worrying about this. He should have thought to reassure her. "I won't say anything."

Alicia looked relieved. "Thanks. I mean, I didn't think you would, but . . . thanks." She sighed. "I had no idea meeting up with Rachel at that stupid event would be so risky. We were almost seen by someone else I know."

Ket Siong had another lesson to get to, forty minutes away in Ealing. He got up, about to make his excuses, when Alicia said:

"A girl called Charmaine. I almost died when she called out to me. Good thing Rachel was in the loo, or Charmaine would have been right on WhatsApp, telling people about her. She's the biggest gossip I know."

"You know Charmaine Low?" said Ket Siong.

"Do you know her? Oh, of course, she's Malaysian," said Alicia. Her eyes widened. "Oh shit, are you guys friends?"

"No," said Ket Siong. "I met her father at the event."

"Phew," said Alicia. Reassured, she went on, "Small world! It's her sister I'm close to. Do you know Clarissa? Charmaine's whatever—just another rich kid who wants to be an influencer— but Clarissa's cool. She's studying a master's in art history. We met volunteering at Kew Gardens, their family's got a place near here."

Ket Siong's investigation into Stephen's disappearance, such as it was, had come to a standstill. There was no word from the *Hornbill Gazette,* a week after he'd messaged them.

He'd contacted a few other people, connections from his family's old civil society circles, though he'd had to be cautious. He could trust the people he'd reached out to wouldn't dob him in to Low Teck Wee and his ilk, but they might well mention it to his brother. He didn't want Ket Hau to know he was asking around about Stephen—not until he'd made better progress on getting answers.

At least it was unlikely that Ket Hau was in touch with any of these people. After what had happened to Stephen, he'd become as hypervigilant as Ma had ever been. Before their move to the UK, he'd deleted his social media accounts and insisted that none of them tell their various friends, neighbours, distant relatives, church acquaintances, or ex-co-workers where they were going. To this day Ket Hau had friends from school who believed he'd migrated to Australia.

The conversations Ket Siong had initiated were unpromising. Almost everyone replied, but they were surprised to be asked.

Would have thought you'd know better than anybody else, said a retired journalist, a former colleague of his father's.

Ket Siong didn't. But he knew who might.

He had not had much to do with God, in recent years. But he still viewed the world as one ordered by a greater power, and he saw this power at work now.

"Can you introduce me to Clarissa Low?" he said.

Alicia blinked. "I—why do you ask?"

How much could Ket Siong safely tell her? He could invent a story. But once he was face-to-face with the Low daughter, he would have to reveal his objective, and knowing he'd lied to get the meeting would hardly incline her to be cooperative.

If Clarissa Low knew what he wanted and who he was, so would Low Teck Wee. It would put a name and a face to what, for Low, had been an anonymous encounter, one he'd perhaps even forgotten by now.

Ket Siong thought of that vigil for Stephen—the attendees' grave faces in the amber glow of candlelight. There were people working to ensure Stephen wasn't forgotten. The least Ket Siong could do was take what leads came his way.

He sat back down on the lowest step of the stairs.

"The Low family own a company called Freshview Industries," said Ket Siong. "A few years ago, they were accused of illicit logging on native customary land in Sarawak, where I'm from. An activist leading the campaign to hold Freshview accountable subsequently disappeared." Ket Siong's mouth was dry. He swallowed. "He was a family friend. Nobody knows what happened to him. Whether he's alive. Or not."

His voice broke on the last syllable, but otherwise he sounded like a news report, or a Wikipedia article. Stephen would have found that funny.

Or maybe not. There wasn't really anything funny about it. Ket Siong drew his arm across his face, drying his eyes on his sleeve.

"OK. Wow," said Alicia. She went red. "Sorry, that was a stupid thing to say. I didn't mean . . . I'm sorry. I don't know what to say."

There was nothing to say. Ket Siong waited while Alicia hesitated.

"I can talk to Clarissa," she said finally. "But do you want me to tell her the reason why you want to meet her?"

"She's your friend," said Ket Siong. "I rely on your judgment."

"Clarissa would never—she would be horrified, if she thought—I mean, she's really into social justice and human rights and all that stuff." Alicia paused. "She's pretty close to her family."

"I'm not looking to blame anybody," said Ket Siong, though this was not quite the truth. "I just want to know what happened to my friend."

"I can't promise she'll agree to talk," said Alicia. "But I'll ask. And . . . I'm really sorry about your friend."

Ket Siong understood, now, why Ket Hau never mentioned Stephen. Nothing anyone could say about it helped. Talking about it only served to bring up all the worst of the sorrow and anger and futility of losing him in such a way.

It was the cruelty and injustice of it that would poison Stephen's memory for the many people who'd loved him—that would make their grief fester unhealed, for the rest of their lives.

Stephen's suffering could not be reversed or made good. But to obtain justice might still be possible. Ket Siong had to believe that, or there would be no point in anything, nothing left to believe in.

"Thank you," he said.

14

The sun shone through the blinds, suffusing Renee's bedroom with a warm golden glow reminiscent of home. There were strong arms wrapped around her, a familiar voice whispering in her ear, tender and low.

The voice was explaining that he loved her. He'd only hurt her by accident, a mistake, easily explained away. For once he spoke, at length, and she was content to listen.

The dream shattered when Renee opened her eyes. She woke up all the way and remembered everything that had happened the day before. Going to the National Gallery and finding Jason there.

It was like plunging into cold water. Renee stiffened all over. Rage and shame churned inside her. She'd managed to escape them for most of yesterday and the night before, but she couldn't run forever. But—

"I won," she said aloud. She gritted her teeth and got out of bed.

A few hours later, she was the possessor of the newest iPhone in rose gold, as well as a new SIM card. She *could* unblock her brother on her existing number, but that was the number she used to send voice notes to Nathalie and speak to her staff, the number she'd given Ket Siong.

Su Khoon could have a different number. She texted him straight away, to prevent herself putting it off.

Hi Er Ge, it's Renee. I want to discuss your offer. I can come to the house tomorrow. 6 pm OK?

Getting to the family's townhouse in Chelsea by six would entail leaving the office earlier than usual, but Renee didn't want to risk getting stuck there with her brother late at night. She didn't feel great about going to the house, but they'd need somewhere private to talk, and there was no way she was letting him in her office again.

At least the house wasn't Su Khoon's. Dad owned it. Sometimes, on their occasional calls, he'd remind her that the house was for the whole family and she was welcome to use it. It was probably his way of making himself feel better about the fact that Renee had run halfway around the world to get away from the family.

So much for keeping her distance. If she was going to win Chahaya, she'd have to let her family back into her life. But that was good, wasn't it? She'd had her ups and downs with them, but they did care about her—Dad did, anyway. Sure, he'd made mistakes, but nobody was perfect. He was the only father she had, and he'd reached out to her. It had to be the right thing to do, to reach back.

Renee was jumpy all day, checking her phone every five minutes for a reply from her brother.

Though she'd recently adopted a resolution to take proper weekends off work, she ended up working, purely for the distraction. She didn't have many other resources. A hopeful text to Nathalie in the morning was answered four hours later with an image of Nathalie with her husband and son at an indoor playground, all three wearing party hats.

Nathalie captioned it, *Hell on earth*. But they looked happy, even if the chocolate smeared on Thomas's chin had made it onto Nathalie's champagne-coloured blouse.

Renee replied:

Did you really wear a silk shirt to a kid's birthday party?

No reply. Nathalie was probably in the ball pit or breaking up a toddler fistfight. Renee found herself typing Ket Siong's name into the WhatsApp search bar.

To her surprise, he had an actual profile picture—a photo of two boys with a grey-haired Chinese auntie dressed in samfu. The younger of the two kids, who must have been six or seven, wore a collared shirt, buttoned all the way up, and a comically serious frown. The soft-cheeked little face didn't much resemble the Ket Siong of today, but the vibes definitely matched.

She swiped WhatsApp off her screen before she could be tempted to send a message. Though she had fond memories of texting with Ket Siong. His messages had been prompt and interesting, always impeccably punctuated.

But he wouldn't want to hear from her now. The shame crashed over her again, suffocating. God, what must he think of her? Messy, pathetic, possessed of incredibly poor judgment and taste in men . . .

No, this was good. If it put Ket Siong off her, that could only be a good thing. Not that he was into her. Not the way she'd want him to be.

Except she *didn't* want him to be into her. Fed up with herself, Renee put her phone screen-down on the coffee table and turned back to her computer. Her lawyer had sent through a thirty-page updated HR policy for Virtu last week, which she'd been procrastinating on looking at. She opened the file and dived in.

Six p.m. came on Monday with no word from Su Khoon, but Renee turned up at the Chelsea house anyway. He had to come back there to sleep sometime. He wouldn't be staying anywhere else. Dad kept a tight leash on her brothers when it came to business expenses, after the Hong Kong junk party drama of 2011, and Su Khoon was too cheap to spend his own money on a hotel.

She still had the keys to the house, though it had taken some hunting to find them, nestled in the depths of a drawer in her bedroom. There was a black Merc parked on the road outside the house when she arrived—probably her brother's hire car; he preferred to drive in London. That must mean he was home.

She climbed up the short flight of stairs leading to the front door, feeling slightly sick.

But nothing happened when she rang the doorbell. The place felt empty when she finally let herself in.

"Er Ge?" she said, and heard her voice echo.

She was going to have to wait. Well, that was fine. She could use the time to knock some emails on the head.

Instead of working, though, Renee found herself wandering around the house, inspecting it like a visitor to an architectural curiosity. It had been years since she'd last been here. It was meticulously clean, with the unnatural quiet of a house that wasn't lived in.

There were signs of her brother's occupation. A pair of trainers on the shoe rack in the hallway. A jacket slung over the back of a sofa. In the ground floor reception room, a bowl on the coffee table filled with apples, pears, oranges, and a banana, supplied by the housekeeping service the family used when they visited.

The pears were the yellow Chinese ones, because Dad liked them. Renee picked up a pear, polished it on her blouse and bit into it.

It was unnerving how little the place had changed. The house had last been redecorated in the mid-noughties, by someone who'd apparently had instructions to make it look as much like a corporate law firm as possible. The walls were dead white, and there was a lot of dark wood and black glass, set off by pristine white upholstery.

Renee came to a stop in front of a large family portrait hanging above the fireplace in the reception room. It had been taken when her eldest brother, Su Beng, had started his undergraduate degree at Royal Holloway. They'd all come over from Singapore for a holiday.

Renee was eight, remote and faintly disapproving in a sequined silver cardigan over a tulle dress. The sight of the outfit spread a ghost itch over her thighs: the underskirt had tormented her, and the black Mary Janes chafed.

Her brothers were in suits, looking solemn and unformed. Like kids. It was hard to see in their faces the towering bullies she remembered.

But she was most struck by her mother. Mom wouldn't even have been forty yet—she'd married at nineteen and had Su Beng a year later—and she looked startlingly young to Renee's eyes. There was a careful distance between her and Dad, Mom's body angled away from him, her expression guarded.

It was a strange picture. No one was touching anyone, except for Dad, who had his hand on Renee's shoulder.

In a way, the relationship between the two of them had always been the least complicated. Su Beng and Su Khoon had run scared of their father, but he'd been different with his daughter— whether that was due to guilt over her unpropitious entry into the world, or simply because he'd had lower expectations of her, as a girl. He'd been a benign if detached parent to Renee, giving her mints and asking about school during his infrequent appearances in her day-to-day life.

It had all gone wrong in the end, when Renee had proved incapable of living up even to the unexacting standards he had for her. Now she had a chance to finally be the daughter he wanted. She just needed to not mess it up.

The rattle of a key unlocking the front door echoed down the hallway, followed by a woman's low laugh.

Renee had set her half-eaten pear down on the coffee table and turned to greet her brother, but she pulled up short. For a moment, she thought, absurdly, that someone had broken in.

Then she heard Su Khoon's voice, murmuring, and the woman squealed.

"Oh *gross*," said Renee aloud.

Clearly she didn't speak up enough, because they stumbled into the room before she could call out to stop them. It was her brother, entangled—predictably—with a blonde woman in a tiny green bodycon dress and vertiginous black heels. Thankfully, Su Khoon was fully clothed, though Renee would happily have lived without experiencing the sight of him with his tongue down a woman's throat.

Unbelievable that he couldn't bring himself to splash out on a hotel for this. There were pictures of Su Khoon's wife, Jessie, and their kids plastered all over the room. Not to mention a huge image from his pre-wedding shoot in his bedroom, right above the headboard. Had he been planning on sleeping with this woman right under that picture of him and Jessie frolicking on a beach in full wedding attire? Why were Renee's brothers so *embarrassing*?

She would have preferred to be pretty much anywhere else in the world, but it couldn't be helped. Renee squared her shoulders and said:

"Do you not check your phone or what?"

The effect was instantaneous and entertaining, if Renee had been in the mood to be amused.

Su Khoon leapt back like he'd been scalded. "Shit!"

Renee could smell the alcohol on his breath from where she was standing. She suppressed a grimace.

The blonde woman whirled around, blanching when her eyes met Renee's. "Oh my God! You are the wife."

"Don't worry, I'm just his sister," said Renee. "That's his wife there, in that picture on the sideboard. Third from the left."

"What the hell are you doing here?" said Su Khoon, though he couldn't really intimidate with lipstick smeared on his ear and his jacket hanging off one arm. He yanked the jacket off savagely, as though the situation was its fault.

"I texted you," said Renee. "I'm here to negotiate." She glanced at the blonde woman. "Should I come another time?"

Su Khoon unbent a little, scenting victory. "If you're ready to be sensible, let's talk." He said to the woman, "You'd better go."

"Oh my God, Er Ge, at least call her a cab," said Renee.

She expected bluster. Her brothers weren't gracious winners, and they were even worse losers.

But Su Khoon seemed unsettled by her reaction, enough that he forgot to be aggressive.

"My phone's not working," he said, looking mulish. "They're getting it fixed in the morning."

Renee managed not to roll her eyes.

"Come on, I'll get you an Uber," she said to the woman. "Where do you need to get to?"

15

After Renee waved Eva off in her Uber, she paused at the base of the steps up to the door to the house, biting her lip.

The Virtu team worked standard business hours. They'd be home, or with friends, or at a bar or restaurant or something—doing normal evening things, not expecting to get a weird message from their boss. She could text Nathalie, but Nathalie never checked her phone in the fraught hours from five to eight p.m., until she finally managed to wrestle Thomas into bed.

And that was it. Renee had exhausted the people to whom she was close enough that she could call on them in an emergency.

Which this was. She was going back into the house to be alone with a furious man who'd had reason to resent her even before this evening's loss of face. A man who had historically shown little sign of caring about her well-being—rather, the reverse. She'd never seen Su Khoon get physically violent, but there was a first time for everything. Andrew Yeoh had never used force with her, until the day he'd pushed his way into her flat and grabbed her phone because he was convinced she was texting a new boyfriend.

Renee slipped her phone out of her bag. She would ring Nathalie.

Or there was one other option. One other person in London who understood the context. Who wouldn't need any explanations about her family history, or what was at stake here.

For the second time that day, she typed Ket Siong's name into WhatsApp. This time, she sent a message.

Long story, but if you don't hear from me in an hour's time, could you ring me? And if you can't get through to me, could you ring the police and ask them to check I'm OK? I'll send you my location.

(Sorry for the drama. I'm meeting up with my brother.)

That was probably the best she could manage by way of precautions. Hopefully Ket Siong would check his phone some time within the next hour. Even if he didn't, the messages were some assurance that if they found her body in the Thames the next day, suspicion would fall squarely on her brother.

She had just placed her foot on the second step up to the door when her phone buzzed.

It was Ket Siong.

Of course. Call me if you need anything.

She was smiling as she came back into the reception room where she'd left her brother. Su Khoon was sitting on the grey moleskin sofa. Renee dropped her eyes when he looked up, ironing out her expression.

Su Khoon had taken off his jacket and rolled up his sleeves. The dampness at his hairline suggested he'd washed his face, and he'd even managed to get the lipstick stains off his ear. An espresso cup was cradled in his hands, the smell of coffee hanging in the air.

He was still pink, but he was probably as sober as he was going to get tonight. Good. That he'd made the effort showed he took Renee seriously. And she wanted him in a state to negotiate.

Renee dropped into a white leather armchair across from Su Khoon.

"Poor Jessie!" she said. "I really thought you loved her." She shook her head. "I always thought she was too smart for you. But I figured you knew that."

Su Khoon put his cup down on the coffee table with more force than was necessary, sloshed dark liquid over his hand, and swore. Renee extracted a tissue from her bag and held it out. He swiped it from her.

"Didn't know you got along so well with my wife," he said, drying his hand off. "You know, it was her idea to get that model on board. The girl who . . ."

"Said I threatened her when she got harassed," said Renee. "I know the one."

There wasn't much Su Khoon could do to hurt her anymore, at least with mere words. He didn't seem to realise that making someone lose all faith in you freed them from caring about your opinion.

"Don't get me wrong. I never thought Jessie liked me," she said. "But I don't have a problem with her. You're her husband, of course she's going to be on your side. You have to admit, though, I might've been a better bet. I may not be a son and heir, but I am loyal."

Su Khoon made an abortive swing, as though he was fighting off a monster in a nightmare. "What do you want? For me to pull out?"

Renee couldn't resist. "I hope you were planning on using better protection than *that*."

"Don't be disgusting," Su Khoon said curtly. He looked in his espresso cup, grunting when he remembered he'd emptied it over his own hand.

"I'm not the one bringing sex workers to the family home," Renee pointed out. She glanced at the family portrait over the fireplace. "I can't believe you were snogging her with Dad's picture staring down at you. Men really are different."

Su Khoon didn't see the funny side. "You think you've won because of this? Go ahead, tell Jessie. Tell the whole world. You think I'll hold back? I'll make sure your boyfriend's photos are all over the Internet."

"Jason's not my boyfriend anymore."

Su Khoon ignored this. He leaned forward, his mouth a grim line. "First place I'll send them is Dad's inbox."

"That's what I came here to talk to you about," said Renee. "Look, I know you don't have the pictures."

Su Khoon raised an eyebrow. "I thought you might try this. You sure you want to call my bluff? That's a risky strategy for you."

Renee leaned back in the armchair, crossing her arms.

"What I don't get," she said contemplatively, "is why you were in such a rush. Why not wait until I *couldn't* call your bluff? Didn't it occur to you I might be able to get ahold of Jason?"

For the first time, doubt flickered across Su Khoon's face.

"I made him a better offer," said Renee. "The photos are off the table.

"I mean, talk about risky strategies," she continued. "It wasn't a great plan anyway. I'm sure the photos would've come from an anonymous source. But if I did get Dad to believe you were behind it, how do you think that would have worked out for you?"

Su Khoon was pop-eyed. The flush fading from his skin returned in full force, creeping up his throat. A vessel throbbed in his forehead. "You—"

"No threats," said Renee. "No shouting. Why don't we try talking like civilised people for a change? Remember, you have no leverage here."

Su Beng would probably have lobbed one of the marble lamps at her. Su Khoon sat snorting like a winded ox. He looked like he couldn't quite believe Renee was saying all these things to him, and he was letting her.

Renee couldn't quite believe it, either. She felt high on adrenaline, her pulse thrumming in her temple.

"What makes you think Jessie would believe you anyway?" said Su Khoon. "You have no evidence."

"Er Ge," said Renee. "Why do you think I waited outside with Eva for her Uber? I was amazed you let me go off with her. Didn't you think we might, I don't know, *talk*?"

This took a moment to sink in. Then Su Khoon reared up onto his feet, his face an ugly red. "If you think you're going to get out of this house with whatever she gave you . . ."

Renee had chosen her seat carefully. She was nearest the door, no obstacles between her and a quick exit.

Her palms were damp, her heart racing. Fear constricted her throat, but she took a deep breath, pushing through it.

"I've told a friend where I am and who I'm with." She was pleased to hear her voice was steady. "They'll call the police if I haven't been in touch in about an hour's time." She glanced at the clock on the wall. "Make that forty-five minutes."

That took the wind out of her brother's sails. He said, "You're acting like—what do you think I'm going to do? I'm your brother."

Renee stared at him. Su Khoon looked *hurt*.

No matter how well-prepared she thought she was, she could never predict how anything would go with her family.

"That's the problem, isn't it?" said Renee. "Er Ge. Don't you think it's time you stopped underestimating me?

"You think of me as your dumb little sister. That's normal, everyone's like that about their siblings. But it's making you make mistakes, like letting me talk to Eva without you around."

She sighed, running a hand through her hair. "Maybe I haven't made this clear enough. I want to work with you. I don't *want* to be gathering blackmail material, or upsetting Jessie and the family. It's not how I do business."

Su Khoon stood immobile. His head was bent, his face in shadow. Renee couldn't make out his expression. He might have been about to slap her, or weep.

Finally he collapsed back onto the sofa. "So what, you want us to shake hands and be friends, just like that?" He gazed at her blearily. He looked rough in the cold white lighting Dad favoured, older than his thirty-nine years. "Look at it from my point of view. I'd be stupid to trust you, no?"

"Why don't you try pretending we're not related?" said Renee. "Give me the same chance you'd give any lateral hire Dad brought in."

Though she couldn't imagine Su Khoon being helpful to any hire of Dad's that he hadn't approved himself. She hurried on:

"Dad wants us to prove we can work with family. Whoever wins Chahaya is going to have to do that, whether they like it or not. It's in both our interests to do a good job. Can't we put aside our personal shit for once and focus on work?"

Su Khoon rolled his eyes. "Don't try and fool me. Like this whole business isn't personal for you. You expect me to believe you won't be trying to sabotage me?"

"No, of course not," said Renee, exasperated. "I'm not an *idiot*. We're competing. But we can either cooperate and get the Freshview deal nailed down, or we can keep squabbling. Then you might as well wrap up Chahaya and give it to Da Ge with a bow on top."

Mentioning Su Beng had the desired effect. Su Khoon went quiet, frowning.

"What happens?" he said. "If I don't agree to work with you."

Renee blinked. "I told you. We both individually try to get Freshview on board. They get a terrible impression of Chahaya as a result and swear off working with us, leaving Dad absolutely delighted with you and me."

"You know what I mean," said Su Khoon impatiently. "What are you going to do with what you got from Eva?"

"What, this?" Renee rummaged in her bag and produced a crumpled Post-it note, placing it on the coffee table.

Su Khoon picked it up gingerly between his index finger and thumb, as though it might explode. He read off the scribble: "'Kip'—what?"

"We were talking about Austrian food. I said I've only had it at the Delaunay and would she recommend anywhere else," said

Renee. "Eva said I should try this place, Kipferl. It's in Angel." She plucked the piece of paper out of his hand and put it back in her bag.

"You were right. I don't have evidence," said Renee. "I didn't ask Eva for anything on you guys. I'm not planning to report you to the family. If you don't want to work with me, I'm not going to force you. You have to be willing, or it won't work."

Su Khoon was silent. Was he actually looking ashamed? Had she somehow managed to prick his conscience? She wouldn't have bet on either of her brothers having one of those.

It should have made her feel triumphant. Instead she felt deflated, grubby and sad. She wished she was home, or on Nathalie's sofa with her feet up, drinking cocktails, or anywhere but here. In this family home nobody lived in.

"I liked Eva," said Renee. "We had a nice chat about her studies. She's obviously bright." She studied Su Khoon, trying to figure him out, as she had done with both her brothers so many times in the course of her childhood. "Jessie's clever, too. You're drawn to smart girls. Why do I piss you off so much?"

There was a long pause.

"You don't piss me off," said Su Khoon.

Renee raised her eyebrows. "Sure."

"It's nothing personal." He was softening, becoming almost human.

So Renee didn't say, *Can't you see, that makes it worse? If everything you do to me isn't personal. If you're not doing it because you hate me or you're mad at me, but simply because I'm in your way.*

She held her tongue. And her family claimed she had no self-control.

Su Khoon tipped his head back on the sofa, letting out a windy sigh. "Dad pits us against each other. Survival of the fittest. Then he expects us to hug and kiss and pretend everything's fine."

Renee's therapist had once put forward this analysis of why her family was so dysfunctional, but it startled her to hear it from

Su Khoon. She'd had no doubt he resented their father for any number of reasons. It had never occurred to her before that any of those reasons might be legitimate.

"I don't think normal siblings kiss," she said. "Hug, maybe. Not *kiss*."

Su Khoon snorted. "How would you know? You don't have any normal siblings."

That surprised a laugh out of Renee. "True."

She let several moments pass in silence. Su Khoon was lost in thought, gazing at the ceiling as though the secrets of the universe were to be found there.

Renee had long given up on being pleasantly surprised by her family. But she'd already been proven wrong once, when Dad had rung her about the Chahaya opportunity. Maybe she should stay open to the possibility of being proven wrong again.

"So," she said. "How about it?"

Su Khoon raised his wrist to check his watch, a handsome Omega Seamaster. If they had been friends, Renee would have asked if it was vintage.

"How long did you say I have?" he said. "Am I about to get swatted if I don't say yes?"

Renee wasn't sure if she was enjoying finding out her brother possessed a sense of humour. Was this a late-in-life development? Part of his midlife crisis, along with cheating on his wife with blonde twenty-year-olds? "Swatting is an American thing, isn't it?"

"Fine," said Su Khoon.

Renee waited. But her brother was getting to his feet, picking up his espresso cup.

"Fine?" said Renee. "That's it?"

Su Khoon looked up, faintly surprised. "What else am I going to say? You've got me over a barrel. You know and I know you don't need evidence to cause trouble for me."

Renee frowned. "I said I'm not going to tell on you."

Su Khoon waved this away. "Sure, sure. Let's leave it at that." He was even smiling.

Renee saw, with a surge of indignation, that he didn't believe she'd never intended to blackmail him, and that had gone some way towards restoring his self-respect. He'd decided the fact she'd decided not to play dirty was a pretence, part of some deep-laid scheme of her devising. Which meant he didn't need to be disquieted or confused, and he definitely didn't need to reflect on how he'd treated her. It was all tactics, from Su Khoon's point of view.

Before she could open her mouth to defend herself, he said:

"Maybe you're right. I need to forget you're my dumb little sister. Let's start over. Clean slate. I'll play nice on this deal, but that's it. You don't expect anything else from me. That's the agreement, right?"

"Right," said Renee.

Su Khoon held out his hand. "Shake on it, then."

Renee reached out and took her brother's hand. His palm was dry, his clasp firm, but not aggressively so. It was the first time she had touched him in years.

She was going to need *so* much therapy.

"No hard feelings?" said Su Khoon. He seemed to have cheered up, now he thought he'd seen through Renee's game.

"No hard feelings," said Renee.

This new, reformed version of Su Khoon suggested Renee could stay for dinner, but he didn't press when she declined. There was a shared recognition that, even if a truce had been achieved, they shouldn't push things too far.

Their goodbyes were civil. Su Khoon said his PA, Penny, would send her the documents for the Freshview pitch the next morning. Renee said she looked forward to reading them.

She took out her phone once she was on the pavement outside, checking the time. It was thirteen minutes past eight. She'd been in the house for just over two hours. It had felt longer.

She clocked the notification as she was about to put the phone away. A message from Ket Siong.

How are you doing?

The timestamp was precisely forty-five minutes after she had texted him.

It was hard not to read something into this. Renee had a vision of Ket Siong, his eye on the clock, waiting till it was no longer too early to check in.

Wishful thinking. Or was it? Ket Siong was a nice, normal person. He'd worry about anyone who was sending him cryptic messages suggesting she might need the authorities to intervene to rescue her from her own brother.

She replied:

All good. Tell you everything another time.

The double blue ticks appeared straight away, but there was no response. Renee decided it was beneath her dignity to wait for more than a minute for a reply, and slipped her phone back into her bag.

She could get an Uber, but she wasn't that far from her flat. About half an hour's walk, which sounded exactly what the doctor ordered. She'd worn comfortable shoes on purpose, in case she needed to run.

The narrow townhouses here had little by way of frontage, with just enough paved yard to place a potted plant or two in. Passersby could peer over the railings right into the front rooms, which was why all the windows facing the street either had blinds or shutters on them, screening out prying eyes. Golden light spilt through the chinks, blotted out occasionally by shadowy figures moving around their homes.

The Gohs were never in London long enough to make their neighbours' acquaintance. Renee wondered what families lived in the other houses, and whether they could possibly be as messed up as hers.

It was a well-lit residential street, quiet on a Monday night. She hadn't seen anyone else on it, so the voice behind her made her jump.

"Renee!"

Renee whipped around. She recognised the tall, broad-shouldered figure crossing the road even before he moved into the amber light of the streetlamp.

Ket Siong looked decidedly sheepish.

"What are you doing here?" said Renee.

"Sorry," said Ket Siong. "I was worried." He looked her over, conducting a thorough and unapologetic survey.

His gaze should have felt intrusive, but it didn't. Renee was reminded of being inspected by her nanny for injuries, when as a child Renee had run to her, seeking comfort for a bump on the head or a skinned knee.

The look, and the association, should have been weird. It wasn't. She felt . . . cared for.

She cleared her throat, pushing down an unexpected swell of shyness. "How did you know where to find—oh, I sent you my location. Of course."

Ket Siong glanced over his shoulder at her family's house. "I wanted to be around, in case . . . I'm sorry. I should have told you I was coming."

"Oh my God, no. I should be the one apologising," said Renee. Necessity had taken precedence over self-consciousness, earlier, but it was coming home to her exactly how bizarre this situation must seem to Ket Siong. "I had no business dragging you into my stupid family drama. I just couldn't think of anyone else to message."

She immediately wished she hadn't said that last line—way too pathetic.

But Ket Siong didn't seem to mind. "I'm glad you messaged." He paused, his eyes searching. "Are you OK?"

"Yeah," said Renee.

How did she keep ending up locking eyes with Ket Siong? There had to be some way to avoid this. It felt like he was about to unpack every embarrassing secret she had, every vulnerability she hid from the world.

She tore her gaze away. "It was fine. As fine as things ever are with my family, you know. Really, you shouldn't have come."

That sent Ket Siong's shoulders up around his ears. "I'm sorry—"

"*Don't* apologise again," said Renee. "I didn't mean it that way. I didn't mean to break up your evening, that's all."

She didn't want to meet his eyes again, in case he saw more in hers than she wanted him to, so she looked at his chin.

Ket Siong had a great chin. She hadn't known it was possible for chins to be that attractive. Men's forearms, yes. Their shoulders and thighs, absolutely. But the male chin had never made it onto her list of physical attributes capable of provoking desire, before now.

"It was nice of you to be worried," she said. "Thank you."

Ket Siong ducked his head. "How are you getting home?"

"Oh, I'm going to walk. It's not far." Renee hesitated.

Ket Siong must have things to do, places to go, people to see. On the other hand, he'd booked it from the outer wilderness of Greater London to make it down here, on the strength of two texts from her. Presumably his Monday night wasn't looking that busy.

"Are you in a rush?" she said. "I haven't eaten yet. I was going to pick up something from Tesco or something. But there's a Malaysian restaurant not too far from here. I've always wanted to try it. My dad refused to go, wouldn't pay Chelsea prices for nasi lemak."

"What is a Chelsea price for nasi lemak?" said Ket Siong.

Renee shrugged. "We can find out. Dinner on me? I can explain what happened." She waved vaguely in the direction of her family's house.

"Sounds good," said Ket Siong, after a moment. "We can split the bill."

"We're not doing the bill fight before we've even gotten to the restaurant," said Renee firmly. "Anyway, I'm paying. I owe you one."

"You don't—"

"I texted you out of nowhere, making it sound like I was going to die," said Renee. "Let me have this one. This evening has been so painful for me, you can't imagine. The least you can do is let me save face."

Ket Siong cocked his head. "You said it went fine."

"I mean, for a definition of 'fine.' I had to see my brother sucking face. It was traumatising." Renee shuddered. "Why are the men in my family such horndogs?"

At Ket Siong's expression, she said, "I'll tell you all about it, but I'm going to need alcohol. Come on, let's go."

16

It wasn't Ket Siong's original intention to walk Renee home after dinner, given how that had turned out last time. Showing up unannounced outside her brother's house was bad enough. He didn't need to add any further reasons for Renee to suspect him of having ulterior motives.

But by the time they got kicked out of the restaurant when it closed at eleven, Renee had had four cocktails, plus half of Ket Siong's when he abandoned it for being too sweet.

"That's nothing," said Renee airily, fumbling with her coat outside the restaurant. The buttons seemed to be giving her trouble. Ket Siong put his hands inside his pockets so he wouldn't forget himself and try to help. "I'm fine. The walk home will do me good. Google Maps says it's only twenty-four minutes."

Ket Siong couldn't bring himself to leave her.

Renee accepted his offer to accompany her without a flicker of doubt. She talked in unimpaired good spirits all the way back—not about her family, but on much more cheerful subjects: her idea for a childrenswear collection; an essay she'd read recently about the pressures of going viral; an extremely boring person they'd both known as students who was now a performance artist in a three-way marriage.

Ket Siong mostly listened. He wasn't much of a drinker. Half a cocktail had been enough to loosen his limbs, dull the edge of his thoughts. He kept getting lost in the low music of Renee's voice, forgetting to follow the words.

As they turned onto the street where she lived, he wondered if he should peel off. But there never came a good point to break off the conversation. He ended up walking her all the way to her door.

"Oh shit, I didn't realise it was so late," said Renee, checking her phone. "Your family's going to be wondering where you are. Are you going to be all right getting home?"

"It's fine. The Tube's still running."

"OK. If you're sure." Renee's eyes were wide and dark, enough to drown in. A floral scent drifted from her hair, reminiscent of summer despite the night's chill.

"Thanks," she said. "This evening was nicer than it had any right being."

"I enjoyed it, too," said Ket Siong.

He wasn't really paying attention to what he was saying. Renee's mouth looked soft, the bottom lip full and red. It would be very easy to bend down and kiss her.

"You should go," said Renee, after a moment. She was blinking a little, as if emerging from a trance. "I don't want you to miss the last train."

Ket Siong stepped back. He felt like he'd had his head dunked in cold water himself.

"Yes," he said. "Good night."

It was good, that Renee knew she could rely on him. She was treating him like a friend. He'd take that and be grateful for it.

Tuesday was a work from home day for Ket Hau. When Ket Siong stumbled out of his bedroom in the morning, rubbing his eyes, his brother was eating cereal at the dining table they'd shoved in a corner of the living room, between the beat-up sofa left there by the landlady and the old Yamaha upright Ket Siong had grown up playing—the single biggest relic they'd kept of their previous life in Malaysia.

"Morning," said Ket Hau. He glanced pointedly at the clock.

It was quarter to nine, more than an hour later than Ket Siong would usually have got up.

Ket Siong was too groggy to sense danger. He made a grunt that could have been a greeting and went into the narrow galley kitchen to make himself coffee.

Ket Hau joined him to wash his cereal bowl. He dried the bowl on a tea towel and put it in the dish drainer, eyeing Ket Siong as he stirred his Nescafé, yawning.

"Ma says you left kind of suddenly last night," said Ket Hau. He'd still been at the office when Ket Siong had left to check on Renee. "Was everything OK with what's her name—the Tan girl?"

"Who?" Ket Siong said, when his phone buzzed in the back pocket of his jeans.

He didn't usually keep his phone on himself, but it had struck him, as he dragged himself out of bed, that perhaps Renee might text this morning.

There was no reason she should be in touch, of course. She was a busy person. She would be on her way to work, if not there already.

Still. She had texted last night, out of the blue. There was no harm in being prepared.

As it turned out, the message wasn't from Renee.

Clarissa says OK to meet, so long as I'm there too. We're free on Friday if that works for you. 10 am?

Ket Siong replied:

That works. Thanks, Alicia. Where do you want to meet?

He emerged into a silence so thick with meaning it was nearly tangible. Ket Hau was looking at him.

"What?" said Ket Siong.

"Nothing," said his brother. "I was just asking about last night. Went OK? Didn't see you when you came back."

"We had a late dinner," said Ket Siong absently.

Alicia suggested meeting at the café at Foyles. He texted back to agree.

"I was thinking," said Ket Hau, when nothing further was forthcoming. "We're definitely filing this case on Thursday—the other side won't give us any more extensions—so I'm planning to take leave on Friday. We could do a day out with Ma? I was thinking of taking her to New Malden. We could have Korean food, stock up on sesame oil or whatever. You know that kdrama she's into, with her third son? They eat a lot of barbeque on the show."

Ma's "third son" was an exquisite young Korean man who was in the process of transitioning from being in a boy band to an acting career. Ket Hau was the only one who tormented her sometimes by calling him her long-distance boyfriend.

"I know you have classes from four o'clock, but we should be done in good time," said Ket Hau.

"I'm meeting someone on Friday morning," said Ket Siong.

Staring at his phone wouldn't magically manifest a text from Renee. On the same principle as the watched kettle that doesn't boil, it was more likely she'd text if he *didn't* look at his phone.

He'd just decided to put the phone on top of the wardrobe, so he wouldn't be tempted to keep checking it, when he realised his brother was speaking.

"What?" said Ket Siong.

Ket Hau took a deep breath. His expression was that of a man pushed beyond endurance. "Siong. As Encik Thiyagu used to say"—this was the discipline teacher at their secondary school, a man with whom Ket Hau had had considerably more to do than Ket Siong—"do some more and you will get two tight slaps. Can you put down your phone for five seconds and talk to me like a human being?"

"Sorry, Ko," said Ket Siong. He shoved his phone back into his pocket. "It was a late night."

His brother rarely ever lost his patience with Ket Siong. It seemed to have wrong-footed Ket Hau almost as much as Ket Siong. He expelled his breath in a theatrical sigh.

"You didn't even notice how good I'm being," he complained. "Didn't try to find out who you saw for dinner, didn't ask where you spent the night. What's the point of virtue? There's no reward."

"Where I spent . . ." Blood mounted Ket Siong's face. "I spent it here! You saw me. I came out of our room."

Ket Hau shrugged. "I only woke up at eight. How do I know? Maybe you sneaked in earlier, like last time.

"I won't pry," he added, before Ket Siong could protest. "You tell us when you're ready. But don't wait too long to introduce the girl to us, OK? Ma will be excited. Even better than a new third-son interview. She used to worry about you, you know. All those girls at church hanging around you after Mass and you didn't go for any of them . . . She started reading these books about what if my kid is gay, how to bring him back to the fold, all that."

Ket Siong raised his head, glancing sidelong at his brother. Ket Hau didn't seem to notice.

"*I* said don't worry," he said. "Siong is just the forever alone kind."

"I'm not—" sputtered Ket Siong. "What about Yi Wen? You all met Yi Wen."

Ket Hau crossed his arms. "You dated Yi Wen for three months."

"It was six months," muttered Ket Siong.

That had been after he'd returned to Malaysia from London for good, as he'd thought then. It had been a strange time. He didn't remember much of it.

Yi Wen was a clarinetist. She was the one who had broken things off: "You're a nice guy, but it's like dating a robot." He'd liked her directness, but he'd mostly started going out with her because she'd seemed interested and he had been lonely. It hadn't really helped with the loneliness.

"I didn't mean 'forever alone' in a bad way," Ket Hau said. "I told Ma, Siong is picky. Once he finds someone he really likes, it'll be OK. It's true, isn't it?"

Ket Siong stared down at his coffee. "It wasn't a date, last night."

Ket Hau snorted. "But just so happens you're seeing her again on Friday?" He settled back against the counter, making himself comfortable. "If a girl's making that much time for you, I'd say she's interested."

"That's not—that's a different thing," said Ket Siong. "I'm not seeing her."

Guilt squirmed inside him. How could he be annoyed? Ma wasn't the only one who'd be excited to hear Ket Siong had found someone. Ket Hau was desperate for him to be happy, too. He knew how much Ket Hau blamed himself for their current circumstances. It would be the best gift Ket Siong could offer his brother—assurance that the fact they'd had to move *hadn't* ruined all their lives.

Instead, Ket Siong was doing the one thing Ket Hau had asked him not to do: risking their peace, on the mere possibility of getting an answer about Stephen.

Ket Hau was not privy to Ket Siong's inner turmoil, of course. He said, "But there *is* a her."

"She's just a friend," said Ket Siong.

Ket Hau said, disbelieving, "Are you telling me a girl has friendzoned you? Yap Ket Siong, the number one friendzoner in the Klang Valley? Stephen used to say if they piled up all the girls you disappointed one on top of the other, they'd reach up to KLCC Skybridge there. 'Climb up like a ladder and you can save thirty-five ringgit, don't need to buy a ticket.'"

Ket Siong remembered. It was a good sign that Ket Hau had mentioned Stephen of his own accord. Maybe he was starting to feel a little better about things.

"I was the one who said we should be friends," said Ket Siong.

Ket Hau hummed at the back of his throat.

"I see," he said, in that annoying tone elders adopted to indicate that what they saw was precisely what you did not want them to see.

Ket Siong knocked back the remainder of his coffee, washed the mug, and put it away. This was intended to indicate that it was time to wind up the conversation and get on with their day. Ket Hau was meant to start work at nine thirty anyway, and it was twenty past.

Ket Hau did not take the hint.

"You want my advice?" he said, just as Ket Siong's phone vibrated in his back pocket.

Once. Twice. A delay, then a third buzz.

"No?" said Ket Siong.

Alicia had no reason to text him three times. It must be the parent of one of his students, asking to reschedule a lesson. It would be rude not to respond promptly to a customer.

Ignoring Ket Siong's subtle attempt to sidle away, Ket Hau said:

"Life's too short, Siong. You and I know, better than most people." He looked Ket Siong in the eye, unexpectedly serious. "If you like this girl, don't go and give her this bullshit about being friends. Ask her out. If she's not interested, go find somebody else. Don't waste your time, OK?"

He clapped Ket Siong on the shoulder and went off to their room, leaving Ket Siong staring after him.

He was roused out of his stupor by his phone vibrating again.

Ket Hau had shut the door behind him. Ket Siong grabbed his phone out of his pocket.

My headddddd

Four and a half cocktails was too many cocktails

A GIF followed, of a bleary-eyed SpongeBob SquarePants getting up off the floor, swaying and burping out a large bubble, accompanied by the caption: This is me

Then, simply:

Thanks for everything, last night

Ket Siong looked at Renee's messages for a long time.

Ket Hau wasn't wrong. There were any number of things Ket Siong could say to Renee, to try to set them on a different path. He went so far as to type some of these things out.

Any time. I was glad to hear from you. Call on me whenever you need me.

But Renee had made it clear what she wanted from him. It wasn't any of this. He deleted the drafts and looked up from his phone. Ran his hand through his hair, breathing out slowly.

No problem. Hope you feel better soon.

17

Renee woke on Tuesday to seven emails from Su Khoon's PA in her inbox, providing the promised information about the Freshview pitch. An eighth email came in while she was reading them—a calendar invite for the meeting at which Su Khoon was to present Chahaya's pitch to Freshview, in two weeks' time.

Then the other calendar invites started coming in.

Renee had picked up her phone to check her emails the moment she'd opened her eyes, a bad habit and one she was deeply regretting. It was only seven a.m. She could've had another hour of sleep if she'd done the sensible thing and rolled over. That wasn't happening now.

She'd thought she might have to fight Su Khoon to gain meaningful access to the Freshview deal, notwithstanding his agreement to work with her the night before. But it looked like he was adopting the opposite strategy—drowning her in detail.

She had to admire it. Taking her at her word meant there was no way she could complain to Dad.

She put down her phone and went and got dressed. COS black jersey dress with an asymmetric draped neckline; hammered gold wrist cuff from an indie designer; BB cream, mascara, tinted lip balm; black coffee; laptop.

Suitably armoured, she took a deep breath and rang her brother on her old phone. She'd transferred her old SIM card—the one she texted her actual friends on—to the new phone.

Su Khoon picked up straight away. "What is it?"

"Your PA's trying to book out the next two weeks to prep for the Freshview pitch," said Renee. "I appreciate the thought, but I've still got a business to run. Can we work out a compromise?"

Su Khoon snorted. "Thought you wanted to be involved? If you're thinking you can just fly in at the end and take credit for the deal . . ."

"That's not what I was thinking," said Renee. "I'll put in the work. But come on, Er Ge. I don't need to be in your office eight hours a day, five days a week, to get a slide deck sorted."

She heard him draw his breath. Before he could launch into a rant, Renee said:

"You don't want to see that much of me, do you? I thought the whole point was to try to avoid killing each other."

This elicited a reluctant huff of amusement. "What are you proposing, then?"

Renee glanced at her calendar on her laptop screen. She was going to have to get Louise to move meetings around, cancel some stuff. And—this hurt—she was going to have to push back the launch of Virtu at Home. She'd been hoping to get the line out in time for Christmas orders, but that had been optimistic even before Chahaya had resurfaced in her life. It was wholly unrealistic now.

She tried not to think about what her team would look like when she told them. She'd cross that bridge when she got to it. You had to be flexible in business, go where opportunity led.

"Give me a day to get through the materials you've sent me," she said. "Then why don't we have a meeting tomorrow and make a plan?"

"I'm seeing some of the Freshview people tomorrow," said Su Khoon. He paused to yawn. "You should have the invite. There's a lawyer there, Lin, she's Jessie's old JC friend. She said she'd introduce me to some of their team who're leading on the London development."

"OK," said Renee, without missing a beat. If Su Khoon was so relaxed he was yawning over the phone at her, she could act like everything was normal and cool, too, as startling as he was being. "Let's meet this evening. Do you have profiles of the people we're meeting tomorrow?"

His lawyer connection hadn't mentioned any names, said Su Khoon. It was an informal get-together. No need to read up.

"You think this is school or what?" he said. "Relax." He yawned again. "Are you done? I'm going to try to get more sleep. Woke up at four a.m."

Renee let her brother go.

What was going on with him? There had to be more to the meeting tomorrow than he'd said. That must be it—she'd show up and it would turn out Freshview were expecting a presentation with slides, data, the lot, and she'd be humiliated.

The alternative was that Su Khoon was being upfront with her and letting her in on the action. Even though it was what she'd been gunning for and what they had agreed, it was hard to believe he was really *doing* it.

Maybe he still thought she was going to tell on him to Jessie and the family. Or maybe he believed her promise to be discreet, and appreciated it.

Renee couldn't afford to get tangled up in speculations about what her brother thought of her. That was too close to caring. There was nothing she could do about tomorrow's meeting except prepare as much as she could and turn up ready for anything.

Focus on the work. That she could do. She picked up her phone to tell Louise to clear her diary.

They met the Freshview lawyer and her colleagues at the bar at the Savoy. It wouldn't have been Renee's choice of venue: it was her favourite place to go with Nathalie for a gossip over cocktails, though admittedly they'd only managed to go once since Nathalie had moved to London.

Besides the cocktail menu, Renee liked the art deco style, plush seats, and impeccably courteous white-jacketed waitstaff. There was no reason having an informal work meeting there with her brother should taint it, she told herself. Su Khoon was being professional, by his standards. And there were outsiders present, which made it even less likely anything unpleasant would happen.

The Freshview team seemed nice enough. Lin turned out to be short for Hazlina, rather than being a Chinese name. She was a curly-haired woman in her early thirties, in an olive trouser suit and nude heels. Besides her, there were two men, around Su Khoon's age.

They spread out over a sofa and three armchairs below a large mirror reflecting the black-and-white photographs on the opposite wall. In about five minutes, Su Khoon had the men launched on a discussion of luxury watches.

It was strange to watch Su Khoon when he was trying to charm. Turned out he had social skills after all. He'd simply never exerted them on Renee's behalf. But then, why would he?

Lin smiled at her. She was wearing bold red lipstick. It suited her, and it was an interesting choice for a work do—it hinted at personality. "You're Su Khoon's sister? Our other colleague who's coming knows you. He said you two met at uni?"

It took a moment for this to sink in. Renee hadn't met many Malaysians while she was at university, and only one of them had had any connection with Freshview Industries that she knew of.

"Ah, he's here," said Lin. She half rose, waving. "Mr. Yeoh!"

Renee made the most of the two seconds she had to rearrange her face. By the time she met Andrew Yeoh's eyes, she was confident it gave nothing away.

She rose, despite Andrew waving at her to sit down. She wasn't the only one—the Freshview team leapt to their feet in a way that would have made Andrew's nepo baby status obvious, if she hadn't already known about it. Not that Renee was in any position to judge him for sliding into a cushy job in the family business.

She was conscious of her brother's eyes on her. So this was

the trap he'd set her. *Come to my informal networking drinks with Freshview, Renee, and meet your nightmare ex-boyfriend while you're at it.*

The stratagem was even more effective than he knew. Su Khoon hadn't been there when Andrew had stormed into her flat, all those years ago. For weeks afterwards, she'd jolted awake every night, her heart pounding—convinced someone was outside the door, in the hallway, shoving his way into her bedroom, coming to get her.

She could be certain Dad would receive a report of how this encounter went. Especially if it went badly.

The thought stiffened her spine.

The last time she'd seen Andrew, he had been about to throw a punch at her. She'd only escaped because the neighbour had knocked on the door. Renee met his eyes and smiled, radiating *Fuck you, asshole* with every fibre of her being.

"Renee!" said Andrew, without so much as a flicker of an eyelash. "How long has it been? Ten years, right? Crazy. You haven't changed at all."

His eyes tracked over her appreciatively. Only the awareness that Su Khoon was monitoring her every microexpression kept the smile on Renee's face.

"It's been a long time," she agreed.

She could have returned the compliment, if she'd felt so inclined. Andrew looked pretty much the same as he had ten years ago. He'd always given off the vibe of a middle-aged investment banker, even in his early twenties. Of all her poor choices of boyfriends, the *most* baffling, Nathalie said.

Was Andrew suffering from amnesia? Did he really not remember how appallingly he'd behaved at their last meeting? If not for the fact that every last detail of that day was burnt indelibly into Renee's memory, she would have started wondering if she'd made it all up.

Andrew held her hand for slightly too long, before moving

on to exchange pleasantries with Su Khoon. They sat down, Su Khoon calling over a waiter so he could order Andrew a drink.

In his place, Renee might have made a *little* more effort to disguise the way he'd transferred his attention to Andrew, as Low Teck Wee's nephew and the most important person in the Freshview party. But the men Su Khoon had been talking to before didn't seem offended. They addressed Andrew as Mr. Yeoh, too.

Was this the reason Dad had asked Renee to get involved in this deal? She'd never told him about what had happened when Andrew came to her flat. Dad had been annoyed enough when he found out they'd broken up that he'd frozen her out for a while—her calls had been declined; her messages went unanswered. By the time they were back on speaking terms, she hadn't felt like raising the subject of Andrew again.

Dad couldn't be hoping for a reconciliation now. Andrew was married. Renee had seen the photos on Instagram, shared by acquaintances who went to the wedding: Felicia Handoko glowing in Vera Wang, Andrew looking justifiably smug over netting the Delima Corp heiress. There'd be no point for Dad in orchestrating this encounter.

This had to be a test of Renee's ability to ingratiate herself, despite her history with Andrew. Or—since it seemed unlikely Dad would risk a deal he wanted by staffing it with someone who'd dumped the chairman's nephew—possibly Dad simply hadn't known Andrew was involved.

Renee would happily have let Su Khoon monopolise Andrew, but after a time her brother was drawn back into conversation with the other Freshview people. One of the other men identified a mutual school friend, which sent them off into reminiscences Renee and Andrew, who were some years younger, couldn't share.

Andrew turned to her. "My uncle said he ran into you recently. You're based in London now, he said?"

Renee tensed despite herself. She rolled her shoulders under her oversized camel blazer, trying to ease the tightness in them.

It was stuffy in the bar, the heating turned too high for the unusually clement weather. She would have taken her blazer off, but she was wearing a black camisole underneath, tucked loosely into an oyster-coloured satin midi skirt, and she didn't feel like exposing her shoulders to Andrew's gaze. It felt like his eyes were leaving trails of slime all over her.

"For the past few years, yes," she said.

"Asia wasn't enough," said Andrew. "You want the UK as well."

"And tomorrow, the world," said Renee lightly.

Andrew laughed, but it was a nice laugh. "You were always ambitious."

"Felicia runs her own business, too, right?" said Renee. "I read the *Marie Claire* profile of her. The restaurant sounds great."

"Oh, Indera's more of a hobby. It doesn't really make money," said Andrew. "She's taken a step back for now. Focusing on the baby."

Renee blinked. "Oh, I didn't know. Congratulations!"

The next twenty minutes passed much more pleasantly than she might have expected, Andrew showing her photos of the baby. The baby was not notable for its beauty, but it was easy to be enthusiastic about it, given some of the other paths the conversation could have gone down.

After an hour or so, Andrew said they should be off—he had a dinner engagement—and they all shook hands again. Su Khoon and Renee insisted the Freshview party take the first black cab that came along the Strand. As they watched the cab move off, Su Khoon said to Renee:

"Not too bad."

Renee didn't pretend not to know what he meant. She inclined her head.

"I didn't know Andrew was coming, for the record." Su Khoon snorted. "Wouldn't have brought you along if I knew. But at least you can be civil."

Renee wondered if she could believe him. "It's business. I'm not going to make things weird so long as he doesn't."

"That's all we need," said Su Khoon. "But don't take it too far, OK? You don't want to piss off his wife's family. Delima's a big deal in Indonesia, that's a growing market for us."

Renee rolled her eyes. "Please, Er Ge. I broke up with him for a reason."

"I'm just saying," said Su Khoon mildly.

It was strange talking to a Su Khoon who was capable of being mild. It reminded Renee of the childhood family holiday when they'd visited the Snake Temple in Penang and she'd had a dozy viper draped over her for photos. The adults promised it had been devenomed, but she could see the creature's fangs when it yawned, and it had not been possible to trust that she would not be bitten.

"You were talking with Andrew for a long time," said her brother.

"He was showing me *baby pictures*," said Renee.

Su Khoon curled his lip, as much as to say, *Don't be naive, you and I both know what men are like.*

But he spared her the lecture.

"I'm going to the office," he said. Su Khoon was renting a tony co-working space in Knightsbridge, not far from the family's townhouse, with a private office for him and desks for his staff. "Are you coming? We should do a debrief."

"I've got an appointment," said Renee. In fact she'd allocated the rest of the day to Virtu, but she knew better than to say so. "I'll send you my notes on the meeting. There were a couple of points you could get the team to look into. I'll see you tomorrow."

Su Khoon gave her a look that suggested he saw right through her excuse. But maybe he really was pleased with how she'd acquitted herself. He said peaceably, "Catch up tomorrow, then. See you."

18

Clarissa Low was plain in a deliberate way, with straight hair down to her shoulders and large, thick-rimmed glasses. She was wearing a black cardigan over a crisp white shirt and dark jeans. Behind the glasses, her face was thoughtful, a little reserved.

She didn't smile when Alicia introduced her to Ket Siong. Once they were seated, she leaned back in her chair and crossed her arms, stone-faced.

The café was on the fifth floor of a bookshop, a pleasant, light-filled space with exposed ceilings and worn wooden tables of different shapes and sizes. It was relatively quiet that morning, with only a handful of other people there, mostly frowning over their phones or laptops.

Alicia had snagged a table by the windows looking out on the brown and redbrick buildings next door. Their closest neighbour was one table over, a young woman hunched over her computer with Bose noise-cancelling headphones on. She was on her second black Americano, counting by the mugs on her table, and was munching through a pain au chocolat while typing with her free hand. They were probably as unlikely to be overheard here as anywhere else in central London.

"Were you OK coming in?" said Alicia, darting an uneasy glance from Clarissa to Ket Siong.

Alicia had insisted on buying everyone's hot drinks, even

though she was technically the one doing Ket Siong a favour. She seemed oppressed by the whole situation.

Ket Siong was keen to make it less awkward for her if he could, but he didn't particularly want Low Teck Wee's daughter to know where he lived. Instead of answering, he said to Clarissa: "Thanks for making the time for this."

After a moment, Clarissa nodded. She still looked forbidding, but something about the pause and the gesture made Ket Siong realise she was simply extremely nervous.

"I don't think I'll be able to help you," she said. "I don't have any involvement in the business. I'm studying art history. My dad's very traditional, anyway. He wouldn't take advice from his daughter on how to run his company, even if I wanted to give advice."

She was redder and redder as she spoke. She went on, stuttering a little, "But obviously, when Alicia told me about your friend . . . I mean, if there's anything I can do . . . I don't know the ins and outs of what happened, but it sounds terrible."

Ket Siong waited, but Clarissa had evidently run out of steam. She gave Alicia a desperate look. Alicia reflected it back at Ket Siong.

They both seemed to be hoping for some form of consolation. He thought about what he should say.

He had been brought up not to make a fuss about things. Even something like Stephen's disappearance . . . its enormity was all the more reason for Ket Siong not to focus on his feelings about it. It was a tragedy, but not *his* tragedy.

But there was nothing to stop Clarissa Low from walking out if he said something that made her uncomfortable. Her guilt was his greatest source of leverage.

So he told the truth. "It has been devastating."

Clarissa twitched. "Of course. I can't imagine . . ." She trailed off, to give him the chance to interrupt.

Ket Siong had a feeling that what Clarissa really wanted was to be saved the act of imagination. Not to have to envision the cost of her family's wealth, the effect on others of their impunity.

"I appreciate that you agreed to meet me," he said. "Shall I explain why I asked?"

Clarissa nodded.

Ket Siong was braced for the words to stick in his throat. He'd expected it would hurt to talk about Stephen, as it had hurt when he'd asked Alicia to arrange this meeting.

Yet he found himself hesitating not because he didn't want to speak, but because there was too much to say. "Stephen Jembu . . ."

Was my brother's best friend—at least, that's what they told us. We didn't ask. It didn't matter. He was part of the family. He came to our house one day when I was sixteen, and after that it felt like he never left. He dragged us to hot yoga and salsa and weightlifting and MMA classes. When he got drunk, he'd sing You'll Never Walk Alone, *and cry. He used to watch kdramas with my mother. He didn't like durian or nasi lemak.*

"The last time I saw Stephen," said Ket Siong, "was around three years ago, when I was still living in Malaysia. He came by our house in the evening, after work."

Their washing machine had been acting up again, and fixing it was a two-man job—one to brace the machine, while the other sorted out the pipes. The original plan had been for Ket Siong to help his brother on the weekend, but Stephen and Ket Hau had put the thing to rights by the time Ket Siong got home from the evening masterclass he'd been leading. Stephen was about to leave, finishing up the mug of Milo Ma had pressed on him.

"How'd it go?" Stephen greeted Ket Siong. "Trained up the new Vanessa-Mae? Very good. Don't get up, eat your dinner."

Ket Siong had only nodded, too tired for chat. There was no need to make polite small talk with Stephen. His brother had seen Stephen out.

"The next morning, around eight a.m.," said Ket Siong, "Stephen drove to the offices of the NGO where he worked, as usual. A van swerved in front of his car, forcing him to stop. Some men wearing masks came out of the van, took Stephen from his car, and forced him into the back of the van. Then the van drove off. He hasn't been seen since then."

He heard his voice wobble on the last line. He paused to take a breath, feeling the dull insistent thud of his heart in his chest.

"Nobody knows what happened to him," he said.

The women were wide-eyed.

Clarissa was pale. "The police couldn't find anything?"

"There were issues with the police investigation," said Ket Siong carefully. "Do you know what Stephen was doing, when he disappeared?"

Clarissa glanced at Alicia.

"You said he was involved in a campaign against Clarissa's dad's company," said Alicia.

Clarissa went red again.

Ket Siong said, "Stephen was from a village called Ensengei in Sarawak. The surrounding forest was a gazetted reserve. Freshview was conducting logging there."

"Freshview held a licence," blurted Clarissa. "I—I looked it up."

Ket Siong wondered if she'd asked her father. He thought not. Low Teck Wee wouldn't have allowed his daughter to attend this meeting, if he knew about it.

"They said they held a licence, yes," said Ket Siong. "But there was no consultation, the local community didn't give their approval. Those are legal requirements. The organisation Stephen worked for was helping the villagers, supporting their lawsuit to challenge the licence. They were successful, at first. But Freshview appealed and won."

He paused. "You'll know it's not transparent, how these things are done. Timber concessions are not tendered. They're not published. The community finds out after the fact, when the bulldozers show up."

"You're overestimating how much I know," said Clarissa. Her

hands were moving restlessly, pleating her cardigan. "My father doesn't tell us these things."

"Maybe it's time you started asking," said Ket Siong.

Alicia broke the ensuing silence by saying, all in one breath: "I'm really sorry, but I'm desperate for a wee. Can we have a comfort break?"

It punctured the tension. Clarissa even laughed weakly.

"Of course," said Ket Siong.

Clarissa shook her head when Alicia gave her an inquiring look. "I'm good."

Clarissa waited till she'd rushed off to turn to Ket Siong.

"I'm sorry about what happened," she said. "I can see Freshview doesn't come off well. I understand why you might suspect . . . But look, my dad and I don't see eye to eye on everything. But there's no way he'd be involved in anything like that. He donates a lot to charity. He's very community-minded. This would be completely against his principles."

She believed what she was saying. Tears were welling up in her eyes.

Ket Siong looked away. Stephen would probably say it was a male chauvinist's instinct, to be discomfited by the mere sight of a woman crying.

"You think your father wouldn't go so far as to do something like that," he said. "Get rid of an activist for causing trouble for his business."

"Yes," said Clarissa, without hesitation. "He's not like that. He's not *greedy*. He'd be the first to tell you, he already has more than enough."

Ket Siong bit back the obvious question of why, in that case, Low Teck Wee had permitted his company to destroy irreplaceable primary rainforest. He wasn't interested in hearing a defence of Low Teck Wee's good qualities.

"There were other interests at play," he said instead. "The rumour was the timber licence was granted by the state premier's son-in-law.

Although the premier's daughter resigned last year, you'll know she was on the board of Freshview at the time."

"What are you trying to say?" said Clarissa.

"I'm not saying Tan Sri Low arranged for it to happen," said Ket Siong. "But he might have closed one eye. He might have been under pressure." He thought of the *Hornbill Gazette* post that had mentioned Stephen. He hadn't heard from the author, two weeks on, though he'd messaged again.

"It may not have had anything to do with your father's business," he said slowly. "Stephen may have known something. Something that threatened someone else, badly enough that they wanted to get rid of him. But if anyone has an idea what that was, your father might.

"Miss Low, I am not an activist or a reporter. If what you say about your father is true, he has nothing to fear from me. All I want is to know what happened to my friend."

Clarissa was gazing down at the table. She raised her eyes to Ket Siong's. "Let's say my dad knows the answer. Let's say he was even involved somehow. Wouldn't you be worried something might happen to you? For trying to find out."

It took Ket Siong a moment to understand that she genuinely thought this was a hypothetical scenario. "I am."

Clarissa stared at him. Alicia reappeared before she mustered an answer.

"I had no idea it was getting so late," said Alicia. "Clarissa, you've got that thing you need to go to, right?"

From the look the women exchanged, it was clear they had arranged this exit in advance. But Clarissa glanced back at Ket Siong and said, "I can stay a little longer, if that would be helpful."

"I think we're done," said Ket Siong. "Thank you."

"I don't—I'm not sure I'll be able to find anything out," said Clarissa. "But I'll try." She hesitated. "How do I contact you? If there is anything."

"Alicia has my number," said Ket Siong. "You can pass on any messages through her."

He stayed at the table after they had gone, staring out of the window.

Talking about Stephen had brought him so vividly before Ket Siong that it seemed strange to find himself looking out on the white skies and brown brick of London. He felt unreal, a ghost trespassing upon the living.

The real Ket Siong was back in Malaysia, leading the life he should have had. Expecting to see Stephen the next day or the day after, whenever he decided to drop by. They'd go for a run together, or a workout session at the gym, or out for a movie and a stint at their favourite mamak stall afterwards—Ket Hau would come if it didn't involve exercise. Ket Siong had spent so many evenings defending his Maggi goreng mamak from his brother and Stephen while they talked about work, politics, football, everyone they knew . . .

But now he was here. And Stephen, most likely, was dead.

"Are you all right?"

It was the woman at the next table but one who'd spoken. She'd taken her Bose headphones off and was looking half-concerned, half-annoyed at being drawn away from her work. "Do you need . . ." She rummaged in her backpack and produced a tissue, holding it out to him.

"Thank you," said Ket Siong. He wiped his eyes and got up to go.

Ket Siong checked his phone as he descended the stairs into the bookshop. Renee had messaged.

As an event, this was no longer as disturbing to his peace of mind as it would have been at the beginning of the week. They had been texting nearly continuously since their unscheduled dinner at the expensive Malaysian joint in Chelsea. Ket Hau had started making pointed comments about how much time Ket Siong was spending on his phone: "Don't tell me you've discovered Candy Crush fifteen years after everybody else."

On this occasion, Renee had sent a video of a small child playing the piano. The accompanying text said:

This made me think of you.

Ket Siong was busy composing a reply when he heard his name.

"Ket!"

He blinked. Nathalie was by a stand of books directly in his line of sight (TRAVEL WITHOUT LEAVING YOUR HOME! said the sign). She was in a floral midi dress and white trainers. It was strange running into her, like being catapulted back in time to his student days.

"It is my mental health day," she said, after Ket Siong apologised for blanking her. "I take a day off every month, so I do not kill either my co-workers or my family. I am buying a book, and then I will go for a pedicure. What are *you* doing today?"

There was a slightly unnerving glint in her eye.

"Just browsing," said Ket Siong. "I'm teaching later today."

"Hmm," said Nathalie.

He wasn't, he concluded, imagining the chill in the air. Nathalie was probably suspicious of him, despite their recent forced rapprochement. At university they had been friendly, but not close. Renee had drawn them together, but when he and Renee had split, Nathalie had picked a side, and it hadn't been his. Whenever he'd seen Nathalie around the Academy buildings after, the look she'd given him had made it clear he should not expect to be acknowledged.

He didn't hold it against her. At the time, Ket Siong had even found her resentment comforting. It was what he'd felt he deserved.

His phone buzzed as he was walking to the Tube station.

Renee again. This time she'd sent a link to a music competition taking place at the Southbank Centre in the spring.

You should go for this! You'd smash it.

Ket Siong hadn't thought of competitions in more than half a decade. None of his students now were at a level to compete.

He was just short of being too old for this one, though he'd squeak in under the maximum age threshold in time for the next round. Given he hadn't performed or practised seriously in years, it wasn't a lot of time to prepare.

And yet . . .

Thanks. I'll check it out.

19

Renee struck a deal with Su Khoon. She'd devote fifty percent of her time in the run-up to the presentation to Freshview working on the pitch. She was free to spend the remainder on Virtu. In theory.

In practice, running Virtu was still a full-time job and then some, and Su Khoon had never respected Renee's boundaries before. He had no reason to start now, with a pitch looming over him that would determine the course of the rest of their lives.

They had enough preexisting materials that they should have been able to work up the pitch in a matter of days. Left to herself, Renee wouldn't have spent more on it. But Su Khoon didn't work like she did. He majored on interminable team meetings at which his staff told him things he would have known if he'd bothered reading the briefing notes they'd prepared for him, and he gave orders he often countermanded the next day.

But the point was to prove to Dad that they could work together. Renee resigned herself to the sacrifice of her time. At least all this face time made it harder for Su Khoon to cut her out, which it had to be expected he would try to do.

This became evident a couple of days into working with him, when they were going through pricing in his office. The phone on Su Khoon's desk went off.

Since the office was rented, nobody had Su Khoon's direct line except the Chahaya team, flown over to the UK to support him. He put the call on speaker without looking up.

"Yes?" said Su Khoon.

"Mr. Goh," said his PA's voice, "you know the dinner with the Freshview team, after the presentation? They say they cannot do that day anymore. Mr. Yeoh has a conflict. Next available slot is the following week, Friday lunchtime. Do you want me to book Friday lunch, or try to find another date for dinner?"

Su Khoon froze. Renee put down the printout of a spreadsheet she'd been puzzling over.

He cleared his throat.

"Let's go for lunch on Friday," he said, with a moderately successful pretence of nonchalance. "Lunch is more fun anyway. But Penny, don't book yet. I need to confirm numbers."

There was a perceptible pause.

"Of course, Mr. Goh," said his PA.

Renee kept her eyes on Su Khoon as he ended the call. He didn't say anything.

"You really lucked out with Penny," Renee remarked. "A PA who doesn't ask unnecessary questions is a godsend." She leaned back in her chair, crossing her legs. "I don't think this meetup with Freshview is in my diary. It was scheduled for after the presentation, was it?"

She was barely even angry. It was too funny seeing Su Khoon with egg on his face, conscious of the need to explain himself.

She'd seen her brother at a disadvantage before, but on every previous occasion he'd been mad about it. Not *embarrassed*. It was a stimulating novelty.

"It's not a work meeting," said Su Khoon. "Andrew mentioned he wanted to try this restaurant, so I said let's go. Just so happened the day of the presentation was the best day for it. But it's not business, it's for fun only."

Renee knew she shouldn't smile—it was too likely to provoke Su Khoon into defensiveness—but she felt the edges of her mouth quirk up despite herself.

"You forget we grew up in the same family, Er Ge," she said. "Everything's business."

Su Khoon didn't try to argue with this. He tugged at the cuffs on his shirtsleeves, collecting himself. "You want to go? It's fine by me. I just thought you wouldn't want to make nice with Andrew. He's going to be at the pitch meeting, so you'll have your fill of him. If you want to come to lunch also, it won't be enough to be professional. You'll have to be pleasant."

Socialising with bloody Andrew Yeoh was the last thing Renee wanted to do. But she should have known this was going to have to happen, from the moment she saw him in the Savoy. Pitching wasn't just about pricing or explaining how you were best placed to meet the counterparty's needs. It was about relationships.

Courting the Freshview team like this was absolutely the right thing for Su Khoon to be doing. If Renee wanted to stay in the game, she was going to have to do it, too . . . or let herself be pushed out.

"Sure," she said. "I'm always pleasant." She smiled. "Where are we going?"

If she had to grin and bear Andrew in order to win, she would do it. At least it was a problem with a clear end date. Either one of her brothers would become CEO of Chahaya, and she could go back to forgetting about Andrew's existence. Or she'd get the job, and—she'd figure out a workaround somehow. Surely she could delegate dealing with Andrew to somebody else.

It became evident, over the next few days, that there were other dilemmas she wouldn't be able to resolve so easily, if she won the contest her father had set them. It was impossible to do any kind of decent job with Virtu, while giving the Freshview pitch the attention Su Khoon—and Dad—expected.

That was fine for now. Her business wouldn't sink from a mere fortnight's neglect. But if Chahaya were to become Renee's full-time job, she was going to have to make some tough decisions about Virtu.

But that was a problem for future Renee to worry about. The Renee of the present day was, fortunately, too busy to think too hard about things that might not come to pass.

Since having therapy a few years ago, she'd tried to change her approach to work. She didn't let her staff stay late at the office and she tried to be as strict with herself as she was with them. But there was something freeing about letting go of that hard-won discipline, succumbing to the siren call of the crunch.

She'd forgotten how *good* it felt—spending late nights hunched over her laptop, surrounded by discarded takeaway sushi boxes and coffee cups. Everything else fell away. Her eyes burned and her back ached, but at the same time she felt electric, alive, running high on adrenaline.

How much of her exhilaration could be attributed to the fact most of her breaks from work involved either texting Ket Siong or catching up on his texts was one of the many things she was avoiding thinking about, with the skill of long practice. Nathalie would have pulled her up on it—so Renee hadn't told her.

Why shouldn't she text Ket Siong, anyway? There was nothing damning in the content of their exchanges. She could have shared any of them with her parents, without a blush. Ket Siong sent her links to long reads about art, culture, and science; she contributed memes, Instagram reels, and gossip about people he didn't know.

She didn't mention the unwelcome reappearance of Andrew in her life. But she did tell Ket Siong that Felicia Handoko had expended a portion of the Delima Corp millions on hiring Michael Learns to Rock to perform at her wedding.

A patron of the arts, he replied, startling a laugh out of Renee while she was engaged in a cheeky under-the-desk phone scroll during one of Su Khoon's endless meetings.

They never texted about anything personal. The closest they got was when, unexpectedly, Ket Siong sent her a video of a piano being played. There was no accompanying message. The pianist's face couldn't be seen, only his hands on the keyboard—but Renee recognised them.

She'd avoided asking about his career, though she hadn't been able to resist sending him that link to the music competition. It was clear something had happened in the past few years, if he'd gone from headlining concerts in Hong Kong—the event web page was the top Google search result for his name, four years on—to teaching kids scales. But natural as it was to confide in Ket Siong, he had a reserve that made it difficult to question him about himself in return.

The video felt meaningful. He was playing Mozart's Piano Sonata No. 16 in C major, one of the few pieces of classical music Renee was able to identify.

That's beautiful.

Then, as if she hadn't known it from the first few notes:

That's Mozart's Sonata facile, isn't it? The one you taught me at Nathalie's party.

Thanks. Yes. I wasn't sure if you'd know it.

I have a good memory when it comes to you, Renee typed out, before she got ahold of herself and wiped the draft.

At some point she was going to have to come clean to Nathalie about the fact she was texting Ket Siong. She'd only managed to avoid it so far because they were both so busy. Nathalie would no doubt demand to see the messages.

Renee was of course aware she had a right to privacy. She was perfectly capable of telling Nathalie so. But still, it was not out of the realms of possibility that Renee might show the messages to her, in a moment of weakness.

Either way, it would be nice to have a clean conscience when she assured Nathalie nothing was going on.

I love Mozart, she said instead, and put her phone down, turning back to the report she was trying to digest on Chahaya's construction capabilities.

She started rereading the paragraph on earned value management that had made her bail in the first place when the phone buzzed. She read the message, felt the blood rush to her face, and put her head down on her desk, pressing her hot cheek to the grateful chill of its surface.

I remember.

Which was a normal thing for Ket Siong to say. Staring at the small hill of Graze snack packets that had accumulated on her desk over the past week or so, Renee was forced to admit that it was she who was not being normal. It was the caffeine, and the pressure of this pitch, and being forced into proximity with her family, who were the single greatest risk factor for her mental health that she had yet identified.

Nothing was going on. There was nothing to worry about. But maybe she wouldn't mention the messages to Nathalie after all.

20

Yap Ket Hau leaned back in his Herman Miller Aeron chair, stretching his arms and sighing. It was midmorning and he was already tired, aching in places he hadn't even known he had when he was in his twenties. There was only so much a £1,000 ergonomic office chair could do for your back when you were thirty-nine and working fourteen-hour days.

He'd hoped for a lull after the team had filed their big case, but he'd had all of a week of quiet—just enough time to clear out the various administrative emails in his inbox and close his open timesheets—before getting pulled onto another department's matter. A big-ticket lawsuit by a Central Asian bank against its former chairman, who had embezzled hundreds of millions before taking off. He was currently believed to be somewhere in the Tuscan countryside.

A case raising crunchy points of law and interesting evidential challenges. As a paralegal, Ket Hau had nothing to do with any of that. His chief contribution was bundling—putting papers in files, in the right order, labelled and divided correctly. For days on end. If he never saw a lever arch file again in his life, it would be too soon.

He'd have to start doing yoga again, for his back. Ten minutes each day, before work.

I promise you, Stephen said, from somewhere in the past. *Do three sessions and it'll become a habit.*

When was that? Right, when Stephen had got obsessed with mixed martial arts and dragged Siong into it. They'd tried to pull

Ket Hau along, but Ket Hau had always been less susceptible than his brother to Stephen's influence in these matters. Exercise had not been one of the passions he'd shared with Stephen.

He detached his conscious mind from the memory of Stephen with a discipline that had become habitual over years of effort. His subconscious would keep gnawing away at it, but there was nothing Ket Hau could do about that. He didn't have the money for therapy. And he wouldn't be able to tell any therapist the worst part, anyway—the part that kept him up at night, when it wasn't giving him bad dreams.

He stood up, scanning the office over the top of his cubicle. Both the pod he was in and the next one were empty. He always chose to work one of his three mandatory "in the office" days on Monday, because hardly anyone else came in.

He'd get himself a fresh cup of tea, then finish proofreading this English translation of a Russian lease. At least he was due some chunky overtime. He'd see where they were at the end of the month, after they'd paid off the bills. Maybe he could take Ma somewhere nice.

And Ket Siong—not that Siong deserved special attention. He was so distracted by this girl he supposedly wasn't dating that he'd probably forget to show up to anything Ket Hau planned. Well, no doubt that would shake itself out in time.

Stephen would have loved watching Siong's little love story play out. He'd always been a romantic.

Ket Hau picked his mug off his desk, when a phone started ringing. It took him a moment to recognise the ringtone. He didn't get calls on his work mobile very often; his co-workers usually preferred to ambush him on Teams.

No Caller ID, read the phone screen. The new partner, Ameera, had said she would call to brief him on a research task. Maybe she was ringing from her landline at home.

"Hello?" It was a woman on the line, but not Ameera, or anyone he knew. "Is this Ket Yap?"

Ket Hau suppressed a yawn. "Yes, speaking."

"It's Clarissa," said the voice on the line. "We talked a couple of weeks ago, at Foyles?" She sounded nervous. Was that a Malaysian accent?

Ket Hau was about to say, *Sorry, you've got the wrong number,* when the woman said:

"Clarissa Low."

Ket Hau froze.

"Give me a moment," he said.

Quiet as it was today, in an open-plan office there was always the risk of being overheard. He stepped out of his cubicle and went into the small meeting room opposite the pod, shutting the door behind him.

He lowered himself into a chair, gripping the phone to his ear. "Right."

There wasn't much of a family resemblance between Ket Hau and his brother. Siong had Ma's willowy grace and enviable bone structure, whereas Ket Hau took after their father. Which meant he was four inches shorter and didn't make people stop dead in the street, staring.

But they sounded almost exactly the same. Even close friends and family were liable to get confused about which of the two of them had picked up the phone.

"Clarissa," he said. "Of course."

"Is now a good time to speak? Great." Clarissa Low paused. "I spoke to my father after we talked. About the Ensengei project. I didn't mention you. And I didn't learn much, he didn't want to talk about it. But it made me realise you were right. I should start asking questions."

"Right," said Ket Hau. It seemed the safest thing to say.

"I managed to get access to the company systems," said Clarissa. "And I found some things. I don't know how much they mean, but I printed them off in case they're useful. I thought that would be better. No electronic trail. Can I pass them to you?

"This week?" she added, before Ket Hau could say anything. "I'm flying back to Malaysia on Thursday. My grandma's not well. That's why I didn't ask Alicia to contact you. She's away travelling, and I don't know how long I'll be gone. I found this number online. I thought there couldn't be that many Malaysian Ket Yaps in London, right?"

"Sure," said one of at least two Malaysian Ket Yaps in London. "So you found this number on the firm's website?" Ket Hau put Clarissa on speaker so he could bring up the website on his phone. "I see."

Turned out he did have an online profile. That was news to him. Historically, the firm hadn't bothered devoting individual web pages to profiles of their paralegal staff.

This had to be Ameera's fault. She came from a tech industry background and believed in doing away with the traditional hierarchies of legal practice. Her team had a stand-up every Monday and she never had ordinary calls, only syncs.

At least his surprise profile was bare bones. The one piece of identifying information on it, besides the shortened and rearranged version of his name he went by at work, was the fact he'd studied at Universiti Malaya. No picture. It was no wonder the girl had been led astray.

"I'm sorry about your grandma," said Ket Hau.

He might be able to bluff this girl into thinking he was Siong for the duration of a phone call, but any face-to-face encounter was going to shatter the illusion.

"You'll be busy," he said. "Rather than meeting up, would it be easier if you courier the documents to me?"

"I think better to hand them to you," said Clarissa. "I could come to your firm? It's near Holborn, right?"

She seemed anxious to put herself out on Ket Siong's account. Whatever he had told her, clearly it had impressed upon her a sense of obligation.

"The thing is, I'm in all-day meetings this whole week," said

Ket Hau apologetically. "Can you drop the documents off at reception? I'll let them know to expect you. Sorry, it's just a busy time."

Clarissa hesitated. "The documents are, you know, they're pretty sensitive. I shouldn't really have them. But after what you told me . . . I want to help. But I hope—I'm trusting you to handle these carefully."

She sounded very young. Wasn't one of the Low daughters some kind of influencer? Ket Hau had seen photos of her before, floating around on social media—a long-legged teenager in Chanel. If this was her, she couldn't be older than twenty, at most.

"I understand," he said gently. "I appreciate your trust. You don't need to worry. If you pass those documents to reception, I'll make sure they come straight to me. This is a reputable firm. We know how to handle documents."

Documents she'd stolen from her father's company and was sharing with an outsider, unbeknownst to her father.

An outsider and a stranger? It didn't sound like Clarissa knew Ket Siong that well. She wouldn't be the girl Ket Siong had been seeing. Would she?

"It's probably the least suspicious way to do the handover," Ket Hau added. "If you're spotted and someone starts asking questions, you can say you came to consult the firm on something."

A nerve-wracking pause, and then:

"That makes sense," said Clarissa. "I'm going to Senate House Library tomorrow afternoon. I'll drop by your firm on the way, if that works? Can you let me know as soon as you receive the documents? I'll give you my number."

Ket Hau took the number down. "I'll let you know the moment they're in my hands."

"Thanks, Ket."

"No," said Ket Hau, with complete sincerity. "Thank *you*."

21

Su Khoon wrapped up work just before seven, the evening before the pitch presentation to Freshview—early, by his standards.

"Go home," he said to the team. "Get a good night's rest."

His staff had either been trained up to low expectations, or had the good sense to pretend. They looked appropriately grateful.

He glanced at Renee.

In the course of the past couple of weeks, there had grown up between the two of them what was not exactly camaraderie, but a functional alliance. Having a common objective to work towards, and being surrounded by witnesses who weren't related to them, had smoothed over their interactions out of all recognition.

Renee knew Su Khoon better, now, than she probably ever had before. She'd learnt he played cricket—*cricket*—for fun; socialised mainly with his circle of friends from primary school; disliked his in-laws cordially, but rang his wife and kids twice a day every day. If he was seeing Eva, or any other girls, in the evenings after work, Renee didn't ask.

She knew better than to think she could trust him simply because they weren't actively biting each other's heads off. But it was nice, not being at loggerheads with her own brother, the sibling closest to her in age.

She tried not to wonder what Su Khoon had learnt about her.

When it came to her family, it was safest to assume they cared a lot less than she did about having a normal, amicable relationship. That wasn't, in the Gohs' view, what family was *for*.

"Dinner?" said Su Khoon. "I'll pay."

Renee smiled. "Thanks, but I've got plans for the evening."

Su Khoon raised his eyebrows. "If you're managing to squeeze in dates even now, I take my hat off to you."

"No," said Renee. "I'm going to go for a walk on Oxford Street, look in the shops, and choose one really nice thing to buy for myself."

She couldn't have said anything better calculated to endear her to Su Khoon, short of *I'm withdrawing from the Chahaya leadership race and will help you sabotage Da Ge*. It was exactly what he expected of a woman.

"Spending the money before you earn it, huh?" he said tolerantly. "Don't break the bank."

"I'm making no promises," said Renee. "See you tomorrow morning."

She took a bus instead of a cab. She wasn't in a hurry.

Su Khoon's joke had made her thoughtful. She was struck by his convenient amnesia about his bad behaviour. It was something she'd seen in both her brothers before, but it never failed to astound her. Of the two of them, Su Khoon was much likelier to be having a date tonight—if booty calls counted.

She was staying off men, at least as romantic prospects. But friends were a different matter. After all, men formed half the world's population. It would be unreasonable of her to decide friendship with any man was out of the question.

And it would be nice to hang out with a friend this evening. She wasn't nervous about the next day—presentations played to her strengths—but she was keyed up, vibrating with energy, with nowhere to put it. A good gossip over a good dinner was just what she needed.

She took out her phone and texted Ket Siong.

Hey, what are you up to? Free for dinner tonight? I know it's super last minute but feel like going out on the town x

The *x* slipped into the message by accident. Renee texted *x*s to all kinds of people. It was one of the British social conventions she was trying to master, like asking people how they were without expecting a real answer, and paying for rounds at the pub.

But Ket Siong was not British, and had made no concession to the pressure to assimilate, so far as she could see.

Before she could get properly launched on tormenting herself over that *x*, however, Ket Siong replied.

What time? Just finished a class in Soho, so I could come meet you.

Renee's heart rate kicked up a notch. Her original plan had been to get off around Bond Street and walk past the designer shops there, peeking in at the windows, before proceeding to Liberty. But she didn't want to keep Ket Siong hanging around.

I'm heading in that direction right now. Going to stop by Liberty. Where do you want to eat? I can meet you at whatever restaurant?

Ket Siong didn't message again, but he would at some point.

Renee got off the bus when it was approaching Regent Street. She walked up along its grand arc, untroubled for once by the tourists and shoppers clogging the broad pavements. She felt young, free, and unburdened, with an evening full of possibility ahead of her.

She'd buy a Diptyque candle. That would be a real treat. Renee didn't mind splashing out on dresses or shoes or makeup, but she generally drew the line at candles: "You're literally burning your money."

"You are paying for the scent," Nathalie argued. "And the flex."

Renee would indulge in the flex on this one occasion, and then . . . she wondered what restaurant Ket Siong would suggest. There was a branch of the ramen chain she liked round the corner from Liberty. She used to patronise the very first outlet when they had opened years ago near Tottenham Court Road, dragging Ket Siong there to wait in the queues.

For the first time, with a pricking of her conscience, it occurred to Renee to wonder if Ket Siong had been able to afford all those restaurants she'd taken him to. He'd never said anything, but his family wasn't that well-off. Presumably that was why he'd had to end his studies at the Royal Academy of Music prematurely.

She had tried to pay for him sometimes, back in the day, but he hadn't liked it. He never got shitty about it—just shook his head, with that affectionate half smile. That was what she'd liked about Ket Siong. No matter what she did—sobbed at him for an hour about her family; hassled him about his janky old shoes—he'd never seemed to mind. She didn't have to be on all the time with him, or dress a certain way, or pretend to be anything or anyone but herself.

She was glad they were able to be friends now. That was what really mattered, after all. Look at Nathalie. Their friendship had outlasted all of Renee's romantic liaisons to date, and it was certainly healthier than her relationship with her family.

Don't use me *to justify this thing with Ket,* said an inner voice that sounded remarkably like Nathalie. *I told you I do not approve. Have sex with him, or block him. Don't do this weird in-between thing where you're secretly in love with him but you're pretending it is nothing.*

"I am *not* in love with him," muttered Renee rebelliously. She glanced down at her phone to check how much time she had before Liberty closed, and heard someone call her name.

She knew who it was before she turned. Her heart sped up, warmth flooding the back of her neck.

"Hey," she said.

Ket Siong was in a charcoal-grey peacoat, worn over a chunky black jumper and jeans, with an oatmeal-coloured scarf around his neck. Renee's embarrassment wasn't quite enough to save her from noticing how his shoulders stretched out that jumper. He looked good enough to eat.

He probably hadn't heard her talking to herself. The steady blare of traffic on the road would have drowned her out.

"Hey," said Ket Siong, glancing up the street. "I was going towards Liberty. Have you already been there?"

"Not yet," said Renee.

She had twenty minutes before the doors closed. But the appeal of elbowing her way past tourists for the privilege of dropping sixty pounds on a scented candle was fading.

The idea of a steaming hot bowl of ramen, on the other hand . . . It had been unseasonably warm the past week, but today there was a bite of frost in the air. It felt, for the first time, like winter.

"But I'm hungry," said Renee. "Let's just go for dinner. Did you have any ideas about where you wanted to eat?"

Ket Siong had his hands in his pockets. There was something so restful about him, thought Renee, looking at his hands. It was the way he made no unnecessary movements, said nothing but what he meant.

"No," he said. "Is there anything you feel like?"

"I was thinking of going to Kanada-Ya. They've opened one near here, did you know?" Remembering her inconsiderate youth, Renee added, "My treat, OK?"

Ket Siong frowned. "You paid last time. Let me cover it."

Renee could fight. It would be the polite thing to do. Ket Siong couldn't be earning that much as a piano teacher, whereas she was objectively loaded, even if it was a while since she'd had direct access to family funds.

"OK," she said.

Ket Siong fell into step next to her. The Christmas lights were up, reliably magical in the glowing darkness of the winter sky. Glittering angels swooped over Regent Street, trailing sparkling webs of light.

Ket Siong was gazing up at them. Renee wondered what he

was thinking. She opened her mouth to ask, but let out a jaw-cracking yawn instead. Tears stood in her eyes.

Ket Siong glanced at her. "Tired?"

Renee blinked away the wetness at her eyes. "Yeah. It's been busy. Luckily my brother decided we should have some rest tonight. It's the big day tomorrow. We're presenting our pitch."

Ket Siong nodded. "How's it been going?"

He was asking about more than work. Renee shoved her hands deeper into her coat pockets. She had on a grey roll-neck cashmere-blend dress that had been, if anything, too toasty in Su Khoon's rented offices, but it wasn't enough to keep her warm now she was outside. The vintage 1930s silk faille coat she was wearing over it was far too light.

"It's weird," she said. "I keep wanting it to be more than it is."

"More than it is," Ket Siong echoed.

His eyes on her made her feel shy. She looked away.

"Yeah, you know. My brother and I have got a common interest in getting along, for now. We both want to impress my dad, and that's what he wants to see. I know that's all it is. But . . . it's pathetic, but there's a part of me that wants us to be friends." She laughed, rueful. "It's the same thing I wanted as a kid. Turns out I haven't changed since I was six."

Ket Siong said, gently, "It's natural to want to have a good relationship with your brother."

Renee shrugged. She felt too exposed to want to meet his eyes. So she looked at the shops lining the street, their window displays festooned with fake holly and ivy and pine, oversized baubles and bright tinsel, reindeer in neon colours with fairy lights tangled in their antlers. The mannequins were decked out in the usual array of dresses and jumpsuits for party season.

She made a mental note to check in with Louise about the arrangements for the Virtu office Christmas party. It was the only festive thing she did around this time of year. There was her birthday, too, a couple of weeks before Christmas, but Renee never did anything for her birthday. Before she moved to London, Dad had always insisted on a ceremonious dinner with all the family to celebrate the occasion. Those dinners—with her brothers sneering on one side of the table, and her mother on the other side doing a great imitation of a block of ice—had given Renee a permanent disgust of birthday parties.

At least nobody had to know when you had a birthday, so nobody expected you to celebrate. Christmas was different. British people especially got a little funny when they heard you were planning to spend it alone, though Renee enjoyed the quiet—just her and her TV, and the KFC meal she allowed herself once a year.

Maybe she'd do some volunteering over Christmas again, if only to avoid getting invited to Louise's family's house for the day. Renee would have accepted being Nathalie's festive charity case, but Nathalie was obliged to divide her Christmas between her family in Paris and Jeroen's in Antwerp: "It is like something out of Dante's *Inferno*. I really think it will be the main topic of discussion at Thomas's future therapy sessions."

"How are things with your brother?" Renee said now. "You guys are close, right? I remember you used to call him and your mom twice a week, when we were at uni."

"They're OK," said Ket Siong, with less enthusiasm than Renee would have expected. She gave him an inquiring look.

He was gazing down at his feet, his eyebrows drawn together. "They're fine," he added. "It's just . . . it's complicated."

"Yeah," said Renee. "Family, huh?"

He smiled. Renee had to stop looking at him; he was too beautiful. This crush was getting out of hand.

Ket Siong was definitely the best-looking guy to have broken her heart, even including Jason. Also the nicest. At least the worst thing Ket Siong had done was change his mind about wanting to be with her.

At the time it had felt like the worst thing that had ever happened to her, but it was several steps up from some of her other exes' greatest hits. It wasn't Ket Siong's *fault* if he was attracted to her but didn't want a relationship. At least she knew now.

Do you know, though? said that annoying inner Nathalie voice. *Sure, he dumped you ten years ago, but this time around he went home with you. And he wanted to keep seeing you after. You're the one who said you weren't looking for anything serious.*

Nor was she, and for good reason. Renee wasn't going to do this now, the night before a potentially life-changing meeting. She was going to have a nice bowl of ramen with Ket Siong and then she was going to go home by herself, watch half an episode of something brainless on Netflix, and turn in early.

"Oh," she said, as they turned a corner onto the narrow street approaching the restaurant. There was a queue going round the building. "Sorry. We could go somewhere else?"

"You wanted to eat here," said Ket Siong. "Let's wait."

Renee glanced back towards Carnaby Street as they joined the queue. The festive lights display this year was on a tropical theme. An arch made of leaping twin tigers loomed over the entrance to the street. Green palm leaves fanned out in a shimmering canopy; monkeys swung off the lampposts. There was even a Rafflesia, monstrous cartoony petals outlined in twinkling red lights.

"I need to take a selfie with that Rafflesia," she said. The lights were less elaborate in the side alley they were on: glowing pink-and-purple bulbs, strung between the buildings. "The lights are so pretty this year."

"Yes," said Ket Siong, but he was looking at her.

Renee's stupid heart skipped a beat. She averted her eyes and pulled her coat closer around herself, shivering.

"It's really feeling like winter now," she said. "You'll have Christmas shopping to do, right? You guys celebrate."

"We don't make a big deal of the presents. It's more about the food," said Ket Siong. But he wasn't interested in discussing his family's Christmas traditions. "You're cold?"

"It's been so warm lately today's taken me off guard." Renee shook her head. "I should've layered up. British weather, huh?"

Ket Siong unwound the scarf around his neck, settled it on her shoulders, and wrapped its length around her neck, twice. Renee couldn't look at his face, so she stared at his throat, her heart fluttering in her chest like a trapped bird.

His fingertips grazed the high collar of her dress, but made no contact with her skin. You could hardly call it a touch. There was no reason for her body to light up all over—as though he had run his hands over her; as though he had kissed her. But it did.

The scarf was soft, warm from the heat of his body. It smelt of him, a clean male animal scent.

Ket Siong's Adam's apple moved as he swallowed. He gave the scarf a final twitch and stepped back.

22

It struck Ket Siong a second too late that he should have asked first. Offered Renee his scarf, instead of putting it on her, as though he had a right to touch her.

The lights overhead were reflected in her eyes. She'd looked tired when he saw her on Regent Street, but under the glow of the lights, her face smoothed out. The dark circles under her eyes and the minute worry lines around her mouth vanished.

Ten years fell away. They might have been students again, at the very start of their adult lives. She was his best friend, and he was in love with her.

He was still in love with Renee.

He hadn't allowed himself to think it in so many words, before now.

Renee reached up to touch the scarf.

He should say something, apologise. But she spoke first.

"Oh, this is the *good* stuff." She ran the scarf between her fingers, her face lit up with delight. "Is this real pashmina? The texture's beautiful."

"Oh. Yes." That was what it was called. An image rose before him: Stephen on the sofa in their small, cluttered living room back home, unwrapping his haul from a work trip, talking about mountain goats. "It's a gift. A friend got it in India."

"Must have been a good friend," said Renee. "Real pashmina isn't cheap."

"He was." Stephen had got two scarves, white for Ma and

beige for Ket Siong. Ket Hau, to his outrage, had received a box of chocolate truffles with durian filling, the kind found only in airports and tourist-trap souvenir shops.

Renee looked cosy in the scarf. Seeing her in it gave Ket Siong a pleasure so intense it felt almost sinful. He looked away to try to hide it, sweetness spreading through his chest.

What was it his brother had said? *You and I know, better than most people.*

It was incalculably precious that he got to be here with Renee, ten years after he'd broken her heart. It was the being here that was important. Renee had drawn her lines. It wasn't his place to ask for anything more.

So he'd been telling himself. But what if Renee had changed her mind?

She didn't want him to leave her alone, that much he felt he could conclude from the memes and the invitations to dinner. But was it simply that she was lonely, or enjoyed the attention? Despite the deceptive openness of her manner, he knew Renee found it hard to trust people. She hadn't mentioned any friends in London other than Nathalie. Even during their university days, she had seemed strangely lonely, set apart from others, despite her retinue of male admirers.

She'd trusted Ket Siong back then. Did she trust him now?

The thought was not pleasant. He suspected he knew the answer.

He hadn't wanted to force a discussion about their past, when she hadn't seemed inclined to go over that old ground. But if he explained himself now, told her why he'd hurt her all those years ago . . .

Maybe it wouldn't make any difference. But he wouldn't know until he tried.

They were at the front of the queue now. The person behind them was on her phone, talking loudly in what sounded like Serbian. A sudden fit of recklessness possessed him.

222 · ZEN CHO

"Renee," said Ket Siong, and who knew what he might have said next, except Renee said:

"I saw Andrew the other day. You remember Andrew Yeoh?"

"Your ex," said Ket Siong, after a moment.

Renee grimaced. "You date a guy for a few months one time and he's your ex for life. Even if he threw your phone out of the window." She blew out a rueful breath. "He's on the other side of the deal."

"On this pitch you've been working on?"

"Yeah," said Renee. "I knew Andrew was Low Teck Wee's nephew, but I didn't know he'd started working for Freshview. Last I heard, he was at Morgan Stanley. I mean, you can't blame him. It's probably an easier ride working in the family business."

"What?" said Ket Siong.

A waitress popped her head out of the restaurant and said:

"Table for two? Right, come on through."

The bustle of getting seated suspended all private conversation. Once they'd been left with the menu to consider their choice of nine different varieties of ramen, Renee took off his scarf and held it out over the table.

"Thanks," she said.

She'd be cold once they got out of the restaurant. But he didn't try to insist she keep it.

"Your pitch," said Ket Siong. "It's to Freshview Industries?"

"Oh, you've heard of them?" said Renee.

The restaurant was tiny and achingly trendy: the walls were painted stark black, exposed pipes hanging low from the ceiling. Their table was shoved right up against their neighbours'. Renee glanced at them—East Asian university students on their phones—then leaned forward, lowering her voice.

"They're leading a redevelopment project here, converting an old factory site in South London. It's a huge job, major investment by the Malaysian government. We're hoping to win the construction work. Dad's an old hand. Chahaya built half the high-rises in Singapore." Renee paused. "It's not public yet, though. We'll only announce if they decide to go for us."

Ket Siong stared fixedly at his menu. Competing aromas crowded the room: tonkotsu broth, pickled ginger, green tea, and soy sauce. Underneath these, the faint scent of roses wafting from his scarf felt like a secret, something Renee had confided to his particular care. "I won't tell anyone."

"I know," said Renee. "I'm not worried about *that*."

"How was it?" he said. "With Andrew."

"Oh. Fine," said Renee. "He was kind of a creep. But it wasn't as bad as I feared. He's married with a kid now. He showed me baby photos." She settled back in her chair, sagging a little. "Hopefully I won't have to spend much time working with him. I'm sure he mostly supervises the people doing the actual work. His staff seem nice enough."

She was probably right. Freshview's employees would be people with bills to pay and families to support, doing their best to get along. Ket Siong was in no position to judge their choices.

The smells of the restaurant had gone from enticing to oppressive. The black walls felt like they were closing in. He took a shallow breath, tamping down on a surge of nausea.

"Ket Siong." Renee's face was concerned. "Are you OK?"

The waitress came to take their order before he had to answer. Ket Siong was glad of the reprieve. It gave him a few moments to think about what he should say.

He had no evidence regarding Freshview's role in what had happened to Stephen. But Renee wasn't a judge sitting in court. He didn't need to prove his suspicions beyond reasonable doubt. Surely anyone, hearing what he knew, would have reservations about doing business with Freshview.

He had to tell her. Ten years ago, he'd broken her heart, and his own, in part because he hadn't trusted her with the truth.

He'd always wished there had been something else he could have done. Well, here he was again, knowing something Renee didn't about her family and his own. He could do something different, this time. He could decide to trust her.

"There's something I need to tell you," he said.

Her eyes flicked up. There was a question in them, one Ket Siong would have liked to answer. "Yes?"

Ket Siong felt a sudden overwhelming surge of protectiveness. He wanted to stand between Renee and anything that might hurt her—including himself. It would be so easy to be quiet, change the subject, tell her something different. Something she wanted to hear.

Curiously, it was not Stephen he thought of then, or Ket Hau, or their mother. It was Clarissa Low whose face appeared before him. Her expression when he'd said to her, *Maybe it's time you started asking.*

"You've never asked why my family came to the UK," he said.

Renee blinked. She looked away, smiling wryly, as though she was laughing at herself. He knew she felt foolish.

Before he could say anything else, their ramen arrived—bowls of noodles coiled in cloudy broth beneath slices of pork belly and generous shavings of black fungus and spring onions, a large square of nori tucked in at the side of the bowl.

Ket Siong had been hungry when he arrived, but his appetite had vanished.

When he looked up, Renee's habitual poise was back in place.

"I didn't like to pry," she said, as though there had been no interruption. "People have different reasons for moving."

"We weren't thinking of migrating originally," said Ket Siong. "My mother didn't want to leave my father. We used to visit him in the columbarium every few months. And . . . it was her home. She wanted to make it better."

"Why'd you change your mind?"

"It was to do with my brother's job," said Ket Siong. "He used to work for an NGO in KL, it did a lot of work with partners in Sarawak. He got involved in a campaign trying to tackle logging on native customary land in Ensengei, in Sarawak. They were supporting the villagers in a lawsuit against the company doing it."

Renee's eyes widened. "That's terrible."

Ket Siong couldn't look at her, or he wasn't going to be able to keep speaking. She'd worked so hard on this pitch to Freshview. So much rode on it for her.

"Yes," he said. "My brother's co-worker Stephen was involved in the same campaign." He swallowed. "He got kidnapped."

"The co-worker?" Renee sat up. "Oh my God. What happened?"

Why had he called Stephen a co-worker? It was hard to explain all Stephen had been to the family, even if he avoided mentioning his suspicions about the nature of Stephen's relationship with his brother.

It was easy to trot out the excuses, harder to fool himself. Ket Siong knew the reason. He didn't want to make this worse for Renee than it was already going to be.

Though who was he really trying to protect? Was he trying to minimise Renee's upset for her sake, or his own? She had already invested so much in the pitch to Freshview. Bound up in this deal was everything her family meant to her, all she'd ever wanted from them and failed to get. How much could he mean to her, compared to that?

He was about to complicate her life. Renee could dispose of that complication easily—by cutting him out of it.

"He was never seen again," said Ket Siong. He went on, quickly, before Renee could speak or he could lose his nerve: "When we met at the V&A, I was there because I saw Freshview Industries in the list of supporters of the exhibition. I went because I wanted to ask Low Teck Wee if he knew what happened to Stephen."

Renee's eyes were huge in her face. Dread roiled in his stomach as he watched understanding dawn on her. He couldn't bear to see her face shut down, not when he'd just told her about Stephen.

"Freshview was the company," she said.

She'd barely had any of her ramen. He should have waited till she'd finished. She wouldn't eat anything now.

"Freshview won the legal case," said Ket Siong. "The forest in Ensengei is gone. They're planting oil palm there now."

Renee took a sip of her genmaicha, placing the cup back on the table with deliberate control. "But your brother's co-worker—what was his name?"

"Stephen. He was a good friend."

Renee's eyes slid past Ket Siong. "The one who got you the scarf?" He'd slung his scarf over the back of his chair.

"Just a guess," she added. "There was something about the way you said the person who gave it to you was a good friend. You know, in the past tense. Like it was someone you'd lost."

She glanced around at their surroundings. The crowd had thinned out a little since they'd arrived. Their immediate neighbours had vacated their table. At the next table over, two men were having an amiable half-shouted conversation in Italian.

"You think Freshview was involved?" Renee said, in a near whisper. Ket Siong had to strain to hear her over the general buzz of conversation. "What did Uncle Low say, when you asked him?"

"Nothing much," said Ket Siong. "He wouldn't have told me, no matter what he knew."

"But you think he does know something."

Ket Siong remembered what Ket Hau had said about his run-in with Low. "There's no way he didn't know. If he wasn't involved, he was complicit."

Renee's expression changed. She said, in a new tone, "Do you have any evidence of that?"

"He wouldn't have left evidence I could find," said Ket Siong sharply.

He regretted this the moment it was out, but Renee gave him no opportunity to soften it or row it back. Her back straightened.

"It's a very serious accusation to make without evidence," she said.

"If Low were an innocent man, Renee, he would have told me he doesn't know what happened to Stephen," said Ket Siong. "He wouldn't have walked away."

"Sometimes all you can do when you've been accused is walk away," said Renee. "If everyone's decided you're guilty, you're not going to change their mind. The only way out is to refuse to engage."

Ket Siong knew what she was talking about. "This isn't like that."

"Like what? You mean, the time my brothers trumped up some bullshit allegations about me and everyone fell over themselves to believe them? Because I was successful and that's the one thing people can't forgive." Renee crossed her arms. "Ket Siong, why did you tell me this? Why now?"

"I didn't know you were planning on working with Freshview before."

"You knew I was working with Chahaya." Renee's eyes were hard. She would give no quarter, would expect none from him. "How do you know Chahaya hasn't done equally bad things? That's what business is like."

Ket Siong frowned. "You don't believe that. It's not how you do business."

"Isn't it just a matter of degree?" said Renee. "Our makers in Cambodia get, say, forty dollars a piece. We apply a three times markup before it gets to the consumer. And I live in the most expensive city in the world, in a flat that could set our makers up for life. Money's never really clean, Ket Siong."

"I know you try to be fair," said Ket Siong. "It's not easy to build a business the way you have. There's a difference between that and Freshview stripping Iban and Bidayuh land. Look, this isn't about you or Virtu—"

"How could it not be?" said Renee. "Tomorrow I'm going to be standing up in front of Low Teck Wee's nephew, trying to persuade him to give us a job on the development. There's millions of pounds of Malaysian state funds invested in that project. How much dirty money do you think is sloshing around in there? Or were you hoping I'd pull out? Tell Su Khoon and Dad, 'Oh no, I can't do it, Freshview is morally suspect'?"

"It's not for me to tell you what to do."

Renee met his eyes. "You'd judge me for making the wrong decision, though."

Ket Siong looked back steadily. Part of him wanted to reassure her, tell her it would make no difference to him what she did.

In a way, it was true. There was nothing he or Renee or anyone could do to change how he felt about her. That was one lesson he'd finally learnt, even if it had taken him ten years. But it wasn't an answer to what she'd said.

"No more than you'd judge yourself," he said.

"You don't understand," said Renee. "Your family's different. You know what mine's like. If I make the call you think I should make, I piss off my dad, my brother—"

"You're not afraid of that."

"Not afraid. No." Renee swallowed. Ket Siong saw, to his horror, that she was fighting back tears.

"I'm sick of it," she said, her voice ragged. "I'm sick of being the outcast. I'm sick of always being in the wrong. This is the first time I've gone so long without fighting with Su Khoon. He offered to buy me dinner this evening, of his own free will. You were the one who said it's natural to want to have a good relationship with my family. Why are you making me choose?"

His heart ached for her. "I'm not trying to make you choose."

"So you'd be fine, whatever I decided?" snapped Renee. "Even if I told you we pitched Freshview and won the deal?"

"You keep saying 'we,'" said Ket Siong. "But you are not Chahaya. You are not your father. You are the decisions that you make. I would not tell your father or your brother what I've told you."

"How do you know I won't tell Dad?" said Renee bitterly. "I could tell him he needs to warn Uncle Low there's a PR storm brewing. Win some brownie points that way."

Ket Siong was getting annoyed. There was no need for Renee to make out that she was worse than she was. It verged on self-indulgence, given the seriousness of what he'd revealed.

But love and pity tugged him the other way. He'd put Renee in a difficult position, and picked the worst possible time to do it. It was impossible not to see her point of view.

"I haven't gone about this the right way," he said. "Give it time. You aren't seeing clearly right now. When you've had a chance to think . . ."

"No." Renee looked around the restaurant, desolate, like someone who had woken from a dream to find themselves abandoned, surrounded by strangers. "I'm seeing clearly now, for the first time." She shook her head. "I've got to go. I've got an early start tomorrow. You stay here and finish your dinner."

"Renee . . ."

"You should get them to pack mine up. Don't want it to go to waste," said Renee. Her cordiality was implacable. Behind it, she'd absented herself. She rummaged in her bag, producing her phone. "She said we could pay by QR code, right?"

"You said I could pay," protested Ket Siong.

Renee wiped her eyes, as though she hadn't noticed they were wet. "Right. I did say that."

She let him cover their dinner with troubling docility, making no objection when Ket Siong said he would leave with her. The waitress took one look at them and refrained from making any comment on the fact she was packing up two untouched bowls of ramen.

He trailed Renee out onto the street, the bowls of soup—no

longer even warm—knocking against his outer thigh. He was trying to think of something to say to hold off the conclusion the waitress had read in their faces.

There was one moment of hope, one moment when it might have gone either way. Outside, Renee paused, lifting her face to the night sky and the lights strung between the shops. She said:

"I'm sorry about your friend. I should have said that earlier."

She wouldn't look at him, but her sincerity could not be doubted.

"Renee," said Ket Siong. "I didn't mean . . ."

But what could he say? He'd thought it right to tell her what he knew. Which meant he had intended to upset her. If she had not been upset by what he'd had to tell her, she would not be the person he knew her to be.

Renee had made up her mind, anyway.

"I don't think we should see each other again," she said. "Good night, Ket Siong."

Before he could answer, she turned and walked away, with a ruthless, unhurried step—as graceful as ever, every movement perfectly judged.

23

Presumably Renee got a taxi home. Ket Siong's journey home was a little more involved, requiring a Tube train and a bus. He had a book on him—a Wallace Stevens collection—but he didn't take it out.

The conversation with Renee replayed itself over and over in his head, but almost without the power to hurt him. He watched it with the bafflement of a viewer of a film in a foreign language, wondering how those people had reached the state in which they found themselves.

He had to get off at Seven Sisters to catch his bus home. He remembered, dully, that he'd texted his family earlier, to say he was going to be late and wouldn't need dinner. He should check whether there had been a reply.

Renee wouldn't have messaged. Though if she'd calmed down and was regretting what she'd said, it would not be out of the question for her to get in touch. Her moods shifted quickly, and she was never too embarrassed to own it.

There were no texts from his family or Renee. But there was a notification of a new direct message on Facebook. He'd forgotten he'd downloaded the messaging app after writing to the *Hornbill Gazette*. Four weeks had passed since then. He'd given up on hearing back.

I'm sorry for the delayed response. Your message went to my spam folder, so I didn't see it before.

> I'm working on an article for a major broadsheet
> here about the situation in Sarawak, and would be
> very interested in talking to you and your brother.
> I hear your brother is in London now. Could we
> meet in person? He can rest assured that I protect
> my sources. I can put you in touch with people who
> could vouch for me, if needed. Let me know.—HD

Which could be none other than Helen Daley—editor in chief of the *Hornbill Gazette* and author of a thousand screeds on the venal corruption of the Malaysian political body. She'd followed up with another message, supplying her phone number:

> Feel free to call me if it would be easier to talk.

She would see that Ket Siong had read her messages the next time she checked. He put his phone away in his pocket.

It shouldn't have been a surprise to hear from Helen Daley herself. That was what he'd been hoping for. If he'd written in thinking the message would be read by an intern, he would have explained who he was and why he was asking. He'd been assuming that would all be understood.

But he hadn't expected this. Mrs. Daley had, at various times, been denounced in Malaysian mainstream media, banned entry to the country, and had an Interpol notice issued against her because she had pissed off the Malaysian government just that much. She had to be careful about giving out her personal details.

Yet she'd given Ket Siong her number, unasked. And she knew Ket Hau was in London. That would, presumably, have taken her some digging to find out. What had she been looking for?

Ket Siong had said to Clarissa Low that Stephen might have known something, echoing the *Hornbill Gazette*'s speculation. It had never previously occurred to him that his brother might withhold anything of importance from him. But he found himself wondering, now, what Ket Hau knew.

It wouldn't be long before he could ask. But the journey home that night felt even longer than usual.

It was past eleven by the time Ket Siong got home. Ma's bedroom door was shut, but Ket Hau was lying in wait for him. He loomed out of the living room, arms crossed, when Ket Siong got to the top of the stairs.

"Come on," he said curtly.

Ket Siong hadn't been planning on talking to his brother about the *Hornbill Gazette*'s messages that night. He'd had enough emotional scenes for one day. But it looked like he was due another, and he wasn't going to be able to opt out.

"What's wrong?" he said, but Ket Hau was already heading to their bedroom.

The first thing Ket Siong noticed, when he entered their room, was the desk. The desk was Ket Hau's domain, since it was his office job that brought in the bulk of their income, his legal studies that were their best bet of financial security in the future.

Usually it was a mess of law textbooks; copious notes on foolscap paper; bills old, new, and overdue; takeaway flyers; and assorted stationery Ket Hau had appropriated from his firm: highlighters, Post-its, sticky flags, and pens.

But the desk had been cleared of its usual chaos. Two manila document wallets sat on it.

"What do you think you're doing?" said Ket Hau. "It's not enough to chat up Low Teck Wee, you have to go look up his daughter as well? Are you playing the fool or what?"

Ket Siong had known he would be in trouble when his family found out, but his imagination hadn't taken him quite far enough in predicting how unpleasant it would be. "I was just trying—"

"To find out what happened to Stephen." Ket Hau's mouth

twisted. "I can tell you, all right? Those thugs drove off with him, they took him to some deserted place, and they shot him in the head—if he was lucky. If he was lucky, he only had a short time to know he was going to die alone and nobody was coming for him. Then those bastards dumped him somewhere. OK? What more do you want? You're so desperate to know every last detail?"

Ket Siong said, "Maybe if we knew the details, you could stop thinking about it."

Ket Hau lowered himself heavily to his bed. "I'm never going to stop thinking about it."

There was nothing to say to that. Guilt lowered Ket Siong's head. But even to apologise would be an insult, at that moment.

"Can I look?" he said instead, gesturing at the manila folders.

Ket Hau no longer looked angry, but sad and tired, older than he should be. "Help yourself."

The folders were crammed with paper. Printouts of emails, spreadsheets, slide decks, reports—the ordinary detritus of corporate operations. Ket Siong was only skimming as he leafed through the documents, but the same two words jumped out again and again.

"'Project Alpha,'" he read aloud.

"That's what they called the Ensengei project," said Ket Hau. "I've looked through the papers. There's not much there. Somebody called 'VVIP' was involved—that must be the state premier, or the daughter, or the son-in-law. Your friend Clarissa's circled some financial transactions, probably kickbacks. Nothing earth-shaking. Do you think it was worth risking our safety for this?"

"When did Clarissa give these to you?"

"She dropped them off at the office today. That's why I went in, instead of working from home." At Ket Siong's look, Ket Hau said, "She found my details online. Thought I was you."

He smiled mirthlessly. "You nuke your social media, move countries, don't tell anybody where you're going, and then your bloody employer outs you to the whole world. Type your name into Google and anybody will know how to find you. Unbelievable." He shook his head. "This time it was documents, but next time it could be a bomb. Who knows?"

Ket Siong sat down on his bed, across from his brother. "Why would anyone send you a bomb?"

Ket Hau shrugged, weary. "Why did they take Stephen?"

"I didn't ask at the time," said Ket Siong slowly. "He was standing in the way of a major project, threatening the reputation of a big company. But the project went ahead and the company is fine. Low Teck Wee had dinner with the mayor of London while he was here. So why would anyone be worried about you?" He paused, watching the play of expression across his brother's face. "Why did they take Stephen, Ko? What did he know?"

Ket Hau went still. "What are you trying to say?"

Ket Siong got out his phone, brought up Helen Daley's messages, and handed the phone to his brother.

"What's this?" said Ket Hau. His eyes skipped down the phone screen, and his face went blank.

"What does Helen Daley want to talk to you about?" said Ket Siong. "Did Stephen know something? Is that why they got rid of him?"

"Is that what you told the *Hornbill Gazette*?" said Ket Hau, his voice rising. "Are you *crazy*?"

"I didn't tell her anything."

But Ket Hau was in no mood to listen. "How does Helen Daley know I'm in London? Why am I even asking, she knows how to Google, too. And now she knows you're here as well. And she wants to write about us in the fucking newspaper. Fuck!" He ran a hand through his hair. "Siong, seriously, do you have a death wish? What's the point of uprooting and coming all the way here if you're just going to paint a target on our backs? Don't you know how dangerous this is?"

Ket Siong should be tactful. Ket Hau had been through a lot

over the past few years. They had all been through a lot, as a family. They needed to be gentle with one another.

But he'd already spent too much of the evening keeping a lid on his feelings to try to avoid some irreversible rupture, and it hadn't even worked. Ket Siong found he was out of tact.

"Obviously not," he said. "If Helen Daley knows more than me! Ko, I can't keep us safe if I don't know the full story."

"It's not your job to keep us safe," shouted Ket Hau. "It's *mine*!"

Ket Siong had never heard this voice from his brother before. It seemed to have bubbled up from some primal, unacknowledged part of him.

They were both shocked. Ket Hau opened his mouth and closed it, looking somewhat at a loss.

"I've been asking and asking you to keep your head down," he said finally. "Instead, you're going off and talking to every Tom, Dick, and Harry in the country. What's Ma going to say when she finds out?"

"Finds out what?" said Ma's voice.

Their mother stood in the doorway in her ancient grey Uniqlo fleece, worn over a batik kaftan. Poking out from under the kaftan were her fluffy polar bear slippers, bought cheap from Poundland. She blinked in the light, looking groggy.

"What are you all fighting about?" she said.

"Ma," Ket Siong began, when it struck him that something was off. It took him a moment to identify what it was.

Ket Siong never got to speak first in this sort of situation. Being the youngest—and the quiet one—meant getting shouted down was an inevitability, even with as kind and equable an elder brother as Ket Hau generally was.

But Ket Hau wasn't interrupting. This was because he was busy staring down at Ket Siong's phone. Ket Siong had forgotten Ket Hau still had it.

"Who's Renee SR Goh?" said Ket Hau.

* * *

Ma sat them down at the dining table. They were not to fight. It was clear none of them was in a fit state to retire, despite Ket Hau and Ket Siong's feeble protests that Ma should go to bed and not worry about them. Instead, they should talk—but not before she had made them all hot drinks.

They waited in silence while Ma bustled around the kitchen, putting on the kettle and getting jars out of cupboards. Ket Siong stared at his phone.

His heart had leapt, absurdly, when Ket Hau said Renee's name, but there was no message from her. Or there was, but nothing so encouraging as a text. Renee had sent him a payment for her half of the bill for dinner.

He'd forgotten she had his bank details. They'd exchanged those after their Chelsea nasi lemak dinner. Renee had reluctantly permitted him to pay for his half of the meal, at his insistence, but then she'd turned around and sent him back an amount covering their drinks. She'd said it wasn't fair for him to have to pay fifty percent when she'd drunk ninety percent of the alcohol.

He hadn't argued. That was what friends did, go Dutch. Maybe when their renewed friendship was no longer quite so new and Renee had relaxed a little, she'd let him treat her once in a while.

So much for that. This time she'd calculated the amount owed down to the penny. The precision of the payment was a statement. Her debts were paid; he had no claim on her.

The notification had come through at five minutes to midnight. Hopefully Renee was asleep by now. She'd have to get up early for her pitch the next morning.

He remembered with a slight start that he didn't want the pitch to succeed. But he didn't want it to go badly for Renee, either. She'd put so much into it.

Who was he to judge her for her choices? Love compromised you. Ket Siong should know.

"So," said Ket Hau, "is this the same Renee?"

Ket Siong's head whipped up. "What?"

"You know, the friend you told us about back then. The one you had a crush on at uni. Come on," said Ket Hau, as Ket Siong gaped at him, "it was obvious. You couldn't talk about her without blushing. You're doing it right now."

Ket Hau shook his head. "So she's the girl you've been seeing. I should have guessed. I couldn't believe you went and slept with some stranger you met at an event—"

Ket Siong glanced towards the kitchen. "Shh!"

There was no sign of Ma emerging, thankfully. The kettle was boiling and the hiss tended to fill the kitchen, drowning out all other sound.

"It was so out of character," Ket Hau went on, though he did at least lower his voice. "I couldn't brain it. You meet some random girl and suddenly you're always on your phone, you're going around humming to yourself . . ."

"I wasn't humming. Was I humming?"

"Oh, and it was a Dior exhibition you went to. Of *course*," said Ket Hau. "She studied fashion, right, your Renee?" At Ket Siong's expression, he added, "What, did you think we didn't know? We were so worried after she rejected you back then."

Ma and Ket Hau had been especially solicitous while he was reeling from the breach with Renee, but Ket Siong hadn't noticed anything unusual in their concern. After all, he had just had to give up his studies at the Royal Academy of Music. If he was crushed, that needed no explanation.

Apparently, it had, in fact, required no explanation. If anyone in this family was allowed secrets, it certainly wasn't Ket Siong.

"She didn't reject me," he said, a little too loudly.

Ma, coming into the room with three mugs on a tray, said, "I told you all, cannot fight."

She placed two mugs before Ket Siong and Ket Hau, brimming with piping hot Milo, made in Ma's irreproducible style. Heated milk poured onto six heaping spoonfuls of Milo powder, with a generous teaspoon of condensed milk stirred in at the end.

Ma had made herself mulberry leaf tea. She sat down, cupping her hands around her mug.

"I wasn't fighting," muttered Ket Siong. "I was just saying. *I* was the one who rejected Renee."

"Which Renee?" Ma's eyes widened. "You mean your uni friend? The fashion student?"

Ket Siong probably shouldn't be surprised at the retentiveness of his family's memory. After all, they remembered more of his life than he did.

"You broke up with her because you had to leave London?" said Ket Hau sympathetically. "I'm sorry, man."

Ket Siong found himself abruptly tired of subterfuge. There was no reason not to be honest. If he'd acted on his impulse to tell Renee how he felt about her earlier that evening, maybe she would still be talking to him.

"No. We weren't dating," he said. "I turned her down, because I found out her father is Goh Kheng Tat."

There was a brief silence.

"Oh *shit*," said Ket Hau.

"Hau!"

"Sorry, Ma." Ket Hau turned back to Ket Siong. "But wait, Siong. You're back in touch now. Are you going out with her, or . . . ?"

Their mother gazed down at her mulberry leaf tea, wearing the expression she used to assume whenever a gossiping auntie visited—austere, yet not quite discouraging. Gossip was not correct and so she would not initiate or encourage it, but it would be rude to interrupt.

Ket Siong wasn't inclined to enlist her help, anyway. It wasn't like there was anything to hide, anymore.

"I don't think I'll be seeing her again," he said.

Ket Hau was agog, more alive than he had looked in a long time. "Why? What happened?"

"I'll tell you," said Ket Siong. He met his brother's eyes. "But I asked you some questions, too, Ko. I think it's your turn to answer."

Ket Hau dropped his gaze.

Ket Siong was experiencing a novel feeling, one he'd rarely enjoyed in relation to his family. It was the sensation of being in possession of the moral high ground.

"Just now you said something," he said.

Ket Hau waved a protesting hand, his head still bent. "Not fair to drag up what I said. Ma said cannot fight."

"You said it's not my job to keep us safe. It's yours," said Ket Siong. "But you can't decide to keep us all safe. That's not under your control. And it shouldn't be on you alone. You have to let us help."

"Correct," said Ma. "I've told you also, Hau. You should listen to Siong. He's so sensible now he's grown up."

Ket Siong had been about to point out that he was an adult and therefore entitled to take on equal responsibility for protecting the family, but Ma's contribution put paid to that. Better to let the fact he was fully thirty-one years of age speak for itself, even if his family seemed incapable of remembering the fact.

"I'm sorry I didn't tell you I was trying to find out about Stephen," he said to his brother. "But I'm going to make mistakes if you don't tell me what's going on. You can't make the decisions for us all."

Ket Hau was quiet, unusually for him. He wiped his face with his hand, and Ket Siong and Ma both realised at the same time that he was crying.

"Boy, what is this?" said Ma. "Why are you crying? No need to cry. Siong, get the tissues there."

Ket Siong was already on his feet, grabbing a box of tissues off the mantelpiece. He passed them to his mother, too obscurely guilty to present them to Ket Hau himself. Ma pulled out several pieces and pressed them into Ket Hau's hands.

"You must be nicer to your brother, Siong," she said. "You don't know. It's not easy, everything that happened . . . And now it's very stressful, his job. Having to earn to support the family. I remember how it was like, when you all were children. You think I don't know?"

"I'm sorry," said Ket Siong.

But Ket Hau said, with a laugh that sounded too much like a sob, "Leave Siong alone, Ma. He didn't do anything wrong. It's just my chickens coming home to roost."

"Chickens? What chickens? You bought chickens? We already have a lot in the freezer, cannot finish—"

"No, don't worry. I didn't buy chickens," said Ket Hau. "There are no chickens."

He was definitely laughing now. Ket Siong sat back down, cautious.

His brother looked at him. "If the worst thing to come out of this is I have to admit Siong is right, I'll be happy. That's considered getting off lightly." Ket Hau rubbed his face on his sleeve and put the tissues Ma had given him on the table, still dry.

"I was trying to protect you all," he said. His voice broke on the sentence.

Ket Siong said, "I know."

Ma's eyes were fixed on Ket Hau's face, troubled. "But what is it, Hau? What are you trying to protect us from?"

"I might as well show you. Hold on." Ket Hau got up and went to their bedroom. They heard him moving around, mysterious creaks and thuds issuing from the room, before he emerged and sat back down at the table.

He was holding a small silver USB drive. He put it on the table.

"What's that?" said Ma.

"This thing is in my dreams every night," said Ket Hau. He was gazing at the USB drive, his expression sombre.

Somehow Ket Siong knew what he was going to say. "Stephen gave it to you."

"The night before they took him," said Ket Hau. "Yes."

Then

Malaysia

"Don't get up," said Stephen, as he rose from the dining table. He picked up the mug Ma had given him, with her old firm's name emblazoned on the side: KHALID AND BALASUBRAMANIAM. The mug was empty now, a brown ring of Milo at the base. "Eat your dinner."

Ket Siong nodded, his mouth full of rice. He had that pale overstretched look again. They wouldn't be getting anything more than monosyllables out of him this evening. It wasn't the late nights he found taxing so much as the long days of social interaction teaching involved.

Siong's reluctance to pass on any opportunity was understandable. It wasn't easy, trying to make a living as a classical musician in Malaysia. But Ket Hau wondered if it was time for another little chat about taking it easier.

Maybe he should force another family holiday on the three of them. If he said it was for Ma's sake, Ket Siong would make the time.

Ma came in, bearing a bowl of soup for Ket Siong.

"Don't wash!" she said, when she saw the mug in Stephen's hand. "Leave it there."

Ket Hau took the mug from Stephen and put it on the table, giving him a pointed look. Eleven years since Ket Hau had first introduced Stephen to the family and he was still trying to impress.

"Thank you, auntie," said Stephen. "Good night."

"No, no, thanks to you," said Ma. "Safe journey home, yeah? I'll see you when?"

"Maybe at the weekend," said Ket Hau. "Stephen wants to go to IKEA, so he might come along on Saturday."

He followed Stephen through their small living room to the door, unlocking the grille for him. Outside was what they called the porch, though this was somewhat overselling it—it was just a narrow tiled area beneath the eaves, where they kept the shoe rack and an assortment of umbrellas.

Stephen's Myvi was parked in the drive, next to the small front garden Ma had crowded with ferns, herbs, bougainvilleas, and birds-of-paradise.

Ket Hau leaned against the wall as Stephen bent down, pulling on his one decent pair of black shoes. They'd come straight from work earlier.

The air was finally cool now it was nighttime. A faint smoky scent lingered, harsh on the throat, though it had rained in the afternoon—a relief, after days of haze. Pleasanter smells exhaled from the garden, of moist earth and green growing things, underlaid by the stink of the drain on the other side of the fence.

Ket Hau observed all of these familiar things without noticing he noticed them. He was preoccupied with the back of Stephen's head.

"Thanks for coming over," said Ket Hau. "That was definitely a two-man job."

Stephen didn't answer. He'd been a little off all day.

It was a strange time, of course. Stephen had dodged the question when Ket Hau asked, but he was pretty sure Stephen was still being followed. That was enough to make anyone jumpy, given the magnitude of the secret Stephen was sitting on.

He'd only started looking into Freshview Industries' links to the Sarawak state government in hope of finding ammunition for the Ensengei campaign. He'd tapped his networks for information and eventually struck gold with a guy he'd hooked up with a couple of times at uni, now the disgruntled employee of a government-linked company. But Stephen hadn't been prepared for the scale of what his contact had revealed.

Corruption was nothing new in Malaysia. Everyone expected politicians to skim a moderate amount off the public purse. But there was nothing moderate about the scandal Stephen had stumbled upon. It was theft on a dizzying scale, implicating not only the Sarawak state premier, but people even more powerful, up to the highest levels of government.

"This stuff is red hot," Stephen had said, as they strolled around the dilapidated playground in a neighbourhood park. The park happened to be near a North Indian restaurant where they'd had a nice meal three years ago. They'd chosen it because it had no connections to their daily routine, or to where they lived and worked. "Regime-changing. If you could get it in the right hands."

"What are you going to do?"

Stephen shrugged. He was frightened, Ket Hau could tell. So was Ket Hau. They hadn't talked about it, each of them trying to put a brave face on for the other.

"I was thinking, right," said Stephen. "All I wanted was to save some plants. That's it. I just want them to leave a bunch of trees alone." He shook his head, blowing out a puff of air. "Crazy, man."

"Everything all right?" Ket Hau said now.

Stephen made a noncommittal noise. Once he'd got his shoes on, he said, "I might not come to IKEA. Better keep my head down."

Ket Hau glanced back at the house. He could hear the distant clatter of cutlery from the kitchen, the gush of a tap, the screech of chair legs scraping the floor as Ket Siong got up from the table.

He lowered his voice. "Has something happened?"

Stephen hesitated. "Johan's worried. I don't know who's said what to him, but he's scared they're going to out him to his family." Stephen's source was a married Malay-Muslim householder with four kids. Johan was less svelte now than he'd been at uni, but no less closeted. "He's not suited to a life of corporate espionage. Got too much to hide."

Ket Hau swallowed, his mouth dry. He hadn't been too happy when Stephen first reached out to Johan, for more than one reason, but he'd already said his piece on that. "So how? You going to be OK?"

"Yeah. But that's why I came over. Wasn't just because I love handling your large appliances." Stephen gave him a crooked smile. "Will you hang onto this for me?"

Ket Hau took the USB drive from him. "What's this?"

"That's got a copy of everything Johan gave me," said Stephen. "I'm going to give him back the hard drive he passed to me. Maybe that will calm him down. And I thought, your mom has some opposition contacts, right? You think they could do something with this stuff?"

Ket Hau turned the USB drive over in his hand, frowning. "I'd want to ask Ma what she thinks. You never know with politicians. It's rival one day, ally the next."

"Don't tell her yet," said Stephen quickly. "Not that I don't trust her, but . . . let's wait first. See how things play out."

"Of course."

Stephen still looked worried. "Is it OK?" He nodded at the USB drive. "I don't want to drag you into this, but I wasn't sure who else to ask."

"I'm in it already." Ket Hau took hold of Stephen's shoulder and gave it a gentle shake. "It's fine."

He slipped the USB drive into the pocket of his shorts. It wasn't heavy, but he could feel its rounded edges against his thigh, through the thin fabric.

"You want to stay over?" he said. Ma wouldn't ask any questions. She was used to putting out a mattress on Ket Hau's bedroom floor for Stephen.

But Stephen said, "Not tonight. Lady from the *Star*'s coming to the office tomorrow morning. I've got to prep for the interview."

He got into his car. Ket Hau opened the gate at the end of the drive, as the Myvi stuttered reluctantly to life.

"You need to get a new car," said Ket Hau.

"It's OK," said Stephen, as he did every time they had this conversation. "It's going now. See? Told you. Only takes three Hail Marys to start."

He backed out into the road and paused, rolling down a window. "You take care of yourself, Hau. And your gang."

He jerked his head at the house. Right now, it contained nearly everyone Ket Hau loved most in the world.

Not quite everyone.

"You too," said Ket Hau. "Good night."

He locked the gate and stood there watching as Stephen drove off, till the car rounded a corner and was lost to sight.

24

After she left Ket Siong at the restaurant, Renee took a taxi home. She smiled dry-eyed at the night-shift receptionist as she passed through the foyer, and went up in the lift to her empty flat, where she lived alone.

She sat down on her pink velvet sofa and burst into tears.

After a while, she got up and washed her face. According to her phone, she'd only been sobbing for ten minutes. It could have been an hour, for all she could tell. The universe seemed to have come off its hinges. Everything felt unreal.

She returned to her sofa, with her laptop this time, and typed *Stephen Ensengei Freshview* into the search bar.

Freshview's PR team had evidently been at work. She had to wade through several pages' worth of corporate guff before she started turning up reports on the local community's campaign against logging in Ensengei.

It did seem Freshview had overseen a project clearing forest to make way for oil palm plantations in Sarawak, but it wasn't obvious from the reports that this had been on a gazetted forest reserve. Freshview denied it. They'd had all the necessary permits, according to their spokespeople, and a court of law had agreed with them.

Even the extent to which the local community disapproved wasn't clear. Against the pictures of villagers protesting, there was an interview with a village headman who enthused about the project. Everyone had been compensated for their land and would be moved into better houses, he said, with access to schools and hospitals—all the benefits of development. It was a great opportunity for the village.

It was hard to know what to think. Cutting down rainforest was definitely not the kind of enterprise Renee wanted to get involved in—but she wasn't going to be involved in anything like that. The factory redevelopment Chahaya was pitching for was going to create jobs, build sorely needed new homes, regenerate an entire neglected part of London. Even if Freshview's money hadn't all been made in pursuits she could approve of, wasn't that a good use of those resources?

Stephen Jembu was mentioned in a few of the articles as a campaigner. Searching his name confirmed this was Ket Siong's Stephen. There were various local news articles and social media posts on his disappearance, all using the same image of Stephen. A stocky curly-haired man in his thirties, dressed for a hike, standing against a backdrop of greenery. He was squinting a little in the sun and smiling, an attractive web of wrinkles radiating out from the corner of each eye.

Renee spent a long time looking at him.

The articles told her less than Ket Siong had. While they set out what had happened to Stephen Jembu, they were frustratingly silent on the how and why. There was nothing linking his disappearance to Freshview, except a solitary Facebook post by some outfit called the *Hornbill Gazette*. Even that only raised questions; it didn't provide any answers.

It transpired the *Hornbill Gazette* had written a lot about deforestation in Ensengei, including a couple of blog posts about Stephen. Before Renee could read them, the app she'd set to switch off her Internet connection at bedtime kicked in.

She tore herself away from her laptop, her mind whirling. She showered and changed and collapsed on her bed.

She should text Ket Siong. And say what? *I couldn't find any evidence of what you told me.* If what Ket Siong believed was true—if

Freshview was complicit in some way in the horrific loss of his friend—they would have covered it up. Renee wasn't going to stumble across a smoking gun through a Google search.

She rolled over and picked up her phone off her bedside table, opening WhatsApp. Ket Siong hadn't messaged. Not that she wanted him to message.

She shouldn't have let him pay for dinner. On an impulse, Renee searched for the restaurant menu, totted up the cost of her dinner, and sent the amount to him by bank transfer.

It didn't make her feel any better. She lay awake for a long time, sleep evading her.

The next morning Renee was puffy-eyed and pale, but it was nothing some concealer and blush wouldn't hide. She put on her Dior trouser suit and her Louboutin heels.

It was only when she looked at herself in the mirror that she remembered she'd worn almost the same outfit to the V&A reception where she'd run into Ket Siong. The only difference was the addition of a mother-of-pearl silk blouse under the jacket, and a pair of diamond stud earrings.

That was rough. Renee breathed shallowly through her nose, her eyes stinging. Her reflection looked wild-eyed and bereft.

She'd felt so *safe* with Ket Siong. She'd told him things she'd never told anyone else, even Nathalie. All the while he'd been privately sitting in judgment of her and her choices. She'd shown him the most defenceless part of herself—the lonely little girl who could never stop chasing affection—and she had been weighed and found wanting.

He's right, said a voice at the back of her head, ruthless. *Nobody loves you, because you don't deserve it. You never have.*

Suddenly the jacket itched unbearably; the shoes pinched. Renee tore off her outfit, kicking off the heels.

She was not going to go to pieces over Yap Ket Siong again.

If there were proof of what he'd told her the night before . . . But there wasn't. No one even shared Ket Siong's suspicions of Freshview, except some fringe blogger with a goofy name.

Yet he expected Renee to blow up her life and relationship with her family on his say-so. Because she was pathetic when it came to him, desperate for his good opinion, and on some level he knew that.

What was the difference between Ket Siong and her family, at the end of the day? They all wanted her to put them before herself. That was her greatest crime, the one none of these men could get over—Renee always acted for herself.

It wasn't like she could trust anyone else to be in her corner. Her family had taught her that. As had Ket Siong, in his own way. She'd come too far to let any of them bring her down.

Do well today, and her life could change. She might, in a matter of a few months' time, be heading up a business whose turnover dwarfed the GDP of some countries. She'd have her father's approval, the respect of her family, access to money and power beyond most people's wildest dreams.

Next to that, what was yet another man she'd disappointed? She'd always known love was a dead end for her.

Nathalie texted while Renee was in the cab heading to Freshview's offices.

Big day today! Feeling OK? Good luck!

Yeah, thanks.

Renee stared down at her phone screen, hesitating. But why not tell Nathalie? If she'd turned to Nathalie as a confidante instead of Ket Siong, maybe she wouldn't now be feeling like someone had torn her heart out of her chest and stamped on it.

Not feeling great, but it'll be fine. You were right about Ket Siong. It was a bad idea.

That was going to drive Nathalie wild with curiosity. Renee added:

Going into my meeting, but I'll tell you another time. I'll need cocktails, though. Like six of them.

By the time Renee was alighting outside the imposing building on the Thames where Freshview had set up their London headquarters, Nathalie had messaged back a string of emojis: three knives, three hearts, and every representation of an alcoholic drink. Renee smiled and put her phone away.

The meeting room was on the top floor, with floor-to-ceiling windows looking down on the muddy brown expanse of the river. Autumn sunlight struck sparks off the waves and rendered the projector screen in the room impossible to make out.

Lin was by the door as Renee and Su Khoon entered, trying to figure out how to lower the blinds. She gave them a harassed smile.

There was a numerous team from Freshview in attendance, as well as stakeholders from local government and the Malaysian state investors backing the project. There were four women in total in the room, if you didn't count the catering staff bringing in tall flasks of coffee and tea, biscuits, and glass bottles of still and sparkling water.

This gave Renee's smile a slight edge as they went through the usual introductions. She was dreading getting to Andrew—he had been the first person she'd seen out of that sea of men, her eyes drawn inexorably to him.

The sight of him still made her body react like she was under threat, her stomach contracting, sweat springing up on her palms. Her heart thrummed in her chest. She hated that fear of him was threaded through her body, when she knew intellectually he was a gutless loser.

She wasn't going to let him ruin this for her, either. When he shook her hand, she smiled, though it felt like a thousand tiny bugs were crawling over her skin.

"Looking forward to this," Andrew said, nodding at the screen displaying the slides she and Su Khoon had wrangled over for the past two weeks. "We're having lunch, when is it, next week? Can't wait."

"Mmm," said Renee. With some men it was not necessary to speak, so long as you were making more or less the right noises and faces, and Andrew belonged to this class. He smiled as though she'd agreed with him.

"We'll start now," said Su Khoon. This was Business Su Khoon—polished and affable, projecting competence. "I wanted to begin by saying how much we value this opportunity and our relationship with Freshview . . ."

As Renee looked out at the faces of their audience, she was swamped by a wave of doubt, so intense it felt like vertigo. What was she *doing* here?

Images from the articles she'd read the night before crowded into her mind. The excavators and bulldozers on churned-up red earth; the gargantuan piles of logs; the groups of protestors, tiny next to the heavy machinery against which they were arrayed. And that picture of Stephen Jembu, squinting and smiling.

How many of these men knew about any of that? How many of them would care?

She put a hand down on the lectern to steady herself, panic constricting her chest. She couldn't do this. She was going to be sick. She'd excuse herself discreetly, go to the bathroom—

She heard Su Khoon say, "Renee's going to take you through some examples of our experience in construction. We think they show why we're the best partner to take this project forward."

He looked at her, expectant. Renee drove her fingernails into her palm, willing the sensation to ground her.

What would she do after she'd slipped out? Flee the building? She couldn't even get to the bathroom without a keycard.

Su Khoon was frowning. "Renee?"

She could just see the contempt in his face if he realised she was wavering, considering pulling out, based on—what? Ket Siong's unsubstantiated word and a handful of old articles.

The thought was like an injection of molten steel down her spine. She couldn't humiliate herself like that, not when she'd fought so hard to have a part in this pitch.

She was here to do a job. She'd reconcile it with herself later.

She shoved down her qualms, pushing away the memory of Ket Siong's eyes when he'd said, *It's not for me to tell you what to do.*

He'd been right about that. Renee was committed now. She couldn't afford to second-guess her actions. It was too late.

She breathed out, stretching her mouth into an approximation of a smile. "Thanks, Su Khoon. Could we have the next slide, please?"

At least it had always been easy to subsume her feelings in work. The script she'd prepared with Su Khoon came back to her, each comfortingly impersonal fact and figure slotting into place. Her nausea receded. Renee set herself aside and let the demands of the job take over.

"What was that about?" said Su Khoon, after the pitch. "You were zoning out when I called on you. Did you forget it was your turn or what?"

Their cab was inching through traffic, bringing them back to Su Khoon's office so they could do a debrief with the team.

"Nerves," said Renee lightly. "I always get jumpy before a presentation. It's fine once I get into it."

"You should work on that. We had a guy come in to train the senior leadership team last year," said Su Khoon. "Personal impact, all that. He was not bad. Ask Penny, she can give you the details."

Renee bristled at his condescension. But it was her own fault for freezing. She swallowed down her irritation with an effort. "Yeah. Sorry, it won't happen again."

Su Khoon waved his hand in dismissal. "You did a good job overall."

Renee already knew this. She felt patronised, but also, despite herself, pleased.

"You too," she said, as a means of maintaining some semblance of dignity.

She looked out of the window, taking a deep breath and letting it out slowly. Any kind of public performance always left her buzzing. But this time, the elation of catching an audience's attention and holding it was underlined by a queasy uncertainty, snaking through her gut.

The day wasn't over yet. And she still had lunch with Freshview to get through in a week's time. She had to stay focused, not let herself be dragged off course.

They had passed Waterloo Bridge and were heading along Embankment: a park screened by greenery on one side of the road, the river on the other. The grey obelisk of Cleopatra's Needle flashed past, the polished black sphinxes on either side just visible behind yellow-crowned trees.

"What do you think of our chances?" she said, watching a police boat race along the river, throwing up plumes of water as it went.

"Should be strong." Su Khoon sat back, adjusting his jacket. "Biggest risk is if we get undercut on costs."

He'd wanted to quote more aggressively, but Renee had insisted on being realistic: "This needs to be profitable for us," she'd argued. "Dad won't thank us if we take a loss on one of the biggest redevelopment projects of the century. And it won't do the Freshview relationship any good if we end up going over budget."

"Every construction project goes over budget," Su Khoon had grumbled, but he'd conceded.

Renee said nothing. They'd had the argument and she'd won. Only time would tell, now, if her strategy was sound.

Fortunately, Su Khoon didn't seem inclined to relitigate the point, either. "We can try to pump Andrew and the rest for intel at the lunch next week."

He took out his phone, so Renee followed suit, scrolling through her emails. Nothing was on fire at Virtu, literally or metaphorically. She needed to speak to the office building manager about the leak in the ceiling.

Maybe she'd be able to make progress on Virtu at Home during the lull while they waited for Freshview to make their decision. Might she even be able to twin the launch with the Chinese New Year womenswear collection? Two simultaneous launches might be too much even for their devoted customer base. But on the other hand, people would be thinking about entertaining around Chinese New Year, possibly in the mood to spend on a fancy bowl or five . . .

A thought struck her. "We should buy lunch for the team. Sushi?"

Su Khoon looked up from his phone, his forehead furrowed. "We haven't won the deal yet and you want to reward them?"

"They've worked hard. We can do a proper meal out if we win the deal, but there's no harm in treating them to a takeaway now," said Renee. "This kind of attention makes a big difference. It makes people feel valued." Su Khoon was looking skeptical, so she added, "Dad always says to invest in relationships."

Su Khoon rolled his eyes. "With people who can get you somewhere. People like Andrew Yeoh. Not *staff*."

Renee would have liked to roll her eyes, too, but she squashed the instinct. "Look, I'll pay for it."

"No, no. If you want to buy their hearts, go ahead." Su Khoon dug his wallet out of his pocket and offered her a credit card. "They'll think they've got it made. They're already having a free holiday on the company account, you know."

Despite the near-inconceivable improvement in their relations, Renee didn't think their rapport was quite strong enough to survive her pointing out that not many people would consider two

weeks of working twelve-hour days a holiday. She contented herself with taking the credit card from him. "Thanks, Er Ge."

"I don't know how your business can survive, if you're so free
with money," said Su Khoon. "You know these people are all
spying on us and reporting back to Dad, right?"

The thought had occurred to Renee, though she would have
insisted on standing lunch for the staff anyway. "All the more
reason to buy them sushi, isn't it?"

Su Khoon blinked. Renee decided to enjoy her triumph discreetly, looking down at her phone.

She'd received a voice note from Nathalie, followed by a text:

How did the presentation go?

Good, thanks. Excited about listening to my new VN!

It's not very exciting. I wasn't sure whether to tell you, but I thought
you'd want to know . . .

The cab was barely moving. Su Khoon was busy making a call.
Renee gave in to temptation and put in her earphones.

Nathalie's voice came through, sounding unusually grave.

"I am sorry about whatever it is that has happened with Ket.
But—look, I haven't been sure whether to mention this, especially
since you decided to be 'friends.'" The quotation marks were perfectly distinct in her voice, as was the disapproval. "But I was at
Foyles a couple of weeks ago, and Ket was there, at the café with a
woman. I am not saying it was a date, but I couldn't tell you it was
not a date. There was definitely something going on.

"I crept away like a little mouse so he did not see me. But . . ."
Nathalie cleared her throat delicately. "I bumped into him later, in
the bookshop. He was by himself. So I asked him, you know, what
he was doing there. And he didn't mention her. I don't think he
realised I saw him earlier.

"Of course, Ket does not have to tell me if he is meeting up
with women. Maybe you know what it was all about, and I have
been worrying for nothing. But"—at this point Nathalie's voice
grew fierce—"I remember always what he did to you and if he

hurts you again, I will track him down and restring a piano with his intestines. You say the word and I will do it."

Renee stifled a laugh. Even to herself, it sounded like a sob. Su Khoon was still on the phone, but he gave her a startled look. She shook her head, pasting a smile on her face. She didn't need to play Nathalie's voice note a second time—every word was seared into her brain—but she did it anyway.

Her eyes were stinging. She wasn't about to cry, that would be ridiculous. But she turned towards the window, away from Su Khoon, so he couldn't see whatever it was that her face was doing.

She felt like she'd been slapped, absurd overreaction though it was. It wasn't like Ket Siong had definitely been on a date— though Nathalie had never been wrong before when she sensed something was going on; her judgment in these matters was un-impeachable. In any case, even if Nathalie was right once again, it was none of Renee's business what women Ket Siong met up with at cafés, or anywhere. She was the one who'd wanted things to stop at a hookup.

But he gave me his scarf, she thought stupidly. *He put his scarf on me.*

So what? jeered an inner voice. *That means he belongs to you now? You're betrothed because he lent you his scarf for five minutes? Don't be pathetic.*

Too late for that. Ten years too late.

She'd had good reasons for not wanting to date Ket Siong. If she'd had the sense to stay within the tidy lines she'd drawn for them, it would have been fine. Their friendship would have been safe, an inconsequential niceness that could never hurt her. But she'd never been able to keep a rein on her heart when it came to him.

The worst part was that she'd had a chance, at one point in time. Not anymore. Even if she reached out to him now, apolo-gised, it was questionable whether he'd want anything to do with her. She'd lost his respect.

Who could blame him? Not much of what Renee had done over the past twenty-four hours was worthy of respect.

She couldn't think about this anymore.

Renee fumbled for her phone.

No gross piano repairs needed, I promise. Got to work, but I'll VN you this evening?

She paused, then typed:

Love you.

This was good, she told herself. It confirmed that her resolution to pull away from Ket Siong had been the right one. At least now she knew where she stood. There was no risk of her being carried away by the tide of her feelings again, wrecking herself against his indifference.

When Renee next checked her phone, after the debrief meeting with Su Khoon's team and the call updating her dad on how the presentation had gone (during which Su Khoon had even let her talk for half a minute), Nathalie had messaged back.

Love you too.

But she hadn't expected anything less from Nathalie. What spiked Renee's heart rate, sent the blood rushing to her cheeks, was the notification of a message from Ket Siong.

I'm sorry about last night. I told you what I did because I trust your judgment, but I didn't handle it well. I'd like to talk to you. Can we meet?

Renee's throat ached. She wanted so much to reply. For things to go differently this time around.

She almost did. But then that snapshot of Stephen Jembu came back to her—his hair ruffled by the wind, eyes creased.

Her heart failed her. What could she say to Ket Siong, if they met? How could she look him in the eye?

Renee felt abruptly sick of herself, sick of her family. Sick, most of all, of Yap Ket Siong. He was one of the only people she'd ever known who'd liked her for who she was, who didn't want anything more from her than she was happy to give. She'd been enough for him as she was, no more and no less. Until she wasn't.

She didn't have time for this. She'd promised to write up a note on the morning's presentation for Su Khoon to circulate to Chahaya's top team. The call with the Virtu office building manager was in half an hour's time, and she needed to email her supplier about the homeware samples that had come in.

She tapped out:

I don't think that's a good idea, sorry.

Then Renee blocked his number, so she wouldn't have to keep thinking about him and all the ways they'd let each other down.

25

The restaurant Andrew wanted to try was in Mayfair. Su Khoon's PA had booked a private dining room for their lunch with him. This had sounded good in theory, but it turned out to be in the basement—something of a letdown after the bright, airy ground floor of the restaurant, with its white walls and high ceilings.

Descending a dimly lit flight of stairs into a windowless room, Renee felt some doubt as to whether this was an improvement. She'd never understood why restaurants thought it was fancy not to be able to see what you were eating, or the people you were eating it with.

But then again, given Andrew was going to be there, the less Renee was able to make out of the company, the better. They weren't that big a party, so it was unlikely she'd be able to avoid talking to him. Only the decision-makers on each side were in attendance.

Fortunately, Su Khoon's PA hadn't been quite so organised as to come up with a seating plan. Renee managed to manoeuvre herself into a seat next to Lin.

Over the past few weeks, she'd gained an impression of Lin as being highly competent and severely underrated. It said a lot about her that she was the only woman visible on the Freshview side of the deal, and the only Malay woman in a predominantly Chinese team.

Sure, Lin was friends with Renee's sister-in-law, who hated

her. But Renee wasn't going to hold that against Lin, if Lin didn't hold it against her.

They were chatting about skincare, exchanging tips on what had and hadn't worked to banish their teenage acne, when Lin cut herself off midsentence. She had been relaxed, laughing, but now she straightened up, an alert wariness passing over her face. Her mouth curved in something that was almost but not quite like a smile.

Renee turned to see Andrew had appropriated the chair to her right. The Chahaya business development guy had been sitting there a moment ago, but either he'd gone to the bathroom, or he'd been prevailed upon to give up his seat for Low Teck Wee's nephew.

"Sorry I'm late," said Andrew. His teeth flashed in what he no doubt thought was a charmingly boyish grin.

Renee cast a desperate glance at the other side of the table, where Su Khoon was sitting. She'd assumed he'd be keen to monopolise Andrew, given his philosophy on building relationships with people who mattered. But Su Khoon was off duty, chatting to his Freshview watch-nerd bros, his face already stained pink from the welcome glass of champagne.

There was nowhere to run. Gritting her teeth, Renee returned Andrew's smile, though hers was probably even less convincing than Lin's had been.

"When are you guys heading back to Singapore?" she said.

Lin was staying for an indefinite time: "Maybe two, three years. I'll be supporting the project."

"You must be desperate to get back," said Renee to Andrew. He was sitting a little too close. She adjusted her chair discreetly to put an extra inch of distance between them—the most she could manage with the space available. "I'm sure Felicia can't wait to see you."

Her emphasis on his wife's name was probably a little on the nose, but this wasn't the time to be subtle.

"Felicia's in Jakarta with her family," said Andrew. "She's got two nannies, her mom's waiting on her hand and foot, and some Indonesian grandma comes to the house every day to massage her. I don't think she's missing me." He laughed. "I'm not in a rush. There's plenty of work to do, and I love London."

His eyes strayed down her front.

Renee was wearing an Isabel Marant V-neck midi dress, black velvet with long sleeves. She hadn't thought the dress was that low-cut when she put it on, but the way Andrew's gaze was dipping downwards was making her wish she'd turned up in a high-collared sack.

It was a relief when the waitstaff brought in the amuse-bouches. Renee turned back to Lin. "What did the waiter say this was? A consommé? Great, I love a consommé."

Renee usually enjoyed a tasting menu, but it was a different experience with Andrew to fend off. She wished she'd faked a cold and stayed home. After the first glass of champagne she stuck to water, but Andrew was subject to no such restraint. Each course was paired with wine and he knocked back a generous glass of every one. By the fourth and final entree, there was a warm, sweaty hand on Renee's knee.

She drew her knee away, but the hand followed. She couldn't shake it off without making it obvious to the table at large what was going on. She didn't want to make a scene.

Andrew was relying on that, of course. Bile rose in her throat.

He waited till Lin was busy talking to the guy on her other side to shoot his shot.

"Renee . . ." Andrew shook his head, smiling. "I can't get over the fact we're here together. Running into you again, on this deal . . . it feels like fate." He moved his mouth close to her ear and said, his voice gravelly, "You were always the one that got away."

Because Renee's brain hated her, a voice in her head said, *Imagine if it was Ket Siong saying this to you.* It was like someone had put their fist in her chest and squeezed.

Nine days had passed since she'd had any interaction with Ket Siong. Not that she'd been wondering how he was; what he was doing; what he thought of her. Whether he was as upset and bewildered by her cutting off contact as she had been over his rejection of her, all those years ago.

He must be thinking she'd ghosted him because he'd challenged her, told her home truths she didn't want to hear. He had no way of knowing how his revelations were haunting her—how many hours she'd spent poring over articles about Freshview's iniquities and Stephen's disappearance.

She'd read through the *Hornbill Gazette*'s archive of posts on Ensengei, including the two entries mentioning Stephen. These shed no light on his fate; they simply quoted him as an environmental campaigner. Renee was subscribed to the blog now, when a couple of weeks ago she'd never heard of it.

Not that her reading had helped her decide what to do. She could see it was simple for Ket Siong. Even if Freshview hadn't been responsible for Stephen's disappearance, by their own admission, they were culpable. Destroying huge tracts of rainforest might be legal; that didn't mean it was right. Anyone involved with Freshview was ultimately profiting off their wrongdoing.

Ket Siong wouldn't care about everything that complicated the matter for Renee. Her dad's expectations; her burgeoning not-quite-friendship with Su Khoon; the way she was doing what her family wanted of her for the first time in her life.

It wasn't just about her family. Getting this deal through was a matter of professional pride. Renee's entire life had been about being good at her job. It wasn't like she had much of anything else to fall back on.

At least Ket Siong only had half the picture. He wouldn't know the other reason she'd blocked him—pure jealousy.

God, she was so pathetic.

She felt drained. The waitstaff were clearing away the plates for the dessert course, the petits fours had come out, and coffees were being served. Maybe she could slip away.

Andrew didn't seem to have noticed her silence.

"I know we had our problems," he was saying, "but the good times were good, right? It's never been the same with anyone else. I've missed you. I miss the person I was when we were together."

Renee had been on the verge of getting up, announcing she had a headache (*not tonight, dear*). But this was too much. "Andrew, when we were together, you used to go through my phone and get upset over my guy friends' messages. You can't call that a healthy relationship."

Andrew seemed to take a perverse pleasure in getting told off.

"It was because I could never believe you really wanted to be with me," he said, wide-eyed. "I was always terrified someone was going to come take you away."

"Well, nobody did," said Renee. "We broke up because you were sexting another girl. Remember?"

Andrew heaved a sigh. "Biggest mistake of my life. But—I'm not saying it was right, what I did, but I never cheated on you. I never met up with her, it was just texting. It was dumb, I should never have done it. But all of that, it was about me, Renee. How I felt about myself. It wasn't that I didn't care about you."

Engaging with him had been a mistake. Renee had thought if she made him mad enough, he'd back off.

It wasn't as though Andrew had ever actually liked *her*. He'd liked the idea of her: her family, their wealth, her looks, her accent. He'd even liked the idea of having a girlfriend who ran her own business. It was the reality he'd had problems with—the fact it meant Renee worked all the time and had a mind of her own.

"I wasn't ready to admit it then," said Andrew. "But being with you made me feel insecure. I knew you were out of my league."

"Look, it was a long time ago," said Renee. "We both made mistakes." For instance, *she* had been dumb enough to date him, whereas *he* had been a giant asshole. "But we've moved on. You've got Felicia and your family, and this great new role. And this project—it's such an amazing opportunity. I want to take it forward on the best possible terms."

Andrew's face darkened. His hand tightened on her knee, his fingers digging into her flesh. "Stop avoiding the subject. You think I can't tell you're trying to fob me off?"

For a moment Renee was flung suddenly back in time. She was in her flat, staring at Andrew's red face as he screamed at her, knowing she was in danger.

"Andrew, you're hurting me," she said, and heard her voice wobble.

"Oh, Mr. Yeoh," said Lin. "Heng Yee is saying he has a contact in local government here, maybe we can talk to them about our issue with planning. Do you want to explain to him?"

Heng Yee was one of Su Khoon's guys. Leaning past the back of Lin's chair so he could catch Andrew's eye, he said:

"I don't know if my contact can help, but I'm happy to connect you guys."

Andrew let go of Renee's knee, forcing a smile.

Renee said, "Heng Yee, why don't you come over here so you can talk? I'm getting up anyway." She pushed back her chair, standing up.

Lin wouldn't meet Renee's eyes, but Renee caught her darting a nervous glance at Andrew. She had a feeling Lin was aware of everything that had happened, down to the hand on the knee.

She thought about making a break for it while she was in the bathroom, but the meal was almost over. She'd tough it out. Su Khoon was bound to make something of it if she retreated even at this late point.

Heng Yee was deep in conversation with Andrew when she returned, as she'd guessed might be the case—he was a talker and keen to make an impression. Renee was able to slip into the seat he'd left vacant next to Lin. She spent the rest of the meal talking to Lin.

Finally the last coffees and petits fours were consumed, napkins discarded on the table, chairs pushed back. The party went upstairs, chatting desultorily while they waited by the cloakroom for their coats and bags.

Renee took up position next to the door, to enable a quick exit. She could no longer see Andrew among their group. Maybe he'd gone to the bathroom, or left in a fit of pique.

She was starting to hope she'd escape any further encounters with him, when, with an unpleasant shock, she caught sight of him through the window. He cast his cigarette onto the pavement, grinding it under his heel, and came back into the restaurant.

He was on her before she could decide what to do. He said brusquely, in an undertone:

"I'm not done with you yet. We need to talk."

Renee put her shoulders back, lifting her chin. "No."

"What do you mean, 'no'?" said Andrew. "I thought you wanted to work together? Or you don't want that anymore?"

He was starting to attract attention, drawing curious glances from the other diners. The Freshview team were looking uncomfortable. Out of the corner of her eye, Renee saw Su Khoon shrug on his coat hastily, preparing to come over.

She should let her brother handle this. She could practically hear him: *Never mind my sister. You know what women are like. I'll handle her.*

But she was fed up. She'd had enough of biting her tongue to spare men's feelings.

"We've made it clear we want this partnership. But you and I are not going to be able to work together if you can't keep our personal history out of it," said Renee. "I'm not the one clinging onto the past. You don't see me telling people about how you broke into my flat and threw my phone out of the window. You got cautioned, remember? I would like to forget, but you are not helping!"

She didn't bother lowering her voice. The Freshview team

heard every word. They sneaked shifty looks at one another, like a class of students getting reamed out by the teacher.

Su Khoon looked furious. At Renee, obviously. But she wouldn't have expected anything else.

A new party entered the restaurant, looking taken aback at the crowd of worried Chinese businessmen blocking their way. Renee pushed past them blindly. She had to get out before anyone noticed the tears in her eyes.

They were tears of rage, but the men would see them as a sign of weakness. She wouldn't give them the satisfaction.

She was nearly at the end of the street when she heard footsteps behind her, quick and purposeful.

She could turn around and face her brother. Or she could keep walking, and he'd probably put on speed and grab her. She turned around.

"What the fuck is wrong with you?" said Su Khoon.

He was a dull red. She could smell the alcohol coming off him. They were on a quiet street, lined with residential and office buildings. In a sense, it didn't matter if they had a scene—but Renee would have appreciated having witnesses.

"Let's talk about this later," she said. "You'll want to say goodbye to the Freshview guys."

"Say goodbye to the deal, more like," said Su Khoon. "Are you purposely trying to fuck us over or what? Just because you don't want to work with Andrew—"

"That is not what that was about. Andrew was the one who—"

"You wanted to work on this pitch," said Su Khoon. "You wanted to come to this lunch. Fine, I let you join, I trust you to be a grown-up. And this is how you behave? You blow up at Andrew Yeoh, treat him like he's nobody in front of his staff. What the hell are you trying to achieve? Everybody knows Low Teck Wee's daughters are not interested in the business. Andrew is being groomed to take over."

Renee crossed her arms over her chest, shivering. She'd forgotten her coat at the restaurant, and it was cold. "He was being a creep! He was groping my knee all through lunch, being a total sleaze—"

Su Khoon rolled his eyes. "Even something like this you can't handle? Managing relationships is not about buying people sushi so you can be popular. It's about dealing with this kind of situation. The man's away from his wife, he had a few drinks, he's trying his luck. It's not like he was going to do anything in a restaurant, with his staff there."

Renee had a lump in her throat, which made her angrier than ever. She should know by now not to let her family get to her.

Su Khoon was never going to see this from her point of view, or give her any credit for exercising self-control. Why should that hurt her?

"I tried being polite," she said. "It didn't work. What did you want me to do, go back to his hotel and fuck him just to shut him up?"

"I don't know why you mind so much," said Su Khoon. "It's not like you're picky when it comes to men."

Heat rose in Renee's face.

"This isn't about me," she snapped. "I was being professional. Andrew's the one who keeps going over the line. I shouldn't have to put up with this behaviour."

"You knew he was coming when you asked to join," said Su Khoon. "If you weren't prepared for it, you shouldn't have come."

"Er Ge—"

"I am not going to let you fuck this up for me," said Su Khoon. "Whatever shit you have with Andrew Yeoh, deal with it, or I'm telling Dad this is over."

He ran his hands through his hair, shaking his head. "I should have known this was going to happen. Dad wants Da Ge to win, that's why he stuck me with you. But there has to be a limit. He can't blame me for you being uncontrollable."

A woman coming along the street glanced at them and crossed to the other side, casting a curious look backwards. Did she think they were a couple having a tiff, or a boss giving his employee a dressing down?

Renee said, with a composure she did not feel, "Let's not do this here. It's been an emotional day, and—" *You've had a lot to drink,* she almost said, but cut herself off just in time. "And we could both do with a break. Let's have the weekend off. We can talk about this on Monday."

"There's nothing more to talk about," said Su Khoon. "You're coming back with me to apologise to the Freshview team."

Renee stared, but he was serious. "Are you kidding me?"

"Why did you think I came after you?" said Su Khoon. "Come on. They're waiting." He turned, not even checking she was following.

"I'm not coming," said Renee.

Su Khoon stopped. He turned his face up to the sky, as if seeking celestial intervention.

"This is the only way to fix the relationship," he said, with strained patience. "I know you're busy throwing a tantrum right now, but we are talking about half a billion pounds here. If you're not willing to swallow your ego for that, you might as well go back to selling overpriced dresses to aunties. Don't fool yourself that you're ready to run a business like Chahaya."

He was probably right that she was putting the deal at risk. Renee had no doubt Andrew was petty enough to use what clout he had to knock them out of the running. Chahaya needed her to turn back with Su Khoon and grovel.

Chahaya had loomed like a mountain over the landscape of her childhood. She had spent the past few weeks labouring in its shadow. But at this moment, it seemed tiny, insignificant, her work to win it meaningless. Renee thought of Andrew's fingers, digging into her knee, and opened her mouth to throw it all away.

Then she heard the clicking of heels. Behind Su Khoon, Lin

was approaching. She had Renee's camel hair coat folded neatly over her arm.

"Mr. Goh!" she said. "Miss Goh forgot her coat."

Lin was breathless, her hair tumbled by the wind. She held the coat out to Renee.

"I—thank you," said Renee.

Su Khoon, too, seemed disarmed by the intrusion of a stranger on their fight. He cleared his throat and tugged at his jacket, shaking out the sleeves.

"Yes. Thank you," he said. "We were just coming back. Sorry to keep you all waiting."

Lin glanced from him to Renee. "Miss Goh is coming, too?"

They had been on first name terms, earlier.

Su Khoon said firmly, "Yes."

Renee was about to disagree, but Lin's expression was so transparently relieved that it gave her pause. Lin threw a glance backwards. There was something hunted about the turn of her head, as though she thought someone might be in pursuit. She hadn't followed them simply because she was worried Renee might get cold.

It didn't take any extraordinary insight to guess what she *was* worried about. Renee could imagine what it would be like for Lin, returning to all those men. Andrew would be fuming, and Andrew was her boss.

Renee would have left Su Khoon to work things out on his own. She wouldn't go back for him, or Chahaya, or herself.

Even now, her stomach turned at the idea of trotting back, docile, to abase herself to Andrew. *Apologise to the Freshview team,* Su Khoon had said, to make it more palatable, but they both knew what he meant.

Why should she have to eat crow because Lin had a shitty boss? Lin had chosen to work for Freshview. Presumably the advantages of her position outweighed the downsides.

But Lin looked over her shoulder again, shifting on her feet. She'd intervened during the lunch, redirecting Andrew's attention, even if Renee could have wished the intervention had come sooner. Renee owed her.

"Yes," echoed Renee. "I'll come."

She shrugged on her coat, belting it at the waist. The three of them walked back to the restaurant together, in silence.

26

Helen Daley of the *Hornbill Gazette* lived in a rectangular white building in West London. The nearest station was Bayswater; the nearest Malaysian restaurant five minutes' walk away.

"Little Malaysia," said Ket Hau, looking up at the building. "You think she moved here before or after the Interpol notice?"

Ket Siong couldn't help feeling relieved at this sign of life. Ket Hau hadn't been himself since he'd told them the secret he had been keeping for Stephen. As though, along with the burden of secrecy, he had felt himself released from the obligation to pretend he was OK.

That was probably a good thing on the whole, even if a Ket Hau who wasn't perpetually cracking jokes didn't feel right.

It had taken him a while to agree to meeting Helen Daley. Ket Siong and Ma had decided it was worth doing long before he was won over. Daley's position meant she received information from all kinds of sources. There were rumblings, she'd told Ket Siong, of an impending downfall of the Sarawak state premier. An accumulation of scandals and the unexpected departure of several allies meant his grip on power was loosening. The state elections were coming up. All that was needed was something to tip the balance.

If she was able to talk to Ket Hau, she thought that might help. She'd supplied her home address:

I can give you a cup of tea and a biscuit.

When Ket Siong showed the message to Ket Hau, he looked at it in silence for a long moment.

"What does she think I know?" he said.

Ket Siong shrugged. "There's one way to find out." He tapped the screen. "Look at the address."

"St. Stephens Mansions." Ket Hau laughed. "You think it's a sign?"

There was a part of Ket Siong that did believe that. "She's trying to show we can trust her."

"OK," said Ket Hau. "When are we going?"

They ended up going on a Sunday, after Mass. They sat at Helen Daley's dining table while she made them tea in her kitchen.

The flat was cosy in a slightly worn, very British way. The kitchen had bottle-green tiles on the walls and a handsome range cooker, the handles draped with the sort of tea towels to be found in National Trust gift shops, faded from use. The place was stuffed with furniture (Ket Siong had already banged his knee on two different side tables). There were kilim rugs on the floors, art on the walls, and stacks of books, magazines, journals, and newspapers on every flat surface. Nothing was from IKEA.

Helen Daley was a brisk middle-aged woman with penetrating blue eyes and flyaway brown hair pulled back in a ponytail. She spoke well and carried herself with a supreme but unfussy self-confidence, like the headmistress of a good girls' school. It was easy to imagine her at her various reported exploits, whether it was grilling politicians or trekking through the Bornean jungle to interview the locals.

"That's one peppermint tea, and one normal tea, no milk, two sugars," she said.

"Thank you, Mrs. Daley," said Ket Hau.

"Please, call me Helen," said Helen. She took a chair across from the brothers and leaned forward, businesslike. "I appreciate your coming here. I have some sense of the concerns you will have had. But I did think it was worth talking in person.

"I'm sure we're all agreed Sarawak cannot continue under the disastrous mismanagement and corruption of the present regime. If there is anything we can do to help people enact democratic change, we have a moral duty to do it. I'm writing a piece for the *Guardian* about what's been going on there, I think that could have real impact. But there are some pieces of the puzzle missing. That's where you could help, if you're willing."

Ket Hau exchanged a look with Ket Siong.

"We'd like to help, if we can," said Ket Siong. "But there are some things we'd like to understand. What made you want to talk to us?"

"I thought you might ask. I'll tell you. Better than that," said Helen, getting up. "I'll show you." She leaned over the back of a sofa, reaching for something out of sight, and went on, in a slightly muffled voice: "If the technology doesn't let us down."

She emerged triumphant, holding a tablet aloft. "I was worried my daughter had taken this out with her. Right, bear with me a moment."

She set the device down on the table, fiddling with the case so as to stand it upright.

"I'll start the call off here," said Helen. "But if you would rather speak in private at any point, you can go into my study, over there. I've got plenty to get on with, so take all the time you need."

Ket Hau had been a little pale, but dignified and professional. At this, his composure wavered. "I'm sorry, I don't understand. What call?"

Helen was busy jabbing at the tablet screen. It was turned towards her, so Ket Hau and Ket Siong couldn't see what was on it.

"I'm ringing the person who told me to look for you," she said absently. "Oh, here we are! Hello there. Can you hear me?"

There was an indistinct crackle from the tablet.

"Yes, they're here," said Helen. "Hold on, let me adjust the volume."

"You invited us here to talk to you," said Ket Siong, glancing at Ket Hau. His brother was thrumming with nervous energy, poised for flight. "You didn't mention anyone else."

Helen wasn't really listening. "He didn't want me to say anything. In case . . . and it does seem better this way. Yes, you can explain yourself in a moment." She paused, looking up at Ket Siong and his brother.

"This may come as a bit of a shock," she said, and turned the tablet to face them.

For a split second, Ket Siong thought Helen had started an old video of Stephen playing, though it was one he had never seen before. Indignation scythed through him. He'd overcome his brother's misgivings to get him here; it wasn't right to subject him to this without warning. He opened his mouth to express his outrage.

Then the face on the screen blinked and said, "Hello?"

Shock stole Ket Siong's voice away.

No one spoke. Ket Hau had turned to stone next to him.

"Stephen?" said Ket Siong faintly, after what felt like a long time. His face felt numb.

Stephen—if it was him, and it could be no one else—had altered since the night Ket Siong had last seen him. He had aged more than three years could account for: his face was thinner, new lines carved into it. And he had grown out his hair. It was shaggy, past his chin, with white strands that hadn't been there before. It made him look like an ageing member of a Malay rock band.

His expression, however, was familiar. It was the same expression Stephen had worn when he used to keep Ket Hau out late watching football at mamak stalls, only to come in for an almighty telling-off from Ma the next morning.

"Hi, hi!" he said, looking relieved. "Hello. Hi."

Ket Siong glanced warily at Ket Hau. His face was perfectly blank. Ket Siong looked back at the screen.

Extraordinarily, Stephen was still on it, the image of his face fuzzy but unmistakable. His eyebrows were practically bristling with anxiety.

Ket Siong must be dreaming. The conviction imparted a certain recklessness. It didn't seem all that important what he said.

"Where are you?" he said, mostly to make conversation. It seemed absurd to care where Stephen was, when he was alive.

"What? Oh, Geneva. Switzerland," said Stephen. "I'm a refugee now. Got the official letter all that. Took a while. Ha! It's been interesting. Interesting few years. Yes. How, uh, how are you?"

Stephen clearly did not have the same feeling as Ket Siong, that nothing he said was of any real consequence. Ket Siong didn't answer, since Stephen's question wasn't for him.

But Ket Hau didn't speak, either. Ket Siong could feel something great and terrible working through him. Behind the blank wall of his expression, he was like a kettle coming to the boil.

"Hau?" said Stephen.

When Ket Hau finally spoke, the wall crumbled all at once.

"You fucking bastard!" he said. It was like an explosive going off. "You fucker! What the fuck, Stephen?"

Ket Siong leaned away a little. Helen Daley suddenly found something of vital interest on her mantelpiece to inspect.

"Sorry! I'm sorry," said Stephen. "Seriously, these past few years, it's been crazy. Then when I could finally start looking for you all, you were gone! Nobody knew where you went. Somebody told me you moved to Perth. I'm damn broke now, or I would have flown there. It's only when I got in touch with Helen, I asked her did she hear anything about you guys. At first she said she couldn't help me, but then DAP messaged her—"

Helen's ears pricked up at the mention of her name.

"DAP?" she said. "I haven't had any contact from anyone there. Are they involved?"

"Ah, no, not the political party," said Stephen. "That's my nickname for Siong. You know, because his name sounds like

Lim Kit Siang. The DAP leader. He's the father of Lim Guan Eng, the guy who—"

"Stephen," said Ket Siong. "Why didn't you contact us?"

Stephen looked stricken. "I was scared you all would think I was a scammer or what. Helen was talking to you anyway, she said she'd set something up. But you all didn't guess? You're not the ones who hired this PI firm?"

"What PI firm?" said Ket Siong.

"I haven't told Helen about this yet," said Stephen. "Happened a couple of days ago. I got tracked down by these guys, called themselves enquiry agents. I thought, shit, that's it for me. But they said they just want to talk to me. Claim they've been hired by an unbiased party or unconnected party or something like that. I thought maybe it was you all, looking for me."

"No, I . . . we didn't know there was something to look for." The term *enquiry agent* was familiar. Ket Siong had heard it before, relatively recently—though he couldn't, at that moment, remember exactly when.

He gave up on chasing down the memory, a wave of self-recrimination rolling over him. He should have thought of hiring investigators. He didn't have the money for it, but he could have come up with some way to raise the funds.

"But Stephen," he said, "what happened? You got taken, right? Who did it? Was Freshview behind it?"

"Who took me?" said Stephen. "Fuck if I know! They didn't give me their business cards. I mean, could be anybody. There are so many candidates. Did Hau show you? It's all in the USB drive. Do you guys have the USB drive?"

They all looked at Ket Hau. Ket Hau opened his mouth, turned away, buried his face in his palms, and burst into tears.

This was not like the time he had broken down while telling Ket Siong and their mother about the USB drive. His sobs racked his body, his shoulders shaking. He was almost howling, with the pure and terrible abandonment of a child.

"Ko!" said Ket Siong, horrified.

"Oh, now, now," said Helen.

But Stephen said, "Baby—oh, baby, I'm so sorry."

"We can end the call," said Helen. "I'm sorry, I should have prepared you better . . ."

"No! Hau, baby, talk to me," said Stephen urgently.

Ket Hau gave his head a savage shake. His shoulders were heaving, his breathing harsh. He said, in a voice guttural with tears, "No."

It was not clear which of them he was talking to. Helen hesitated, but then Ket Hau grabbed the tablet and stalked out of the room, banging the door shut behind him.

Ket Siong and Helen Daley stared at each other.

"Well," said Helen.

"Stephen *is* his boyfriend," blurted Ket Siong.

"Right," said Helen, after a moment. "I'm going to make myself a cup of tea, with sugar in this time. Would you like something? Another peppermint tea, or something stronger? I really think you ought to have something stronger. And then we can chat. I'm happy to answer any questions you have. I suspect," said Helen, glancing at the door, "we're going to have plenty of time."

There was no noise coming from Helen's study, where Ket Hau had shut himself up with the tablet.

"I'm sure they're just talking things out," said Helen. "We've got excellent soundproofing. My daughter plays the guitar."

She was a comforting person to be around when your world had been turned upside down several times in the space of twenty minutes. Once she'd made herself a fresh cup of tea and confirmed Ket Siong didn't want any of her husband's eighteen-year-old single malt, she sat down and told Ket Siong what she knew.

"I don't know how much you've been following local politics," she said. "In Sarawak, I mean. But I've been hearing for a while now, from people in the know, that they think the time is coming. There's a real groundswell of dissatisfaction with the regime. What Stephen found out before he got kidnapped could make all the difference in the elections. Not just the state elections, either. That's why he reached out to me. It's the evidence we need. Stephen lost the documents his informant passed to him. He didn't have the chance to get his things before he left the country."

"But what happened?" said Ket Siong. "There were eyewitnesses, they said they saw him get kidnapped . . ."

"Oh yes, that happened. But he managed to escape," said Helen. "I don't know the full story, but I gather it was quite dramatic. He fought off his kidnappers and got away—they probably weren't expecting a trained martial artist. He managed to get on a plane out of the country. He's been in hiding since then. He thinks his attackers made out they got rid of him, so they could collect their fee, and that's why he hasn't had much trouble. Everyone thinks he's dead."

"We thought so, too," said Ket Siong. He thought of his brother's face before he'd left the room. His heart twisted. "Stephen could have told us."

Helen's face creased with sympathy. "You must try to understand. He was terrified. Your brother was the last person he wanted to expose.

"It was only very recently that I heard from him," she added. "Only a few months before you contacted me. He was very cagey, he used a pseudonym. I had my suspicions from early on, but it took him a while to trust me enough to admit who he was. Getting asylum was a big deal. I think he's felt much more confident since then.

"He's been worried about you. Ket Hau most of all, but all of you. He told me you're the closest he's got to a family."

Ket Siong realised Helen was trying to plead Stephen's case with him. That she, a stranger, should feel the need to do this made everything feel more surreal than ever.

"He's part of our family," he said.

"And family is complicated," said Helen. "I know you haven't asked for advice, but you'll forgive me for giving it. I'm much older than you and I feel that gives me the right to speak, you know. Stephen did what he thought he needed to. He really was planning to fly to Australia, after he was granted asylum. He even asked me for a loan. I told him he could have the money, but he should wait until he had a better lead. And now here we are. You will forgive him, won't you?"

Evidently Ket Siong's attempt to explain had not worked.

"There's nothing to forgive," he said. "We've been worried about him, too."

"Right. I'm glad to hear that," said Helen.

They both looked at the door to her study. It betrayed no hint of what was going on behind it.

"I wasn't sure . . ." she said. "Your brother seemed upset."

"He's just shocked," said Ket Siong.

But it was true Ket Hau still looked furious when he eventually rejoined them. His eyes were red and swollen, though at least he wasn't crying anymore. He merely looked mad as hell.

He handed the tablet to Helen. "Thanks."

Helen and Ket Siong exchanged a glance.

"Was it all right?" she said.

"The technology worked," said Ket Hau.

Ket Siong wanted to be respectful. But after all, Stephen was his friend, too.

"What did he say?" said Ket Siong.

"Who?" said Ket Hau.

For a moment Ket Siong wondered if his brother had actually lost it.

Then:

"Stephen? You want to know what he said?" said Ket Hau. "I'll tell you what that bastard said. He said gay marriage is legal here. Three years, not a single word, me having nightmares every night. And that's what he's got to say for himself. Fucking hell. He's lucky he's in Geneva. If he was here, I'd kill him myself."

On any other day, Ket Siong might have been staggered at the idea of Stephen proposing marriage to Ket Hau. But it was the least unlikely thing that had happened since they'd arrived at Helen Daley's flat.

"Are you getting married?" said Ket Siong.

"What do you think!" snarled Ket Hau. He flung himself around and went to the window, standing with his back to them.

"If you want," said Ket Siong, "I could talk to Ma." Another thought struck him. "So is Stephen coming here? Or are you going to move to Switzerland?"

"I'm not going anywhere," said Ket Hau. "I'm never talking to that bastard again. Unbelievable."

Clearly this was not a point to pursue until Ket Hau had had a chance to cool down.

Now that Ket Siong thought about it, he was not sure Ma had not known about Ket Hau and Stephen all along. If he had had his suspicions, so must she. But how she would feel about gaining Stephen as a son-in-law was hard to predict.

Ket Hau turned around. "Mrs. Daley—Helen. You've been very patient while we've been subjecting you to our drama."

"Not at all," said Helen readily. "It's been a pleasure hosting you. I'm only sorry I couldn't persuade your brother to try some Glenmorangie. Would you like some? I find a dram steadies the nerves wonderfully."

Ket Hau declined, but only after an extended pause that suggested he was seriously considering the offer.

"About the USB drive Stephen mentioned," he said. "I don't have it on me right now. But it's in our possession. I can tell you what the evidence consists of, if that would be helpful."

"I would be very interested in hearing that," said Helen. "Stephen wasn't able to tell me much of the detail. It's been so long since he had access to the documents. But are you sure you'd like to talk about it now? You've had rather a trying day. We could always speak another time."

"I'm fine," said Ket Hau. He drew out a chair, sitting down at the dining table. "I should have tried to do something with the information three years ago. But better late than never."

"It couldn't be a better time if you had planned it," said Helen. "So let's say it's all for the best, in this best of all possible worlds. You're sure you don't want another drink? All right. Do you mind if I record this conversation? Perfect." She smiled. "Take it away."

27

*R*enee *was working* when she saw the notification. A new blog post had been published on the *Hornbill Gazette*.

She clicked on the link because she felt in need of distraction. Her supplier for Virtu at Home—a family-run studio in Japan that had taken long searching to find—was folding, after the sudden passing of the patriarch. Forget about rolling out the line at Chinese New Year. She might not get to do it at all. It was a crushing blow.

At least sales in the run-up to Christmas were robust, but it was always a crunch getting orders out and everything done before Virtu closed for the break. Shutting the office from Christmas Eve through to the new year was something she'd introduced as a well-being measure, but it made the weeks before wildly stressful. Chinese New Year was bearing down on them, too—it was in late January next year, earlier than usual—and their New Year womenswear collection had to be perfect. It was their mainstay, vital for cash flow.

At least Renee had had three weeks of relative peace since the Freshview pitch to focus on Virtu's problems. They were waiting to hear about the outcome of the pitch, though they should be getting the news any day now. Freshview had said it would take three or four weeks.

In the meantime, Su Khoon had taken himself off to Europe, where he was travelling with his family. They were due to return to London next week, and Dad was flying in from Singapore

284 · ZEN CHO

to join them for a few days. He'd made it clear the reason he was coming was to tell Renee and Su Khoon in person about his choice of CEO—the assumption was that Freshview would have announced *their* choice by then. But the plan was also to have a big family get-together to celebrate Renee's birthday.

That was something to look forward to. They'd booked a nice restaurant—Renee was particularly fond of Yauatcha's patisserie—but she was considering whether she might invent a bout of stomach flu to get out of the meal.

Dad, Su Khoon, and his family were going to travel back to Singapore together afterwards. With a lesser man, one might be inclined to wonder whether the fact Dad had elected to share a plane with Su Khoon and Jessie for thirteen hours indicated he was leaning towards choosing Su Khoon.

But Renee had decided not to read too much into the choice. She was avoiding thinking about the Chahaya leadership contest as much as she could. It was a topic that only led her down dead ends.

It didn't occur to her, as the *Hornbill Gazette* update loaded, that its contents were unlikely to be soothing, given the reason she'd subscribed in the first place. It had been years since the *Gazette* had blogged about Ensengei or Freshview. Even the Facebook post mentioning Stephen's disappearance dated from seven months ago. Renee didn't expect to see anything relevant to her in the new post.

The *Gazette* began by apologising for its silence in recent months, before offering an explanation:

> We have been busy working on a piece, to be pub-
> lished shortly in one of the UK's major broadsheets,
> detailing a shocking corruption scandal implicating
> the highest levels of the state and federal govern-
> ment. The main players will be familiar to those
> who have followed Sarawak's woes over the years.

They include a prominent company, run by one of the premier's cronies, whose rapacious exploitation of Sarawak's resources and flagrant disregard of the law have been covered in this blog before. The article will also present, for the first time, a full account of the enforced disappearance of a local activist, with proof of the complicity of corporate interests and state forces. As always in Malaysia, money works hand in hand with politics to serve the powerful.

Renee read the post over again, pressure gathering in her chest.

There was no reason to think the *Gazette* was talking about Freshview. If there was one thing she'd learnt from reading through the blog's archives, it was that prominent companies run by political cronies abounded in Malaysia. The post could be about any number of shady businesses.

If not for the detail of the disappeared activist. There weren't *that* many of those.

Renee's throat closed up, her heart banging against her ribs. She got up and staggered to her kitchen, fumbled for a glass of water, and drank it down.

She had been working so hard not to worry about the Freshview deal—though it *had* struck her a couple of weeks ago that she had the resources to do more than Google obsessively for evidence of what Ket Siong had told her. She'd reached out to the enquiry agents she'd hired a few years back when her brothers had engineered their campaign to sabotage her and Virtu.

The agency had said they would see what they could find out. So far, they hadn't come up with anything she hadn't already read about online. They'd said they were investigating a potential lead in Switzerland, of all places, but there hadn't been an update on that yet.

If they found anything . . . but until they did, until there was some concrete evidence she could show her family, there was nothing Renee could do. The pitch was done. Their proposal was going through Freshview's corporate machinery. Freshview would decide what they decided.

It wasn't likely they'd decide for Chahaya, anyway, after that debacle at lunch. Andrew had accepted Renee's apology with oily condescension, but the incident would hardly have endeared Chahaya to him. And if Chahaya lost the pitch, then there was nothing to worry about. Su Khoon would blame Renee; Dad would be scathing about her emotional incontinence; Su Beng would saunter into the top job to which he had been born; and they would all go back to their lives.

Renee wasn't going to lose it over a deal that would probably never be signed.

She sat back down at her desk. It was only three o'clock. If she buckled down, she should be able to get four or five solid hours of work in before clocking off for the evening.

But for once, work proved ineffective as a distraction. Her concentration was shot. Every time her mind drifted back to that *Hornbill Gazette* post, her chest started hurting, darkness crowding at the edge of her vision.

When she found herself rereading a draft press release for the Chinese New Year collection for the third time, Renee made a snap decision.

She'd go for a run. She hadn't been exercising much of late. That must be why she was like this, so jangled and nervy that merely reading a blog post had sent her into a spiral.

She'd burn off her restlessness, get out of her head, and come back refreshed, ready to tackle her inbox. Things would seem less bad then.

The sun was low in the sky by the time Renee set off, heading for her usual route in Hyde Park. It would be dark soon, but so long as she stuck to the main paths, with their rows of lampposts, she'd be all right.

It was a clear, crisp day. There would be frost on the grass in the morning. Her breath steamed in the air. She let the movement take over: the steady beat of her heart; the thud of her trainers on the path; the rhythm of her legs.

It didn't take long for her to get winded—she was out of shape. Too much work and worry, not enough physical exertion. But she pushed through, relishing the burn in her chest and the ache in her muscles.

The lamps were coming on along the path when her phone, strapped to her arm, started buzzing. The ringtone interrupted the true crime podcast she'd been half listening to—a recommendation from Nathalie, who had ghoulish tastes in nonfiction. Renee glanced at the screen.

It was Su Khoon.

"Hey, what's up?"

"They've gone for us," said Su Khoon, without precursor.

Renee was already slowing down. She came to an abrupt stop.

"What?" she said, though she already knew what he meant. What else could he be talking about?

"We got the deal." Su Khoon's voice was exultant. "I've told Dad. He wants to have a call tomorrow morning. Can you come over to the house? Penny's looking at flights for me, I should be in London by tonight."

There was a fair amount of background noise on the line. He must be in a café or something. Maybe that was why his voice sounded like it was coming from so far away. The syllables landed against Renee's ears, weightless, deprived of meaning.

"You're coming back?" she said.

"What's that? Yes," said Su Khoon. "There's some kind of lag, you're taking forever to come through. Yeah, might as well get to work. I've seen enough of lakes. I'll see you at eight a.m.

tomorrow? I'm going to ring the lawyers now, get them to clear conflicts, all that."

"Right," said Renee.

"Bye," said Su Khoon. "Good work. We got there!"

He rang off, to Renee's distant relief. He probably hadn't heard her breathing change, though she could hear herself, hoarse and laboured.

No matter how hard she fought to breathe, it wasn't enough. The pressure in her chest was crushing, her heart in a vice. Her vision narrowed.

She crumpled over onto the path, gasping for air. Pain sparked in her knee as the tarmac scraped the skin off through the thin fabric of her leggings. She thumped her fist against her chest as if that might shift the obstruction, her other hand scrabbling for purchase on the path.

Dread shook her in its jaws. It felt like she was going to die.

It took a while for the voice to penetrate.

"Are you all right?" A man's voice. Then it said, shocked, "Renee?"

It came to Renee that she knew the person speaking. It was Ket Siong.

She choked out, "Panic attack."

She'd had them before, though not in a while. This was probably a recurrence, and not that she was dying, bad as it felt.

She was remotely conscious of Ket Siong hovering, not quite touching her.

"How can I help?" he said.

Let me crawl in a hole and die, was what Renee would have said, if she could. She shook her head, or tried to.

Either none of this got through, or Ket Siong wasn't inclined to respect her wishes, for once.

"Come on," he said.

He raised her to her feet, his touch light but decisive, and walked her to a bench. The wool of his coat was scratchy against her arm. She could feel the solid warmth of him through it.

She collapsed onto the bench. Ket Siong moved the arm that had been holding her up, letting her fold over onto herself.

"I'm going to count," he said. "Try to focus on my voice."

He started counting, unexpectedly, in Mandarin. "Yi. Er. San. Si. Wu . . ."

Renee's Mandarin wasn't great, despite the Chinese for Business course she'd taken a few years ago. But numbers she could follow.

"Liu. Qi. Ba. Jiu. Shi."

More than the numbers, it was his voice she clung to—deep, gentle, infinitely familiar. She followed the thread of it until her breathing evened out and her chest unlocked, her heartbeat slowing.

When she could feel all her limbs again, she said, "Sorry." Her voice came out as a croak. Her mouth was dry.

"Here." Ket Siong held out a water bottle, then paused. "I've drunk from it. But I could get you . . ." He looked around.

It was properly dark now. They were by the Serpentine, its waters illuminated by the yellow glow of the night sky, reflecting the million lights of London. Trees made irregular patches of shadow on the mirrored surface.

During the day, there were booths where Ket Siong could have bankrupted himself to buy a bottle of mineral water. They'd be closed now.

A hush lay over the park. There was no one around, for once. It felt like they were the only two people in the world.

"It's OK," said Renee, and took a swig from his bottle. She felt drained and trembly, light-headed.

She handed the bottle back to him. "Thanks."

Ket Siong put it away in his messenger bag. "How are you feeling?"

"Fine," said Renee, and burst into tears.

She wasn't planning on doing that, or on explaining herself. The moment she was able to pull herself together, she was going to get out of here, hide away in her flat, and never show her face to the world again.

Except Ket Siong put his arm around her, as naturally as though it was a thing they did. She found herself leaning into his warmth, talking.

"We won the deal," she said. "With Freshview."

"I thought you wanted the deal."

"That was before you told me—before I knew—" Renee's voice hitched. She drew her arm across her eyes. "I don't know what to do. The pitch was bad enough. Virtu's a mess. If I have to work on nailing the deal down, I'll never get to launch Virtu at Home, and our CNY collection is fucked. But I'm stuck. Freshview's made their choice, and now you hate me, and Chahaya's going to be partnering with the company that killed your friend—"

"That's not right," said Ket Siong. "I don't hate you." He paused. "And Stephen's alive. We found him."

"What?" Ket Siong was blurry; her eyes were still full of tears. Renee blinked, scrubbing them. "You found him? How? Where has he been?"

"He's in Geneva," said Ket Siong. "It's a long story."

Renee hadn't been in a state to notice much about him till now. His face was too close for her to be able to make out his expression. She pulled away so she could look at him. He withdrew the arm he'd put around her, clearing his throat.

He looked different, in some indefinable way. There was something new about him, but also something familiar. He was more like the Ket Siong she'd known when they were students. Freer, less sad.

She found herself missing the warmth of his arm around her. It took her a moment to process what he'd said.

"Wait," she said. *"Stephen's* the lead in Switzerland?"

Ket Siong's forehead furrowed. "The lead . . . ?" His eyes widened. "You hired the PI firm that contacted Stephen."

Renee looked away. "It's not that I didn't believe you. I tried to read up online, but it was hard to piece it all together. I thought if I had more information . . . I don't know, I thought it'd help me figure out what to do. But it's too late now."

Hopelessness bore down on her again, the sense of being trapped with no way out. She shivered, her breathing speeding up.

Panic rose in her. She couldn't break down again, not in front of Ket Siong. Renee opened her mouth to give some kind of excuse, lay the ground for an escape.

But Ket Siong spoke first. "You shouldn't stay out here in the cold. You were running?"

Renee nodded, though it had to be obvious. She was in running leggings and an ancient, pilling T-shirt, near-translucent from the washes it had been through. Her hair was a mess, and the state of her face didn't bear thinking of. She must be looking like a complete wreck.

Ket Siong, of course, looked great. He had on the same charcoal-grey coat he'd been wearing the last time she'd seen him, the evening before the pitch to Freshview, though this time he was wearing a green hoodie under it. She'd registered all of this before she realised he was shrugging off his coat.

"No, no," said Renee. "I'm all gross and sweaty. I don't want to stink up your coat."

In fact the sweat had dried on her skin. Any warmth generated by her run was long gone. She clasped her hands, noticing for the first time that they were freezing.

Ket Siong paid no attention to her protests. He draped his coat over her shoulders. "Come on. Let's get you home."

"I'm fine," said Renee feebly, but it would have taken far more energy than she had to resist Ket Siong in this mood. The moral force of his concern was irresistible.

Without quite knowing how it happened, she found herself

scudding along the path, with him beside her. It was like she was being borne along in the wake of a large ship. Ket Siong wasn't even touching her.

Renee glanced up at him. "Do you know where we're going?"

It was harder to navigate now darkness had fallen. Around them, the amber glow of the streetlights picked out trees and benches and patches of grass, casting them in sharp relief. Beyond, the surrounding parkland fell away into mystery.

This didn't seem to worry Ket Siong. "I've been to your place before."

It felt weirdly natural being with him like this, despite how they'd last parted. In a way, it always felt natural being with Ket Siong. Maybe that was why it hadn't occurred to Renee before to wonder how he'd happened to stumble on her.

"What were you doing here?" she said. "When you found me, I mean."

There was a brief pause. Ket Siong said, "I was on a walk."

Renee had been expecting him to say he'd been teaching a class nearby, or had been meeting a friend. She blinked. "Really?"

It would have taken Ket Siong an hour to get here from Edmonton. It was an odd place to choose for a stroll.

Ket Siong seemed aware of this. He looked a little embarrassed. "I've been coming here a lot. I was hoping I'd bump into you." He paused. "I would have texted, but you weren't receiving my messages."

"I blocked your number," admitted Renee.

"I thought so." He gave her a sidelong look, his brows knitted. "I know you said you didn't want to see me again. But I wanted to apologise, for what happened last time. It wasn't fair to you."

"Oh, Ket Siong, no." Renee touched his arm. "It was my fault. I shouldn't have flown off the handle like that. I knew I was in the wrong. I was just so mixed up, with everything going on."

Ket Siong's eyes dropped to her hand where it was resting on his bicep. Renee had reached out without thinking, but she was suddenly conscious of the muscle under her palm. They had been closer less than ten minutes ago, her head resting on his chest, but this touch felt more intimate, somehow. As though she'd transgressed a boundary.

She lifted her hand, heat flooding her face.

But Ket Siong caught her hand in his. His eyes were fixed on her. The look in them made Renee's heart start beating wildly. He opened his mouth.

At this pivotal moment, Renee's body elected to let out an enormous sneeze. This was followed by two more sneezes, equally seismic, in rapid succession.

"We'd better get indoors," said Ket Siong.

This was disappointing, but less crushing than it might have been, because he forgot to let go of her hand.

Perhaps it was just that he needed it to tow her along. Renee had to work to keep up with Ket Siong's pace. By the time they arrived at her building, she had warmed up.

He slowed to a stop in the foyer, releasing her. Renee put her hand in her coat pocket before remembering it wasn't her coat. She took it off, fumbling a little with the buttons.

Dragan was on holiday. The reception desk was manned by a haughty-looking blonde woman Renee didn't recognise. She eyed them without interest before turning back to her computer screen.

Renee passed Ket Siong's coat back to him. "Thanks." A thought struck her. "I could get it dry-cleaned."

"No need," said Ket Siong. He glanced at the glass door that separated the foyer from the residents-only parts of the building. He looked uncertain, now they were here. "You've got my number. You could let me know, when . . . if you're ready to speak."

"Ket Siong," said Renee. "I'm ready now. Do you want to come up?"

Ket Siong's ears were pink. Presumably he, too, was thinking about what had happened the last time he'd accepted that invitation. "Do you want me to?"

"I wouldn't ask if not. But I need a shower," said Renee. "Sorry. Can you wait until I'm done? Or do you have somewhere else to get to?"

"I can wait," said Ket Siong.

28

Renee felt better for the shower, cleansed and calm. After the day's extremes of feeling, she was wrung out, too tired to be nervous about the man waiting in her living room. She pulled on black leggings, an oversized grey cable-knit jumper and her fluffiest bed socks, and went to see what he was doing.

Ket Siong wasn't in the living room, where she'd left him nursing a barley tea. He was in her kitchen, apparently busy poking through her cabinets.

"Looking for something?" said Renee.

"I thought you might want something to eat," said Ket Siong. He shut a cabinet door.

"And then you found out I live on Nespresso pods and Graze packets." The pot of barley tea she'd made for Ket Siong before going off for her shower was still hot. Renee got a mug out and poured herself some. "I don't really cook. There's a Whole Foods nearby if you're hungry. We could pick something up."

"It's OK. I'm not hungry." Ket Siong hesitated, looking her over.

It was more of a checkup than a checkout. He said, "How are you feeling?"

Fine, Renee was about to say, automatically.

But Ket Siong had found her crouched and shivering on the ground like an injured animal, barely capable of speech. There wasn't much point in lying at this stage.

"Better," she said. "I'm sorry about all of that."

Ket Siong waved the apology away. "I'm glad I found you." He paused. "What you said earlier . . . I know you were upset. But you know, you aren't stuck. It's not too late. You can make a different choice."

Renee stared down at her tea. She'd chosen her favourite hex- agonal mug, hand-thrown in a celadon glaze by a former CSM coursemate. In it, the barley tea took on an unearthly green tint.

"The Freshview deal's going ahead," she said. "There's nothing I can do to change that, now. If I hadn't apologised to Andrew, maybe . . ."

Ket Siong's eyebrows drew together. "What did you apologise to Andrew for?"

Renee told him. "I should have refused to go back with my brother. Apologising seemed like the right thing to do. But it's not like anyone could blame Lin for me telling off Andrew. What's the worst that could have happened to her?"

Ket Siong listened with the completeness of attention she was used to from him, his hands cupped around his own mug.

Staring at them, Renee was visited by a vivid sense-memory of him hoisting her up against the kitchen island, those long fingers digging into her thighs. Warmth flooded her cheeks.

She pushed off the counter like it had scalded her. "Shall we go sit down? I'm pretty tired."

"Of course," said Ket Siong, looking concerned.

He showed no sign of experiencing inconvenient horny flash- backs. She might have imagined him holding her hand all the way back to her building.

In the living room, he chose an armchair a decorous distance from the sofa where she was sitting.

"Going by what Andrew tried with you, it could have been even worse for Lin," said Ket Siong. "You've been trying to win his business, but you're still the daughter of Goh Kheng Tat. She has fewer protections. It was a good impulse, to want to shield her."

Andrew was full of shit, obviously, but till now, Renee had not questioned one aspect of his story—that his outrageous behaviour was due to the history between them. Renee had dumped Andrew even though he'd felt entitled to her, and that was why he hadn't gotten over it, ten years on.

It had not previously occurred to her that she was probably not the singular recipient of Andrew's sense of entitlement, out of all the women he knew.

She sat up. "Ket Siong, you're right. If Andrew's willing to harass me, what's to say he's not doing the same thing with his staff? I don't know why I never thought of it before. I thought it was about me, like I'm special. How self-absorbed is that?"

"You are special," said Ket Siong.

Renee blinked.

She waited for him to make it into a joke, or change the subject, but he didn't. He was blushing, but his gaze on her was steady.

"I thought you'd never want to speak to me again," Renee said, after a moment. "After how I behaved."

"You're the one who stopped talking to me."

"I'm sorry—"

"That's not what I meant," said Ket Siong. "I know I put you in a difficult position. Hearing all that, the night before your pitch . . . I knew how important it was to you. I made a serious accusation about someone you know, a friend of your family's, and I expected you to just take my word for it."

"But we're friends," said Renee. "You're entitled to expect your friends to trust you."

Ket Siong tried to suppress it, but she caught his wince. Guilt twisted in her chest.

"It was a big deal," she said. "That you trusted me enough to tell me about Stephen. I'm not proud of how I reacted. I should have been there for you. I'm sorry I let you down."

Renee looked down at her hands, empty now she'd put her tea on the coffee table.

"I don't know what to do," she said. "I don't know how to make a different choice."

"You'll figure it out," said Ket Siong. He got up and crossed the living room, sitting down next to her. "Renee."

His voice was low and tender. Renee felt hypnotised. She couldn't look away from him.

He reached out and touched her hair. Just the lightest brush of the fingers, but it went through Renee like a hot knife through butter. It felt like her bones were dissolving, like she might melt into the sofa.

Ket Siong was looking at her like she was something magical, like he couldn't believe he was allowed so close.

He was going to kiss her. Renee's heart was racing, but she felt at the same time profoundly calm, as though nothing could go wrong. Everything that had happened between them was meant to lead up to this. Every misunderstanding, every hurt, every time she'd doubted his feelings: it all fell away, insignificant, compared to the supreme importance of this one moment . . .

"Do you have a hair dryer?" said Ket Siong.

Renee's eyes snapped open. "What?"

Ket Siong had that perfect little crease between his eyes that always made her want to kiss him, first there, and then on his mouth.

"It's just," he said apologetically. "Your hair's wet."

Renee had towelled her hair off till it was no longer dripping, brushed the worst of the tangles out, and bundled it up in a bun. It was true it was somewhat damp, but . . . "You don't believe that stuff about leaving your hair wet? Like, it's bad luck or you'll get rheumatism or something?"

Ket Siong frowned. "I get headaches when my hair's wet."

Renee must be down bad. Ket Siong was pouting—there was really no other word for the stubborn curl of his lip—but it suited him.

"You are the most Chinese person I have ever met," she said. She flopped back onto the sofa, glaring at the ceiling.

She was so deluded. At least Ket Siong was busy looking embarrassed over having been revealed to hold beliefs at least a generation too old for him. He probably hadn't noticed Renee's own embarrassment.

"I'm too *tired* to blow-dry my hair," she said. "It's not going to kill me if I let it dry by itself, this one time."

Ket Siong muttered something unintelligible.

"What's that?" said Renee.

Ket Siong looked at her, then away. His ears were pink.

"If you tell me where your hair dryer is," he said, "I can do it."

Renee moved to one of her rattan armchairs, close to a power point.

Ket Siong took up position behind her, turning her hair dryer over in his hands. "I've never seen one like this before."

"It cost three hundred pounds."

"What?"

"My hair's important." Renee leaned back in the chair. "No pressure."

She wasn't sure why she was letting Ket Siong loose on her head. She could have done it herself, or insisted on letting the air-drying process complete itself, Chinese superstitions about wet hair be damned.

But then Ket Siong touched her, running his fingers over the curve of her ear and lifting a damp coil of hair in his hand. And—well.

Ket Siong was gentle and thorough. He took his time, dividing her hair into sections and blow-drying each one separately until the strands were slipping through his fingers. His touch was almost impersonal. Almost.

By the time he was done, Renee felt drowsy and loose-limbed. She could have laid her head down on his lap and gone to sleep.

She carded her fingers through her hair. She had to admit it was nice having it dry.

"That seems to have done the job." She yawned. "Happy now?"

Silence. Renee turned around. "Ket Siong?"

Ket Siong unplugged the hair dryer, set it down on a side table, and came to sit by her. He was looking thoughtful.

"You haven't asked why I kept coming to Hyde Park," he said.

Renee's brain had been tiptoeing around that particular revelation. Getting to the park and back home meant a two-hour round trip for Ket Siong. It was a lot to take in.

"You wanted to apologise," she said. A thought struck her. "Why didn't you come to my building? You know where I live."

"That would have been . . . I didn't want to cross the line."

Renee tried to suppress her grin, but from the way Ket Siong ducked his head, she wasn't that successful. He went on:

"Apologising was part of it. But it wasn't just that. There were some other things I wanted to talk to you about."

Renee nodded. "About Freshview?"

"What? No." Biting his lip, Ket Siong looked away, as though casting around for something to help him.

She realised he was nervous.

"Renee, I haven't been honest with you," he said. "I was trying to respect what you wanted, from—from our friendship. But when we stopped talking, I regretted not telling you how I felt."

He paused, his eyes slipping down to the coffee table where their two mugs of tea sat, side by side.

Renee wasn't feeling sleepy anymore. She could hear her own heartbeat, a rushing in her ears.

"I hope we will stay friends," said Ket Siong. "But that's not what I want from you. My feelings for you haven't changed. I know you said you weren't looking for anything serious. But if you've changed your mind about that—or if you think you might change your mind, sometime—"

"Wait, wait," said Renee. "What do you mean, your feelings for me? What feelings?"

The colour in Ket Siong's cheeks deepened.

"You know," he said.

Renee's blank stare must have made it evident that she did not, in fact, know.

Ket Siong said, "I—I'm in love with you."

"Did I know that?" said Renee. "I don't think I knew. You never said. I would definitely have remembered."

Ket Siong was very red. "Wasn't it—I thought it was obvious. Everyone else seemed to know."

Renee's head was spinning. "They did? Who's everyone else?"

"My family. And . . ." Ket Siong cleared his throat. "Dragan."

"Dragan?"

"Your concierge," said Ket Siong, unnecessarily. "We talked when I left your flat last time. After the V&A reception. He remembered me."

"What do you mean, you talked?" said Renee. "What did you talk about?"

"How he's been doing, his family. His daughter's studying engineering at Bristol now," added Ket Siong. "At the end he said, um, 'I always thought you were a good match, you two.'"

Renee found herself feeling glad that Dragan hadn't been on shift that evening.

"But when did this happen?" she said. "I mean, it's not like it was love at first sight, so . . ."

Ket Siong scratched his eyebrow with his thumbnail. "Well."

"Ket Siong."

"Is this such a surprise?" said Ket Siong—dodging the question, Renee noticed. "I said I wanted to keep seeing you, after the V&A."

"OK, I'll buy you were in—" The word "love" stuck in Renee's throat; it was too big. "I'll buy you were interested, from that point." In retrospect, she had to admit the signals he'd been giving since they'd run into each other at the V&A had been pretty clear. "But you can't have liked me since uni."

"I did. I told you, back then."

"No, no. I told *you*," said Renee. Her recollection of that particular conversation was perfectly distinct. She'd gone over it so many times in subsequent years, trying to figure out where she'd gone wrong—what she could have done differently, to alter the outcome. "And you nodded, because you didn't feel you could say I'd got it wrong. You told me you were my friend. That's what you wanted from me."

Ket Siong raised an eyebrow. "And then I kissed you."

OK, he had a point there.

"But you changed your mind," said Renee. "You dumped me."

"That wasn't because I didn't like you," said Ket Siong. He leaned back, his expression sombre. "I found out your father was the reason my mother lost her job. Her firm was representing Chahaya at the time. She was blocking a deal, so they fired her."

"Shit, are you serious?" said Renee, before realising how that might come off. "Sorry, it's not that I don't believe you. I mean, it sounds like Dad. If somebody was holding up a deal he wanted, he wouldn't think twice about getting them fired. But why was your mom blocking it?"

Ket Siong hesitated. "My mother found some irregularities when she was working on the transaction. She made an internal report under the firm's anti–money laundering policy. But it wasn't a popular move."

"I can imagine." Renee dug her thumbs into her temples, pushing her hair back. "So my dad told the firm to fire your mom."

Ket Siong nodded.

Renee was remembering being in his narrow room at halls. Ket Siong saying, *I have to go back*, refusing to look her in the eye.

"That's why you had to break off your studies," she said.

He shrugged. "We were already stretched. It was better for me to go home."

It wasn't a denial.

"Oh my God," said Renee. "Ket Siong, this is terrible. No wonder you resented me."

He'd been so different, after coming back to his room. Renee could summon his expression even now, could recreate every detail. It was the way he'd flinched away from her, like he couldn't bear to look at her, much less touch her.

Even now, the memory stung. Even with an understanding of Ket Siong's reasons, and Ket Siong himself gazing at her with his heart in his eyes.

The change had been so complete and shocking. She'd felt like a piece of garbage, thrown aside.

"I couldn't understand why you were acting that way," she said. "I thought I'd made a mistake. Like I'd pushed you into it, or something."

"No," said Ket Siong. "I think I fell in love with you the day we met. When you sat next to me at Nathalie's piano. Do you remember?"

Renee had asked Ket Siong to teach her the Mozart sonata he'd played for her. She remembered watching his fingers on the keys, trying to reproduce what they did, complaining when she fell short. Ket Siong had tried to help, showing her what she should do with her hands, taking her through each bar. He had been utterly charming.

"A pretty girl sitting next to you, letting you show off," said Renee. "You never had a chance."

"No," Ket Siong agreed. He reached out and took her hand. "The day we first kissed . . . I've never forgotten it. What happened with your father didn't make a difference to how I felt about you. I knew it wasn't your fault. But I felt I owed it to my family to break things off."

He traced the veins in Renee's wrist with his index finger. The touch was light, barely there. Every brush of his fingertip against her skin sent a shivery thrill racing from the back of her neck down her spine.

She swallowed. "Why didn't you tell me?"

Ket Siong's finger paused, resting against the thin skin of her wrist, just over her pulse.

"I promised my brother I wouldn't tell anyone," he said. "I'm sorry, Renee. I know I hurt you. I didn't feel I had a choice, at the time. I've always regretted it."

His hand was large and warm. It felt right, cradling hers. Renee never wanted to let it go.

She made to disentangle their hands. Ket Siong released her, sitting back. She didn't want to see hurt or wariness in his eyes, so she didn't look up.

"I wish I'd known," said Renee. "But I get it. I get why you did it."

A thread had come loose on her jumper. She played with it, twirling the thread around her finger before letting it go.

"But what's changed?" she said. "My dad's still the reason your mom got fired. I don't agree with everything he does. It'd be more accurate to say I disagree with almost everything he does. We have different values. And . . ." She hesitated. "I don't think this thing with Chahaya is going to happen."

"You don't think he'll choose you?"

It was hard to read Ket Siong's tone of voice. Renee couldn't stop herself from sneaking a look at him.

He was waiting for her answer, clear-eyed and calm. She could tell him anything, and he'd listen.

"I think my chances are pretty good," she said. "We got the deal, and I'm still on speaking terms with my brother. I've done everything Dad wanted. That doesn't mean he'll go for me, but . . ." She shook her head. "It doesn't matter. Whatever happens, I don't think I want to do it.

"I don't want to run Chahaya," she repeated, and knew it was true. It was the first time Renee had admitted it to herself. "It's not even about the Freshview deal. I mean, that's what got me thinking about it. But if I took on Chahaya, I'd have to give up Virtu. I couldn't keep running it myself. I could hire somebody else to do it, but . . . and I'd have to move back to Singapore. Back to dinner with the family every Sunday."

She tipped her head back, closing her eyes. "Oh my God, you can't imagine. There was always some stupid fight, every time. Su Beng or Su Khoon would start squabbling about Chahaya, or money, or something dumb one of them did. And I'd be right in the middle of it, this time around. No way out."

She opened her eyes. Her artisanal light fitting twisted on the ceiling, the fluted golden-brown petals of wood casting arced shadows on the wall. Watching the shadows, she said:

"I was so blown away when Dad asked, I didn't think it through. But it's not what I want."

She would have thought the admission would feel like failure. As though she was giving up, not only on all the work she'd put into the pitch, but on her relationship with her family.

At the end of the day, everything she'd done to win Chahaya had been for that. To prove she deserved a place in the family. All she'd wanted was to belong.

So much for that. She'd left Singapore and stopped talking to her family for a reason. If they didn't love her now, as the not particularly wayward daughter whose main offence was that she'd built something of her own and didn't mean to give it up to anyone else, they wouldn't love her just because she was CEO of Chahaya. They'd respect her, maybe, but respect was a cold thing to walk away from a life for.

The thought was painful. But it was a relief, too. She felt like she'd put down a burden.

"But they're my family," said Renee. "That's not going to change. I'm not planning to cut them off, unless they do it first."

Ket Siong said, "I wouldn't expect that of you."

Renee turned her face so her cheek was resting on the back of the chair. The rattan cane was cold against her face, but it meant she could see Ket Siong. "So what makes things different now?"

"It's been ten years," said Ket Siong. "My mother moved on, she found a job she liked better. She's retired now. And what happened, with Stephen . . . it changed things for me." He met her eyes. "It made me realise love isn't something to give up easily."

This time, it was Renee who reached out. She sat up, perching on the edge of her chair, and trailed her fingers along the arcs of his eyebrows, stroking the bridge of his nose. The pad of her finger fit perfectly into the dent above his upper lip.

He was very still, watching her. Renee traced the shape of his mouth, memorising it as though they were going to test her later.

Ket Siong's breathing was harsh. She could feel him trembling under her touch. She leaned over and pressed her lips to his mouth.

The kiss started out gentle, almost chaste, but it didn't stay chaste for long. She wasn't sure if he pulled her towards him, or if she clambered on top of him, but she ended up sprawled across his lap as they kissed. Long, languorous kisses, stealing her breath, Ket Siong's chest moving rapidly under her.

There was something she should say. Renee pulled back so she could remember what it was, giving Ket Siong a little push when he tried to follow her.

"I like you, too," she said. "By the way."

Ket Siong's smile spread across his face like sunlight. He ducked his head and then he was dropping delicate kisses along her neck, tracing a line down to the place where it joined her shoulder, his hands stroking warmth down her back.

Renee said against his hair, "Do you want to move to the bedroom?"

Ket Siong nodded. He slid an arm under her knees, the other around her back, and stood up, surprising a squeak out of her.

"Sweeping me off my feet," said Renee, laughing.

Ket Siong pressed a dreamy kiss to the shell of her ear. A shock of sensation zinged through her, earthing between her thighs. She pressed them together and turned her face to his shoulder, found his collarbone, and bit down.

It occurred to her a moment later that possibly she shouldn't distract him while he was bearing her full weight. But Ket Siong only shivered a little and carried on, through the hallway and into the bedroom. He laid her on the bed carefully, as if she was something precious, before drawing back.

"What is it?" said Renee, with a twinge of apprehension.

The expression in Ket Siong's eyes reassured her.

"Just looking at you," he said.

"Come here," said Renee, pulling him down.

There was a lot of kissing before anything else happened. Ket Siong didn't seem to be in a rush, which was nice, but after a while Renee started getting impatient. She managed to get his hoodie off and the T-shirt underneath. But when she got to work unbuttoning his jeans, he wriggled out of her grasp, pulled off her leggings and underwear, and tossed them over the side of the bed.

She made a noise of protest. Ket Siong looked intent, engrossed in what he was doing. His big warm hands holding her thighs open, he lowered his head and licked her.

Renee forgot about complaining. She fisted her hand in his hair, thrilling when he groaned against her, and gave herself up to pleasure.

She might have been a little noisy when she came. Ket Siong certainly looked smug when he hauled himself up the bed. He didn't seem sure if she would want to kiss him. Renee kissed him a few times to put that beyond doubt, tasting herself on his lips.

"I want you inside me," she said, and felt his cock jerk against her thigh. "There are condoms in the bedside cabinet. In the bottom drawer."

"OK," said Ket Siong breathlessly.

So then they did that. And it was good. It was very good.

Ket Siong was a postcoital cuddler. Renee had forgotten that about him.

"We should have dinner," she said. "Do you want to order in?"

Ket Siong murmured something contented and indecipherable into the back of her neck.

"Can I ask you a question?" said Renee.

"Hmm?"

"What was up with this woman you had a coffee with?"

Ket Siong didn't react to this particularly. Renee would have been able to tell—they were touching all along the length of their bodies. Any tension in him would have communicated itself to her.

"What woman?" he said sleepily.

"You know, when Nathalie ran into you at Foyles. She got worried because you didn't mention you were having coffee with someone when she asked what you were doing there."

That did get a reaction. Ket Siong stiffened—not in a good way. Renee turned, wriggling away a little so she could get a proper look at him.

His eyes were open. He was frowning. "Was Nathalie spying on me?"

"She just happened to be there," said Renee. "But for the record, she absolutely would spy on you. Nathalie's hated you ever since you broke my heart. She made me burn your pictures."

"Really?"

"She thought I needed to move on," said Renee. "I had a hard time getting over you."

Ket Siong's eyes softened. He brushed Renee's hair back, tucking a lock behind her ear. "It was Low Teck Wee's daughter. The woman I was meeting. I was trying to find out about Stephen."

"*Oh*," said Renee. "Is that how you found him?"

Ket Siong shook his head. "It was through a journalist. Helen Daley. She writes a blog called—"

"The *Hornbill Gazette*." At Ket Siong's look, Renee said, "I told you, I did some research. Is she writing an article about Freshview?"

"Er . . ."

"It's OK, you don't need to answer that. You're really bad at lying, by the way," she added, kissing him on the chin. "It's cute. Can you put me in touch with her? Just to talk."

Ket Siong was looking like he couldn't decide whether to be miffed or not. "Talk about?"

"Business," said Renee. She was buzzing with energy, the beginnings of a plan coalescing in her head. "You told me I'd figure it out, and I think I have."

She rolled over onto Ket Siong, pushing him onto his back, and kissed him. Partly because it was thanks to him she'd had her idea, but mostly because she could. His mouth opened under hers. She nipped his bottom lip, licking it to soothe the sting. Ket Siong hummed deep inside his throat, sliding a hand up the back of her thigh.

Renee had been starting to feel a little peckish, but she decided she wasn't *that* hungry—not for food, at least.

For once, Ket Siong didn't seem inclined to worry about her food intake. She wasn't about to remind him. Dinner could wait.

29

Renee insisted on walking Ket Siong to the station in the morning. He put up some resistance, but not much. He wasn't ready to say goodbye to her yet.

Their route took them down a street lined with elegant nineteenth-century buildings. There weren't many other people around, early on a Friday morning, so Ket Siong took note of the guy walking behind them. He was in a light grey puffer jacket and jeans, with a bulky cross-body bag slung over a shoulder. Asian, but what kind of Asian was hard to tell, thanks to the cap pulled low over his face.

Ket Siong wasn't in a temper to pay attention to anything that wasn't Renee, but it struck him that there was something vaguely familiar about the man. They'd passed the Zambian High Commission and the Korean Consulate when he worked out where he'd seen the guy before.

There had been a man in a light-coloured puffer and a cap, with a cross-body bag, in Hyde Park yesterday. Ket Siong had passed him just before he'd seen what had turned out to be Renee, hunkered down on the path.

There began to be, in Ket Siong's mind, something that was not quite suspicion, but the hazy outline of a question mark.

He turned his head to slide a look at the man out of the corner of his eye. The man sped up, overtaking Ket Siong and Renee on the pavement.

Something about this, and the way the man was holding his shoulders, solidified Ket Siong's growing suspicion.

"Excuse me," he said.

Renee glanced up at him, surprised.

The man's pace quickened.

Ket Siong raised his voice. "Excuse me." He let go of Renee's hand, taking a step towards the man.

The man broke into a run.

Ket Siong did not pause to think about what he should do next. He lunged after him. But the man had about a yard on Ket Siong, and he was fast, despite the bag bumping on his back. He pelted down the street, running flat out.

Ket Siong was at risk of losing him, when a van pulled out of a driveway ahead of them. The man checked, stumbling. That delayed him just enough for Ket Siong to get close. He threw himself at the man and they went down together.

The man jarred his shoulder against the pavement, swearing fruitily in Cantonese. His accent sounded Malaysian, but Ket Siong had assumed it would.

"Why were you following me?" he said, in the same language. "Who are you?"

"Motherfucker! Are you crazy or what?" said the man. "I'm not following you. Who the hell are you? Get off me!"

He tried to throw Ket Siong off. Ket Siong slammed him back to the ground and said, "I saw you last night, at Hyde Park."

"So what if I was at Hyde Park?" said the man belligerently. "Are you the only person who's allowed to go to Hyde Park?"

Renee caught up with them, looking alarmed. "Are you OK? What's going on?"

Ket Siong switched to English for her benefit.

"If you weren't following me," he said, "why run away when I called after you?"

The man glowered. "Let go!"

"I'll let you go if you answer me," said Ket Siong. "Who told you to follow me?"

"I don't know what you are talking about."

"Was it Low Teck Wee?" Another possibility occurred to Ket Siong, far more disturbing. "Are you Special Branch?"

Ket Siong would have expected this to elicit a furious denial, if it was anywhere near to the truth. The man's expression was reassuring: he merely looked baffled.

"Special Branch?" he said. His eyes flicked to Renee. "Special Branch also wants to follow you? For what?"

"What's in your bag?" said Renee.

The bag was under the man's body. Ket Siong hadn't thought to look in it. There was a minor scuffle while he remedied the oversight.

"Don't break!" said the man. "It's expensive!"

"Camera," said Ket Siong. It was a serious one, too. Ket Siong could imagine it would record decent footage, even in a park at night.

"Thought so," said Renee. She folded her arms, turning on the man a coolly assessing gaze, like that of a gardener who has come across a particularly unpleasant slug.

Ket Siong had seen versions of this look on Renee's face before, mostly when she was discussing Andrew or her brothers. He found himself disturbingly into it.

"Who was it who hired you?" said Renee. "Goh Su Beng, or Goh Su Khoon?"

"Who are you?" said the man. "Why so many people want to follow you? Are you famous or what?"

"Tell us, and he'll let you go," said Renee. "Otherwise, we can all go to the police station together. Stalking is a crime, you know."

The man opened his mouth. Renee said, "And if we have a look at what's on that camera, it might be hard for you to argue you haven't been following us."

"The client won't give me their name," said the man sulkily. "You think they're so stupid?"

"Somebody has to be making the arrangements," said Renee. "Is it a lady called Jessie Chan?"

The man scoffed. "You really think everybody wants to know your business—"

"Or Penny Ooi?"

The man's expression froze. After a moment, he said, "I won't tell you anything. You let me go, or I'll call the police."

"It's OK," said Renee to Ket Siong. "You can let him up. I know who it is now."

"Who's Penny Ooi?"

"Su Khoon's PA," said Renee. She passed a hand over her face, sighing. "Here I was, thinking we were getting along better."

Ket Siong considered the situation. "Should I take the camera?"

"It's fine," said Renee. "It's not like there's going to be anything on there that's going to make a difference to anything." She shook her head, wry. "My brother's problem is he can never predict what I'm going to do. What I'm planning is going to piss Dad off more than any blackmail material he could come up with."

Ket Siong got off their follower. The guy stood up, shook himself, glared at Ket Siong and stomped off, back the way they came.

"I'll have to tell Dragan to keep an eye out for him," said Renee.

"Do you think . . ." Ket Siong hesitated. "Your brother wouldn't do anything worse."

"Oh, he wouldn't hire someone to hurt me. Not physically," said Renee. "Not unless I really pissed him off. Don't worry."

Ket Siong did not find this reassuring. He wished he hadn't let her come out with him.

314 · ZEN CHO

"I can hear you worrying," said Renee. "That's a direct contradiction of orders."

When he didn't smile back, she said, "Look, I'll take a cab home from the station if it really bothers you. Are you sure you're OK?"

She checked him over, brushing his shoulders to rid them of some microscopic contamination, visible only to her. He found himself relaxing under her touch, despite himself.

"Are *you* OK?" he said.

Renee shrugged. "I'm fine." She wouldn't meet his eyes. "It makes me feel better, in a way. I was feeling bad about what I'm going to do—you know, with the Freshview deal. My brother agreed to work with me in good faith, and I'm about to turn around and blow that all up."

It was important not to criticise Renee's family to her. She would only feel obliged to defend them.

But Ket Siong couldn't let this pass.

"As I recall," he said, "he agreed to work with you after it turned out he couldn't blackmail you. After you caught him with his mistress."

"I think she was just a hookup," said Renee. "It's OK. Really. I've always known what my brothers are like. It's not a shock, like if your brother did something like this to you. You guys actually trust each other."

A woman in running gear jogged past them, her face pink and set. Across the road, two men got out of a van and started extracting a ladder and buckets of paint from the back. Ket Siong put his arms around Renee, slightly tentative. He wasn't sure yet how she felt about public displays of affection.

She was stiff at first, her shoulders locked with tension. Ket Siong was about to release her, step back to give her space. But all of a sudden Renee melted into the embrace, turning her face into his chest.

"I'm so stupid," she said, in a low voice. He had to strain to catch the words. "I don't know why I keep setting myself up for this, every time."

Ket Siong wished they were somewhere private. He needed to go home. Before falling asleep the night before, he'd remembered to text Ket Hau not to expect him back, but he hadn't supplied a reason. Ma would be worrying. And he had classes to teach, later that day.

But left to himself, he would have turned around and gone back to Renee's flat with her. He didn't want to let her go. The appearance of Su Khoon's hired man had broken the unthinking optimism to which he had woken that morning. It seemed now all too likely that something would go wrong, that someone would snatch Renee away from him, shatter this extraordinary happiness.

"Why don't I walk you home?" said Ket Siong. "It would only take a few minutes."

Renee shook her head. "I said I'd walk you to the station and I'm going to." She drew back, wiping her eyes. "If I let my family stop me from living my life, I might as well give up now. They're never going to change. I can't let them intimidate me."

This was admirable, in principle. In practice, Ket Siong would have liked to pack Renee up and keep her somewhere safe.

Renee slipped her hand into his. "Come on, let's keep walking. I've got a call at half nine. Trying to resolve this supplier nightmare we've got."

Ket Siong wavered, but the reference to her work got him moving, as Renee had probably known it would.

"Tell me," she said, "what's up with all this chasing people down? Seems a strange hobby for a classical pianist. Did you do a stint at a police academy or something?"

"I got into martial arts after I went back home. I used to go with Stephen."

"What kind of martial arts?" Renee brightened. "Could you teach me? I've always fancied being able to kill someone with my bare hands."

Ket Siong frowned. "It's not really about that."

Renee glanced at her phone.

"We've got ten minutes before we get there," she said. "Tell me what it's about."

30

$\mathcal{S}$u Khoon had slides for their meeting with their father up on an iPad, positioned on the dining table so Renee and their father could see them.

It was the first time Renee had seen her brother since they'd found out they'd won the Freshview deal. She'd begged off the meeting he wanted to have when he was back from Italy, claiming illness, and ignored the subsequent messages and emails from him and his team. There hadn't been that many, before Su Khoon had suddenly gone quiet. Renee assumed his hired man had reported back on being found out.

She hadn't bothered following up. She'd been busy with other matters. It had been a crowded week—but a productive one.

It was just the three of them in the family's Chelsea townhouse. Su Khoon's wife had taken the kids out, at Dad's command. Su Khoon had tried suggesting that Jessie join them, but Dad was traditional about daughters-in-law: they had all the obligations of a daughter, none of the rights. Jessie wouldn't dare come back before dinnertime.

Su Khoon obviously hadn't worked with Renee on the presentation, so he was doing all the talking.

"I just thought of doing slides last night," he said offhandedly to Dad. "Haven't had a chance to coordinate with Renee."

He couldn't quite stop himself from shooting Renee a quick glance at this point.

Renee was leaning back in her chair, her arms crossed. She kept her smile bright.

She'd have her chance to speak. In the meantime, she was interested to see what Su Khoon had to say.

It was an impressive presentation. Su Khoon went through the deal they'd struck with Freshview, their plans for working together, the projected returns for Chahaya, and future opportunities they could explore. He even remembered to say "we" some of the time.

Dad asked a couple of questions, but mostly he listened, leafing through the briefing pack Su Khoon had supplied. When Su Khoon was done, Dad turned to Renee.

"You've been very quiet," he said.

"She's been busy," said Su Khoon quickly. "Got a launch for Virtu coming up."

"That's next year," said Renee. Her tone was light, but the reference to Virtu at Home smarted. She hadn't found an alternative supplier yet. "Next year" was optimistic.

Well, she'd have all the time in the world to devote to putting Virtu in order, after this.

"Did you, uh, did you have anything to add?" said Su Khoon. He nodded at the slides.

He was evidently in some suspense about how and when she was going to introduce the fact he'd been having her followed. In his place, Renee might have tried to get ahead of the revelation, announced it herself. That way, Su Khoon could frame it in a favourable light. After all, he could always fall back on claiming he was worried about Renee, had hired a guy to follow her around London with a camera for her own safety.

But of course, that wasn't the only secret Renee was keeping for him. Maybe he was wary of trying her patience too far.

Though in that case, he really should have resisted the temptation to do a solo presentation effectively taking the credit for the deal they had won together. Careers had been ruined for lesser offences.

Part of Renee was enjoying his nervousness, not least because it was a distraction from her own trepidation. Dad was not going to be happy about her news.

Oh well. No point in putting it off.

"I do, actually," said Renee. She turned to her father. "I'm afraid the deal's off. Freshview's going with someone else, a British player. Er Ge should be getting the email soon. It's an easy choice for them to justify. They'll say we don't have the local contacts. That was always the weakness of our pitch."

The two men stared at her.

"What are you talking about?" said Su Khoon.

Dad looked from him to Renee. "I thought you all were working together?"

"We were," said Su Khoon, correcting himself: "I thought we were. *I* was being collaborative."

"Oh yes," said Renee. "You've been paying very close attention to my business."

Su Khoon went red.

Dad said, "Then?"

Renee uncrossed her arms, clasping her hands and resting them on the table.

"Around the time we were pitching Freshview, I received some concerning intelligence about the company," she said. "I hired some people to look into it, and I talked to contacts at Freshview. The group has a chequered history in Malaysia. They're the subject of a lawsuit accusing them of illicit logging in Sarawak, and there are rumours they were involved in the disappearance of an activist in KL some years back. In my view, they're not a company Chahaya should be doing business with."

She reached over to her bag on the chair next to her, pulled out a plastic folder, and slid it across the table to her father. He picked it up gingerly, as though it might bite him.

"I printed off some documents, in case you want to look through them," she said. "I can email the materials to you, Er Ge."

"What the hell?" said Su Khoon, his voice rising. "Dad, I don't know what this is all about. This is the first I've heard of any of this." He turned to Renee. "What's wrong with you? You told me you wanted to work together. Now you're trying to blow up the deal? Because, what, Andrew Yeoh rubbed your knee at lunch?"

"What did Andrew Yeoh do?" said Dad, looking up from the folder.

"That's a separate issue," said Renee. "Andrew Yeoh has a record of sexually harassing his staff. Turns out there have been quite a few complaints by Freshview employees."

"That's what you were getting so cosy with Hazlina about," said Su Khoon, his lip curling. "I suppose you encouraged her to report Andrew. So long as you get your revenge, you don't care what happens. What's Lin going to do if she gets pushed out of the company? Did you bother to ask yourself that?"

"Funny you should mention it," said Renee. "Lin's decided to leave Freshview. She's going to be joining Virtu as our new business affairs manager. I've been feeling the need for someone who can take on the strategic side of the business, free me up so I can focus more on the creative side. It's a new direction for Lin, but I think her skillset's a good fit for us.

"Anyway," she went on, having struck Su Khoon speechless, "the sexual harassment allegations are a problem for Freshview's HR department, not us. It's the *Guardian* exposé you should be worried about."

That got Dad's attention. "What exposé?"

"Do you know the *Guardian*, Dad?" said Renee. "It's one of the big UK newspapers. They're planning to publish an article on corruption in Sarawak. Freshview features heavily."

Dad was frowning. "How do you know that?"

"I spoke to the journalist," said Renee.

Dad flicked through the papers in the folder she'd given him, his eyes darting over the pages. "You told Low Teck Wee all this?"

"I haven't had any contact with Low Teck Wee," said Renee. "Though I did DM Felicia Handoko and mention some of the things her husband's said to me. I wasn't sure she'd believe me, but I guess she must have had her suspicions. We had quite a long chat. It was a few days after that that I heard Freshview are looking for a new construction partner."

Renee inspected her nails. They were growing out. She needed to make an appointment for a manicure.

"But who knows what's going to happen after the *Guardian* piece is out?" she said. "Freshview would have given warranties when they won the project. The government here's been bigging it up, it's a showpiece for them. They're not going to enjoy being embarrassed. It's not too late for Freshview to get kicked off the development."

Renee should probably leave it there. It wasn't any of her business any longer. She'd declared her position by doing this— and that was firmly outside the circle of family entrusted with Chahaya's interests.

But it was impossible to resist the temptation to be clever, with Su Khoon snorting and turning purple on the other side of the table. She added:

"Of course, Chahaya has contacts with the Malaysian state investors, too."

Dad had been looking like he couldn't decide whether to rage out, or to find a dark, quiet place where he could lie down and try to forget he'd ever had children. He perked up.

"You think we can take over the development," he said.

"It's speculation at this stage," said Renee. "But Chahaya would be well placed to do it."

Su Khoon finally found his voice.

"Selling crap on Instagram is good PR training, huh?" he said. His fingers were twitching slightly where they were resting on the table, but apart from that he was remarkably controlled. "Teaches you how to present your fuckups as wins. Since you're being so upfront, telling us about what's been keeping you busy, why don't you tell Dad about your little boyfriend?"

Su Khoon probably didn't expect Renee to roll her eyes.

"Why don't *you* tell Dad?" she said. "Since you know so much. I'm sure Dad's going to be shocked to hear that sometimes I go on dates."

Su Khoon glared at her. "You know there's more to it than that."

"Oh, please enlighten me," said Renee.

Su Khoon was already leaning over to grab the iPad, bringing up an image on the screen.

It was a shot of Renee with Ket Siong as they left her building together, the morning after he'd found her in Hyde Park. Su Khoon's guy must have taken the shot mere minutes before Ket Siong clocked him.

Dad squinted at the iPad. "I thought you're with that singer? What's his name, Jason?"

"That's over now," said Renee. "For the record, the reason why Er Ge has this picture is because he had me followed." She added to Su Khoon, "That's messed up, by the way. No wonder you think Andrew's behaviour is fine."

Su Khoon shrugged. "I didn't know if you could be trusted. Who knows what kind of nonsense you might have been getting up to? Turns out I was right, no?"

Dad ignored their bickering with the ease of long practice.

"Who's this, in the photo?" he said to Renee. "He's Singaporean?"

"His name's Yap Ket Siong. He's from Malaysia," said Renee. It wasn't like it mattered what Dad thought of Ket Siong. But moved by some obscure impulse, she said, "His mom was a lawyer, but she's retired now."

"Lawyer?" Dad picked up the iPad so he could bring it closer to his eyes. "Looks like a decent boy. What firm was the mother at?"

"His mother is Chang Yin Lok," said Su Khoon sharply. "Ten years ago, she was working at Khalid and Balasubramaniam in KL. You remember, when SB Permata was trying to acquire the land for Uptown Mall? The deal almost got called off." He pointed at Ket Siong's blurry image on the screen. "His mother was the lawyer who was causing the problem."

"You told the firm to fire her," said Renee.

She wasn't sure why she said it. It wasn't like Dad was going to admit to having done wrong.

"Oh, the activist," he said. "I remember."

He didn't seem overly perturbed. Given some of the other boys Renee had brought home, maybe it struck him as a nonissue. Derek Lim's mother had sold laksa in a hawker centre.

"It's clear what's happening here," said Su Khoon. "This woman, Chang Yin Lok, has a grudge against Chahaya. Renee's seeing the son and he's fed her some rumours about Freshview. Do you think she's up for the job of leading Chahaya? What's to stop her from sabotaging the business if it doesn't meet her boyfriend's approval?"

Renee began, "The *Guardian* wouldn't be publishing an exposé about Freshview if it was simply rumours—"

Dad crooked a finger. It was the signal he used when he wanted silence. Renee shut up despite herself.

"This boy, what's his name—he's your new boyfriend?" he said.

Renee's cheeks warmed.

She and Ket Siong hadn't talked about their relationship status. They'd barely even spoken since the day the picture on Su Khoon's iPad was taken. She'd been so busy laying the ground for this meeting, the only time she'd seen Ket Siong in the intervening period was when he'd taken her to meet Helen Daley.

She knew how she felt about him, even if she'd yet to say it out loud, but this thing between them was so new and fragile. Could she really trust it was serious?

Then she remembered the way he'd looked at her when they'd

last parted—a long, steady look, as though he was drinking her in, trying to imprint her image on the back of his brain. Her chest flooded with light.

"Yes," she said.

"Hmm," said Dad. Su Khoon opened his mouth, but Dad said, "I've heard enough for now. I called this meeting because I wanted to tell you two about the succession planning for Chahaya. I spoke to your brother already."

He rubbed his temples. "Su Beng has been taken off his project. I'm putting somebody else in his place. If he could do the job, he would be the next CEO, but he cannot manage it. It must be one of you. But if I give it to Su Khoon, it will be Jessie who runs the business."

Su Khoon said, "That's not—"

"You had your turn," said Dad. "Right now, I'm talking."

His very mildness was a warning. Su Khoon quietened down, looking disgruntled.

"Jessie is a clever girl. But she is not a Goh," said Dad. "Su Ren is too emotional, and the way she makes decisions is hard to predict. But in business, you need somebody who can work hard, who can sacrifice, and who is willing to take risks. So I was planning to appoint her."

Renee caught her breath. Her heartbeat was thundering in her ears.

She'd imagined the triumph of this moment so many times, craving the recognition it would represent.

None of her fantasies had involved her blowing up the Freshview deal. She'd given up on the idea of being chosen when she'd decided to do that. But that yearning for validation remained, woven through her body, even if her mind knew Chahaya wasn't what she wanted.

"But now you tell me you've pulled us out of the Freshview deal," said Dad. "Some more you went and interfered in the family affairs, talking to the nephew's wife and all this." He sighed. "So I don't need to ask Low Teck Wee if he wants to play golf anymore."

"Dad," said Su Khoon and Renee, at the same time.

"Wait until I finish first," said Dad. He settled back in his chair, looking weary. "You shouldn't have run off to do all this by yourself. This kind of major decision, you must get the stakeholders on board.

"But," said Dad, "I can see the problems with Freshview. Singaporean government is very sensitive about corruption. We have to be careful. And if the development goes out for retendering, that will be interesting for us."

He gazed into the middle distance, seeming not to see either of his children.

"It's too early to decide," he said. He straightened up and took off his glasses, putting them in the front pocket of his shirt. "Su Ren will be acting CEO for one year. Then we'll see how. If you can win this London development, we will formalise the appointment. Otherwise, it will go to Su Khoon."

"But—" said Su Khoon.

Dad got up. "I'm going to rest. Call me when the children are back."

When Dad was done with you, you were done. That didn't stop Su Khoon from saying, "But *Dad* . . ."

Dad ignored him, lumbering off to the stairs. He had a foot on the first step when he checked and turned around.

"Of course," he said, "you must finish with this boy. What's the name, Yap—? The lawyer's son. Your mother has a friend, her eldest is divorcing his wife. Forty years old, no children. The father owns a media company in Hong Kong."

"I'm good, thanks," said Renee.

"At your age, you should be thinking about getting married," said Dad. "Otherwise, it'll be too late to have children. We can arrange a meeting with the man when you're back in Singapore." He yawned, about to head off up the stairs.

"Dad," said Renee. "You haven't asked me yet."

He looked back again, surprised. His eyes were red and a lit-tle watery, the lids drooping. Dad had been straight-backed and strong for as long as Renee could remember, but as he stood there by the stairs, she saw that he was stooping, his shoulders curving in. Her heart failed her.

Her father's force of personality, his power, his position as the head of the family all made it hard to remember he was a human being, subject to human frailty. But for once Renee looked at him and saw not Goh Kheng Tat, a man possessed of more wealth and resources than most people ever dreamt of having. She saw an old man, worn out from jet lag, the burden of responsibility, and the intransigence of his children.

"You know how many people work for Chahaya Group?" he'd said to her once, when she was a teenager. Su Beng or Su Khoon had messed something up—she couldn't remember what, now. "Fifteen thousand. If I don't work hard, or I make a mistake, fif-teen thousand families will lose their rice bowl. Means it's worth taking seriously, right?"

If only she could have left this conversation for another day, put off the moment when she had to disappoint him yet again. But there wasn't time. Dad was flying off in a few days' time, and once Jessie knew about the outcome of this meeting, there would be no hope of keeping the news within the family.

Dad's brow furrowed. "Asked what?"

"If I'm going to accept the job," said Renee.

31

No one responded when Renee texted Dad, Su Khoon, and Jessie to ask what time they were leaving for the airport. But she had their flight details from Dad's PA, who was acutely conscious of the fact that rebooking the flights at Dad's demand meant they were leaving on Renee's birthday. Miss Adibah already had a guilty conscience over all the times she'd cancelled birthday dinners and scheduled business meetings against school plays and graduation ceremonies. Getting the information out of her had been easy.

Dad liked to be at the airport early, so Renee turned up at the Chelsea house midafternoon, five hours before their evening flight back to Singapore. It was Jessie who opened the door.

"Oh," she said.

Renee had come for reasons no one could fault, but there was no denying that Jessie's expression was a reward for her effort. She'd never seen her sister-in-law quite so much at a loss before.

Renee smiled. "Came to say goodbye." She raised a shopping bag. "I got some things for the kids. Nothing big. I thought they could play with them on the flight."

"Oh, you shouldn't have," said Jessie, recovering. "The kids will be so excited to see you. Kai made you a birthday card, we were going to post it. Guys, Gu Gu is here!"

Renee followed her through to the reception room, where Su Khoon's three kids were watching TV. Dad was on the sofa, frowning over his iPad.

"Your brother's upstairs," said Jessie. "I'll tell him you're here."

She slipped out of the room before she could be detained by either kids or in-laws, and who could blame her?

Dodging enthusiastic greetings from her nieces and nephew, who recognised the Hamleys branding on her shopping bag, Renee said:

"Hey, Dad. All packed?"

Without looking at her, Dad got up from the sofa, tucked the iPad under his arm, and went out of the room.

"Where's Gong Gong going?"

"He's going to get ready," said Renee. She had been prepared for the snub, so it only hurt a little to watch him leave the room, back stiff with affront.

She knelt, turning a smile on the kids. "You guys want to see what I've got for you?"

Su Khoon came downstairs while she was distributing her gifts. It was their first meeting since it had been decided that Su Khoon would be CEO of Chahaya. He looked as dubious about having the pleasure of Renee's company as Jessie had.

The kids' presence was helpful. First it was necessary to mediate between the girls when they fought over which of the two nearly identical Disney Princess arts-and-crafts kits they wanted. Then it transpired the youngest boy had concluded from Renee's sudden appearance that she was coming back to Singapore with them. Soothing him when the truth was broken to him consumed all of Renee and Su Khoon's attention.

By the time Jessie and the nanny showed up to whip the kids away for a pre-departure snack and shower, any awkwardness was gone.

Renee said to Su Khoon, with feeling, "I don't know how you do it."

"Two helpers and a nanny," said Su Khoon. "It's like a bloody zoo." He collapsed onto the sofa. "You've seen Dad?"

Renee inclined her head. "And he saw me. Didn't talk to me, of course. That would be going too far."

Su Khoon humphed. "Why'd you come? You know what Dad's like."

"I know. I thought he'd be more upset if I didn't come, though," said Renee. "Anyway, I haven't congratulated you yet."

Su Khoon slanted a suspicious glance at her. "Are you trying to make me feel bad?"

Renee met the glance head-on. "Is it working?"

Su Khoon looked away first.

"I hope you don't think I'm going to apologise or whatever," he said. "I told you from the start. Just because I'm working with you, doesn't mean I'm not going to try to win. We were in a contest. Blame Dad if you want to blame anyone."

"I'm trying not to," said Renee. "Blame anyone, I mean."

She gazed up at the family portrait over the fireplace. At least she hadn't annoyed anyone badly enough yet to move them to cut her out of it.

There they were, five strangers crowded into one place, for the duration of a lifetime. She could step out of the picture, or she could try to make the best of it.

"I don't want to do business with you," said Renee, her eyes on the portrait. "But I want to have a relationship with my family."

The teenaged Su Khoon in the picture was pale and lanky, eyes wary behind his glasses. She wondered if he'd got bullied at school. If he had, she'd be the last person he would admit that to.

It was a slight surprise when the Su Khoon of the present day spoke.

"I told Dad we should stay," he said gruffly. "It's your birthday and all that. And the kids haven't had a chance to try Yauatcha. Ridiculous to rush off like this, just because he's angry."

"It's OK," said Renee earnestly. "Really. Don't feel bad about that. I'll take the kids to Yauatcha another time."

Su Khoon snorted. "You probably don't want to spend your birthday with us anyway."

Renee didn't bother denying it.

After a moment, Su Khoon said, "Don't worry about Dad. He'll get over it. You're his daughter, at the end of the day."

Renee nodded. She got to her feet. "You guys will want to sort yourselves out. I'll leave you to it."

She was at the door when Su Khoon said, "Eh. Renee."

Renee looked back.

"Good luck," said her brother. "With your new guy and all."

"Thanks," said Renee, after a pause. "You too."

She paused in the hallway, hesitating. The stairs to the other floors were to her left, the front door to her right. She turned left.

Dad's study was on the first floor. The door was shut. Renee knocked and opened it without waiting for a response.

Dad was at his desk, with the iPad propped up in front of him. His reading glasses were on his forehead. He adjusted them hastily, sitting up as she entered the room. She had the impression he hadn't been doing much reading.

"I'm going now, Dad," said Renee. "Have a safe flight."

Dad stared down at his iPad, his mouth locked in a straight line. Renee lingered well past the point of discomfort—but if Dad didn't want to speak to her, there was nothing she could do about it except wait him out. She'd done it before.

She was turning to go when Dad cleared his throat.

"You're going where?" he said. He clamped his mouth shut, looking annoyed at himself.

"Back to the flat," said Renee. "I took leave today." *For my birthday*, she didn't need to say.

She half thought Dad might acknowledge it was her birthday. But he just said, "Hmph," resettled his glasses on his nose, and bent his head studiously over his iPad.

She felt it counted as a win, all the same. Descending the stairs, Renee decided she was glad she'd come.

When she got back to her building, it was to the somewhat surprising scene of Dragan hanging out with Ket Siong on the sofas in the foyer, chatting.

Ket Siong saw her first. He was surrounded by tote bags bulging with groceries. A leek stuck out of one of them. He said something to Dragan, who got up, clapping him on the shoulder. Renee got a nod and an approving smile as Dragan went back to his post.

It was a little weird getting more emotional validation from the concierge than her own father. Dad would say it was easy to praise other people's children.

Ket Siong stood up at her approach. Renee could see that one of the tote bags had a bouquet of flowers in it.

"This is a nice surprise," she said.

Ket Siong ducked his head. "You said you weren't seeing your family for your birthday anymore. I thought I could make you dinner. If you want."

Renee put her head on one side. "What are you going to do with all of that if I say no?"

Ket Siong considered his shopping, strewn around him. He appeared to have bought enough to cater for a football team. "My family could have it tomorrow. My brother's taking my mother out for dinner tonight."

"Come on," said Renee. She reached out for the bags, but Ket Siong intervened before she could pick any of them up.

"I can manage," he said, so Renee left him to it.

Ket Siong was unenthusiastic when Renee offered to help with the cooking, but he did allow her to snap the roots off the bean sprouts.

"That's about my level," said Renee. She took a picture of their shining white stems, heaped in a metal bowl on her marble table. It was the kind of thing her Instagram followers would go wild for, with its nostalgic associations with Chinese grandmas at work.

The flowers he'd got her were clearly visible in the background. A bunch of gerberas from Tesco, more cheerful than romantic, costing all of five pounds. She touched a bright pink petal and smiled.

That would pique interest, too. Let Instagram speculate. She'd do a soft launch of the new man in time.

Ket Siong was moving around her kitchen as though he'd lived there for years, taking out pots and pans and cooking utensils. Renee moved to the kitchen island so she could watch him better, bringing the bean sprouts with her.

"I didn't even know I had a colander," she said. "What are those? Cooking chopsticks? Those must be from Auntie Mindy's time. How did you know where to find all this stuff?"

Ket Siong went pink. "I had a look the last time I was here. I used to wish I could cook for you, when we were students. Like Derek Lim."

Renee laughed. "Derek said it was his secret weapon."

"His food was OK," said Ket Siong repressively.

"Ket Siong," said Renee, charmed, "were you jealous of Derek?"

Ket Siong didn't dignify that with an answer. He filled the kettle at the tap, put it on to boil, and said:

"I've been meaning to tell you. I sent in a video to that competition you told me about. I got into the next round. Auditions are in March."

Renee's eyes widened. "Ket Siong, that's fantastic!"

That made him bashful. He drew his head in a little, like a turtle withdrawing into its shell. "We'll see what happens."

"This is a double celebration, then," said Renee. "We should get cake!" She abandoned the bean sprouts, picking up her phone. "There are a couple of Japanese patisseries nearby. I wonder if they deliver . . . Do you like crepe cakes?"

"I got a cake," said Ket Siong, nodding at the bags he hadn't unpacked yet. "Nothing special, though. Pandan chiffon cake. I picked it up in Chinatown."

"OK, that is my *favourite* kind of cake. Forget Japanese patisserie." Renee put down her phone. "How do you know all the things I like?"

Ket Siong gave her a sidelong glance, smiling a little. But he only said, "If you want to have those with your noodles"—meaning the neglected bean sprouts—"you'd better keep working."

"OK, *fine*," said Renee. She felt suddenly, absurdly happy.

They were quiet for a while, Ket Siong chopping vegetables—he'd even brought a knife sharpener with him—and Renee working through her pile of veg.

It was Ket Siong who broke the silence. "Did you manage to see your family?"

"Yeah." Renee nipped the root off a bean sprout and tossed it into a bowl. "Dad's pretty mad at me. And my brother doesn't know whether to send me a Fortnum & Mason hamper or a turd in a box. But it was worth going."

"They're angry about the Freshview deal?"

"It's not just that." Renee paused. "You know, Dad's devoted his entire life to Chahaya. He spent more time growing the business than raising us. He was asking me to take over his life's work, and I turned him down. Of course he's unhappy with me. I get it."

Ket Siong said, "I wish your family put in as much effort to try to understand you."

The look in his eyes made her shy. Renee looked down at her phone and saw a notification on the screen. "Oh hey, Nathalie's sent a voice note. Do you mind . . . ?"

She put it on speaker so she could keep going with the bean sprouts. Nathalie's voice filled the room.

"Happy birthday, babe. I hope you have had a perfect day and got yourself a nice treat or three. My present is on its way, I ordered it online. We need to go for cocktails very soon, I have so much to tell you about my nemesis. Are you free next week? Let's go to the Savoy, we need to cleanse it of Andrew's presence. I will bring sage and sixty litres of bleach. Don't worry about that yowl, it is only Thomas whose father is very cruel, he is giving him a bath. I have to go, but let me know when you can go for drinks, and I want to know all your news. How is it with Virtu and your family whom I hate, and have you started sexting with that knobhead Ket or are you still pretending you are just friends?"

The voice note ended before Renee could pause it. She bent her head over her bowl, avoiding meeting Ket Siong's eyes.

"She really doesn't like me." Ket Siong sounded more puzzled than offended. It was probably a novel experience for him, being disliked.

"It's only because she thinks you're two-timing me," said Renee. "Can I tell her about Stephen? If she knew you were having coffee with Low Teck Wee's daughter that time, that might help. I don't want her to hate you, if you're going to be my boyfriend."

This elicited a much stronger reaction from Ket Siong than overhearing himself being called names. He stiffened, his knife hovering midair above the chopping board.

"Am I your boyfriend?" he said.

"I have a vacancy," said Renee lightly. "Would you like to fill it?"

Ket Siong put down the knife, wiped his hands on a tea towel, and came over to her. Renee was feeling a little too exposed to want to look at him directly, but once she glanced up, she couldn't look away. Under his gaze, fearlessly loving, her levity seemed cheap, revealed for the flimsy protection against hurt it was.

"Please don't hurt me," she whispered.

Ket Siong put his arms around her, drawing her close. She could feel the steady beat of his heart under her cheek. She closed her eyes.

"I'll try not to," he said. "I'll try my best."

Epilogue

Christmas Day

*W*hat do you think?" said Renee.

Ket Siong had stayed over at her flat the night before, relying on the somewhat thin excuse that Renee might need help finding his place on Christmas Day. They'd said they'd arrive midmorning, so they could help Ma and Ket Hau prepare the lunch, but Ket Siong was regretting that agreement. They were running late.

He'd been imagining a luxuriously slow start to the day, involving a protracted lie-in. Instead, he'd spent the morning sitting on Renee's bed while she stressed out about what she should wear for two hours straight.

This dress was black, with a pattern of blowsy white roses. It had long sleeves and a square neckline, low enough to reveal an enchanting glimpse of cleavage. Renee smoothed the fabric over her hips.

"It's nice," said Ket Siong. Watching the movement of her hands, he wondered if that was something he could offer to help with.

Renee glared at him. "You said that about the last one, too."

"But they've all been nice," said Ket Siong, bemused. Renee didn't usually need reassuring about her appearance. "You always look nice."

"I'm meeting your family for the first time," said Renee. "*Nice* isn't enough. I need to look right." She turned back to the mirror, tugging at the dress and grimacing. "I think it's too low-cut. Can you help me unzip it?"

Ket Siong would happily have assisted with taking the dress the rest of the way off, but the moment he was finished with the zip, Renee vanished into the depths of her wardrobe. When she re-emerged, she was tucking a high-collared cream blouse into a floaty midi skirt in a peachy beige.

This outfit was indeed more demure than the previous one, but somehow it was even sexier. Before Ket Siong could start day-dreaming about pulling Renee down onto the bed and reaching up underneath that skirt, she said:

"Your mom loves Stephen, right?"

Ket Siong thought he knew where this was coming from. "She'll like you, too."

"No, but," said Renee. She went to the mirror, pulling her hair back and pinning it up in a chignon. "Does she have any issues with, you know, him and your brother?"

They hadn't discussed it as a family. Ket Hau had made no further mention of marriage, though he was talking regularly to Stephen now. Ket Siong and Ma were careful to give him space during their calls, but Ket Siong hadn't noticed any difference in Ma's manner when she happened to see Stephen on Ket Hau's phone screen.

She had been very quiet when they'd told her Stephen was alive. "God is good," she'd said, and crossed herself.

"I don't know," said Ket Siong, remembering her face. "She cares about Stephen. I don't think that would change, just because . . . She might need some time, that's all."

"Right," said Renee. She applied lipstick to her mouth and turned around. "How do I look?"

She looked fresh and wholesome. It brought the Renee of ten years ago vividly back to Ket Siong. He got up off her bed and took her in his arms.

"You're beautiful," he said truthfully. He leaned in for a kiss. She smelt nice, too.

The plan was to sit down to lunch around two p.m. Maybe it didn't matter if they were late.

Renee gave him a little push.

"Don't mess me up," she said. "Oh my God, is that the time? You should've told me. Let's go."

They took a cab to Ket Siong's place—a wild extravagance, but unavoidable, since public transport had shut down for the day. Renee didn't talk much during the drive. She spent most of it on her phone.

"Is something happening at work?" said Ket Siong.

Renee was busy texting in silence.

"Hmm?" she said. "No, Virtu's closed for the week. It's just a friend. Aww, that's cute. Look!"

She tilted her phone screen. Ket Siong was allowed a second to admire the image of Nathalie with her husband and child, beaming in matching Christmas jumpers, before Renee whipped the phone away.

She wasn't any less jittery once they arrived, though Ma and Ket Hau were suitably welcoming. They relieved her of her coat and settled her on the sofa with a mug of Milo. But Renee kept jumping up, going to the window to gaze out at the street, wandering to the door, inspecting the pictures on the walls and the books on the shelves.

She was waiting for something. But what?

When the doorbell sounded, Renee nearly jumped out of her skin. Then she glanced at Ket Hau—a look of trepidation.

Ket Hau didn't notice. He was busy setting out drinks on the dining table: orange juice, Ribena, and a bottle of Chardonnay they'd picked up when doing their big Christmas shop at Asda, in case Renee wanted wine.

Ma poked her head out of the kitchen. "What's that? Are you all expecting anything?"

"Nobody's going to be delivering on Christmas Day," said Ket Hau. "Must be Roberta."

The landlady had come round a couple of weeks ago to complain about the noise. Ket Siong only played the piano during business hours, when the neighbours were most likely to be out of the house, and they'd done all they could by way of sound-proofing: hung heavy blackout curtains over the windows; used a draught stopper to seal up the gap under the door. He couldn't very well be less annoying without cutting down on practice, which he was loath to do. After such a long break from performing, he needed it.

On this point, at least, he had good news. "We can tell her I'm going to start practising at Renee's place."

"OK," said Ket Hau. His brow furrowed. "Wait, do you mean Renee bought you a piano?"

"I couldn't think of what else to get him for Christmas," said Renee apologetically. "Ket Siong's so hard to buy for. Why don't I get the door? You guys are busy."

She'd nipped out of the living room and down the stairs leading to the front door before they could say anything.

"Is she always like this?" said Ket Hau.

Ket Siong suppressed the instinct to defend Renee; he knew what his brother meant. "Something's going on."

"Like what?" said Ket Hau. He looked up as Renee came up the stairs, and saw who was with her. The blood drained from his face.

Renee ushered the man into the living room. He was looking unnaturally tidy, in a batik shirt and long trousers. His long hair was tied up in a ponytail. In person, he was startlingly thin.

"Hey," said Stephen. He was holding a tub of Quality Street, and he looked anxious.

Ma came in, carrying a glass dish containing her famous macaroni casserole, saw Stephen, and dropped the dish. It bounced off the side of the sofa and landed casserole-down.

"Stephen!"

"Oh shit!" said Stephen. "Sorry, auntie." He abandoned the

Quality Street and dived for the casserole, scooping it up. "It's OK. Didn't even spill, look. Blow off the fluff and it'll be fine."

"Give me that!" said Ma. She swiped the baking dish, put it on the table, and flung her arms around him, bursting into tears.

Ket Hau and Ket Siong looked at each other. The last time Ma had hugged Ket Siong was after a triumphant concert he'd done in KL, years ago, and she'd had the excuse of being under the influence of the music—Chopin always made Ma emotional. He couldn't remember the last time he'd seen her hug Ket Hau.

"I didn't mean to intrude," said Stephen, his voice muffled. "Renee invited me—"

"I know it was presumptuous," said Renee. "But he was going to spend Christmas alone in Geneva and I thought you wouldn't mind—"

"I can go if you all want to have a family dinner by yourselves—"

"What are you talking about?" said Ma. "You flew in yesterday? How long are you in UK? Until New Year. Where are you staying? Hotel, why are you staying in hotel? Hotel is so expensive. You can stay with us, we have space in the living room."

This was more an expression of hope than of fact—the living room could barely accommodate the five people in it—but spatial reality was not going to get in the way of a determined Ma.

"The table can go in the corner there and we can put a mattress on the floor by the sofa," she said. "We can buy air mattress, air mattress is quite comfortable. Auntie Shirley used to have one. We can WhatsApp her and ask what brand to buy. Oh, but the shops are closed. When will they open? Tomorrow? You're so thin now! Are you eating properly? You cannot just eat Maggi mee, I told you boys it's not real food. Have you eaten? Come, sit down. Hau, go and get the plate for him."

Stephen wiped his eyes and said, "Don't worry, auntie. I can help myself. Where's the kitchen?"

"You won't know where everything is," said Ket Hau. He was perched on the sofa. For a while he'd been bent over, his breathing suspiciously uneven, but his colour was better now and he seemed more or less back to normal. He got up.

"I'll come with you," said Stephen.

They went out of the room together. Ma looked at the dining table, sizing up the possibilities.

"We have the macaroni and the drinks," she said. "The turkey is out already, just needs to rest. Everything else, Hau and Stephen can take out of the oven when it's ready. We can start eating now. Let them talk by themselves. Oh, thank you, thank you. What's this?"

"I brought champagne," said Renee shyly. "And zero-alcohol bubbly, in case anyone's alcohol-free. Sorry, I should've put them in the fridge when I got here, but I forgot."

"Champagne is perfect," said Ma. "It's still cold." They glanced towards the kitchen.

"I'll open it in the garden," said Ket Siong.

Stephen and Ket Hau didn't take that long. The bubbles were still racing in their glasses of champagne when they came back to the living room, bearing plates heaped with roast turkey, stir-fried vegetables, roast potatoes, curry simmered for many hours till its smells filled the flat, wonderfully rich and savoury and complex, and—

"Is that roti jala?" said Renee, brightening. "Did you make that, auntie? Oh, amazing. You've been working so hard."

"Rendang for Christmas," said Stephen blissfully. "When the smell of auntie's rendang hit me, whoof! I was almost going to cry, man."

"You must pack some and take back with you," said Ma to Renee. "We have so much, we won't be able to finish. But Stephen, your hotel, can you get a refund? Tonight you can stay there, then tomorrow we'll see if the shops are open and we can get the mattress . . ."

"You want water?" said Renee to Stephen. She scanned the

crowded table. "I don't think there's a spare glass. Let me get you one."

Ket Siong went after her. Once they were in the kitchen, well out of sight of the living room, he put a hand on her wrist. She looked around and he pulled her close, kissing her.

Kissing was still new and delicious. When Renee's mouth opened beneath his, he felt it all the way up his spine, heat licking up his back.

Renee emerged from the kiss flushed, wisps of hair straying out of her bun. Ket Siong smoothed the wisps back, tucking them behind her ear.

"What was that for?" she said.

"I love you," said Ket Siong.

"I love you, too," said Renee. Her tone was matter-of-fact, as if this was pre-agreed between them, as if he already knew.

This was true, in a sense, but still. It was the first time Renee had ever said it to him, in so many words.

She didn't seem to have noticed.

"Come on," she said. "If we leave your mom to it, she's going to go off and order that air mattress off Amazon. I'm covering Stephen's hotel room, it's fine."

It was of course necessary to kiss Renee again after that. She permitted the liberty, smiling against his mouth, before nudging him away.

"Keep your hands to yourself, Mr. Yap," she said, in her most princessy mode. "I've got a job to do."

She flicked a look of challenge at him through her lashes, grabbed a glass out of a cabinet, and turned back to the living room, where—from the sound of it—a heated argument was underway about whether there was or was not space left on anyone's plate for macaroni casserole. He followed her, smiling.

ACKNOWLEDGMENTS

A thousand thanks to:

The fantastic Bramble team, including Devi Pillai, Monique Patterson, Mal Frazier, Erika Tsang, Tessa Villanueva, Tyrinne Lewis, Hannah Smoot, Desirae May Friesen, and Shawna Hampton.

Ellah Mwale at Pan Macmillan for bringing the book home to the UK—and the kdrama chat!

My literary agent, Caitlin Blasdell, and her colleagues at Liza Dawson Associates, as well as my film agent, Angela Cheng Caplan, and her assistant, Sasha Shulman, for their support, guidance, and advocacy for my books.

Bo Feng Lin for an absolute dream of a cover.

My family, as always, both the Chos and the Augers, and of course the Auger Chos, who do their best to help Mummy miss her deadlines. Special thanks and love to Peter Auger, of whose love and care the best kdrama heroes remind me.

Beloved friends Rachel Monte, Samit Basu, Juliet Mushens, Maxine Lim, Tai Cheh Kuan, Karen Lord, Aliette de Bodard, and Alis Rasmussen, as well as invaluable group chats the Idlers by Bamboo and the Great Malaysian Aunties, for listening to all my moans and ramblings in the course of writing this book. Particular thanks to twice-doctor Audrey Soo for supplying a key location and to Rae for persevering in recommending kdramas to me until one finally clicked.

Total strangers Park Ji-eun, Lee Jeong-hyo, Hyun Bin, and Son Ye-jin, for showing me the power of truly committing to an epic love story between two really, really good-looking people.

Clare Rewcastle Brown, whose book and blog *The Sarawak Report* provided inspiration for several key aspects of the plot, and also did a lot for Malaysians generally.

This book is dedicated to my cousin Lina, one of the first people who gave me the greatest mark of respect a writer can receive—the attention of an intelligent reader. Thanks for everything, over the years.

ABOUT THE AUTHOR

Zen Cho is the author of the Sorcerer to the Crown novels, *Black Water Sister,* and various shorter fiction. Her work has won the Hugo, Crawford, and British Fantasy Awards, and the LA Times Ray Bradbury Prize, as well as being short-listed for the World Fantasy, Lambda, Locus, and Astounding Awards. Born and raised in Malaysia, Cho now lives in the UK.